# 80% DONE WITH STRAIGHT GIRLS

Mari SanGiovanni

Bywater BOOKS

2022

Bywater Books

Copyright © 2022 Mari SanGiovanni

Print ISBN: 978-1-61294-239-1

Bywater Books First Edition: July 2022

Printed in the United States of America on acid-free paper.

Cover designer: Mari SanGiovanni
Book layout designer: Ann McMan, TreeHouse Studio

Bywater Books
PO Box 3671
Ann Arbor MI 48106-3671

www.bywaterbooks.com

This novel cites lyrics from the Italian folk song, "C'è la luna
mezzo mare"—related music and lyrics appeared as early as 1835
in the art song "La Danza" (Tarantella Napoletana) by Gioachino
Rossini and Carlo Pepoli. In 1927, New York City's Italian Book
Company arranged and recorded a version by Sicilian sailor Paolo
Citorello—an American court upheld their copyright in 1928. The
song lyrics quoted in this novel are in the public domain.

For my sister, Nisa, and in loving memory of Kim.

A Lot Has Happened Since You Left...
Here Are the Highlights

My sister Lisa sped her Jeep along the highway playing a live game of Frogger (only not from the view of the frog) with my brother Vince and I held captive in the vehicle. I see from the look in my brother's eyes that he is also sure our bodies are shifting the maximum amount a seat belt allows before we blow an airbag. Of course, I don't know a soul in the cars we blow by, yet I feel a camaraderie with them as they join our long-standing fate that nobody, not ever, could keep up with our sister.

I wondered how many ways a person could die, and to distract myself from our imminent doom, I took a roll call. To my amazement it was one for each vowel: Accident, Emptiness, Illness, Old, & Unlucky. Today my chances of dying from O were extremely low, and if I didn't die in the next few minutes from A or U, I would keep my original bet on E. My stomach lurched, and it may not have been from my sister's driving.

Could you actually die from a constant feeling of emptiness? Was the sickness I felt this realization, or was I simply going to lose the lunch I barely ate due to her driving? Either way, if I barfed in her Jeep, I would get killed because my sister loved her damned truck. She had even rigged the car alarm to accidentally go off every time she opened the door so people would not miss her getting into it.

"I think I know what my next venture will be," my sister announced while she bobbed and weaved the three of us

1

through traffic with her trademark relaxed hand loosely guiding the bottom of the steering wheel. Instead of venture, she should have said adventure, because when Lisa talked business, she had a way of landing something that was really quite the opposite.

"Want to hear?"

Vince and I knew a rhetorical question when we heard it, and Lisa never asked any other kind. We also knew without speaking about it that although my sister's tone was casual, as if the thought was just occurring to her, it was much more likely she was already full steam ahead on her plan, and the whole point of this car ride was to have a captive audience.

"I'm going to open up a gourmet meatball-themed food truck. It will be high-end, no cheap food, and I was thinking, for example, of starting with a truck on Nantucket Island. Lots of cash to be made there; those people are not newly rich like us. Want to know what I am going to call it?" (Another rhetorical.)

When we didn't answer, she said, "Wait for it . . . wait for it . . ."

We were waiting for it.

"*Balls!*" she said and roared at her own announcement, Vince bursting with a laugh right after.

I was laughing too, but I knew from past experience a good crazy idea from a bad one when it came to Lisa. Compared to her past ideas, this one sounded quite doable.

"I have the entire business plan already in my head. Do you want to hear?"

(That didn't matter.)

Vince played along. "What else do we have to do today, except survive?"

Since Lisa was driving us to a destination unknown, we didn't know the answer to that question either. It was at this moment I noticed we had careened off the highway and entered one of the sketchier parts of Providence that my sister had a warm affection for.

Lisa said, "Even though the food truck will be based solely on meatballs, it will have something for everyone. Ready? Ready?"

"Ready?" meant hold on to your seats, which we already were.

"*Go!*" Vince said, already starting to giggle.

Lisa's voice grew louder as she spewed out her list.

"Meatballs with sausage links will be called: 'The Ball & Chain.' The vegetarian meatball: 'No Balls!'"

Vince started howling and I couldn't help joining in, especially when Vince cut her off to add, "Chicken meatballs: 'Cock 'n Balls!' And a ground beef, sloppy joe version: 'Ball Breaker!'" As Vince yelled, he continued to slap Lisa's shoulder from the back seat as if she needed encouragement. (Read: never.)

"*Yes!* But wait, wait, there's more!" Lisa yelled like a bad infomercial. Of course, there was *always* more.

"Lamb and feta version will be 'Greecy Balls'—get it? *GREECE?!*"

We got it, and I couldn't help but laugh along with both of them, even knowing these ideas were going off the rails into a depth my sister would not see until she was in way over her head. Lisa was trying to compose herself by slapping her steering wheel since she couldn't reach Vince.

When she caught her breath, she said "An arrabbiata-extra-spicy-sauce version: 'Great Balls of Fire!'"

"Damn!" Vince yelled, and I knew he was ready to climb aboard. "Wait—wait," he said, "your meatballs with spinach and blue cheese—'Blue Balls!'"

Lisa barked her deep husky laugh that transitioned not so gracefully into her trademark snorting. "Maybe you should pull over," I said.

"No, no, there's more! Meatballs with turkey meat—" Lisa couldn't speak, she was laughing so hard, and when he fell silent, I knew Vince was trying to beat her to the punch line, but he didn't quite make it when Lisa shouted, "Gobble Balls!"

Vince and I joined her with fresh peals of laughter, as he added, "What about a plain, no sauce version: 'Bare Balls?'"

Lisa was wheezing as she wiped her eyes along with Vince,

while I was seriously thinking of taking the wheel. "One more, one more," Lisa said. "Meatballs inside a pita pocket: 'Balls to the Walls!'"

Vince slapped her again, this time with no sound escaping from his hysterical laughter. He had inherited from Dad the silent cry-laugh followed by a "hee hee" choked out at the end. It was a laugh our Uncle Tony had as well.

Like all of Lisa's ideas, there was always a back-and-forth flipping, knowing she was going too far, but wondering if maybe the idea wasn't so crazy after all. I was thinking this as Lisa yanked her Jeep into an adult toy store parking lot and said, "Can you even imagine our promo T-shirts?"

As a matter of fact, I could, and the "our" did not escape me. Of course this would be another family project. The idea of it both interested and exhausted me. A lot had happened since I had bought a campground with my sister, and her last crazy business adventure had turned it into the extremely successful LGBTQ resort, Camptown Ladies. Except for the huge success of the business, which felt more like a hobby for our entire family, nearly everything else in my life had changed for worse. While the campground was wildly successful, my personal life had been just as wildly destroyed. Lisa would say it was not a surprise as, technically speaking, Erica had been yet another straight girl, like my ex-girlfriend before her, and Lisa had predicted it wasn't such a stretch that Erica would leave me, too, one way or another, and she had been right.

I could have bought ten campgrounds if I had a dollar for every time my sister had said, "There's something about straight girls you just can't put your finger on," and of course she had meant it in the dirtiest way possible, but in another way she had been right about that, too.

My track record was not good. I had crashed and burned with straight girl number one, television actress Lorn Elaine, who came before Erica. She was not just any TV actress, but an Emmy winner at that. Turned out she was a better actress than I'd realized, and it had been no surprise to me or least of all my sister when it finally ended after many false attempts. Lorn was a still-in-the-closet actress petrified to protect her career, but with Erica—well, she really fooled me. She fooled all of us. It took years, but I finally believed her when she said she would love me forever, and I think even my sister had started to believe it too.

Of course, Lisa didn't believe it at first—I mean, who believes a love story like the one we had? Dumped by my first girlfriend, I fell in love with my brother's girlfriend and somehow it had all worked out. Until the end.

My whole family believed in Erica, and us as a couple, and that was saying something as the Santoras are not an innocent or trusting bunch. It had been so complicated in the beginning that when we finally took the chance to be together, I believed neither of us would ever give up what we had. By the end of our five years together, Erica had me completely convinced that should you be lucky enough to have it, love was actually a real thing you could count on over the long haul, long after the first-date U-Haul.

Lisa interrupted my thoughts by jumping out of the car and slamming the door. My sister was at her candy store. She hadn't noticed that I hadn't moved, and that I was a million miles away. When she noticed I wasn't following, she doubled back to impart sage advice.

"Stay in the moment, douchebag."

"Trying," I said.

Lisa didn't miss a beat and tossed out another meatball name to Vince who was waiting at the front door only seconds after the car had stopped. He was nodding with approval and pointing at the way the windows were obstructed by shouting signs completely blocking the view, always a good sign, he said, still laughing at Lisa's genius business plan.

I didn't have the heart to tell Lisa that what I heard was a menu, not a business plan, but that wouldn't make a bit of difference. Also, if I had to pinpoint the most perfect spot on a map of New England to *not* start a business named *Balls*, it would be the island of Nantucket, Massachusetts. Nantucket was a billionaire's playground, designed most certainly, and not subtly, at a cost of living high enough to keep the riffraff out. Our family's money didn't count, as we had no connections to the Mayflower at all, which made us ineligible to hold a wedding at certain places on the island. Therefore, getting a truck named *Balls* over on the ferry seemed a long shot. When it came to Nantucket, the Santoras would be the riffraff, Balls or no balls.

Lisa's "douchebag stay in the moment" aside, there had been real affection in my sister's voice, which made me uncomfortable. It was hard to miss how everyone was treating me so carefully these days. And I hated it, especially from my sister. As they headed into the store, I yelled after them, "Maybe you two should wait for an adult!"

But Lisa and Vince were already inside.

Vince had disappeared by the time I caught up to Lisa. She was staring at the first aisle of product with the complete awe of a seven-year-old in a candy aisle.

I said, "It's so weird in here."

Lisa didn't hear me as she was totally in the moment, but probably for the best or she might grab something unspeakable shaped like a woman's nether regions, shove it in my face and say, "No, Marie, its weird in *here*."

I watched my sister walk ahead of me along the racks, touching each blister pack of mysterious products, making her usual commentary. If there was a way to make me laugh again, Lisa would find it here, and I could see by her pace that she was seeking, rather than shopping. Lisa turned into the second aisle and was out of my view for a few seconds. By the time I caught up she whipped around with a dildo strapped to her face with a thick black chinstrap and nearly swiped my nose with it. I pulled my head back just in time, like a skilled boxer with many years of the dangers of shopping with my sister under my belt. Even grocery stores were a danger, as I had been bonked in the head or poked in the backside with a cucumber more times than I could count.

Uh-oh, I thought.

Lisa said, "I mean, I don't get the point of it. Oh, wait, I get it," and she bobbed her head(s) up and down in a *yes*. "It's like Bluetooth for sex! Totally hands-free."

She snuck a peek at the price.

I tried to look away, but, witnessing a train wreck, I had to keep looking, along with a few others in the store. I also knew from experience that ignoring my sister would only make her raise her voice, and in a sex toy shop the *last* thing I wanted was all eyes on us. Lisa, on the other hand, not so much.

"Seriously, look at this thing," she said, as if I could miss her making the penis bob higher and lower as she shook her head up and down, then side to side. I knew from experience circles and a figure eight would be not far behind.

I could tell she was pleased how good she was getting at it, so it was not going to end any time soon. Lisa said, "Awesome idea, this multitasking, but how many other things do you really have going at the same moment that you have to strap a rubber dick to your face? I mean, are you texting? Baking a ham? And even if your partner thinks it feels good, how do you not get laughed at when you are charging at your partner's crotch like a Polish unicorn?"

"*Lisa!*" I said.

"What? Am I stereotyping?" she said, looking around the sex toy shop for offended Polish people, but I knew she just wanted to make the dildo anchored to her chin swing wildly until she was making perfect figure eights. "Look, the symbol for eternity!" Lisa shouted, which was ironic since I was worried she would never stop.

Lisa said, "Hey, if someone stereotyped me because I was Italian and assumed I would knock someone over for a meatball, am I gonna argue with them about it? Look at me." She felt along the sides of her broad body. "I didn't get this body from being polite around food; of course I will knock you down for a meatball. I'm a big girl and maybe there are some Italians who don't swear like truck drivers and eat every meal like it's their last fucking supper, but I sure don't know any."

I started to walk away from her, but that may have been a mistake because she yelled down the aisle, "Mare, where you going? Okay, okay, I'm sure there are tons of brilliant Polish people! Hey, wait, I have a great idea!"

A better idea better than parading around a store in a dildo chinstrap?

Where the hell was Vince? I made a note to myself to kill him for leaving me alone with Lisa in a toy shop. I scanned the room and spotted him in the far corner, in the spanking section, testing the sound of a leather paddle against his palm. He wore a sneaky grin. I wanted to grin, too, knowing his wife, Katie, would knock him into next week if he ever brought that thing home.

Vince was too absorbed in his own thoughts to help me with Lisa so I braced myself.

"Hey, Mare," she shouted down the aisle as if I were a mile away. "They should design a dildo shaped like a sausage and with two meatballs hanging from it and call it the Italian Stallion. Hell, I'd buy it!"

Shocker, I thought. Would this be the second business plan of the day?

By now, a group of twentysomething ladies in the store had already keyed into our conversation and started to giggle, and this was all Lisa needed for encouragement. Lisa could sniff out a pack of giddy bridesmaids quicker than a veteran truffle hog.

I knew two things would happen now: with an audience, Lisa would get louder and raunchier. And, miraculously, the bridesmaids would find her as irresistible as a seventeen-year-old high school football hero—cocky, macho, yet still charming and funny to the straight female species. My sister never ceased to amaze me.

As predicted, up went her audio another notch. "I have another idea, a dildo with ribbing like a giant screw, called *The Big Screw!* Wait—no—we'll call it the *Screw You!*"

I had no choice but to raise my eyebrows, nod yes, and flatten my mouth as if I agreed she had just invented the next Post-Its while Lisa pretended she had just noticed she had an audience. The next thing she'd say would be to make sure they knew she was single and luckily still up for grabs.

"Oh, hi, girls! Hey, I need your opinion, especially since my sister here won't be honest with me. How else am I going to start my sex toy business without doing a consumer survey? Please be honest." She turned to the side, "Does this dildo make me look fat?"

The young women laughed, encouraging her as Lisa turned so they could see every angle for the full effect. "Thoughts?" Lisa said.

"No, no, it's perfect," one of girls said, laughing.

"Yes?" she asked, nodding her head again to get a good rubber bounce going. "Excellent. Good to know, ladies. One more thing." She tried to sound as clinical as possible, "Sometimes you ladies can be tricky for the men . . . you know, finding the right spot and all. What if we made a version for men only, modeled after a miner's helmet with a light strapped to the forehead?"

They were already laughing hysterically, a few of them covering their mouths, but Lisa wasn't nearly done.

She said, "Maybe we could add a GPS . . . Global Pussy System!"

I tried not to, but even I cracked up as Lisa tried to look as innocent as you can with nine inches of rubber pointing directly at a group of young women. "What?" Lisa said. "Too much?"

Like answering a bat signal, Vince appeared on the scene to watch the ladies busting a gut laughing at our sister. I noticed he forgot to put down his black leather paddle trimmed with brass studs, and one of the girls whispered to her friend, clearly goofing on him, but of course Vince thought they were flirting with him. I also noticed that the most attractive girl of the bunch, who had first zeroed in on Lisa for the comedy, was now ignoring Lisa and Vince to zero in on me. The young woman stared, unblinking (not usually a sign of high intelligence) and smiling with perfect teeth that cautioned: These bicuspids are bi-curious. Never, never, again. I thought for the millionth time: I am 100% done with straight girls.

At this thought I turned away, my stomach also turning. Done. So done.

"Try to enjoy the show," Lisa whispered to me as I passed by her leaving the aisle. She galloped closer to the pack of girls, like a male unicorn who fears he's on the verge of extinction. They circled her, laughing and hanging on each other, and I tried to enjoy the show as best I could, even though the last eight months had slowed my sense of humor to a painful crawl. Before my world stopped, before my heart was shattered, before Erica left me . . . before Erica died.

Past memories flooded in as they do, with no rhyme or reason as to where I am, or what I am doing. Like now. I might be standing in a sex toy shop, watching my sister clowning around, but my mind was actually meeting Erica for the first time in California; then I was working with her at the campground, believing all that time that she was to be my brother's true love . . . all the while as I fell for her . . . my mind spun as I remembered trying to ignore my feelings for her as we worked together, handing her supplies from the height of a ladder on the edge of the roof that I pretended not to mind the height of . . . and how that night everything changed for us, as I clutched the shingles at the roof's edge when the ladder slipped from under me. Erica had saved me from falling that night, and that was the moment I confessed I had fallen for her. How had she miraculously found the speed and strength to grab me in time and pull me up over the edge? How could we have ever thought we could let each other go to spare my brother the pain of losing her?

Later, at home, I am still torturing myself, sparking more memories by holding Erica's ancient flip phone in my hand, running my finger across the worn and raised buttons, tracing them with my fingertips as if they were hieroglyphics. My nostalgic feeling for real buttons on a phone made me feel older than my thirtysomething years.

How many times had Erica's fingers pressed right here . . . or here? She had the most beautiful hands, strong and pretty, such a rare combination.

I thought about how back in the old texting days, when Erica and I first worked together as contractor and contractor's assistant (I called myself her Homo-Depot runner), texting was not really a functional way to communicate. I imagined how I would explain this to my little nephew, Buddy, in my best grandpa impression (if grandpa were a lipstick lesbo with a giant rack o' boobs): "You see, Buddy, back in the old days, phones looked like this, and you used to have to text a series of numbers just to make one word. These are real, honest-to-goodness buttons, and something actually happens when you push them. In the old days, you might have to push the numbers many times just to spell a small word; can you even imagine that? Kind of a Morse code if you will." I thought about how Vince's son would have looked at me like I had grown an extra head with a dusty set of abacus teeth.

I would not have told him the rest of the story, the real reason I was tracing the button numbers 2229. It was out of that ancient texting system that came the nickname "2229," which spelled out the word: BABY. Once I slipped up by leaving Erica a love note addressed to 2229 and the note was discovered by Lisa who shared it with my brother, so they could team torture me about it for years.

This phone still works. I plugged it in yesterday and watched it come to life with cold white-blue lights outlining each of the buttons. I thought to myself . . . should I do it? It would be damned funny. "I shouldn't do it," I say out loud, but even as I say this, I know I'm going to do it.

The idea came to me innocently enough. I had been scrolling through Erica's messages, and there, sitting among all the restricted and blocked calls, was an old text message to Erica from my sister Lisa, announcing she planned to take a break from her Camptown Ladies publicity tour. My sister's idea to make the unlikely combo campground/gay resort/Italian restaurant had taken off like wildfire, and although she threatened it, Lisa never did take that break. One TV interview led to another, and by the time she could break away from the paparazzi to make time to come back home, with very little warning Erica was dead and my world had changed forever.

But I still had Erica's phone, and I had charged it, and on this day I had thought it would be a good idea to type a text message, inspired by my sister's trademark all-caps (text yelling):

HI LISA, IT'S ME, ERICA

I knew the timing was perfect since Lisa was home, so I hit the worn-out "Send" button before I could change my mind. It occurred to me this was how I did most things these days. The "quickly . . . just do it" method . . . before logic had a chance to take over and talk me out of doing anything at all.

I waited. The house was dead quiet, as it always was.

Would Erica have been happy to see me teasing Lisa like this? I thought so, yet did it really matter? I had done it regardless and Erica was gone. A moment later Erica's phone beeped and vibrated in my hands as if acknowledging my decision, and I nearly dropped it as if her ghost had texted me back. Of course, it was a return text from Lisa, who had just gotten a text from Erica, and I laughed in anticipation as I flipped the phone back open to read:

U FUCKER

I knew, several miles away, Lisa was laughing, too.

I continued my search for random messages I may have missed, but there weren't any left to find. It had been almost a year, so everyone already knew Erica was gone. No need to call. Who would answer?

Me, that's who.

Lisa texted again:

SOMETHING IS SERIOUSLY WRONG WITH U

I knew things I had been doing weren't normal behavior after someone leaves. Especially when everyone knows it's coming, even when you know it's coming, too, and you have plenty of warning. After all, Erica had been the beautiful straight girl who fell in love with a woman and really should not have been mine for the last five damned-near perfect years. Shouldn't I be grateful that I'd had that much time with her? Why should I have expected more when I had been the happiest person I'd ever known for those years? I had lived in a fantasy world, and it all had to come to an end at some point, didn't it?

But this end . . . I had not expected this.

I texted back:

Hahaha what's wrong with me texting from Erica's phone?

I was feeling a bit entitled; it was one of the few things I had left of her, and she had carried it with her always. Mine now. It had been five perfect years, followed by many horrible months. I texted:

It's not like I know she isn't gone.

A few seconds later, Lisa wrote:

ERICA IS NOT GONE, SHE'S DEAD.

Classic Lisa, but still, I was surprised to feel my two fingers already at my right cheek, strangely soothing myself as if my hand had anticipated all on its own, ready to catch the first tear that rolled down my cheek and skidded over my wrist as the phone buzzed again.

My sister surprised me by texting:

SORRY

I wrote back:

I know. See you next week at Mom's.

Divine Intervention

"The thing is," my sister said, as she stirred her saucepot, "I believe life sends you signs." I knew where this was going. "Like one time, just a few years ago, I had just finished messing with my Magic Wand, Lisa-Lisa," (she had named her vibrator after herself . . . twice), "and was a little miffed at the less than stellar result. So, in my fit of rage, I yanked the plug and the fucker whipped the cord back right at my face, and the plug chipped my front tooth."

Okay, that wasn't where I thought her story was going.

"You chipped your tooth at Rocky Point Park. I was there."

Lisa laughed and said, "You only thought I chipped it there. I had it covered with a piece of my Chiclet gum until I could fake the incident on the park ride." Come to think of it, she had been weirdly covering her front teeth that day . . . pretending she was George Foreman before he had a panini grill biz. I just shook my head at her.

"What do you mean 'less than stellar' result? Did you expect it to buy you dinner first? You were thirteen. Wait, you had your vibrator back then?"

Lisa gave me her classic *duh* look and said, "I stole it when I was eleven. But that chipped tooth was a turning point for me. I knew I had to get back out there with girls and try a relationship, I had gotten so numb to it all."

"At thirteen years old your vibrator chipped your front

tooth and that made you realize you needed to have another relationship?"

Lisa said, "No, you idiot, I made myself numb from the vibrator, so I realized I needed to get a girlfriend. The point is, when are you going to realize you need to get back out there?"

"My teeth are fine, and I threw away my vibrator when Erica died."

When Lisa gasped in horror at the waste of a perfectly good vibrator, my whole family turned to look at her.

I lowered my voice and said quietly to Lisa, "I don't need a girlfriend," and walked out of the kitchen. Rookie mistake because when you walk away from Lisa, she just yells after you.

"You're numb in more ways than one." She took another swig of her drink before she yelled across the room, "And you're afraid!"

"Speaking of which, I have the balls to admit I'm a little freaked out about my surgery this week," Dad said. "People die under the knife every day you know . . . especially at my age." His voice trailed off when he realized he was talking to me about death; then he muttered something about spring chickens as he walked away. I could feel everyone in the room look at me for a reaction.

I called after him, trying to sound playful, "It's a wisdom tooth, Dad. You'll be fine." Then I vaguely wondered why everyone was still staring, and more incredibly nobody was eating.

I wasn't eating either, but that was my norm. What was strange, was nobody was pestering me about it. Lisa's lasagna had been ready since we arrived, and even after she brought out the pot of meatballs and set it dangerously close to Dad (who stood by, fork ready) Lisa had not insisted on fixing me a plate. She also had not started her threats to shove food directly into my mouth. Instead, she went back to her bubbling pots of sausage and peppers swimming in tomato sauce lined up on the stove, sitting untouched. I could tell by the way she was stirring the pot there was something going on. Nobody stirred the pot like my sister.

Instead of making preparations to serve our family, Lisa had been patrolling the perimeter of the kitchen like a dyke cop, allowing nobody to enter to sniff anything, except Dad, since that was never worth the police work needed to hold him back. Everyone else was weirdly hanging in the living room, like guests.

I yelled over to Lisa, "Are we going to eat, or what?"

I saw her shoot a look to my brother, Vince, then over to my mother, who signaled to everyone that they should move to the far side of the living room. Uncle Tony, Dad's brother, was visiting with wife Katherine, and in an even bigger surprise my Uncle Freddie had been a surprise guest, visiting from Italy. He had come back when he heard of Erica's death and had stayed for over a month, and seemed oddly not in a hurry to rush back to Italy, his first love. I looked around at the gathering, noticing how quiet it was for a Santora event. Nobody was eating, and not a bit of sarcasm to be heard.

Dad distracted me again.

"It's not the surgery; it's the anesthesia I'm worried about," Dad said. I watched Mom hover closer, and, more alarmingly, Lisa abandoned her post in the kitchen. What the hell was going on?

"You'll be fine, Dad," I said.

"Seriously, though. It's that whole not waking up thing."

I may have raised my voice just a little. "You've had anesthesia before. You'll be fine. But if you do die and you run into Erica, can you ask where she used to keep the coffee filters? I'd really appreciate it. I can't fucking find them."

Dad's eyes went wide and he was speechless, maybe for the first time in his life; then he looked like he was about to burst into laughter until Mom thudded him hard in the side as she pushed past him to get right in my face.

"What?" I said. "We all talked about this; it's not a secret she's dead."

Mom said, "Marie, your anger . . . and your sadness, this is

16

exactly why we're all here."

"Wait . . . it is?"

Lisa rolled her eyes, "Good one, Mom. That's exactly how we wanted this to go."

"Wanted what to go?" I asked, but they all ignored me like they were in some kind of a play and I was the only one without a script. I caught the eye of my brother Vince, who froze when he saw me glaring at him.

"What the fuck is going on?"

Vince said, "Marie, the thing is, we think you have been acting really strange lately . . . you know, lots of ball-busting, lashing out and stuff."

I gave him a little shove. "From you? That's ridiculous!"

Vince teetered back, then kept his distance. I had seen him do this so many times, but it had always been in fear of our sister.

I said, "Is this an anti-ball-busting intervention? If so, why is this gathering hosted by my sister and brother, king and queen of the ball-busters—Lisa being the king, of course—or is this some sort of lame family intervention?" I laughed, but I was laughing alone.

At that, Dad walked into the living room, noisily smacking on a heel of crusty bread, his saucy lips staining it with an orange kiss. "Oh . . . you guys told her," he said, disappointed he had missed the big reveal.

I found myself yelling. "Told me what? You have got to be kidding me right now."

I yelled louder. "Does anyone else but me see the irony? *Lisa and Vince* are concerned I am acting out? This. Is. Hysterical!"

Nobody seemed to see the irony, or find it the least bit hysterical. "If Erica wasn't dead, she would be laughing her head off right now. Hell, maybe she is!"

I raised my voice, but it was more in amusement than anger, and I hadn't planned for the laughter that came out of me now to sound so maniacal, yet that's how it erupted, one wave after another, unrecognizable even to me, until I felt a hand gently take my arm.

It was Vince, and he wasn't laughing with me, which was so strange that it kicked off more of my crazy laughter, and now I was finding it hard to catch my breath or to speak. Truthfully, I was a bit light-headed.

"Mare . . .," he said.

"No, no . . . this is funny," I choked, "just . . . let me explain."

Then I looked just past my mother's shoulder and dramatically widened my eyes, horrified, pointing over her shoulder as I spat out the words as if I were seeing a ghost: *"OH. MY. GOD. ERICA!"*

Mom whirled around, but of course there was nothing behind her, and my laughter ramped up another notch at her gullibility and I was laughing at my own joke, gasping and snorting.

Lisa let out a snicker, but caught herself when Uncle Tony's usually unheard, gentle voice cut through the room in an unfamiliar tone. "Marie, this behavior has to stop. We all know how much you're hurting. More than anyone, I know what losing someone is like."

He did know this.

Before he found Katherine, he had been drowning after losing the love of his life, Auntie Celia. The silence in the room bore a strong testimony to the truth he spoke. Still . . . couldn't I handle my grief my own way? It was my pain to bear any way I needed to, right? Maybe my way was to laugh like a crazy person.

If it had been anyone but Uncle Tony, I would have said all this in my defense.

Instead, I cleared my throat and struggled to make my voice sound sane and gentle, like his. "Uncle Tony, I'm fine, really . . ." But my voice came out high-pitched and wobbly. "Can we all just eat?"

Uncle Tony wrapped his arms around me in a bear hug. I was embarrassed, and I imagined he could feel my bones. His voice was another level of gentle when he said into the top of my head, "I don't know, Marieooche, can you? Can you eat

18

something for us?"

I didn't answer, but I thought: No way. Today was not a good eating day, now that he mentioned it.

Vince moved alongside me, and I could tell before he spoke that he wanted to defend me. "Mare, we all know how strong you are. You'll get through this. You'll survive losing Erica if you just let yourself be hurt and talk about it so you can let her go. Wasn't it Woody Allen who said the heart is a resilient little muscle?"

I snapped at him, "Woody Allen fucked his girlfriend's adopted daughter, so he would know all about resilient little muscles."

Vince stepped back from me as if I had taken a swing at him. There was no mistaking the anger in my voice that time, and the fake laugh I attempted fell as flat as a bug on a windshield.

Vince said, "This is what we're talking about, Mare."

Mom piped up, "And just last week, when we were at the supermarket and I mentioned Erica, you gave that little boy ten dollars to come over to me and whisper: *I see dead people.*"

"Well, that one was funny, Lisa piped in. "We have to give her that one."

"Come on," I protested. "She's dead, right? So why can't I talk about it, joke about it if I want to?"

"But it isn't funny, Marie," Mom said. "It's just sad what happened to you. Not funny at all. You are so deeply, darkly sad."

And just when she said that, something in me cracked, and I realized deeply and darkly sad was *exactly* what I was.

"Tough room," I said, trying to hang on. "Listen, all the jokes can't be winners."

Vince approached me again.

"Mare, that's what we're trying to tell you. You don't have to be that way around us. It's okay . . . you are allowed to be devastated. When somebody is gone so fast like that . . . it was a shock . . . to all of us. We all lost Erica."

It was then that I felt something I had never felt before. It was rising in me, starting like anger . . . but now it was a full-blown panic attack. I eyeballed my bag on the couch and the ten paces to freedom, but in the flick of an eye I saw that my sister had figured me out. Thankfully, she was across the room, with several elderly relatives between us.

I bolted.

I heard the shuffling behind me as I passed them all and hurtled through the front door. I could hear Lisa yell at Vince that he should have grabbed me, the yelling getting farther away as I ran, and now the pounding of the blood pumping in my ears stifled the yelling, and the sounds of my name being called out by Dad, Uncle Tony, and Mom were all growing fainter until they closed off completely when I slammed the door of my car and sped off.

Lisa had tried so hard to get me to agree to let her pick me up at my cabin, but thank God I had insisted on driving. Thinking back, I may have unconsciously planned my fast exit. For months I had been always the last to arrive, and the very first to leave. Dying to get back to my cabin, for what I never knew.

On the chance that one of my siblings would follow my usual path home, I ditched the highway and drove blindly away from the condo where Vince and Katie now lived. It was the same condo that Vince, Lisa, and I had shared when we all came together to work on Camptown Ladies, the once dilapidated campground (transformed miraculously by Erica's expert contracting skills and Lisa's insanely great Italian cooking and quirky people skills). In just a few months it had grown into a gay mecca resort, mostly due to the fact that it featured a casual camp style open-air atmosphere, with a five-star Italian food menu. The restaurant, buried in the woods and converted from an old camp recreation hall, was the first of its kind and made it to the top of every reviewer's *must not miss* list, thanks entirely to my sister.

My eyes burned and filled with tears now that I was off the highway and I could afford the risk of crying. The woods looked similar to the woods where my cabin was, the one I had shared with Erica, and the reason all the woods in Rhode Island reminded me of her. How could I ever escape her memory, when all roads led back to Erica?

I had become pretty good at this, carefully scheduling my breakdowns. I had done this expertly since she was gone, and before she left, I never let her see me upset. There had only been one time right at the very end when I stupidly told her to fight harder for me, and she told me she just couldn't. It didn't make sense. If it was so hard for her to leave, why didn't she fight harder to stay?

I vaguely noticed my car was racing, so I slowed down, not for my own safety, but in fear I would kill an animal. I was on a side street now, and the smell of pine blasted into the vents of my car like a cardboard tree-shaped freshener. The sun was going down and I was alongside a part of the lake I didn't know. How far had I driven? Had I been going in circles? I wondered how long I had been out here. Ten minutes? An hour? I noticed the sun hadn't fully set.

The passing of time had changed so much since Erica died. Pre-Erica time flew; post-Erica time crawled, with every minute an eternity. When people said things like, I can't believe she's been gone six months . . . or a year, I wanted to punch them in the mouth. To me it had felt like years. Captain Janeway of the Starship Voyager would explain it by saying there must have been a fracture in the time/space continuum.

I waited for the feeling of panic to lessen, but my eyes were still filling as I drove and my vision had now blurred beyond what my Dunkin' Donuts napkin could stop. I decided to pull over. I pictured my tears as the lower levels of the Titanic filling . . . and Erica and I were the elderly couple on the bed holding each other, waiting patiently. Then I imagined me closing my eyes for just a second, and Erica slipping off the bed and disappearing from me. We used to hold hands every night, but not this night, or I didn't think so since I never felt her leave. When I dreamed about it, she would look back at me and evaporate like a ghost into a fog. Where did she end and the fog begin? Gone without a trace. I would wake up gasping for air as if the fog had been choking me.

After she was gone, even on prescription sleeping pills, I didn't ever fully sleep. I floated above sleep, aware of each passing, agonizing hour, trying not to open my eyes and knowing, even in my half-sleep, that her side of the bed would remain empty when I woke, so I kept my eyes tightly shut not to see the empty side in the moonlight.

I supposed my side of the bed didn't look much more filled than hers, since my sister kept reminding me how I had gotten "creepily thin." Sometimes when I would wake, I only half opened my eyes, enough so I could leave the bed without seeing Erica's empty space. I never cried in bed. Instead, I would get up and go to the bathroom to cry, always with a doubled bath towel across my face, as if the scream that slipped out could somehow wake someone that had already gone.

I finally pulled over to stop on the side of the road and wished I had a towel for my tear-stained face. "Time to let this go, let her go . . ." I had said this out loud in a whisper for the millionth time . . . *I can't keep doing this.* I was so exhausted I thought for just a second that I might be able to actually let her go.

So why right then did I have to see a sign from the universe that Erica was somehow still around? I had taken a random exit, far from my family's campground and the cabin we had shared, and something caught my eye. On my dashboard, the multiple numbers flicked with an odd symmetry, grabbing my attention as they rolled over. I knew I wouldn't believe it later, so I reached for my phone and snapped a picture of the odometer, which read: 102229.

This was weird enough. Except I was sitting in front of a house with the number 2229. What were the odds? It had to be some sort of a sign.

I tossed the soaked napkin in the back seat and reached into my glove compartment to hunt through the many packs of nearly empty Kleenex to wipe my streaming eyes. The sun was nearly down now, but I could see in the distance that I was parked in front of a huge lake house. A compound, really. I also saw it was for sale, and before I even considered what it might look like inside, or even if my plentiful inheritance from my long-lost grandmother would be stretched thin to pay for a house this size, I strangely knew beyond any doubt: I would buy this house.

On some level I believed Erica had found a way to send me here during this dark moment. What else would have explained it? Had she somehow reached out to pull me along to the exact place I needed to be? Maybe I had been right. All roads did lead to Erica . . . and this time by some numerical impossibility my odometer read 102229 at the very same moment it sat in front of 2229 Lakeside Drive.

Bait & Switch, & Tackle

Being a Santora, my timing could be a little off on most things, but my timing was nothing next to Lisa's. It was always a high priority for Lisa to be the Cool Auntie (which she was), and last year when our eleven-year-old nephew, Buddy, had come running home to give a wide-eyed retelling of the thrilling moment his teacher actually *swore* in the classroom, Lisa was there for a visit and only too happy to offer her perspective.

Buddy broke the story to his mom and Daddy Vince, carefully avoiding saying the actual offending word. I kept my mouth shut, but Cool Auntie saw swearing as a bonding moment, so she pulled Buddy aside, so our brother and Buddy's mom wouldn't overhear. Lisa whispered to Buddy, "Really, your teacher swore? Out loud so everyone could hear?"

"Yup," Buddy said, "in front of our whole class."

Lisa whispered as a co-conspirator, "That must have been awesome. You know, you can tell me what she said."

Buddy grinned devilishly at the thought, but politely shook his head no. No, he couldn't.

"Come on, Bud," Lisa goaded him, "you can tell me. You know I won't tell your mom or dad. It'll be our secret, like always."

Buddy looked across the room at his dad, and he judged he was a safe distance away before he whispered, *"It was the C-word."*

"What?" Lisa yelled, and of course now the room had her

attention. Vince walked over, alarmed he had not pressed his son for the full story.

"Yup," Buddy said, covering his mouth even though he hadn't said the horrible word, "the whole class heard it."

"Wow!" Lisa said, "That's the worst swear word ever!"

Buddy looked puzzled, which would have tipped me off that Cool Auntie better proceed with caution, but Lisa's caution button had been on the blink since the age of two.

Buddy asked, "Really?"

"Yes," Lisa said, and she whispered into his ear, "cunt is the worse swear ever."

When a child is hit with a new swear word, you see the impact first in their saucer-wide eyes. Then Buddy's head snapped back like a cartoon character as he let a high-pitched shriek escape before he could cover his mouth again, as if he had just said the word himself. Daddy Vince approached like the dad of a grizzly bear cub, and I stepped back a few seconds too late to pull off being uninvolved.

Vince knew from the delighted look in Buddy's eyes what had gone wrong. "Lisa, what did you just say to him?"

Lisa said, "I—I—nothing his teacher didn't already say."

Buddy was furiously shaking his head no, pointing at Cool Auntie as if she were a criminal, serving her up to save himself. "My teacher said *crap!*"

"Buddy!" his mother yelled at him, coming over, horrified.

Lisa whispered to me, "Oh crap."

It was every man for himself so I left Lisa in a hurry for the door, saying, "I will leave you guys to appreciate that crap swear word Buddy just said for at least a few seconds more . . ."

Since Erica left me, my timing for a lot of things had gotten worse than my sister's. For instance, it was a bad time for me to take up running. When you are down to 103 pounds and still losing weight, running may not be the best thing for you, yet it was the only thing that made me feel alive. It got my heart pumping again. The buildup, the tensing of the muscles, the rhythm of it, the exhaustion later . . . It felt a bit like sex, or at least from what I could remember.

But it was something else too. Something I couldn't quite place. There were times when I pushed myself running, past mile seven and on to mile eight, after not having eaten all day (all week in fact), my head spinning gloriously and the feel of the deep thudding in my chest that felt like a dark promise, and I hadn't desired anything else since she had gone. Could I run away the pain? Could I run to Erica, wherever she was?

I whipped around the track, on course to go farther than I ever had in my new addiction. I was already on mile eight and the possibility of going farther seemed much less crazy than standing still and letting life continue to crash over me.

As I rounded one of the corners, I got a bit dizzy, the ground tilting once then twice before I realized it had not actually moved. I stumbled. I should have eaten something, but I knew if I didn't, the high from running came more quickly, and I had stopped craving food so long ago, and I rarely felt hunger anymore. Even Lisa's cooking couldn't entice me, and that, I was just now realizing, might be a danger sign.

I had felt this need to keep running before, many days in fact, but why was today so different? I wondered if it was because today I knew I had no plans to stop.

Lisa had delivered the news that the family (of course) would not be spending our collective fortune to buy 2229 Lakeside Drive, and the reality was that it would be impossible to afford a compound that large on my own, but I still couldn't let it go. I wasn't even sure why I wanted a place that could cause me to go broke trying to float a giant house and grounds like that. The taxes on the land alone would be enough to bury me in the place. I wondered why this sounded weirdly comforting, and I had tested to see if the banks would possibly be dumb enough to give me a loan that size. If they had, I would have given it a shot. Several banks later, I had the same answer as the first.

Before this, I had pitched to Lisa and Vince the idea that we collectively buy 2229 Lakeside Drive as a Santora compound, just like the Kennedys—minus the politicians, the celebrities, and the sex scandals. Well, minus the politicians anyway.

As it turned out, the Kennedys must have wanted a bit more togetherness than the Santoras. Understandable. If Erica were still here, I would never be thinking of us all living under one roof. I had loved my privacy with her, but now the log cabin was the last place I wanted to be, and I would exhaust myself stalling anywhere rather than go home to sleep . . . or, not sleep. Even if my sister agreed, would we kill each other living that close?

As I ran, that creepy yet comforting feeling blanketed the tightness building in my chest. I looked down at my hands, heard my distant and ragged breathing. Even in the low evening light, I could tell my hands had turned a bizarre purplish color. Was that the right color of hands on a runner?

Somewhere in the back of my brain was another nagging thought. Was I supposed to be somewhere? Maybe, hours ago? Was someone expecting me . . . somewhere?

No, I corrected myself. Not anymore. Nobody expects you at home, Marie. In fact, if you never come home, you won't be missed for days. What else was there to do but run?

I ran harder, but the feeling in my chest (was it pain?) had now spread to my arms, or maybe just one arm. I was alone on the entire track. I thought, what if I dropped?

I had a foggy memory from last week when there was a young boy on the track. He was maybe thirteen years old and he kept cutting halfway across the field so he could pass me as if we were in the final leg of a race. Again and again, right after he would pass, he would shoot me a look over his shoulder that said: "Victory . . . bwah-ha-ha-ha!" and I would stifle a smirk, because, honestly, it looked like the kid had spent most of his days cuddled up to a bag of Doritos and just the quarter of the track he would run ahead of me seemed his limit.

At the time, I had two concerns. One, that the kid would leave that day believing a fantasy of conquering me at the track, and another, more pressing, that he might see me spitting off to the side, as it was as necessary as breathing, and I had to do it right then. On his fourth time attempting to cut me off, he had the misfortune of timing, and my spit landed square on his neck as he attempted to pass.

In my defense, it hadn't been on purpose. However, I knew I had done it, and yes, I kept on running that day. Truth be told, I was so impressed with the razor-sharp accuracy of my spittle whack to his young jugular (unintentional, or otherwise) that it distracted me from the fact that I had just spat on a child. At the time I didn't want to interrupt my run, so I told myself that with this kid's ability to conjure up fantasy scenarios, he may have thought the hit he took was from an awesome bird with mind-blowing horizontal-shitting skills in order to get him on the neck like that.

I took another misstep as I relived the memory, but I didn't go down. Still, I had stumbled twice now, and I was dizzy from the adrenaline of my almost-fall. I thought, I should run one more mile, or maybe a couple more, or three should definitely do it. During all this I was battling the foggy, nagging thought that I was supposed to be somewhere . . . and I was having a bit of trouble seeing the track, and it wasn't the light. There was water in my eyes and no sting of sweat. Was it raining, or had I simply decided to cry?

I was imagining someone calling my name in the distance . . . All I knew was that it wasn't Erica, so I ran faster and the voice got farther behind me on the track. I could always outrun people these days; my weight loss meant less boobs to lug, and I flew around the track unencumbered. The voice was an echo far away now, so I turned to see if it was real, but it had gotten dark.

Was that a shadow cutting across the track? Was it that damned kid again?

I ran faster, but I could see that the kid anticipated this and cut across the football field at a sharper angle, and my heart, lungs and legs would not let me go faster . . . they were on fire and at this rate the kid might just pass me. The worst thing was my mouth was so dry I couldn't even fantasize about spitting on him. What the hell was wrong with me, running without water? And I couldn't remember the last time I'd eaten, but I knew it had been Lisa who forced me. She didn't know I had become an expert at ditching food into a plastic baggie, kept open and ready in my pocket. No stains, I thought, remembering how proud I was when I thought of it.

If it was the same kid, he was bigger than I remembered, much bigger, and faster too . . . and now, as he was barreling towards me, a sharp pang of fear weakened my stride: maybe it was someone else.

My last thought before I was tackled was that only my sister had ever tackled me like that.

I was thinking this as I was tumbling across the grass, feeling the familiar strength, as I was expertly rolled off the track, cushioned by the body of my attacker as I rolled to a stop on the grass without even scuffing an elbow. Only at rest did my breathing finally turn to gasping and my legs fall into spasms from the lack of fluids. I was trapped in a bear hug from behind when Lisa said, "You didn't show up for my lasagna. You okay? I have water in the car . . . did you spit on anyone else today?"

"Not yet," I croaked.

"Good day, then," she said, still hugging me as if she thought I would bolt again. She had no idea how impossible that was right now.

I would have puked in the grass if there had been anything in me, but my stomach just tightened as if I were doing a set of high-speed imaginary sit-ups. Lisa loosened her grip and after my fruitless heaving was done, she rolled me back so that I was in front of her. I had caught a glimpse of a defeated smile on her face. This was not something I had ever seen on my sister before.

"I've decided to sell Camptown Ladies. It doesn't fit into my future business plan. Besides *BALLS*, the gourmet food truck, I have other ideas. You and I will buy 2229 Lakeside Drive, and if Mom and Dad want to join, they will have to kick in."

My body relaxed against her until she was the only

thing holding me up in a seated position. "There goes the neighborhood," I croaked.

I felt my sister's head nodding against mine as she whispered, "Fuck, yeah."

With all the publicity Camptown Ladies had received over the last several years, Lisa found a prospective investment buyer for the campground in just a matter of weeks. I found it strange she had agreed as part of the deal that she would have to stay on for an additional year, even though she would retain no financial control of the place. The buying firm was based out of Boston, and had offered a lucrative, non-negotiable deal. Lisa seemed happy she would still have a year left in the contract to run the camp, and I tried to ignore the idea that she didn't really want to let Camptown Ladies go.

A sticking point came when it was revealed during negotiations that it would also include the neighboring camp for the gay boys, Camp Camp. This had over the years turned out to be Lisa's favorite part of the venture, and I was surprised she had allowed the investors to throw that in. How would Lisa give up the rave parties in the rec hall, the made-up camp holiday Medical Marijuana Daze, and of course the pet costume parades, which included an assortment of delicate dogs and fabulous cats led by more fabulous men, with the most fabulous men dressed to match their pets.

"I didn't think they would find out about Camp Camp," Lisa said. "Those shysters."

"You really thought you could keep thousands of pine trees and a bunch of rec halls hidden after all the articles written about the place?"

"They're rich people, not rich like we are, but REAL rich people. The type who buy things without ever having seen them, so it was worth a try to not mention it."

"And they're the shysters."

"It would have been the perfect deal," she said. "I figured I could hang on to a piece of it to build on later . . . I thought I could hide a few other things, too. Now I have to dig up the Bone Yard."

The Bone Yard was the cannabis garden, and I did not want to be anywhere near when she broke this news to her best gay boyfriend, Eddie. He would cry pink flamingo tears just thinking of the parties that would no longer sprout from that garden. Lisa could tell him. I was used to expecting my sister to deliver all the bad news. Although, when it came to the campground, there had been so little bad news, and nowhere else on Earth was there a place where my sister had shone so bright.

The guilt was eating at me, but before I could convince her to call it off, the entire deal was done through our family lawyer and a Boston bank, all in a matter of weeks. Lisa didn't let these guys win on all accounts, however. For just about any circumstance, Lisa knew a guy who knew a guy and had convinced the Boston Boys (as Lisa called them) to package in the purchase of the newly classified "dilapidated" 2229 Lakeside Drive. Lisa played her cards right to add this property to the deal, and the Boston Boys bought it and flipped it over to her in the same transaction as the sale of the campground. She knew in their rush to buy, the chances were good that nobody would bother to show up in the woods of Rhode Island to get a closer look at the place. Lisa played hardball, and they agreed to use her inspector for the house. "Rookie mistake!" she cackled, as she signed the papers that rolled 2229 Lakeside Drive into the deal, and keeping Lisa's inheritance somewhat intact.

I ignored a gnawing guilt that my sister would have gone through with the sale even if she hadn't fallen in love with 2229 Lakeside Drive just as I had. I knew she may have even done it sight unseen, and knew this the night Lisa tackled me on that football field track. I hadn't known exactly how she would buy it (how could I, when nobody on earth thinks like my sister) but I knew as sure as I had been lying flat on my back on the turf looking up at the early evening sky that Lisa would fix things for her little sister, no matter what. I was too desperate to think about what she had given up to do so. She loved that campground, and I had chosen to forget this part, to be selfish and grab hold of a new distraction.

Immediately after, I had been so distracted by the lure of Lakeside 2229 that it had been easy for me to bail on any last responsibilities at the campground. If my heart hadn't already left it with the loss of Erica, I left it the moment I saw that lake house. What was it about the place? Why was I able to imagine memories made there before I had them? Even with nobody in my life except my family to share memories with, the lake house was the first time I had felt excitement and hope since Erica.

It had such a strong hold on me, and I knew my family was bewildered how I could be leaving my beloved log cabin, and Mom, Dad and Vince were even more confused how Lisa could give up the campground. To me, it made sense. Erica had built the house for me, and with her gone, that house remained my last connection to her. Wasn't letting it go the healthy thing to do?

I felt my time there had passed, and the universe was telling me to live somewhere else. That place was not far, and since it also hugged the back end of the same lake our entire family had become attached to, I was convinced my new home should be Lakeside 2229. The house also shared the same connected pine tree forest as the Camptown Ladies, though a few miles away, but when I closed my eyes and breathed in, I knew the familiar scent of the pine would always smell like home.

It could have been that—the deep feeling low in my chest like you feel when you are falling in love (or fainting from lack of food). More likely it was because there had been a hurricane just one week prior to me finding it, and the storm had stuffed one of my beloved campground pine trees into the back ass of my log cabin. I had been forced to live in a trailer on site during the repairs. It was a bizarre feeling to be in that trailer, looking out at the log cabin as if I were observing someone else's life from my trailer window. When it first happened, I had taken the storm as a clear sign that my life was over.

A similar electrical storm five years ago had brought Erica and I together, and maybe this one was signaling, officially, our end. It was the first moment I thought I needed a dramatic change, away from the log cabin she built for me, farther away than the driveway . . . farther away from the ghost of Erica. She was welcome to stay in the log cabin we once shared, but I knew I needed to leave, even though the tree damage had had the opposite effect I had been hoping for. Seeing the wounded place from my trailer window brought a new physical pain, a sense of longing and pity as if I could feel the pain of the house while the tree was cut apart and wrenched roughly from the roof of the log cabin. The screeching of the branches dragging on the roof made me wince, and later I felt each nail being pounded into the roof as it was boarded up and covered with a bright blue tarp bandage.

I kept thinking how the contractor in Erica would have loved to dig into a repair project like this one, using the opportunity to tweak and update a house we both loved—one that didn't need any updating at all. It was an authentically built log cabin, but to an overachiever like Erica five years was a lifetime for a home and long overdue for things to be changed. Five years had indeed been a lifetime, and everything had, in fact, changed.

Now, the log cabin was sold along with the sturdy bones of Camptown Ladies and her more flamboyant brother, Camp Camp. It had been Lisa's grand venture, and although our entire family had been a part of it all, it was Lisa who had to pull the trigger to sell, and although it was too late, I began to worry how she would feel once the victory of her grand manipulation of the Boston Boys faded. Too late now for me to be wondering if my sister would be hit with regret long after she had signed the papers.

House Call

I crossed the length of my house at Lakeside 2229, and realized how every time I did this I would be struck by its magnificence and the disbelief that it was actually mine. (Well, not just mine.) The large home was simple on the outside, nothing visibly special except the size. What's to love about vinyl siding on a sprawling two-story home? Only that it was protecting a home sprawled out along acres of property on a lake, and the vinyl was perfectly manufactured to look like Nantucket gray wood, faux sun-bleached and God's gift to waterfront houses. The realistic wood grain and matte finish, no-upkeep plastic, says "Chill out . . . nothing to do here, I will outlive you." And you do chill out because as hard as you look at it, there is nothing to repair, paint, or clean, because God (or a plastics company in Columbus, Ohio) figured out how to stop dirt or mold from clinging to it. Erica would have hated it. Back in the day when I worked with her, I saw her tear plenty of it off houses she had renovated. "Vinyl is final," she would say, as if that were a bad thing, and then follow that with a "my ass it is," as she pried off each strip from the structure as if it were a parasite and flung it to the ground. "Now *that's* final."

Lakeside 2229 was much like the Boston-born Toll House cookie, simple and rustic casual on the outside, and secretly rich in its guts. The warm cream walls with sky-high vaulted ceilings were joined by thick wood beams the color of dark chocolate chips, in an expanse of space typically seen only in public buildings and cathedrals. When Lisa first walked inside, she said, "Wow. If a beach house fucked a church, this is what you would get."

"I wonder why the agent didn't list it that way?"

Lisa shrugged, "Missed opportunity," she said as she walked through the house.

It's the light of the place that gets everyone, and she walked through it just as I had, as if she was feeling the sunlit air in the house bathing her like a spa treatment.

Each time I walked through, I felt the overabundance of skylights above, a ridiculous amount, until you are taken in and enchanted by the light and how it uniquely bathes each room in the ever-changing colors of the day. It appeared that the first part of the house was built on all one level, street level from the front door, but as you walked through the house you became aware of how high up it was perched, over a long lakefront yard, which dropped down to the lake. There was a wide lake view from every room, the house constructed in a giant L shape, to take full advantage of the water. Erica would have appreciated that part, and maybe forgiven the vinyl.

When we first moved in, my sister and I giggled like idiots whenever we called the sides of the house the Left Wing and the Right Wing, the way we imagined real rich people might do (with the giant deck dubbed the West Wing, even though it didn't face west.) The deck spanned the length of the Left Wing, half nestled in the pine trees, and the other half suspended out so far from the house that the illusion of the view when you sat down at the patio set was that there was no giant yard, and instead my sister, mom, and dad were magically hovering over the lake as we sipped our evening wine. For the entire first month we were there Vince made it a ritual to join us each early evening before heading home to Katie and Buddy.

Mornings like this were my favorite, when the sunrise bathed the non-lake side of the house in a warm orange glow, filtering though the kitchen and spilling gently into the living room. Even after being here for several months now, I could not get over how the color of the light magically cooled as you walked from the Right Wing to the kitchen, the heart of the house, and then toward the Left Wing, where the glass sliders facing the lake gathered the coolness and changed the light as if water saturated the air, turning it a cooler shade of pale orange. It was there that I noticed a new habit I had of actually eating my breakfast, instead of tossing it away when my sister left the room.

Eating food . . . what a novel idea.

On most days the wind tunnel on the water decorated the lake with perfect wave patterns like whipped cake-frosting shapes in bright reflections across the entire length of the living room. When I first moved in, I would sit on the floor and binge-watch as if it were Netflix. I loved it so much I argued with my sister that we didn't need a couch, or any other seating in the living room for that matter, since it might block the spectacular and ever-changing show on the walls. Lisa won that battle, with the help of Mom, but we compromised with a long, low-profile couch in a color that sat perfectly in the middle between sand and sea, and complemented the reflected waves dancing around our living room.

Heading out from my bedroom this morning from the Right Wing, I was in my typical haze admiring the house as I padded across the wood floor of the bedroom, then the stone floor of the kitchen, then back to warm wood again toward the front door. I loved everything about it, the look and the feel of the slight temperature change as I moved from one end to the next. The thought struck me that I was feeling something I had not felt in a very long time. What exactly? It took a few moments, but I realized this unfamiliar feeling creeping about me was that I was feeling *lucky*. I was in a beautiful place that spoke privately to me in ways I didn't understand, and for the first time in a year I wasn't thinking (at least not constantly) about how much Erica would have loved this or that, too.

The only thing I cared to change about the place was the

sound of the doorbell, and as I heard it now, it left me wanting to change it from something so generic to something more lake-like . . . was there such a thing? Maybe the clanking of that mooring in *Jaws* just before the naked swimming lady clung to it with one less leg . . . though that was less lake and more beach. As I passed the living room, I glanced down the long span of wall toward the front door as I always do to catch the waves, and it reminded me of the other thing I wanted to change. I wanted a glass window on my door, because I hated surprises, expecting a package, and getting a begging Girl Scout. I also hate the way my mouth drops open when I am shocked, and how I take in a sharp breath like someone just punched me in the stomach when I see something unexpected. Like a killer . . . a ghost . . . or a nurse. I wasn't (or was?) grateful that of the three, there was a nurse standing in my doorway.

To be more accurate, it was Lorn, dressed like a nurse.

My ex-love (several times over in fact), ex-Hollywood actress (I had read), was standing in my doorway, all her most attractive features conservatively played down by her new role, long auburn hair pulled away from her face, hiding from view. So professional, I forced myself to think, as I stifled the thought, so unearthly beautiful, as if six years had not passed. Was she pulling a Clark Kent with the glasses? Did she need them or were they to stop people from recognizing her? Or maybe to make her electric green eyes a little less celebrity, a bit more nurse-like.

"Hello, Marie," she said, her face concerned, unsmiling, "you're so thin."

"And you're so lost." I pointed to her outfit. "New TV role?"

"No," she said.

The truth was, Katherine, her mother and my Uncle Tony's wife, had told me Lorn had quit Hollywood and gone back to school to become a nurse. That had been years ago, and I never asked about her again, though I had a million questions at the time. I could not imagine it, and yet here she was, a live update on the Hollywood actress turned nurse.

I felt my jaw tighten as I said, "I heard you gave up your career, the one you so fiercely protected." Lorn-the-actress had made her choice back then, several times, and I couldn't compete with what Hollywood had given her. And now she had thrown it all away.

"Marie, I'm not here to cause trouble for you. I—"

"If you were, you're too late. No trouble to cause. Erica's gone; she died . . . or maybe you knew she's gone?"

"I'm sorry, I didn't know," she said, but her face never changed, no surprise, no sadness, only her usual and fixed compassionate stare, no more, no less than how she looked at my weight loss. Lorn appeared to have adopted the steeliness I imagined a nurse must have to do her job.

"If you were going to come uninvited, showing up before I already lost everything would have made much more sense."

"Marie, no—"

"Save it," I said. You were late trying to come back the first time, and the second . . . third, and now this house call. Erica has been gone for a year now, and if you were worried what that did to me, I hope to hell you give speedier care to your patients."

I have never slammed the door in someone's face in all my life, but I felt the door fly from my hand and slam closed harder than I had intended. I imagined her on the other side, jumping back, thinking the door frame might break free with the impact.

I turned to walk away as there came a soft knocking.

Even if I didn't know it was her, I thought from now on I would recognize her knock, and debated for a second before I flung open the door, my anger ignited by the colossal gall of this woman. I said, "You come here, to my home, after dumping me . . . sorry, how many times?"

"I don't know," she said.

"Then, after I finally find happiness, you show up after she's gone—dressed like the porn version of Nurse Fucking Ratched? And not the hot Sarah Paulson one, the creepy *One Flew Over the Cuckoo's Nest* one. You have got to be f'ing kidding me!"

"Marie—"

If she said anything else, I didn't hear her, since I slammed the door again and walked away.

This time she rang the bell, twice. Anger flared as I thought how this would wake up my mom, who hadn't been sleeping well.

I felt a fury rise in me that I feared. Actually, I feared for her as I flung open the door again, my eyes wild, and this time she did step back at the sight of me.

"You don't get it. You are not welcome here," I said, and I would have said it louder, if only the message hadn't been trapped behind clenched teeth.

Her expression softened. Was it pity? I had been overloaded with that expression lately; everyone had it when they looked at me, and so I easily recognized it. It was the same expression that forced me to drive two towns over to a grocery store so if I ran into somebody I knew, I would not have to see that *look*.

She put both hands up in surrender. "I'm sorry," she said. It was the same soft tone in her voice that I remembered from long ago, so sincere, so loving . . . so unwelcome.

"I don't want your sympathy," I spat, and would've considered slamming the door again if it didn't seem so redundant. As if she read my mind, she threw her heavy medical bag between her and the door jamb, and backed it up with her foot. Lorn Elaine was a feminine woman, but she was not a slight woman, and as slight as I was these days, I was not going to move her if she didn't choose to move. About my only ability these days was to run from life with my weightless body, but now even that was impossible with someone blocking my doorway.

Lorn said, "I am not here in sympathy, but I'm sorry. About so many things." Her voice trailed off and she looked down at the front step. I stared at her for a long time, squelching the flickering thought that her sadness seemed genuine, as it always did, yet each time she would leave me again.

But there was something else . . . I could feel it deep in my bones, moments before she said it. I saw the pity she had for me. I saw it so clearly in her eyes and instinctively knew there was something far worse coming my way. I tried to settle my nerves. She had no hold on me or any connection to anyone in my life. Still, I held on to the door just in case.

"Marie, I'm sorry. I'm not here for you. I'm here for your mother."

I didn't remember letting her in, though I must have because soon after, we were walking down the hallway together toward my mother's room, and now I was thinking how funny it was that the sea-foam green color Mom had picked for the walls in the corridor leading to her bedroom in the Right Wing resembled a slightly more cheerful hospital green with a nurse walking through it. And not just any nurse. This nurse had eyes the color identical to the sea-foam of the walls, which I had noticed when Mom first picked the color. I noticed this in that irritated way you would notice a faded spot on a rug, wondering if you would learn to live with it until you didn't notice it anymore.

As Lorn walked ahead of me, I had a strange feeling in the pit of my stomach that rushed to my head in a dizzying spin, causing one of the hallway walls to tip toward me. I ran my hand along the wall to steady myself as I walked down the corridor, thinking: how many times have I told my nephew Buddy not to do the same? I followed weakly, hoping it was just the familiar scent of her making me woozy, but fearing it was something much worse.

Why was Lorn here?

At the end of the long hallway Mom's door was closed, as it had been until late morning and then again in the afternoon on most days. As we approached it, I was thinking how Dad got up hours before Mom and how she had been prone to naps lately, so unlike her, and I wondered why I had not noticed until right this moment. I was also wondering why I hadn't noticed Mom had been going to bed shortly after *Jeopardy*, saying she was going to read in her room, when she was more of a late-night *Law and Order* girl, rather than a read-before-bed girl . . . and that was when I knew.

I stopped dead in the hallway, realizing my mother must have called her, and whispered, "Is Mom sick?"

But Lorn didn't answer, kept walking, rather professionally I thought, and I was weirdly grateful. Was this to be the last moment where I could believe Mom was fine? Coursing through me was a flashback of a feeling I had just before I realized Erica was gone forever. I instinctively knew then too. Doesn't all trouble start with a confused thought, followed by a flash of panic, before the dreaded reality can seep in?

Lorn was leading, but now she hesitated down the end of the hall when she was met with several doors. "Last door at the end," I said, but I didn't follow, and instead, I turned and wobbled into the room just before Mom and Dad's.

I heard Lorn walk further down the hall and so I felt safe to let myself slump against the adjoining wall to get my balance and then decided to lower myself, worried I might make a sound if the side of my head thumped against the floor. Good catch, I thought. If this was what fainting was like, it felt so very nice and cool with my cheek against the tile, and finally the room stopped spinning and I was nestled under a blanket of dark.

I woke up staring at the back of the most stunning long, wavy auburn hair, trying to enjoy the spectacular sight as it came into focus, wondering about the familiarity of it, the sensuality of it, before I was plagued with a nagging feeling that something was very wrong. That thought dissolved as quickly as it came, and now I was concerned that Lorn was wearing her hair pulled back when she knew I preferred it down. But she wasn't here. My eyes darted around to be sure and I saw I was still alone in the room.

My memory tried to make a comeback: Erica was still gone —dead (always my first thought) and Lorn was gone—or was she? Did Lorn ever leave? Was my love for Erica just a faraway dream? Then I remembered seeing Lorn at my front door and of course I couldn't feel what I used to feel about Lorn because I was still in love with Erica, but now I was failing miserably at remembering which one of them I was with last, or still with. How could I be having any thoughts about Lorn when I had squelched all my senses regarding women, even a stunning auburn-haired woman dressed as a . . . nurse?

Hadn't I loved her once, twice . . . several times before it was finally over? So long ago, and yet I could hear her talking not so far away from me. I wished she could just come back so I could see her face . . . just to make sure it really was her.

My eyes fluttered open and I realized Lorn was not in the room with me, and I could hear her softly knocking on Mom's door, and I could feel the panic rising inside me to get up, but I was too dizzy to rise right now. So, instead, I lay still on the floor, and listened down the hall to Mom's voice from behind her door, "Come in," followed by her strange little cough, which had been lingering for weeks (or had it been months?) and now, from the other room without a view of her, I finally let myself notice that Mom had become very weak. Even her voice had gradually become almost undetectably warbly, sounding like a woman so far removed from the mother I knew even just a month ago. I had told myself that the move into the lake house had exhausted her. I knew now it was something else.

I had been distracted by the loss of Erica and then distracted by my entire family with the impact of my loss. *It was my fault nobody noticed this.*

"Mrs. Santora, it's Lorn. Lorn Elaine," I heard Lorn say, and I wondered if Lorn's muffled speech meant she had on a face mask. No, I thought. Bad dreams are like this . . .

I heard Mom's sleepy voice say, "Lorn? So nice to see you; please come in here before Marie lays eyes on you."

"Don't worry, Marie let me in," Lorn said, and I could tell, yes, without even seeing her, that her voice was indeed stuffed under a face mask.

If I had been able to see my mother, instead of just the floor, I would see Mom as Lorn must now be seeing her. Mom, like me, had shrunk down thin, and thin was even more unseemly for an Italian woman her age, who should be wearing her plumpness like a badge of honor. Mom was the proud matriarch of Camptown Ladies, Camp Camp, and the nearly famous Chef Lisa.

I heard my mother let Lorn in her room and felt my head spin again as I tried to lift it. When had my mother called her? I wondered if Mom had a plan to hide Lorn in her room among a bunch of old dolls she kept in a storage cabinet, dressing all the dolls like nurses to hide Lorn among them, like E.T.? Except my mother would know I would not want Lorn in my house.

I strained to hear the conversation, and squeezed my eyes tight. It was easier to hear with the room not spinning.

"Lorn, honey, you look beautiful," Mom said. "I'm very proud of you. We heard you were a nurse . . . please sit. I don't have a temperature, dear. I have been checking. I see Marie took you right though the kitchen without getting you a nice cold drink. I don't have to tell you how she sometimes takes after her father. Lorn, honey, if you sit over there, would you feel safe to remove your mask to have a drink?" Mom didn't wait for an answer and sounded stronger as she shouted out the balcony slider, "Sal!!! Bring Lorn a drink!"

The windows were cracked open in the spare bedroom I'd landed in, so I heard Dad's voice come from far down below in the yard. "What the hell did she say?" Dad was either talking to himself or to Lisa's dog.

The door was shut to the corridor and I held my breath, hoping I would still be able to hear them, but I couldn't. I would keep my cheek against the floor and just rest here a minute, I thought, give them a while to talk, and then I would get up. This seemed a good plan since the dizziness wasn't going away.

When my eyes opened again, most of my family was looking down at me and there was a heated debate about whether I had fainted or if I'd had a heart attack from the "horrible" weight loss, followed by several other guesses as to why, Lisa said, I was drooling onto the tile grout.

All this was happening while Lorn Elaine, current nurse, former girlfriend, hovered over me, checking my vitals. I stared up at her blinking as if it was 4 a.m. Christmas morning. With a face mask covering her mouth, there was nowhere to look but into those green eyes for answers. Thoughts rushed and swirled in my head as they always did when a woman was on top of me for any reason. I had not had a woman lean over me for such a very long time . . . over a year, in fact . . . before that, of course it had been Erica, but before that, the woman who had leaned over me, in a sexual position, had been *this* woman, sans mask.

I stupidly searched her eyes to see if she had the same thought, but she was staring at her watch, counting seconds, with her two fingers pressed against my wrist. Then she moved a stethoscope to my chest. What was wrong with me? Usually when a woman opened up my shirt, I noticed.

"Well, I'll be the first to say it," Mom said, "Lorn, I'm so grateful you came today."

Dad chimed in, "Yeah, and I'll be the first to say that your timing was downright . . ."

"Creepy," I mumbled.

Lorn looked away and over at them, the turn of her head brushing a loose chunk of her hair across my neck. I imagined asking, "When you are dressed like a nurse, how often do women drop to the floor in front of you?" I would've bet it's a lot. There aren't too many ex-celebrity actress-nurses, and fewer with soft auburn hair brushing across their patient's necks.

This gave me a burst of energy and I tried to get up, wanting to show everyone that there was no reason for Lorn to be there at all. The fact that I had a cheek planted on the floor and that my ex-girlfriend happened to be wearing a nurse uniform, while an amazing coincidence, was irrelevant. She, along with Erica, were both not in my life anymore.

Lorn turned to Lisa and Dad. "It's been a rough time for

your whole family. This weight loss around here must have everyone concerned."

"Of course," Dad said. "It's just not natural for Italian girls; my daughter looks adopted and my wife looks like she did in high school."

Mom came into view now, and the guilt flooded back. How could I have not noticed? It was so painfully obvious. I looked at her. Mom's face was slightly gaunt, her skin seemed slack and pale, and the worry on her face was for me. Another pang of guilt.

Why hadn't I seen it?

Dad said, "Does she need to go to the hospital?"

Lorn flicked her eyes at me, but only for a moment before looking back at Dad. "She just needs to take better care of herself. Eat better . . . or simply eat by the looks of it. Is she sleeping?"

"Um, I can hear you," I said from nine inches below Lorn's face.

Lorn straightened up. "I know this will sound strange to you all since Marie is lying on the floor, but she is not who I came here to—"

Mom spoke up as if someone had pricked her backside with a needle. "Sal, you never got Lorn that damned drink!" And off Mom went to the kitchen, with Dad in tow.

Lorn tried to protest, but Mom had already made her escape. Lorn flipped her mask below her chin and we were left staring at each other, her lips finally within view again. I stared at the mask instead. She noticed.

"Neither you nor your mother have a fever. The mask is just habit."

I worked on calming my frustrated expression while Lorn looked as calm as the Road Runner in an ACME store. Surrounded by lunatics and chaos, Lorn had always appeared as if she had prepared her whole life for moments like this, and the thought struck me that this might make good nurse material. Lorn put her arm around my shoulders and helped me sit up. Now it was her familiar perfume (or maybe shampoo?) making me dizzy. When Mom could not avoid coming back in the room any longer and I noticed her thin face again, I wondered if Lorn had come back just in time.

Lorn stood up from me at last and I was able to breathe as Mom handed Lorn an iced tea. I abandoned the floor as Lorn signaled for us to go back to Mom and Dad's room where there was more room. There, she signaled for Mom and Dad to sit on the couch. They did without question. Lisa, Vince, and I stayed hovering in the doorway, all blankly staring at each other like a reunion of dementia patients until finally Mom dropped the bomb.

"So at first I thought I had The Covid since I refused the vaccine."

"What?" Dad said, turning to her. "You said you went."

"Well, I didn't. I got a little spooked reading about it on the W-W-W-dot."

Dad leaned over to his high school sweetheart and kissed her forehead while I just stood there with my brother and sister, not saying a word because I felt like I wasn't really there at all.

Mom continued talking as if she were telling a story about a coworker's distant cousin. "Whatever it is, it will be what it will be," she said. "How long does a person really need to live, anyway?" she asked to nobody in particular. "My doctor said it could be a touch of lung cancer." She waved a bony hand as if she was pushing the thought away, a female, elderly Tom Cruise in *Mission Impossible*, clearing the virtual reality stats to the next screen. "Which would have to be God's will, since I've never smoked a day in my friggin' life . . . not like your father here with that *medical* marijuana silliness." She rolled her eyes in Dad's direction as he sheepishly shrugged at Lorn. I was trying to distract myself from the conversation, thinking, Mom is embarrassed by the following things: pot, sex, loud people. How on earth did she make Vince, Lisa, and me?

"If I do have it, maybe I got it secondhand. That would be you, Sal," Mom said.

Dad laughed at her. "You can't get lung cancer from

secondhand gummies." Mom waved this idea away as well. I wondered, if you strung together all the times Mom had waved Dad's comments or theories away, would we be able to get rid of the ceiling fans? Our parents were crazy and it was made more obvious by Lorn sitting and listening like their reactions were perfectly normal. I thought I saw the flicker of a smile before she put her game face back on.

Mom said, "So, anyway, kids, they want to take another peek at my lung to see if there is anything they want to take out, and I would have to decide if I will have treatment, but anyway cancer is my doc's first guess unless it's some other viral thing that just won't go away."

Since my sister was silent for the first time in her life, I finally found my voice, "Mom, did you just say—"

"Yep, maybe a touch of lung cancer, or, what do you think, Lorn, maybe a new strain of virus?" She dismissed her own words with another wave, but smaller this time, like she believed in it less.

Lorn pulled her face mask from under her chin over her head, and stuffed it into her uniform pocket. I liked that she did that.

"Let's not get ahead of ourselves," she said.

Quietly, to Vince and me, Lisa whispered, "Jesus . . . the C word."

Mom brushed off nothing visible from her polyblend pajama pants and straightened the edge of an invisible wrinkle before she said, "Bad news is if it's cancer, I won't be able to blame the Republicans."

Lisa said, "That's the bad news? Mom, what do you mean that you have to decide *if* you will have treatment? You will have whatever treatment they want to throw at you." Lisa put her hand on Mom's shoulder gently, like she was afraid to touch her. "What if you are supposed to live to be a hundred years old and love every minute of your old age?"

Mom waved away double-time. "One hundred? No thank you. I don't want to smell."

Dad chimed in, "One hundred could be amazing! You don't want to find that kind of thing out too late. It's like that old joke: you don't want to find out the day before you die that you love sucking——" Dad made a lewd graphic motion behind Mom's back to clue us in to the punchline. All I could do was shake my head as Vince and Lisa burst out laughing.

"Not helping, Dad," I said. "Read the friggin' room. You *are* the old joke!" Dad was laughing harder than anyone as usual.

Mom said in an exaggerated tired voice, "Lorn, honey, do you see what I have to deal with?" and she raised her hand to slap Dad on his arm and shoo him away like a fly. I was happy to see her enthusiasm was back.

Lorn said, "Ten percent of all lung cancer patients have never smoked, so it is not out of the question. But at your mother's age, depending on location and type, a treatable cancer could be the preferred choice over a virus."

"Thanks for the stats, Nurse Ratched," I heard myself snap. "Any other interesting facts regarding my family's shit luck?"

"Marie!" Mom raised her voice, "Behave yourself. Lorn was kind enough to come, and I did look at the statistics after we spoke. I snuck onto Marie's computer to search what was on the W-W-W-dot and it doesn't really matter; it's going to be whatever it is, and I will deal with it my way."

And with that, Mom got up from the couch and stepped out onto the balcony. I knew Mom was pretending to get some air when in fact she probably worried she could be contagious to the rest of us. With her out of earshot, we all started talking at once, firing questions at Lorn.

She patiently tried to answer all of us until my brother Vince said he was so happy Lorn was here and Dad turned on him.

"Vince, did you know anything about this?"

But of course he didn't, and now it was clear that Dad didn't know either, and the shock of hearing it sent Dad reeling. He was staring out at the balcony at Mom, careful to make sure she didn't see the worry on his face, but Mom was ignoring us all.

Vince joined Dad and me and we all took turns lobbing

questions at Lorn Elaine, ex-Hollywood actress, full-time nurse. What was the prognosis of lung cancer patients her age? What were the treatment options? Would she be in terrible pain? Which should we be more worried about? Would surgery avoid chemotherapy?

The severity of the situation sat upon us as Lorn tried to answer the barrage of questions bubbling up, while I considered my options. My top choice was running across the room and jumping off the balcony, and I felt my body respond as if it was a reasonable option. But my flight or fight subsided with the thought that the balcony was likely only high enough to give me a broken leg, or maybe two, and of course my sister's wrath for making things more difficult.

As if on cue Lisa took control. "Everyone stop talking at once—and—wait—why the hell—*is Mom smoking?*"

We collectively turned to see our mother standing on the balcony, awkwardly holding a cigarette between her fingers. She struck more the pose of a gay man than an elderly woman, taking tiny puffs between lips so tight they could not have allowed much in. Still, she stifled a cough.

The silence of the room got Mom's attention. She turned back to us slowly as if she was in one of Lorn's made-for-TV movies. "I figured, if I was going to have lung cancer, I might as well do what everyone will assume. I've decided to take up smoking. Starting today." She took a micro-puff and gave a micro-cough.

"Hey, I think that's one of mine," Dad said.

Mom faked one more tiny drag and stumped the cigarette out on the railing of the deck.

"What the fuck?" Lisa said.

In typical fashion, my sister assessed us all in five seconds, maybe less: Mom, coughing from her new hobby; Dad, distraught, confused, and pissed Mom stole from his hidden stash of butts; Vince, eyes watery, looking down, wanting to be alone so he could cry like he used to as a kid; and me, wannabe balcony diver, dizzy from lack of food and sleep, yet inebriated by ex-girlfriend exposure that made me feel more like an angry drunk than a panicked daughter. If only that damned balcony had been ten feet higher . . .

Lisa clapped her hands together, and I knew she had completed her assessment. She began in a voice we knew all too well. "Unless The Actress is heading to a gig, I am supposing Lorn is now officially a nurse." She turned toward Lorn. "I'm also thinking Mom will be more comfortable with you than with a stranger, so let's make this work, especially since somebody is already making noise about not getting treatment."

We were all silent.

Lisa turned to Lorn, who seemed to be ignoring us all to stare calmly at my mother with a nurse's analytical gaze.

"Lorn," continued Lisa, "I'm guessing you must have huge nursing school bills, what with giving up the acting gig, coupled with the ancient gay scandal stalling your career, so this should work out for you. Congratulations, you're hired. You'll be our mom's private nurse and you'll stay right here in a guest room in the Left Wing. This way you can help Mom with whatever she needs."

Lorn didn't take her eyes off our mother, and I realized she was looking for a sign that this was agreeable to the patient, and Lisa took this as a sign that she was playing hardball, something Lorn had never played in her life (while my sister invented the game).

"It's just that I have a job," Lorn said, but it was said in a long-ago-far-away voice, as if it were somewhere buried deep in Sherwood Forest, and she couldn't quite remember if it was real or a fairy tale. Our family had a way of doing that to people. When the characters surrounding you are this colorful, real life no longer seems real.

"Did I mention we'll pay you a ridiculous amount of money? So don't even insult us by asking. Plus free room and board, of course; this includes my cooking, which, as you know, makes the deal priceless. On second thought, maybe you should be paying us."

Lorn turned toward Lisa, unblinking. This was the look most people gave to Lisa during her Italian version of *Let's Make a Deal,* which is: I talk, you shut up.

Lisa went on, "You'll be free to live your own life, dating men, women, or cats or whatever you're doing these days, and I'll make sure my sister won't interfere." I looked at Lisa with dagger eyes, which never did a bit of good. "And," she said, "we'll also have to concoct something for Dad to do to keep him out of your way."

"Um, I can hear you," Dad said.

Lisa ignored him. "I assume we will all have to wear masks, to be safe."

I knew by Lorn's casual shake of her head that we were either safe or already exposed.

Lisa continued to address Lorn. "So, we'll get Dad out of the way, just to be safe, and for Mom's sanity. There are rooms in this giant house we haven't even walked into yet." She turned to Dad, widened her eyes, and spoke to him as if he were a twelve-year-old. "Dad, you're getting a new room."

Dad tried to nod as if it was a sacrifice, but I saw the Man Cave glint in his eye. Mom patted his hand in case he needed soothing. "No problem," he said. "I'll do whatever Doctor Lorn says."

"I'm not a—"

"Lorn, you don't have to worry about Vince getting in your way," Lisa said. "He's such a pussy about medical things, the first time you whip out your stethoscope, he'll wet his pants and run from the room."

Vince looked at his shoes, but nodded, and I could see him blinking watery eyes.

Lisa whipped her attention back to me. "And you are going to cut the bullshit and start getting well or I'll kill you. I didn't sell Camptown Ladies to help you buy this house for MY health!" Lisa took a deep breath. "Now, everyone, got it?"

Everyone got it, but I stood with heat in my face rising like a furnace about to blow, as there was no way Lorn was going to move into this house even if she agreed to. We didn't even know if Mom needed that much help . . . but as I thought this, I noticed how pale she was and hoped it was from the cigarette. When I turned to my sister to protest the live-in nurse idea, Lisa's hand went up like a bull-dyke crossing guard and stifled me with a healthy dose of childhood fear.

"Shut the F-up. It's settled," she said, an inch from my face. And when Lisa says that, two things always happen: I shut the F-up, and it's settled.

Still, it occurred to me that none of us had bothered to see if this deal was okay with Mom, and when I looked over at her, a thought struck me, how the rebellious side of Erica would have appreciated Mom lighting up for the first time in her life. As if she had read my thoughts, Mom smiled at me defiantly. "I'll save this for later," she said, sticking her crushed butt in her pajama pocket and giving her pocket an affectionate pat for safekeeping.

I felt my eyes stinging at the corners, my index finger already catching the first tear and flicking it away as if it were a bug. I also fought the desire to laugh at my mother's ridiculous strength, and at the craziness of it all. When I looked back at Lorn, she was staring at me, and I could tell she was thinking the same thing. I still felt anger at her in the pit of my stomach, but there was relief there, too, a relief that only Lorn's presence could bring. I took my first deep breath since fainting.

Just Too Damned Much
Vagina Around Here

When Lisa goes into panic mode, things happen, and her average runs about 80/20. Most for the good, some for the bad, but one thing you can say about Lisa, when she is around, nothing will stay still for very long. Also, that the 20% of the time she failed would be the most entertaining.

From birth, my sister has operated under the assumption that some action was always better than no action. And she'd been acting stranger than usual the last few days, leaving me wondering what she was up to, and feeling the deeply unrealistic hope that she would fix everything.

The doorbell rang, but before I could get to it, Lisa intercepted me in the hall, grabbed me by the elbow, and pulled me into Dad's makeshift bedroom, still in progress. I noticed for the first time that Dad had already outfitted it with one too many things that should never come inside a house. Lisa glanced over my shoulder at the far corner of Dad's new bed and asked, "Is that a tree limb?"

"Yeah, saw that. I was just getting the door," I said.

"I have to catch you up on something."

Uh-oh.

"A while ago I told Lorn she needed to use her influence to score an at-home test kit for Mom. And she did. A few days ago."

"How—"

"Doesn't matter, she did it. You were out canoeing with Dad."

Lisa had told me Dad desperately needed a canoe ride since the self-imposed quarantine was making him hyperfocus on Mom, which was, in turn, driving Mom crazy. Lisa had said, "After three days at home, Dad is already losing it. Mom says it's your turn to take him fishing." It was only as I was loading the canoe stuffed with fishing equipment into the lake that I thought, Lisa had never taken Dad fishing in her life, so how was it my turn? Since Lisa was more the "I'll hang back to make us a nice lunch" type, at least Dad and I had that to look forward to.

As we dined later that day, flashbacks of the Covid virus devastation ran through my mind. The overwhelmed hospitals, the tragic stories one after another on the news. How, at first, our family seemed to be so lucky that nobody we knew had contracted the virus. Then that started to change over the second half of the year. Families flocked from crowded cities like Providence, Boston, and New York to spend time outdoors at Camptown Ladies when we were finally allowed to reopen.

Lisa served hundreds, maybe thousands, of free meals she had personally cooked and our family donned N95 masks as we served the dishes, staying six feet apart under the pine trees. Camptown Ladies and Camp Camp were busier than ever, and the gay boys gave away cotton masks made of rainbow and glitter fabric, while the lesbians made camp-themed masks with trees, tents, axes, and campfires. Weirdly, Mom had taught me how to sew just two months prior to the arrival of this modern-day plague, so while my sister cooked long into each night, prepping for the following day, I sewed hundreds of masks to cover the faces of the campers as they stood in line for food. They happily wore them when they weren't stuffing the best Italian food in all of New England into their mouths.

It was a strange time among all the tragic stories . . . but there were good times too. The forced closeness made our family grow closer, and we all felt lucky to be able to be of service to so many people who were out of work and in need of a meal. We opened up undeveloped land for anyone in need, BYOT (bring your own tent), and Erica had her crew build more open-air shelters where people could easily social distance by playing cards in gloved hands with their families on rainy days. Donations were collected from anyone who could afford to pay for a meal, and all kids ate free, including college kids. For adults, all the pasta and vegetable dishes were complimentary, and Lisa established a pay-only-what-you-can policy for her award-winning meat and seafood dishes.

This went on all season, and when the virus continued, it went into the next. Finally, when it all started to look like the virus might come to a manageable end, our family took the next winter off, sleeping through most of it like exhausted bears in hibernation. At every family gathering for the following year, we shared stories of that incredible time when millions of people were sick and hundreds of thousands died from what our then-president had convinced people was a hoax.

After it was all over, it was Mom who took it upon herself to declare all health-care workers, emergency workers, teachers and law enforcement workers and their families welcome to eat at the campground, where their money was no good. Shortly after that, the once-depilated recreation hall converted into Dove Mangia: Fine Italian Restaurant in the woods was in dire need of an expansion. If any of us had needed a job, it would have been a lifetime of job security, especially for Lisa. This was 2020, and just when I thought things could not be more upside down in my world, Erica was dead.

"Lorn is here," Lisa said, "with Mom's Covid report," and I knew by her tone she was worried.

I nodded slowly. "Good news arrives by phone."

I walked toward the front door, with Lisa trailing atypically behind me.

My sister and I held our breath as I opened the front door. At once I saw at the corners of Lorn's eyes a telling smile a second before her full lips shaped into a grin. I also knew the way her green eyes sparkled that she was fighting back happy tears, nodding without saying a word. Lisa and I exhaled in unison, and my sister promptly shoved me aside to barrel a hug into Lorn, who dropped her medical bag when trapped in the bear hug. I looked down at the bag in the doorway and remembered how such a short time ago she had used it to stop me from slamming the door on her. I caught her eyes over Lisa's shoulder, and the tiny lines at her eyes deepened as I thought they might, and I knew she was wasting one of her unearthly beautiful smiles against the bulk of my sister's shoulder. She seemed to be looking to me for approval, and I silently mouthed, *thank you*.

A brighter sparkle flashed as she nodded with a tear spilling from the corner of her eye and disappearing, ironically, into my sister's camouflage shirt. One hurdle jumped, I thought, and breathed deeply again. Recent victory for Mom aside, I must get back to not wanting Lorn here. I would be talking to my sister about the concept of plenty of other nurses in the sea . . . if she ever let her out of that hug.

Lisa finally released Lorn. "Thank you," Lisa said, "from all of us. Just in case my thick-headed sister doesn't say it." I saw Lorn hiding a smirk as she looked at me. There had been a finality in my sister's voice that made me hope this was it, and it was time for the Santora family to say our grateful good-byes— until Lisa swooped to grab the medical bag before pulling Lorn through the door. "Now, let's talk about this pesky cancer scare business . . ."

One victory in our pockets was not enough to calm the household until (and maybe not after) we knew what was really going on with Mom, so we were all in a tailspin to fill our time. With quarantine not mandatory, with Campground Ladies now sold and our mother's medical bills set to pile up, Lisa had a fire under her ass to start a new venture. Her days of running a five-star restaurant in a gay and lesbian campground were not her top priority anymore, especially since the new owner had worked in a stipulation to close the property for a full renovation before they could open again.

Lisa was using the time to cook up bigger ideas, and while she had the talent and what Uncle Tony would say was *sefere di acciaio* (balls of steel) to back it up, what she didn't have was a plan, though this never stopped Lisa from taking action.

We were all gathered outside on the main porch deck overlooking the lake, and strangely there was an odd calm about our family, led by Mom. Having agreed to whatever treatment would be decided, she had given all appearances of going back to ignoring the fact that anything was wrong at all. Mom was doing her best to hide her exhaustion, and she and Dad were both acting like the virus-shaped bullet she had just dodged would be the last.

I wasn't sure if I should be grateful or pissed off because I wasn't having any such luck. It was mind-boggling to think of the journey my mother could be facing so late in her life. Instead, I chose to fester on the fact that Lorn was to begin her first day of work at the end of this week as Lakeside 2229 Temporary Live-in Nurse. I had insisted on the T-word, and Lisa had agreed just to end the discussion. My first order of business was to have something to do to get me the hell out of the house when Lorn moved in this Friday.

Lisa, of course, had a plan brewing, and when I heard her inform Dad she would be setting off for Boston for the day, I invited myself, not even caring about what I might be in for. All I knew was that after birthing the idea of a fleet of gourmet catering trucks named *BALLS*, Lisa's most recent brain fart was to focus on parlaying her past TV appearances from her five-star campground restaurant days into an appearance on a cooking show. This, of course, could feed into the business of getting Lisa's *BALLS* off the ground. By sheer bullying (Lisa's version of networking) she had coerced an old college friend to finagle a meeting with a well-known agent to discuss the possibilities of taking on her "brand" and possibly scoring an appearance on a network morning show.

I watched as Lisa cornered Dad on his chair, which was set apart from us on the deck. It was unsettling how, since we had all learned about Mom, Dad had been keeping to himself. We were all used to the Dad who stayed in everyone's business, the Dad you had to make a wide path around to get some space, not this six-feet-apart Dad. This Dad sat off by himself, like he was being punished and had his favorite toy taken from him: Mom.

Lisa said, "How about you come with us today, Dad. You don't ever get to Boston, and seeing a TV studio will be fun."

"Mom might need me here."

"For what?" Lisa busted him. "You have been useless around here, and Lorn is moving in today. You're coming with us so you can stay out of Lorn's way. Besides, there'll be all the cute newsgirls from Channel Five."

A twinkle sparked in his eye. Dad had a thing for the ladies on Channel Five.

"It would be great TV," he said, "because if one of those beauties comes within ten feet of me, they can film my heart attack." He looked around and lowered his voice. "You know your mom doesn't let me watch them." Then he yelled over to Mom, "Hey, honey, who is that hot little number on the news, the one with the nice fun bags?"

"I'm shocked Mom doesn't like you watching them."

"Don't honey me," Mom yelled from across the deck, "and you leave those sweet young women alone, Stan. No career girl needs an old man prowling about, scaring the hell out of them." I thought, #TimesUpDad.

Lisa said, "Don't worry, there will be security at the studio. They will spot him in a second."

"Nope," Dad said, "I can't go anywhere today because I'm breaking ground on building my shed."

Lisa cocked her head at him like a giant Saint Bernard as she repeated, "Your shed?"

Dad said, "Like I had at the last house. I need a place to put my tools."

Mom got up, a bit unsteady, but made her way over to the

tray of fruit Lisa had served. Mom reached for some grapes as she said under her breath to Vince and me, "You mark my words, your father will be the only tool in that shed."

"Every guy wants his own space," I said. "A place to work uninterrupted."

Mom snorted. "Your father is building another clubhouse. Only this time he's not even bothering to disguise it. He wants it to have full electrical and plumbing."

"Electrical, yes; some of my yard tools have to be plugged in," he muttered to nobody in particular.

"So what did the kids hire the landscapers for?" Mom asked.

"So we have someone to bet against the Patriots games," Lisa answered.

Dad wouldn't quit. "I am investigating my options for all the bells and whistles. Once the plumbing is in, if I have to go to the bathroom, I won't have to go all the way back in the house."

"Tell your daughters about the entertainment system," Mom said.

"Helps to keep the gardeners entertained while they're working," Dad answered. "Besides, I need a place I can hang out with my grandson. This house is not beneficial to a little boy's well-being."

"Buddy shouldn't be witnessing an old man squandering money," Mom said, "and he doesn't need a clubhouse. When he comes over to visit, he has an entire yard the size of a football field . . . and a lake."

Dad answered that with, "Just too damned much vagina around here. He'll need a place to get away from it all once in a while."

"I'll never understand that thinking," Lisa said.

Vince whispered to me, "There goes our sister, pretending she doesn't have a vagina again."

I whispered back, "Well, it is Thursday." Vince and I laughed until Lisa scared us silent with a deadly glance.

"It's settled. Dad's coming," she said.

"I'm not going anywhere," Dad answered, with a tone that

made us all turn to look at him. "Sorry," he said. But he didn't look sorry. He looked angry. Dad was never angry, so on him it looked weird, and sad. He got up and left the deck, but I heard him stumble a bit when his garden man-clogs hit the pile of the carpet. I'd begged him not to wear those, but since we had all inherited Grandma's loot, he insisted that rich people could wear whatever they wanted, and he certainly did.

When Dad refused to join us on the trip, Lisa roped in Vince to do the driving so she could work on the way. (This meant control the radio.) It wasn't until we were on our way that Lisa teased Vince that she invited a second man to join us since he barely had enough testosterone to be considered her brother. On our way, we picked up Lisa's pal, the fabulous Eddie, who coached Lisa on all things feminine. Truthfully, Eddie was more feminine than either my sister or I could ever hope to be, even on our best days.

When Eddie floated to the car, Lisa said, "Thanks for coming, Eddie. I needed a man on this trip."

"Oh, I'm so honored, but I need a man on this trip too, honey. Why hello, Vince," he said, playing the honorary butch boy by rolling up his sleeves. On Eddie rolled sleeves had more the look of bracelets.

Eddie said, "I know what I need for my sleeve; anyone have a box of butts?"

Lisa said, "If we had them, I assume you would be able to sniff out the butts."

Vince and I laughed our heads off.

Lisa knew Eddie lived to be teased and she also knew Eddie would playfully cuddle up to Vince on the ride, telling him how handsome he was and reveling in watching him squirm. It was his favorite pastime, Lisa's favorite, too.

I was just happy for the distraction.

"I need a proper posse so I can represent for my fans," Lisa said.

"Girrrrrl," Eddie said, as he adjusted himself in the car. Out of nowhere he whipped out a thin, shimmering scarf "just for show" to drape around his neck. "To draw attention to my shoulders," he said, before frowning like an eight-year-old. "I know you didn't think this through, that the prettiest pony would be sitting in the back of the bus." And with that, he catapulted over the seat and plastered himself between Vince and Lisa in the front. "With us three boys up front, Marie gets the back seat all to herself."

"Usually your department," Lisa cracked, as Vince tried, without success, not to have his body touch Eddie's since for Eddie just a man who was breathing was encouragement. Lisa worked against Vince by playfully shoving Eddie against him at any given turn of the wheel. Eddie squealed in ecstasy at every turn as if it were a body slam at a club, and Vince stepped on the gas in an attempt to shorten the torture. We arrived at the station a hair-raising forty-five minutes later.

She Used to Prefer Sausage

The receptionist said Lisa's agent friend from college could not join us, but she had arranged a meeting with a producer from the channel. A few moments later, the second we saw her, I knew we were screwed.

"God, I hope that's her," Lisa groaned, growling like a bull in heat when the woman stopped at the receptionist's desk before turning to look at us. She was an attractive type A corporate woman in a tight business suit and stylish long hair and funky black-rimmed glasses perched on her head. Cute look, I thought, and randomly wondered if Nurse Lorn ever wore her glasses as a hair accessory. Lisa whispered to Eddie and me that the woman looked like a more voluptuous version of Sandra Bullock if Sandy had gained an extra fifteen pounds, mostly in her bra.

Lisa wasted no time strutting over to the producer who met us halfway. "Sandra," the woman said, and I saw my sister was impressed with her quick-on-the-draw hand. My sister and Eddie each made an identical noise to acknowledge there was another Sandra in town, so move over, Bullock. There were more aggressive handshakes all around, after which Eddie absently rubbed his soft, wounded paw. Only the faintest sense of reality must have been what stopped him from grooming himself like a wounded cat (the Broadway version) because Eddie was never one to properly read a room.

"I have to be on set for a few more minutes," Sandra said,

"but rather than keep you waiting in the lobby, you can tag along for a tour if you like, if you are all good with the rules of the sound stage—total quiet during takes."

Sandra would have had no way of knowing this was a ridiculous request of my sister and Eddie, but I didn't feel it was the time or place to say so since I valued my head.

"Oh, yippee!!" Eddie said, flapping his hands together, as I saw an expression pass over Sandra's face, already second-guessing her offer.

"Our crew is filming a cooking show," she said, her expression one of fruitlessly hoping it wouldn't appeal to our clapping friend. Eddie clapped double time. "Oooohhh, sssssnacks!" he said, adding a little hop. "I love food, and the attention of a camera; just ask anyone!"

"It's true, Eddie will eat anything, and do anything in front of a camera," Lisa said, and Producer Sandra shot my sister a raised eyebrow so Lisa would know the comment didn't sail over her head. I got the impression not much did.

"They're filming a cookie episode, nothing fancy," Sandra said, but there was no deterring Eddie's excitement.

"L.U.C.K.Y!!!" he spelled out, like a cheerleader or the winner of a gay spelling bee.

As we headed to the elevator, Lisa said, "Sandra, I appreciate you agreeing to see me with your busy schedule, what with making cookies and all."

I winced. Sometimes my sister took this tack.

Sandra stopped walking and turned to Lisa. "Huh. Starting with an insult?" she said, cocking her head. "An interesting choice. Sometimes I like that. It's not like I wasn't warned about you," the producer said, turning her back to Lisa to keep walking.

"Whatever you heard is true," Lisa said. "The good, the bad. All of it."

Producer Sandra ignored this, which left Lisa uncharacteristically quiet as we all rode the elevator to the sound stage, floor twelve. Out of the corner of my eye I could see Lisa looking the producer up and down like a late lunch panini.

Oh boy.

The crew had just finished shooting a scene in the kitchen when we walked in. The host of the cooking show was an annoyingly perky woman I vaguely recognized with a Joker-like smile at the ready to help sell the cookware (or dishes or bedding) that bore her name in a bold cursive script she must have insisted on. When she saw us walk in with Sandra, she gave a heavy sigh as if she had been digging a ditch all morning, which contrasted fiercely with the act of her nose being powdered by another human being.

She waved the makeup person away and clicked over on her heels. "Sandra, they can't seem to get this shot. Is there anything you can do? I don't know how many more times I can scoop this same cookie batter onto these trays."

"Dough," Lisa said, and everyone turned to her.

I thumped her on the back in a futile attempt to shut her up.

"Excuse me?" the blonde host said.

"It's not batter. It's cookie dough. It's okay; a lot of people make that mistake."

The blonde looked like she smelled something bad. "Oh, it's okay?" Then she spun around to Sandra. "Who are these … people?" With that, she tossed back a chunk of perfect long blonde hair as if it had been obstructing her vision.

Sandra looked at Lisa with an equal blend of annoyance and amusement, recognizing that within seconds Lisa had insulted her and her staff. This was a look Lisa gets often from attractive straight girls. The blonde cooking show lady was not amused, and she looked my sister up and down as if Lisa had just splashed the woman's bright yellow weather-girl dress with mud from her metallic granite gray Jeep.

Lisa asked Sandra, "Should you tell her a cookie sheet is not a tray?"

Blondie fumed. "How do you feel about spoons?" she yelled as she flung one the length of the cross-section TV kitchen, spattering cookie dough shrapnel across the faux kitchen sink. In seconds an intern scrambled over with a wet dishtowel to mop it off the wall.

"Oh, too bad," Lisa said. "I'm pretty sure that was a Williams-Sonoma cookie dough scoop."

Sandra's voice boomed out to the room, "Take twenty!" which sent Blondie and everyone but the cleanup crew scurrying off. Sandra turned to Lisa. "I mean, if it's okay with you that they take a break?"

Lisa shrugged. "I'm good with it. It will give us a chance to chat," my sister said cheerfully as she made herself comfy on one of the set's living room couches. She specifically chose the one that had the never-sat-in look. When nobody followed her, she thought better about where she had propped her feet up and made a beeline back to the cooking stage as if she was refreshed from her sit.

Sandra looked at me with raised eyebrows for an explanation. I had none. I never did.

Lisa was now perusing the countertops and opened a few doors to see what was in the cupboards. I knew her nodding and "uh-huh" sounds meant she was pleased with what she found.

"Make yourself at home," Sandra said. "This studio is free for the next hour, so why not?"

I couldn't tell if Producer Sandra was moving from amused to angry, but perhaps she was more confused than anything else. Lisa saw that look also, and to her it smelled like potential. I have seen this look on so many people before. My sister outraged people, but equally entertained them, and usually (*usually* . . .) the latter won out. I wondered what would happen in this particular case.

"Well, it's almost lunchtime and I see from the fridge that I could make you an omelet right now that will be better than your last three orgasms. Combined."

"Lisa!" I said. My Mom-like shout was purely reflex, and automatically emerged whenever my mother wasn't around to do it. My heart sank to the pit of my stomach as I wondered if I would someday always have to be that voice . . . and, more alarming, would I have to be Lisa's sole reality check?

65

Eddie's and Vince's giggling pulled my morbid thoughts away, knowing their laughter would only encourage Lisa.

"Pretty confident, this one," Sandra said to me, but before I could answer, she walked over to Lisa, who was still rummaging through the cupboards for supplies. Sandra leaned on the kitchen island, saying, "Better than my last *three* orgasms?"

Lisa planted her hands on her hips like a field hockey coach whose player forgot a part of the game plan. "*Combined*," Lisa corrected.

Sandra stayed silent for a few seconds while I imagined her pressing a secret security button under the island. My sister stared her down.

"That's a bold statement," Sandra challenged.

"Not really. I mean, how good could the orgasms be since I assume everyone is straight until they prove to me otherwise." I knew that part not to be true. Again, not the time to mention this.

Sandra didn't blink, didn't smile, and instead slid past the island and moved one step closer, until only the distance of her clipboard was between them.

"Well, Chef Lisa, you could give it a try . . . but I've never been much of an omelet girl. I prefer sausage."

"Oh me too!" Eddie said clapping for Producer Sandy and gasping with delight over some sausage-laden memory.

The look on my sister's face read: *RESPECT*. Not a look I have seen often.

"Well, you will love this omelet, I assure you. You will love it so much you may end up preferring eggs to sausages. You wouldn't be the first."

Sandra couldn't stop a laugh from escaping as she walked away toward a member of the security crew. I wondered if we were about to get bounced out, but Lisa, who was not reading the room at all, had already crossed back to the fridge to fling a brick of sausage links onto the counter. It skidded into the stainless sink with a loud thud. "That is the sound of sausage taking a back seat."

"Oh, I know that sound," Eddie cackled, with Vince slapping my arm, laughing.

Sandra stopped dead in her tracks, turned to look at Lisa and Eddie for a second before a smirk spread across her face. She nodded to a camera guy who started filming without moving a muscle.

Lisa called out, loud enough for the crew to hear, the order. "If you give the crew an extra ten-minute break, I'll give you the best sausage you've ever had in your mouth."

Sandra waved the approaching security guard away and turned back to Lisa. "Fine, but I should warn you, as a general rule I don't eat omelets."

"Not even once . . . maybe in college?" Lisa asked.

The producer flinched and this time couldn't hide the laugh.

"Maybe once. In college," Sandra said. Lisa lifted one eyebrow in my direction, her way of keeping score.

"Well then, the taste of this might bring back some amazing memories."

And with that, Lisa stepped into high gear on the kitchen stage, ignoring us, as was her process, quickly assessing the equipment and grabbing glass jars from the wall-mounted spice rack, spreading them out with the dexterity of a casino dealer. I kept my eyes on Sandra who, despite having her arms folded tightly in front of her, seemed keenly aware that she had lost all control of the room . . . and didn't seem to care. Round one: Lisa.

I forgot the rest of the crew was still there until Sandy said, "Take an extra ten," and except for the camera guy they all dispersed just as the blonde headed toward Sandra to protest. When she saw she was alone, and walking against the tide of crew, Blondie spun on her heels and stomped off.

Vince took a seat in the empty audience chairs to watch at a safe distance while Eddie followed after Lisa like a prancing poodle gracefully balancing on his shapely back legs, hoping to be in a position to catch any falling scraps.

Lisa went back to the fridge and I heard her say to him, "Okay, moment of truth, if they are out of tarragon, I'm cooked."

Eddie tried to help her look on the shelves, but she swatted him on the ass, saying, "You wouldn't know what you were looking for if it bit you in the behind . . . well, maybe if it bit you in the behind."

Eddie cackled and strolled back to the industrial-sized Wolf burners on the kitchen island, making a disgusted face. "All these knobs . . . and not one the right size. What does one *do* with all of them?"

Lisa laughed and, typical of her luck, scored a twist tie of fresh tarragon and unleashed it with one hand while gathering a few herb bundles from a basket near the fridge. She elbowed Eddie aside and he yipped like a terrier. "You just stand there and look pretty," she said.

"I can't help that, but what if I want to learn?" he asked in a high-pitched whine.

"If I knew this kitchen better, I'd get you some cheese to have with your whine."

Lisa glanced over at the producer, who had taken a seat at the sound desk, as if being sucked into a reality show she hadn't intended to watch. Absently, she glanced down at her clipboard, but her attention was so clearly on Lisa and Eddie. I could tell by the way Lisa was strutting that she knew it too. My sister was in full-blown showboat mode.

Lisa said, "Okay, Eddie, you can stay and learn, but you have to let me be the boss."

"And this makes today different, how?"

"Shut the hell up and hand me those eggs. Unless you're opposed to touching eggs."

Eddie said, "No, we are cool with touching and eating them. Darling, how else could my people brunch?"

"Is that the royal *we*?" Lisa asked.

"It's just the fertilizing of eggs—*this we won't do*—gaaay-ross, gross!"

Vince and I laughed and I glanced over at the producer, who had forgotten her plan to feign disinterest and was using her clipboard to hide a permanent smirk.

As Lisa and Eddie slipped into their usual slapstick act, what I saw was a producer whose wheels were turning. Unlike me, she was not seeing my wiseass sister bossing around her gay boyfriend. I was pretty sure she was seeing dollar signs.

Lisa whipped something into the bowl, her skilled hands blurring as she said, "You know what's weird, Eddie?"

"This?"

"I think this is the first time I've made eggs for a woman without first getting the prize the night before." Eddie squealed as Lisa winked at the producer while skillfully breaking four eggs for emphasis, cracking them all at once, with perfect delivery into the bowl.

Eddie looked at her deadpan. "Oh, honey, maybe you've hit the wall. Making the morning-after eggs before the morning after? *Never.* You've lost it."

"Hand me that larger whisk, bitch, if you know what it is."

Eddie smirked at her, "Oh I know what a bitch is." He was as puzzled by the assortment of kitchen tools splayed out in front of him as he would have been if Lisa had asked him to go find Waldo in an ocean of tiny US flags.

"Sorry. I got nothing," he said, shaking his head with a bored sigh. "Oh, wait, I found wine!" He tossed back a short glass of merlot-colored liquid before Lisa could stop him. Eddie followed that by running to spit it in the sink as we all laughed at him. "It had turned!" he said, horrified.

"Eddie's not a fan of balsamic," Lisa said calmly, watching Sandra because she didn't need to watch her bowl. "Eddie, I need a whisk; just pick the one that would leave the most interesting marks after a good spanking."

He giggled, and in a flash he was back and proudly handing her the whisk. Lisa patted him on the head and he clapped for himself like a baby seal.

The producer was sitting now, leaning forward in her chair, her eyes widening to take it all in as she scratched notes on her clipboard. Lisa was in her zone in the kitchen and appeared to have forgotten all about the producer, but I knew better.

Lisa said to Eddie, "Okay, Flipper, stop clapping for yourself. While I bust up these bits of sun-dried tomato, you're going to go in the fridge for me." When Eddie, with a deadpan expression, didn't move, Lisa said, "That's the big cold box in the kitchen where you keep your vodka."

"Aaahh," he said, nodding with dramatic recognition before trotting off. I saw the producer shield her mouth from exhibiting a full-blown smile.

Lisa continued. "In there, fetch me a stick of butter. If you're unsure what that is, that's the thing you might use in a pinch to make things slippery."

Another light bulb went off on Eddie's face. "Got it!" He galloped back from the fridge, proudly holding the stick. Lisa snatched it from his wildly waving wrist, but not before he held it just out of her reach.

Lisa said, "It's easier if you just pass things to me, instead of doing the fairy wand thing."

"Hey, look at me in the kitchen! My mom would be so proud!"

Lisa laughed, pointing at him and addressing us as if we were the audience. "Who could have known that pretty girls could cook?" she said as she broke up the tarragon, pitching the spiky greens into the beaten egg with an exaggerated toss from behind her back. Sandra noticed not one speck of green missed the bowl. She sat up straighter.

Eddie made a face. "Why are you playing with weeds when we're supposed to be making your future girlfriend an omelet?"

Lisa laughed, glancing at the producer. "Now, now Eddie, we mustn't make assumptions . . . and I'm not playing with leaves. Tarragon is an herb that has a flavor similar to anise."

Eddie perked up and clasped his hands together. "*Oooohhh*. While I love the sound of that, I have no idea what you're babbling about. What does a butch lesbo know about anise?"

Lisa folded over the sizzling omelet perfectly in half as she said, "Imagine if I took an omelet, then spanked it silly with a black licorice whip. That's the flavor we Italians are raised on."

"Oooooooh, yum-yum. Wait, what did you say after the word spanked?"

"Never mind, you're going to smell it, right . . . about . . . now."

And just then, we all got our first sniff of the omelet as the pan-seared tomatoes, egg, and tarragon folded together into a fluffy half pancake. Eddie swooned. "So this is what you make all your girlfriends when they sleep over?"

I noticed the producer was leaning farther forward in her chair, hanging on their every word, and I knew, without my sister even turning her head, that she had seen it too.

"Depends," Lisa said. "Sometimes they just get coffee in a biodegradable to-go cup."

Eddie nudged her arm like a drinking buddy and said, "Very earth conscious of you."

"You don't want a coffee cup that outlasts your relationship."

"Ha!" Eddie spewed, laughing before regaining his snotty composure. "Really? *Relationship?*"

Lisa glared at him, deadpan, and the vision of her shorter, stockier frame looking up at his long, wiry one, totally intimidating him, was hysterical.

"I just mean, I bet there's a story there you would love to share with our audience . . . or . . . not?" Eddie said in a tiny voice.

Lisa said, "Hand me a serving fork . . . it's the thing with the four pointy ends on it, like your pitchfork."

"Everyone loves my devil costume," Eddie said, resting his hand on his hip, "and I know what a serving fork is. Oh. Wait. There's *soooo* many choices . . ."

"Hurry up or you will get the *mopine* treatment." Eddie's eyes widened as she reached for the dishtowel, twisting it in preparation. Eddie backed away, having found himself at the wrong end of that towel too many times to count. "For the people at home, *mopine* is an Italian word for dishtowel, and in this case a very effective motivator."

Eddie frantically picked through the serving utensil cup,

keeping one whale eye on my sister. "I'll give you a hint," she said. "Hand me the one that looks most like your last boyfriend: tall, skinny red neck," she said.

Producer Sandra failed at muffling a laugh.

Eddie nodded, closed his eye, put his hand to his chest, and fanned his face with the horrid memory. He slapped the red-handled serving fork hard into Lisa's hand as she yelped from the slap to her palm. This time, Vince, myself, and the producer all laughed out loud.

When Sandra finished laughing, she glanced over at Vince and me before she jotted down notes on the desk in front of her. I could tell by the way she was writing excitedly and afraid to look away like she would miss something that she was already making detailed decisions about my sister's new career.

Lisa loosened the omelet with a spatula, choosing to flip it from the frying pan, sending it into a perfect double airborne flip before landing it back on the pan to sear one more time. She flipped it in the air once more with her other hand, before it landed perfectly on a serving plate in front of Eddie, who clapped like a cheerleader. When Eddie attempted to grab the plate, Lisa whisked it away, busting Eddie about his ignorance of garnishes. "Eddie, just pretend it's a pretty bow in your hair, place it off to the side, like this, near the edge of the plate without touching it, never, never smack in the middle."

Next Lisa swooped it up and headed toward Sandra in that smooth and speedy way my sister moves only when she fears her cooking might get cold. (That, and on a random football field to tackle me.) I smelled the food again as she cruised past and I knew Sandra was the one who would be toast.

It really wouldn't have mattered what the thing tasted like at that point, but I knew Sandra was in for my sister's astonishing cooking. I had been by her side so many times when the simple ingredients used fooled you into thinking she could not possibly deliver any magic to the meal, and yet your taste buds sang a different story. Where did all the flavor come from?

Before digging in with her fork, Sandra glanced back over to

Vince and me with a question on her face I could easily answer. "Yup," I said. "It will taste like the best thing you have ever eaten."

My sister snorted.

And it did.

There was a delay in the business talk while we waited for Sandra to finish eating every last bite of her omelet, a delay Lisa thoroughly enjoyed. After all, my sister was eating her favorite dish too, feasting on a platter of "I told you so," and it was a taste she liked ingesting more than food, second only to women. Lisa didn't miss witnessing one single mouthful of that omelet as it passed by Sandra's lips. The producer missed her staring, however, since her eyes were mostly closed as she chewed.

When the last bite disappeared, Sandra surprised all of us by refusing to set up any guest appearances on any major talk shows. Instead, Sandra spent the rest of our time in Boston negotiating with Lisa about signing to do her own national cooking show, including Eddie as her clueless co-star and kitchen helper. "Every great cooking show has a stooge to play the part of the non-cooker at home. No offense, Eddie."

While Eddie dove for the pen on the table to sign a document that didn't yet exist, I didn't understand my sister's hesitation. Lisa saw an obstacle I hadn't thought of.

"Once the network censors the hell out of us, I would have nothing to say. I can't be one of those stupid airheads on those shows. You already have a slew of them here."

Sandra smiled, calmly, confidently, and in her answer I saw a tiny glimpse of how she had gotten to this level in her career. "Don't misunderstand, Lisa. I want *this* show. The exact show I just saw today."

"That was just me busting Eddie's ball. He only has one you know."

"Lies!" Eddie shrieked.

Sandra pointed at him and yelled, "*That* is the show I want!"

Lisa smirked at her. "Sweetie," she said in her most condescending voice, "are you trying to wreck your career?

Middle America would find what Eddie and I think funny downright pornographic."

Sandra said, "Listen, sweetie, don't you worry about me. I plan to sign you with our cable network, at the soft porn-safe eleven o'clock time slot."

I saw my sister's gears turning.

"So, me and Queen Eddie over here can say whatever the fuck we want?"

Sandra stared at my sister and slowed her answer. "Whatever ... the fuck ... you want."

Although Eddie's squeal was deafening (the gay seal clapping for himself), I saw my sister doing her own version of celebrating at the sound of this attractive woman cursing in her direction. Producer Sandra had my sister's full attention, a rare occurrence indeed.

As Lisa walked by me, she whispered, "Any steam coming off my tits?"

"Yep," I said, "careful near that gas stove."

As my sister continued her inspection of the cooking stage, Sandra said, "Sounds like Eddie might be agreeable to a deal. Now, what about our star?"

This woman knew how to get to my sister, but still Lisa held her ground.

"I have a concern," she said. "We have a deal on one condition. If this network has a policy about its stars dating producers, I'm out."

Sandra met Lisa with an equally cocky gaze and said, "You wouldn't believe what I can crowbar into the fine print . . ." Sandra took a dramatic pause, then moved closer to Lisa as tit-smoke turned to sparks, ". . . no matter how ridiculous."

"I like having all options open and in writing," Lisa said.

"And then you'll sign?"

"Maybe. We will see what happens when next we meet. When next we meet will be in my kitchen."

Later, as the three of us walked to the car, I said to my sister, "Really? 'When next we meet'?"

Lisa swatted Eddie hard on the ass, yelled "You're it!" and ran half the parking lot to the car as he chased (read, bounced) after her. I can't speak to why, just then, she needed to spank a gay boy's ass, but it was clear she needed to cool her tits with a breezy victory lap.

A Dick By Any Other Name

Several years ago when my Dad's cantankerous sister, Aunt Aggie, died, it had been unfortunate that it happened during a nasty fight with Mom. Perhaps more unfortunate were Mom's last words to Aunt Aggie: *"Drop dead!"* Suffice to say that Mom carried some guilt about this, and, of course, we mercilessly teased her about it. Who could resist teasing one's mother about commanding a death wish toward our most pain-in-the-ass relative and then actually getting her wish? Not any of us, certainly not Dad, who affectionately referred to Aunt Aggie as Devil Sister.

Over the years Mom had so much guilt, she made trips with Dad to visit his still-living sister, Etta, Aunt Aggie's twin, despite the fact that she was in a coma. This would be normal, except Etta was worse than Aunt Aggie, and before she had taken to snoozing in a coma for the last eight years, Mom hadn't spoken to her for over a decade . . . and now, after fearing she had cursed Etta's sister Aggie into an early grave, she was trying to reconcile with her. Every once in a while, Dad would inquire why they were visiting, given that if Etta ever did wake, it would be highly likely she'd believe Mom had something to do with her beloved sister's death. Vince and I were not so sure.

Etta had been in the coma ever since she arrived at a house party and mistakenly thought her twin sister had shown up as well. The twins, Etta and Aggie, were very close, though a

76

spat had Etta not having seen her sister in weeks. Legend had it that Etta sprinted across the house to greet her sister in a wildly enthusiastic hug, both sisters extending their arms at the same exact moment, winding up with Etta (the less bright half of a pair of otherwise identical twins) having crashed headfirst into—wait for it—a full-length wall mirror.

Spoiler Alert: sister Aggie was not actually at the party though Etta had enthusiastically shouted her sister's name before the crash.

Ironically, it had originally been Mom's mirror, which she had given to our neighbor who had thrown the party. That made two sisters whose doom Mom was peripherally involved with, all points my sister could not resist teasing her about.

Dad hated visiting Etta in the nursing home, which he called Coma Calls. Over the past year he'd managed to convince Mom to go without him, hoping that just being around one of his cantankerous sisters, coma or not, would do Mom some good.

"Your mother is at her best when she has someone to spar with," Dad had said, "and for the first time she has a fighting chance against Etta."

Mom was off the hook for the Coma Calls now, and Dad had been going on his own. He was there now while Mom was napping and Lisa was God knows where, and the house was quiet.

I had successfully avoided Lorn for the first three days after she arrived. Pretty easy to do in a house this size; however, it became more difficult once Mom's doctor called saying she flunked her lung scan and would have to see an oncologist.

We all agreed to take Mom up to Dana-Farber in Boston to get their opinion on her case. It didn't surprise us that Mom scheduled her appointment for the exact time Dad had workmen coming for his shed project so he couldn't join us.

"Your father doesn't need to be around any of this," Mom said, but what she really meant was she did not want him around her during this. I heard her tell Lorn in a hushed voice as she got ready to leave, "Men are unfairly categorized as the stronger sex. We all know that's a bunch of bullshit."

"True story," Lorn said.

Despite her secret chats with Lorn about his shortcomings, Mom was being uncharacteristically sensitive to Dad's soft side, and it made me wonder if Dad was taking it harder than any of us even knew. That was, until I heard Mom say to Lorn, "Cancer isn't very sexy. If I ever hope to have a normal sex life again, we need to keep Stan out of the details."

When I told my sister, she said, "I wish I had been kept uninformed on that one."

When we arrived at Dana-Farber, for some reason they looked right past Mom and zeroed in on me, asking my name for the admitting form. "Marie Santora," I answered automatically. The woman searched her computer log.

Lisa jabbed me with an elbow. "They need Mom's name, you *cavone.*"

When the administrator found Mom's name, within seconds the head nurse came over to look at all the paperwork and smiled at my mother. "Ah, Mrs. Santora, you're a VIP. So nice to meet you."

"VIP?" Mom asked. "Oh, I don't think anything of the sort. You should check your clipboard again—make sure you have the right person; don't cut off my arm or something."

"Way to go, Mom; hospitals love when they hear things like that."

"It says here we are making an exception, you will be entered into a clinical trial which has been closed to new patients for over a week. The hospital rarely, if ever, allows that to happen."

"What does this mean?" Lisa asked the nurse, all business since the nurse was not her type.

"This is very good news," the nurse said. "There have been some amazing breakthroughs in lungs, and this same trial was successful the first time we ran it, and we know so much more now. You must be special to somebody really important here."

The admitting nurse insisted we take a wheelchair for Mom

for the long trip over to the adjoining buildings for tests, but Mom, of course, would not hear of it.

"I walked in here and I can walk out just as easily," she said, crossing her thin arms.

"Mom," I said, "what harm will it do for you to be wheeled around like a queen for one day?"

"No. I'm not an invalid. Save the wheelchairs for the people who really need them. I'm stepping outside for a cigarette," she said as she defiantly walked away.

Lisa signed out the wheelchair, explaining to the woman that while our mother might have lung cancer, she really didn't smoke. "If you don't stop her, she will get kicked out of the trial," the nurse said, and she meant it.

I tore after Mom.

I caught her just outside the door, lighting her cigarette under the huge Dana-Farber Cancer Institute sign. She lit the cigarette, not in her mouth, but at her waist, so she would not have to inhale, she told me later. Faker, I thought. But there was something in her eyes. Mom was deep in thought.

She asked, "You kids still do The Facebook?"

"Yes, Mom, we sometimes still do The Facebook. On the WWW dot," I said, quoting her.

She glanced up at the sign again. "You have a camera phone with you?"

"It's called a phone, but sure," I said, immediately regretting it.

"I want you to take my picture under this sign smoking a cigarette."

"No!"

"You will do it, or I will ask a stranger walking by to do it. Your choice."

I knew there was no persuading her so I reluctantly snapped a quick picture, and I have to say, it was a good one. Lisa came outside with the wheelchair just as I snapped it. "What the fuck?" she said.

Mom informed her, "I'm getting on The Facebook. I will be representing all the women with lung cancer who have never smoked."

"But you are smoking," I said.

"Don't be an ass," she said. "I'm not really smoking. I'm going to have all those women take pictures of themselves holding a cigarette. Maybe even flipping off the camera with it as their middle finger."

"Why are you doing this, Mom?"

Mom had a smug expression on her face. "Because when I told a few of my friends that I might have lung cancer, every single one of them assumed I had been a secret smoker. It was the first thing they said to me. Not, 'I'm so sorry,' or 'oh, my God, how terrible.' Every single one of them said, 'I had no idea you smoked.' One even said, 'didn't you know the risk you were taking?' Can you imagine if people said something like that to women with breast cancer? 'Did you exercise enough? Too bad . . . you must eat a lot of fatty foods. You should have known the risk of not having children and not breastfeeding . . .' Lung cancer is like AIDS was back in the day. Now lung cancer is the only non-sympathetic cancer you can get. So, I've decided it will be my job to call *bullshit!*"

Lisa and I just stared. Where did Political Mom come from? And, the bigger question, where can we return her?

"I want women with lung cancer everywhere to take outrageous pictures of themselves fake-smoking in wickedly defiant places and send them to my Facebook site. This one should start it off nicely."

"You don't have The Facebook," I said.

"That's where I will need your help. Can you get me on The Facebook?"

"Sure," I said, already planning to make sure it was an account closed to the general public.

Lisa said, "Great speech, Mom," taking the cigarette from her hand and chucking it into the trash. "When we go back in, you need to tell the nurses this was your idea of a joke so they don't kick you out of this trial. Now sit your bony ass in this wheelchair. It's like you always say, your house, your rules. Well, it's their house, their friggin' rules. Now, sit down."

Throwing Mom's own rule back on her did the trick. She took a seat, not without her Darth Vader sigh, and off we went. As the automatic doors opened for her, she said, "Well, perhaps I was too hasty. This is pretty comfy getting around like this. You girls think I could get your father to cart me around if need be?"

After a full day of testing every inch of her body, Mom was summoned back to the waiting room to meet with the clinical testing group once more before we were allowed to go for the day. I had a bad feeling about this last-minute meeting as we wheeled Mom over to the packed waiting room. She had had enough of the wheelchair and wanted out, insisting that sitting in a waiting room chair wouldn't be breaking the rules.

"Mom, I will embarrass you," Lisa said quietly.

Mom looked at her sideways, hesitated, then called her bluff as she stood up from the wheelchair and defiantly started to walk away from it.

Until Lisa yelled in a booming voice: *"It's a miracle!!! My mother is walking!"*

The entire waiting room turned to see our startled mother and Lisa, looking as if the miracle of her walking had blown her away.

"Funny," Mom said. "That's my daughter, The Mouth."

Several younger ladies with colorful scarf wraps on their heads started laughing, which spread the giggles to the rest of the room. Mom doubled back to Lisa to give her a playful tap on the back of the head, while Lisa put her hand up in surrender, laughing her ass off. Only my sister could turn a cancer unit waiting area into a comedy club. All that was missing were the drinks to go with all the drugs.

Eventually, we were called in to see the doctor, and when he entered the room, I could tell that the news was not good by his apologetic tone.

81

"Sorry to put you through such a long day," he said while two interns took their places at his side as if he were a crisp and handsome French fry lying on a beach, and they were starved seagulls.

Mom said, "Uh, oh, they're voting me off the island, I bet. Am I out of the trial?" She whispered in a tone that all could hear, "Lisa, go ahead and tell them my smoking was a publicity stunt for The Facebook. These young nurses will understand."

Doctor hunk shook his head. "These young women are two of our best and brightest interns, doctors in training," and he pulled a chair close to Mom to share a chart as the interns adjusted their positions to get closer to him like birds on a wire.

I braced myself.

Lisa asked matter-of-factly, "Cut to the chase, right, Mom? We want to know where else it spread."

"Not really I don't," Mom said.

"That's just it," the doctor said. "Yes, we are kicking you out of the trial, but this is actually good news. We checked every inch of you, and the growth is precisely contained, only within the left lobe of one lung. Nothing in your lymph nodes."

"What does this mean?"

"This is good news," he said, as we all instinctually leaned nearer, "because even if the biopsy comes back positive for cancer, we could just remove the part of the one lobe since the tumor is safely nestled and contained."

There was a knock at the door, and a nurse stepped in. "Sorry to interrupt. Doctor, you asked me to let you know when Ms. Elaine was leaving."

"Please ask her to wait."

"Ms. Elaine? You mean our Lorn?" Mom asked, before I could. "Is Lorn here?"

Lisa and I had no idea what was going on.

The nurse left the room, and the doctor said, in a lowered voice that was a bit too dramatic for my taste and his position, "Your friend Lorn didn't want you to know she was pulling strings for your family, but she was very persuasive, and with my help, she got Mrs. Santora considered for this trial, even after it was closed. This trial is for patients who have a probability of at least two locations of invasion, and you, Mrs. Santora, are lucky enough to have been kicked out because you only have one, and a small one at that."

His handsome smile flashed as the flanking interns swooned. "I hope you don't mind that I invited a few of my doctors-in-training. They often have to be by my side when I am delivering bad news, so I thought they should also hear the delivering of good news." He was cocky, but I liked this doctor and I glanced at his name badge, knowing I would not remember it.

"Poor dears," Mom said as she looked back and forth between the two young women, as if any of the cancer news had not been about her. "What a stressful job for two young ladies."

"Some extraordinary measures were taken to get you into this trial, Mrs. Santora, and now I'll have to tell Ms. Elaine that regardless of how I'm a huge admirer of her work, both on TV and here at the hospital, all her work to get you in this trial was for nothing."

Vince said, "Thank God!" and he and Lisa slapped each other on the back as if the Patriots had just made a first down.

I was lost in my thoughts, imagining my mother's body as a battleground and her sheer will were keeping the cancer trapped within one space. Like the old guy in *Harry Potter*, I imagined her holding her hand up, shouting, "Thou shall not pass!" and the cancer, if it was cancer, tucking its tail between its pathetic legs and retreating, preferring to take the easy way out rather than face Momma Santora. (That's what I would have done.)

For the first time in months, I felt myself take a full, deep breath. It was a breath my body sorely needed, and Lisa didn't miss the moment.

The doctor smiled and said, "If she didn't want what she did to be a secret, I would ask one of you to tell Ms. Elaine I'm going to have to hold her to honoring her original promise. I did get her into the trial, after all."

"What promise?" Lisa, Vince, and I all asked at once.

"The one she made to get you into the trial. Just to make sure, I'm going to get you into another trial after the biopsy, so we can more closely monitor your treatment, all in the name of science, of course."

Who says that? It made me worry that it was actually not all in the name of science.

"We have been testing a drug that has had phenomenal results on stopping any reoccurrences in cases where the cancer is isolated only in one lung. It's much harder to get into that trial, reserved seating, but if you qualify, I'll make sure I get you in."

Cocky bastard. "What does this have to do with Lorn?" I asked, trying to ignore the douche chills I had listening to him.

"We're building a new unit on this wing of the hospital, and Ms. Elaine agreed to be auctioned off as a date at our fundraiser. I told her it would really help since she will certainly fetch a pretty penny." I glanced at his badge again, this time rhyming it with a rude word I would remember.

Of course, this had nothing to do with my mother. It was about Lorn, and I wondered further if it wasn't even for the hospital, but for his own gain. This was a guy who was used to getting his way.

He smiled at me, but something in his eyes cooled as if he registered I was somehow immune to his charms. Not exactly gaydar . . . maybe he had hate-dar? He turned back to my mother, who was positively swooning; the eldest seagull in the flock was not immune.

Mom said, "I don't know . . . Boston is a very long drive from Rhode Island."

"Mrs. Santora, if there is a surgery needed and you need any post-op treatment, you can return under the care of your primary doctor in Rhode Island, with no hard feelings of course. Unless you especially like us here?" He winked at our mother and she smiled, absolutely charmed by him. I thought he was laying it on a little too thick.

Mom said, "Of course I do, Dr. Rickland—"

"Please Mrs. Santora, we are friends now, call me Dr. Rick." (I noted that the shortened rude version of his name worked even better.)

Mom said, "Dr. Rick, we need to save all seats in the trial for the people who really need them." Mom stepped out of the wheelchair, both to show off and to shake the doctor's hand, and this time Lisa and I didn't argue with her.

The doctor said, backpedaling out of the room, "If you don't have any questions, I'm going to catch Ms. Elaine before she leaves."

"Just one question. Do I have to have the biopsy right away?" Mom asked, burying the fear in her face under her warm smile.

The surgeon looked at my mother sternly and said, "Yes, you do. And just in case, we will schedule a surgery date to follow, as a precaution. Now, don't fight me on this, Mrs. Santora. Even though I gave you some good news today, timing could still be critical on this one."

Critical wasn't usually a good word to hear. Mom noted this as well and nodded as her smile faded. I heard a whisper of "Oh fuck" escape from behind her teeth. I didn't like the word, but if Lorn were in the room, she would have reminded us all that the word could have been *terminal,* and next to that *critical* sounded damned good. *Terminal* is a flat line on a computer screen, gravestones, lost loves, and plagues. By comparison *critical* merely required our respect.

I reached for my mother's hand and realized it was a hand I had not held for any length of time, not since I was very young. "Piece of cake," I lied to her, not knowing really, what we were in for. I looked at my sister and brother, and their faces looked too pale to be Italian. I widened my eyes, smiled, and shook my head at them, indicating they were going to scare her if they didn't each put on a brave face.

As the doctor matter-of-factly gave a few details of the biopsy, I was now annoyed by how attractive he was, and decided he looked more like a Hollywood version of a doctor. He went on to explain the procedure if she needed surgery, as if the partial removal of one lobe of her lung was as simple as removing a package of burgers from a grocery meat counter.

"So, how do you all know Lorn Elaine?" asked Dr. Dick.

Since men like him rarely invite a topic of conversation apart from themselves, this gave him away. How many times do you walk away from meeting a guy, knowing everything about him, from his entire resume to the addition of some random factoids he wants to pass along to fill out the amazing character that is: Him. This man had plans that included Lorn.

And I shouldn't care.

I answered flatly, "I met her a long time ago on a Jamaica vacation. She became my—a family friend. Now she's my mother's nurse."

I realized I was missing something. When I spoke Lorn's name, anger was no longer lodged in my throat. At the very least, Lorn was a family friend, and is *still* a family friend, even though I had not been so friendly to her. No doubt Dr. Dick had been.

I heard Erica's voice in my head. I had been hearing her voice a lot lately. *Don't be so thick. Lorn has paid her dues, not the least of which has been her own loss and loneliness.*

How do you tell a dead person to stay out of your business?

Later, when my sister and I were sitting outside alone, she nudged my arm and said, "So, Dr. Dick has a thing for the ex-actress."

"Hey, that's my name for him!"

"Maybe, but you didn't say it out loud first."

She's Not Here for You

On the day of Mom's biopsy, Lorn insisted on going early to the hospital and meeting us there. She said she would be more useful there, but when we arrived, she was not in the admitting area and I couldn't help wondering if she had gone early to meet up with Dr. Dick.

We still hadn't seen her, even after Mom had been prepped and they let us back into her room. Mom chattered on with nervous energy, asking the nurses questions about their personal lives, their kids, their husbands and, especially, their jobs. She was sympathizing with them about their long hours and stressful days and she sounded as if she were the lucky one. She continued to do this as they prepared her to be wheeled down for her anesthesia, but I heard my mother's voice starting to shift to a higher pitch and my stomach shifted in the same direction. I realized I couldn't ever remember seeing my mother afraid.

When the nurses and Dr. Dick left the room, I said to Mom, "Your hospital clothes make you look like a reject from *Grey's Anatomy*." Now, away from strangers, it was harder for Mom to keep the brave face, and instead of laughing at my lame joke she reached for my hand.

Or maybe I reached for hers. Before she could say anything, and I'm not sure she would have, there was a soft knock on the door and it opened.

Lorn walked in, and I caught my breath. I told myself my

reaction was from the relief of seeing it was not some orderly come to wheel Mom away. When I saw my mother had the same reaction, the feeling of seeing Lorn there sent warmth to the center of my chest. She brings Mom comfort, I thought. It made sense I would still feel affection for her, yet I heard my chest loud and clear, and if Lorn could hear it, she would have wondered if the thumps tapped out: *Thank God you came back. Not just now, but that you came back to us . . .*

Reminder. She's not here for you.

"Just checking in on you, Mrs. Santora," Lorn said. Almost ready to take you for a short ride. Is everyone treating you all right?"

Mom smiled and nodded like a child, looking over at me. "I'm almost as happy to see you as my daughter."

Traitor. A thought occurred to me, so I said it out loud. "You have a uniform and a badge."

"Marie, she is a nurse. Keep up, will you?" Mom said.

I was trying.

Lorn looked a bit guilty, saying, "I pulled a few strings so I could head down with your mom. No nonmedical personnel allowed in the surgery area." Then Lorn finished the thought I had in my head. "I will be able to stay with her right until she falls asleep."

I hadn't planned to exhale the way I did, so I tried to sound extra casual. "I'll go for a bit and let you two visit. Mom might have some questions for you," I said, giving Mom's hand a quick squeeze and excusing myself to let Nurse Lorn work her magic. When I passed by Lorn at the door, she gently caught my arm.

She smiled warmly. "Mom will be fine," she said, and for the first time today I believed something a medical person said.

"Thank you. You know, for Mom." She nodded. Before I turned to go out the door, I said, "And for all of us." But Lorn was already at my mother's bedside, patting her arm and listening as Mom was thanking her.

"No place I would rather be," Lorn said, and the warmth I was feeling spread.

Weirdly, as I stepped outside into the hallway, I was hit with a flood of memories, not about Lorn, but about Erica.

Before finally taking the flying leap into lesbian life, Erica had been terrified of only one thing, and that was needles. It was a secret she had kept from me and one I found out about one time as I leaned against the door that separated the lobby from the clinic room she was in. I had heard so clearly Erica's voice. Her casual chatter didn't fool the nurses or me anymore than Mom's had today. I had finally convinced Erica to go for a blood test after she had not been feeling well for weeks, and actually had to drag her there to make sure she got it done.

I remember hearing metal trays and the sound of paper being ripped off to sanitize some kind of single-use item, which probably was not going to be pleasant. The nurse kept interrupting Erica's chatter to ask if she was doing okay, and telling her she did not have to look. The nurse on the other side of the door had been able to tell, just like I had, that the tightness in her voice meant she was *not* okay at all. I had been in the hallway, straining to hear and finally, finally, they told her she did great, that they got plenty of good blood samples and that she would be out of there soon enough. It was all I could do not to burst through the door to rescue her. Enough already, I thought, enough. I hated to see Erica like that, the strongest woman I had ever known, in pain and so afraid.

I didn't know it then, but her pain was ending and mine was just about to start . . .

Back then, all that stopped me from sneaking through the door when they were taking her blood was that I didn't want to embarrass her. Her secret was finally out: Erica was petrified of needles. I tried to think of a way to let her know that I was near, so I used our signal. It was a birdcall copied from our little yellow cockatiel with bright orange cheeks who we named Daffy, short for daffodil. Daffy had learned only one whistle, a short repeating catcall, always whistled back in sets of twos. For years Erica and I used that call in public places when we lost track of each other, a chirping little GPS. I loved calling for her with it, almost as much as I loved hearing her return it.

When Erica and I lost that bird, we both mourned the loss of her sweet whistle, a call the bird had used for hello and good-bye and good morning and feed me (and everything else since she was vocabulary challenged).

That day at the clinic was the last time I had used it, softly whistling the Daffy call to Erica from the next room, hearing her weak little return whistle, *Whoet-whew, whoet-whew* come back as quick and cheerful as she could, but even in this I could hear her stress, and it tightened around my heart.

All those years together, how had I not known her fear of needles?

When Erica finally came out, almost an hour later as I was starting to worry they had found something really wrong, she walked toward me, smiling sheepishly.

I tried to make light of it by teasing. "You really are so ridiculous. You climb second-story roofs of decrepit buildings without batting an eye, but you freak out over a little needle."

As I drove home, I looked over and saw that she still looked queasy, but forced a smile back at me. "How come I didn't know this about you? The whole needle thing?"

"Can we stop saying the N-word? And it wasn't little!" At the next red light I leaned over and kissed her in agreement.

"What did they say about how tired you've been?" I asked.

"When you whistled, I thought maybe you could hear."

"After you whistled back, I left my post," I said, but actually I was made to sit down in the lobby when one of the ladies at the desk had given me a dirty look for pressing my head against the door.

Erica still sounded nervous even as she gave a dramatic sigh and said a bit too cheerfully, "They expect a clean bill of health."

I believed her. And a month later she was gone.

Now, in the hallway of the hospital, I thought about how we had kept Daffy's memory alive by still using her call for years after the bird was gone. Now that Erica was gone too, I hadn't realized how much I had missed using that sweet call. There are still times when I hear a high-pitched creak of a door, and I swear that I still hear that little call, and I wonder, is it my long-lost bird? Is it my long-lost Erica?

When I came back from getting coffee, Mom and Lorn had already departed for the biopsy. I made a production of nervously gathering Mom's things in case the test went faster than they had prepared us for.

"What's the rush?" Lisa said, coming into the room, watching me scramble for Mom's things.

"Just . . . hospitals," I said. "Sometimes they leave you waiting forever, and then they can come fetch you with no warning. I don't see why she just couldn't stay here."

"It's not really a room," Lisa answered back, pulling back the curtain to look down both corridors. I didn't know what she was looking for, but there was still no sign of Lorn. She said, "They don't do lung biopsies behind a flimsy curtain next to the nurses' station." However, I could tell, like me, she wished they did.

Later, much later, I whispered to my sister, "Is there such a thing as 'safely nestled lung cancer'?"

My sister looked as doubtful as I felt. "I suppose . . . if you can trust a Doctor named Dick."

I laughed in spite of my nerves. "No, I don't."

"But you should trust Lorn," she said.

Magical Nurse Pocket

Lisa and I flanked either side of Mom, whose steps mimicked the urgency of a fugitive. When Mom pulled slightly ahead of us, I said to Lisa, "Who's in a rush now?" and my sister smiled for the first time since we had entered the hospital.

Mom had waved off the wheelchair and was making her escape before they forced her back into it. "Never again," she said, "and if you want me to sign something, I will." They did, and she did. I was proud of her defiance and made a note to be that way some twenty-five years from now.

When Mom reached the outside air, her body began to shake all over. I was alarmed, and looked to Lisa for reassurance, who mirrored me instead with wide eyes of her own. She braced Mom and tried to get her to say what was wrong, but she couldn't speak clearly through chattering teeth. Lisa tried to apply some logic by talking her out of shaking. "What's the matter, Mom? It's not even cold out."

"You got her?" I said to Lisa and when she nodded, I doubled back inside to get help and crashed into Lorn when the automatic doors slid open. I gripped both her arms, and all I could think to say was "Help," but her eyes were already on Mom. As she pushed me aside to get to her, Lorn's hair nearly whipped across my face. I leapt past the inappropriate flashbacks as I stumbled after her. Lorn paused to whip an abandoned wheelchair out of the corner of the entryway, and had it behind Mom before

I caught up. Lisa gladly handed Mom off to Lorn, who seated her gently in the chair. She signaled one of the nurses inside with a raised finger, not unlike you would summon a waiter, but followed up by bear-hugging herself. I was no nurse, but this seemed to be the universal sign for "this woman should have had a wheelchair; now get me a fucking blanket."

"Lorn, what's happening?"

"She's fine," she said gently.

"How do you know that?" I hadn't planned to sound angry at her, but Lorn was not easily rattled when wearing the badge, L. Elaine, RN.

The other nurse arrived with a warm blanket, and Lorn wrapped Mom up, holding the blanket together at the front until the chattering of her teeth stopped.

"Tell us what's wrong," Lisa demanded, while I stood still as a rock, and just as useful.

"Lisa," Lorn said smoothly, as if my sister were her child, "hold this blanket around your mother, just like this. Her shaking will stop in a few seconds; trust me."

I didn't trust her. "We should take her back in," I said, but Lorn turned to me, and this time she took me by both arms. "Marie, your mom is fine. She is just relieved."

"But—"

"What looks like violent shaking is really just her letting go, finally allowing her fear to take over for just a bit. She was holding onto that brave act a bit too tight, and this is what happens. She will let it go."

I felt a tear roll down my face, saw it hit Lorn's arm, and was grateful she pretended not to notice.

Lorn gave both my arms a gentle squeeze. "Your Mom was holding onto that brave act a bit too tight, and so are you. No matter how strong you are, in the end everything catches up with you if you don't let it out."

The compassion in her voice and soft smile broke my heart again, as it always could, but I pushed that thought away. I think she felt it because she let go of my arms, pulled a Kleenex out of

93

some magical nurse pocket, pressed it into my hand, and let me go. I squeezed the tissue, wishing it had been a note, and shook my head at my own stupidity.

Vince had already pulled in with the getaway car, and even with the stress of the long day and the tinted car windows, I could see he had been watching me and Lorn with a raised eyebrow and his signature smirk.

Mom had stopped shaking, just like Nurse Lorn said she would, and now Lorn was kneeling right down on the pavement in front of Mom's wheelchair, nodding her head with a smile. "We're better, right?"

Something about the softness of her voice made me feel threads were being pulled from inside me. I noticed the back of her auburn hair, so rich against the white of her uniform, a few strands coming loose and blowing softly in the breeze. "Mrs. Santora, you had your girls all scared, but we know you're fine, right?"

Mom smiled. "Of course, dear. You're a professional. You say I'm fine, then I am fine. I think I just need some more meat on my bones. Should we go somewhere for some dessert?"

Lorn clasped both of Mom's hands and gave them each a soft kiss. "Oops, I could get in trouble for that, not very professional." Then she whispered, "Don't tell anyone."

Although she wasn't facing me, I knew she had winked at my mother, who awkwardly winked back with a happy snort.

As I watched, I thought: Stop it. Do you have to be so damned good? Do you have to look so damned good? As if she read my thoughts, she looked over her shoulder at me with a smile, green eyes sparkling in the late afternoon sun. When I didn't say anything, she turned back to Mom.

"Thank you," I whispered to her back, but it came out with no sound, and so Lorn didn't turn back around. Thank God, I thought, I didn't need to see those eyes again . . .

Lisa and I helped Mom up from her chair, and Mom let us capture her in a rare hug. When we pulled back, Mom's eyes had teared up from what she explained must have been the damned ammonia they used to clean the floors. "Probably cancer causing," Mom said.

"Good for business," Vince said, helping her into the car.

"Those fuckers," Lisa said, and we all laughed.

By the time we got home from taking Mom to Gregg's Restaurant for a slice of Death by Chocolate cake ("now that's how you want to go," Mom said), Lorn had already retreated to her room. We had agreed beforehand this would be a day off for our live-in nurse. Lisa and I would take care of anything Mom would need. As it turned out, Lorn's day off had started with an early drive up to Boston to offer herself up in trade so our mother could have VIP care at one of the best hospitals in the country.

Once Mom was situated and my brother and sister were out of sight, I went to the door of Lorn's room and raised my hand to knock, but my hand froze there, knuckles poised just in front of the door. My stomach tightened as I imagined trying to thank her. That was, in fact, what I told myself I was going to her room for, and I almost believed it. I didn't knock, guessing it would have been a mistake . . . one I had made several times with her so many years ago.

I didn't need to thank her. She was being paid, and I reminded myself that her commitment and the entire reason she was here was for my mother. I walked away, ignoring the knot, which tightened further in my gut. I reminded myself how my gut had been wrong so many times before about her.

Leave her alone . . . don't go there. She is not here for you.

Days later, just before Mom's follow-up appointment with her doctors in Rhode Island, I was playing over and over the words Lorn had said. How Mom might also get kicked out of the second trial to track reoccurrence chances, since Lorn said Mom's doctor had not believed the biopsy would find cancer. Only then did I allow myself just a sliver of hope.

The tiny sliver felt terrifying. After all, I had vowed never to hope for anything again. Why gamble your heart that way? Seems a better choice to choose to simply think the worst and be surprised if things take a turn for the better. I should be going with that.

I had done nothing but cling to the hope that love conquers all, and this had been dashed again and again for the better part of my adult life. First with Lorn, when I wished that my love had been strong enough for both of us, and that she would find the strength not to care what her publicists, fans, and producers thought of her personal life. Then, after five years of bliss with Erica, once again wishing and hoping had failed me. Wishing that my love could somehow keep her here with me, when it hadn't. Over the last year, since Erica's death, my hope stubbornly wouldn't die and appeared stronger in irrational dreams, where I would wake with the lingering hope that it was strong enough to bring her back. I woke from those dreams only to feel it gradually melt away all over again. She was gone. She would not be back. I went to bed at night and only wasted prayers that I would not dream about her again.

But I hadn't dreamt about Erica, not once since Lorn had come back. God only gives you what you can handle, and it seemed that God had taken pity on me and washed Erica from my dreams. I still prayed every night like it was an insurance policy.

And now there was Mom. Was it worth risking hope that she could be completely well? That I would someday hear again the sounds of her bickering with Dad? When hope flickered up, anger with Lorn ignited in my heart as well. It started the night Lorn had told me one or two encouraging details the doctor hadn't mentioned. Lisa had missed it, but I heard her and it made me wonder if Mom could totally recover.

I knew in my heart that Lorn was not a woman who played

games, but how cruel that she would risk giving us hope. How cruel that she would come back after all the pain she had caused. How dare she make me want to believe in her again? While consumed with the risk of having hope for Mom, lately my dreams had drifted away from the constant memory of Erica and loss . . . and without her memory consuming me, did this leave me wide open to take other risks?

Guess Whose Coma to Dinner

Mom floated into the kitchen as if it were any other day. "Good morning; oh, I smell coffee. Did Lorn make it?"

"No, it was me. I couldn't sleep," I said.

"No reason for that, dear, if you're worried about me."

"Don't know why I would be," I said, handing Mom a mug of coffee. "Sit."

"I don't need to sit. I just got up," Mom said, strolling to the sun streaming in the kitchen window. It was her favorite spot to sip her coffee while zen-staring at the lake.

"My handsome Doctor Rick called early this morning. He said the rest of my tests came back, and he seemed quite relieved. You know, your father is jealous of him," she said as she giggled into her cup.

I set my mug down a bit too hard on the counter, and Mom looked up. "What? You think your father is too old to get jealous?"

"I think you buried the lead," I said, slowly walking over to her. Was this bad dream coming to an end?

"I'm not totally off the hook. I still need to have a bit of surgery, but it will be only to remove the growth, not the piece of the lung. Dr. Rick says all signs point to all *this business* being nicely contained. Worst-case scenario: if they get in there and need to, they just lop off the lobe from the lung, and off I go."

This business? I hadn't noticed before now that Mom never

once said the C word.

"Hi, good news travels fast."

Mom and I both turned to see Lorn, uncharacteristically still in her robe, her hair loose at her shoulders, sun streaming in from the skylight and bathing her in warmth. It was the first time I had seen her smile *that smile* since years before when we had been together. And in a robe, no less. I turned away from the golden warmth of her and wondered if I should have that skylight removed.

"I don't know how much you heard, but Mom's medical assessment is they will put her in a drive-through, and either snip out the growth or lop off a lung lobe, and off she goes." My voice was sarcastic, but my face couldn't manage it. I was beaming at Mom so I walked over and plunked a kiss on her cheek.

Mom said, "What was that for? I didn't do anything; it's Lorn's handsome doctor friend."

I fought the urge to turn around to see Lorn's reaction, but held steady with my eyes on Mom.

Lorn said, "I hope you don't mind, Dr. Rick called me just a few minutes ago. He said he could not give specifics, except that if the news had not been good, he wouldn't have called me at all."

I doubted that.

It was a few days before her surgery, and Mom had surrendered to a nap in the afternoon while Lisa, Vince, and I were sitting on the highest porch out by the lake, trying to avoid talking about it. Instead, we sat considering the options of ordering pizza or pressuring Lisa to make some dough boy pizzas from scratch and throw them on the grill. Lisa did what she was best at, changing the subject.

"This must be so weird for you, Mare, because I certainly can't help thinking about it. I look at Lorn and all I can think about is this whole nursing thing."

I said, "Yes . . . so strange she tossed away her acting career."

Lisa said, "No, no. It's her breasts in that uniform . . . I can't stop thinking about nursing."

While Vince laughed like a lunatic, I gave Lisa the expected smack across the back of her head. "Pig," I said, as she kept laughing at her joke, rewarding both her knees with congratulatory slaps. "I kill me," she said.

"Someone should."

"I have a question," Vince said, looking at the text that had just come in on his phone.

"What?"

"Why do you suppose Dad said to make sure only Mom answers the door later when he comes home?"

"I have no idea, but whatever it is, I'm troubled," I said, and Lisa nodded.

"A normal family might think their father was coming home with a bouquet of flowers," Vince said, and the silence that followed spoke volumes.

"I liked it better in the dark ages," Lisa said, "when parents didn't know how to friggin' text."

"Those were such good days," I said with a sigh.

Much later, it was Mom's scream that brought us all rushing to the front of the house, the images in my head ranging from an alien-like explosion from her lung, to much, much worse. What we saw when we converged at the front door made Mom's reaction seem quite mild. It's not every day you see a ghost, and what Lisa, Vince and I saw was the disheveled and gaunt ghost of dead Aunt Aggie perched in a wheelchair in the doorway.

"F-fuck!" Lisa yelled.

"Holy sh—" I whispered.

Vince said nothing, but tried to run in the other direction so quickly he fell backwards on his ass and crawled sideways like a crab until he hit a wall that had been there since we moved in. Against the safety of the wall, he finally found his voice,

"*W-WHAT T-T-THE-F!*"

When the ghost started laughing from its eerie smile, it chilled me to my bones, with my feet going numb, not only because her mouth did not move with the laugh, but because it was a deep man's laugh, and it seemed to come from beyond . . .

Mom, not usually the dramatic one in the family, choked out, "She's here to avenge her death!"

The ghost smiled wider, showing a toothless mouth. When she rolled toward us, I screamed again, along with my mother, as Vince crawled a few more steps, attempting to scale the wall, leaving his siblings to die at the hands of this ghastly ghoul.

And that's when I recognized that the deep laugh from beyond was actually coming from behind the wheelchair. It was Dad's laugh, getting lower, not in pitch, but closer to the floor, since he was laughing so hard he'd rolled onto the floor behind his sister in the wheelchair. It was not the dead Aggie, but the oddly alive Auntie Etta, apparently out of her coma, wearing a housecoat identical to Aggie's floral sleeveless one, smiling and and enjoying playing the part of her dead twin sister.

The miraculously cured Auntie Etta grinned wider, nodded her head as if it was a job well done, and stole Lisa's trademarked slap to her own knee. She signaled impatiently for Dad with her bony hand. "Get off your ass, Stan, and move me closer."

Dad hopped to it, getting to his feet and rolling Auntie Etta forward until she was close to Mom, who hadn't moved since she had opened the door. Auntie Etta stabbed both arms at Mom for a hug. I realized now that the thin hospital blanket draped over her arms had completed the ghostly scene.

Auntie Etta said, "Surprise! Stanny here says you need me here, which is damned lucky timing since the hospital was planning to kick me out. They tell me I've been snoozing for years, can you beat that? Just tell me anything you want except that the horrible actor Reagan is not still president."

We all looked at each other, but nobody wanted to take that one. Lisa finally said, "Nope, not that horrible actor; we moved on to reality TV."

I assumed Mom was just too stunned to give Dad a dirty look, and I think Dad thought so too as he cheerfully piped up, "Auntie Etta will be staying with us for a while." When he was met with stunned silence from us all, he continued, "Which we are all grateful for, aren't we, since we were all missing Aunt Aggie so much. Right, kids?"

I could only nod; I was too distracted studying Mom's expression. Here she was, faced with the identical twin of the woman she felt responsible for cursing to death. On the surface it read: "Oh my God, anything but this . . ." Underneath, I could see that there was a new fire in Mom's eyes that I hadn't seen in a while. I wondered if thoughts of future battles were feeding her adrenaline.

Mom could always surprise us. Just when you thought something might actually give her pause, you were forced to remember that nothing has ever given Mom pause. When Covid 19 first hit, and the news exposed a more critical situation day by day, she had a pleasant sense of acceptance (or was it denial?) about the whole thing. Mom would chirp, "Your father and I aren't living all that differently in lockdown, except we are watching less news, you kids get us groceries, and I only have to wear a breathing mask if I need something in the *library* when your father's in there." We knew "library" meant the bathroom, where Dad reads the newspaper.

But still, Dad bringing home his fresh-from-a-coma sister should have rattled her. Since it didn't, I wondered if Mom thought she had been given a chance to make things right with her.

Dad looked over to Mom and said, "Sorry, honey. I knew about this a few weeks ago, but Etta thought it would be fun to surprise you. They think she will do better here."

"But Stan, we were both just there—"

Auntie Etta thundered with laughter, the slight rattle of nineteen years of sleep still caught in her chest, but she didn't seem to mind. "I was fake-sleeping last time you came! Stan and I thought surprising you was best since they wouldn't let me out right away."

"I see," Mom said, shooting Dad an *I will deal with you later* look, before saying, "Auntie Etta is family. Welcome home, Auntie." Then she ended the discussion as she bent down to carefully give Auntie Etta a mostly genuine hug. Aunt Etta was still laughing as she hugged Mom, patting her back and shooting Dad a shaky thumbs-up from behind Mom's back.

In typical Santora fashion, I knew there would be much more that would be said later, and not so quietly. Meanwhile, before each of us leaned in to give Auntie Etta hugs, I gently gave Mom's shoulder a "proud of you" squeeze. She shrugged it off with a whisper. "Surgery will be nothing compared to living with Etta."

Lisa sized up our aunt and said, "Holy shit, Auntie Etta, between you and my Marie, I'm not sure which one of you looks worse. My project will be to fatten you both up to your pre-coma-pre-mourning-chubby-Italian-sized selves. Etta, what the heck were they feeding you?"

"How the hell would I know?"

She focused her attention on Lorn who'd just entered the room. Her eyes widened. "We've seen you before."

I wondered who "we" was, but opted not to ask.

"No, Auntie Etta," I said. "This is Lorn Elaine; you have never met. She came along years after your accident. She's a nurse and, like you, she'll be staying with us—for a while."

Etta made a "smells bad" face. "My sister Aggie says she's an actress, but she's not acting anymore."

WTF? Her dead sister had said something? My mouth hung open, useless, as I imagined the ghost of Aunt Aggie coaching her from behind her wheelchair. I was wrong, because Etta turned to the blank wall right near me to ask, "Aggie, is she really a nurse . . . or just acting like one? Well, I can't tell that," she grumbled impatiently.

As she turned back to Lorn for one more look, Etta was silent while we all stayed frozen. Auntie Etta broke the silence by replying to the blank wall again: "Well, dammit, how would I know, Aggie? She's not *wearing* a frigging uniform!"

Dad's sheepish shrug said it all. Etta was not exactly as she had been before the coma . . . or . . . was she? If I were being honest, she sounded exactly how she did when she had conversations with her live sister.

Then Etta said, "Hmm. Aggie says the nurse is not here for me."

A chill ran up my spine, and my sister made a cuckoo sign with her finger to her head. When Auntie Etta scanned the room and her eyes landed on me, I blurted, "Well, she's not here for me either." I used an icy tone I regretted.

"Hmmm," Auntie Etta said.

I braved a quick glance at Lorn who, gratefully, had her nurse face on. I could see the way her eyes darted around Aunt Etta's face, down to her bare ankles in her slippers and back to her face again, that she was evaluating Auntie Etta's color and condition.

What Lorn didn't have on was her uniform. She was in an open robe wearing a whisper-thin nightshirt, which said anything but nurse.

Why is it so hard to unflip a switch once it's turned on?

My sister and I locked eyes and I could tell she was exactly where I was, confused and wondering how Etta could know *anything* about Lorn. Vince was too busy admiring the wheels on Auntie Etta's chair to catch the particulars of the conversation.

"Well, isn't she a very attractive lady," Auntie Etta said as she indicated Lorn, yet still addressing her odd comments toward me. She was sizing Lorn up like a thoroughbred horse on the auction block.

Apparently Lorn appealed to anyone with the power of sight, and likely her voice captured the rest, so this was not so unusual. Thankfully my sight and other senses had been impaired since the day I lost Erica. Back when Lorn and I were together, I would teach her that blondes (especially the stunning strawberry blonde actress variety) don't live the way the rest of us do. I told her this once when a door was held open grandly for her and slammed just as grandly into my brunette head. Lorn had turned, confused as to why I was howling with laughter on the other side of the door, not for a second imagining that a door could close in this way.

My years with Lorn had been filled with moments like that, plus many less subtle than a slammed door to the face. I had witnessed from Lorn's adoring fans countless unapologetic sweeping hand signals and verbal requests for me to kindly step out of photos. I had seen Lorn showered with exaggerated (and fabricated) excuses or apologies from men admitting to some faux faux pas, just for the chance to speak with her. I had seen grown men almost come to blows to fight for the chance to hand her a shopping cart, or to carry something she was easily transporting and, on more than one occasion, had nearly tripped over men who dived in front of me to retrieve something Lorn had dropped. At first I had told myself it was her fame, but it was mostly women who watched her wildly popular soap-like drama; the men were enamored simply by the look of her, and who could blame them? Certainly not me as she had attracted me long before she had landed that popular show.

Lorn had that rare combination of looking beautiful yet absolutely approachable, an intoxicating combo that would make any man (or woman) feel eligible, while at the same time inviting elderly women to stop dead in their tracks to comment on her hair, eyes, or smile. I once witnessed an elderly woman who seemed too frail to walk safely with her cane, yet once she set eyes on Lorn, her cane floated from the floor, pointing like a divining rod seeking beauty. "Well, dear, aren't you just beautiful! That smile . . ."

If a husband had been by an admiring woman's side, he would nod dumbly, but he knew to control his enthusiasm in front of his wife.

"Just look at her, Harold; doesn't she look just like an angel?"

And Lorn would smile in that radiant, yet genuinely shy way, and I could see the beauty beams hitting them square in their slack-jawed faces. The beams would convince them. *She has no idea how pretty she is. Tell her, tell her!* And they would. "All that plus that smile!" they would say; it was all too much for them, too much for anyone. Add the nurse's uniform, and old Harold would have needed defibrillator paddles.

But it was never too much for me back then. I loved all of it. I loved other people's admiration of her, and I loved my own. I had been charmed by her, in awe of her from the moment I saw her, and I was part of a devoted club I easily understood. Telling Lorn she didn't live as the rest of us do got me only a "What do you mean?" and, best of all, she meant it.

I would tease her in my best impression of her innocence by saying, "Don't all people experience instantly smitten, fumbling men and awestruck women who want to be your best friend just because they laid eyes on you?" Then I would laugh, muster up a look of half pity and half understanding and answer as if she had been the one to ask the question, "No, Lorn, they really don't."

Truth be told, I had thoroughly enjoyed it, the knowledge that Lorn, the same woman who had the ability to charm men, women, and children alike, would at the end of each day be crawling into bed with me. It would be the Italian brunette whose hands would be rolling up the back of her nightshirt so I could feel the full of her naked backside pressed along the front side of me as I slept (if I could sleep). With all the attention that came to her naturally, I would never once think: How lucky was she? Instead, I would drift off to sleep thinking: How lucky was I?

People reacting this way to Lorn had happened recently at the hospital with Doctor Dick. It likely happened at the drugstore when Lorn picked up something to help Mom sleep ... and it was happening right now with the historically straight, and recently comatose.

Auntie Etta looked back and forth at Lorn and me, now with an intense expression that sent another chill up my spine, as if she could hear my thoughts.

Vince said, "Auntie Etta, you'll have to wait for the book. You've missed a lot around here."

Auntie Etta smiled at Vince. "I haven't missed a thing. My sister tells me everything."

"Oh," Vince said.

As if to prove a point, she said to Lorn, "My sister tells me you haven't been a nurse for very long. She says you were an actress?"

Lisa whispered to me and Vince, "But her sister was dead ... way before ..."

I shook my head to silence her, not wanting to miss a second of this strange play unfolding in front of us.

Lorn answered as if it was perfectly normal for a person to come out of a coma not missing one beat of the family business. "That's right," she said. "I haven't been a nurse for very long, but I know a good patient when I see one."

Auntie Etta laughed, and she had an "aren't you clever" look as she said, "Don't worry dear, we always say we are in exactly the right place at exactly the right time. No matter what condition we are all in."

We again.

Lorn smiled at her without a trace of pity. It didn't seem to register with Lorn that our aunt was a confused old woman who thought her dead sister was in the room with us. Instead, Lorn nodded her head at Auntie Etta in agreement, although I suspected Lorn never felt she was in the right place at any time.

Vince elbowed Lisa and whispered, "Ask why she says 'we' all the time."

Lisa, who always had the balls to ask anything, got more than she bargained for when she asked.

Auntie Etta answered, "Why don't you ask Marie? She has known about all this since you all came to Italy when she was chasing that Erica girl. Aggie told her what to do with her years ago. And now Erica is gone again."

Lisa and I were stunned, wearing identical wide-eyed looks. I had shared with Lisa my belief that Aunt Aggie had come to me in a dream to tell me *exactly* what to do about Erica, and we were in Italy when it happened.

Auntie Etta wagged her finger at all of us as she said, "The whole time I was resting in the hospital, I've been with my sister. And unlike all the secrets you keep around here, Aggie tells me *everything*."

How could it be that Aunt Etta, who had been tucked away in a coma for so many years, knew all the latest Santora family dramas? Then it finally occurred to me, with a great sigh of relief. "Dad must have filled you in on the way home," I told Etta.

Except one look at Dad told us he hadn't filled her in on anything. He was about as white as an Italian ghost could look.

Maybe it was because Etta was back from a nineteen-year coma, or maybe it was because we thought she was gone forever, or maybe it was because Lorn was here as a witness that this crazy thing was happening to our family. But we collectively held our Italian tongues in silent agreement as Lisa offered the guaranteed solution of gravitating toward the kitchen.

When Lisa was around, the kitchen (at any time of the day or night) meant food would miraculously appear and happiness would soon follow. Discussing messages from dead relatives would have to stay on the back burner while Lisa whipped up some pasta and meat sauce on the front two.

Auntie Etta created some fresh drama right away by refusing to share her diet restriction paperwork with Mom and Dad, but revealing its whereabouts while clutching her hard clamshell circa pre-coma pocketbook. Luckily, we pulled Lorn into the kitchen as a consult, whereby Lorn sealed a solid friendship with Auntie Etta by noting that as long as her portions were small, and light on the sauce, she could still eat a bit of macaroni with the rest of us.

"You and I are going to get along just fine," Auntie Etta said, both affectionately and dismissively patting Lorn's arm. "Can you fetch me the meatballs?"

Lorn answered, "Next week. Let's start with pasta and when that goes fine, we graduate to meatballs soon enough. Deal?"

Auntie Etta was thinking she should take that deal while I was thinking about the nurse's skills. She could talk me into never eating a meatball again, and with Lisa's cooking that was saying something.

After dinner I listened to the familiar sounds of the kitchen: plates being scraped of tomato sauce; dishes and clattering flatware being shoveled into the dishwasher; wine glasses being hand-washed in the sink; and the familiar, almost musical sound of Mom and Auntie Etta bickering and finding their groove as if the extraordinary coma-emerging had already been forgotten.

Auntie Etta supervised Mom's dishwasher loading from her wheelchair, "That's not the way you load it. It's supposed to be like a plane, from back to front."

"Is supervising why you got the bum's rush out of the hospital?" Mom sniped back.

"Oh, I miss that place already . . . no *yap-yap-yap*. I was asleep the whole time, so peaceful," Auntie Etta said.

"There's always the old folks home if you think you'll get better care. We aren't experts at this you know," Mom said, awkwardly maneuvering Auntie Etta's wheelchair out of the way.

"I can tell by your driving," Auntie Etta snipped with a chuckle at her joke.

Mom said, "This isn't how I would prefer to push you around, believe me . . ."

Aunt Etta laughed, then flung back, "My sister says you pushed her into an early grave. Oh, don't worry, we'll get to *that* discussion one day soon."

Lisa let out a long, low whistle followed with an "Oooohhh . . ."

Round one: Auntie Etta.

Vince, Lisa, and I watched as Mom waved Dad off and slowly but capably pushed Auntie Etta's wheelchair down the hallway toward the spare bedroom Dad had recently abandoned. "Let me guess," Aunt Etta said as if Mom had the hearing problem, "this place is a castle but you're sticking me in the smallest room? And what the devil is that giant stick doing there in the corner?"

I watched as Lorn walked a safe distance behind them, ready to assist if needed, as my heart betrayed me by thudding at the sight. I thought *I* might need the assistance.

Auntie Etta spotted her and said to Mom, "Why don't you ask Nurse Lorna Doone if she can make this rickety old thing go any faster?"

"Lorn Elaine," Mom said, "and there's nothing wrong with this chair."

"I wasn't talking about the chair," said Auntie Etta.

Mom made an indignant "humph" followed by a chuckle that was music to our ears. She had been far too upbeat lately, and it was creeping us all out. I looked over to see Lisa grinning and stifling a laugh as Mom snipped back at Aunt Etta. "You know, it isn't too late to change your mind about staying here if you liked the nursing home so much. We could find you another one."

Auntie Etta said, "Santoras never change our minds. You're not really a Santora, so maybe you haven't learned by now there are only two things in life: Either you're *in*, or you're *out*. And when I say I'm *in*, I'm *in*."

"As long as I don't throw you *out*," Mom said, which sent Auntie Etta cackling with laughter.

The cheerful bickering continued all the way down the hallway, with Lorn just shaking her head behind them, smart enough to keep well out of it.

When they finally rambled out of earshot, we all burst out laughing, thrilled that Mom had herself a project to keep her fears of surgery at bay. "Either you're in or you're out of a coma!!" Lisa squealed.

Dad was caught in a continuous laughter that brought tears to his eyes, as nothing brought Dad more enjoyment than listening to two ladies jabbing at each other. Especially these two old ladies. Bickering, so much a part of our family recreation, had finally found its way back into our home again.

Regardless of what my mother still had to go through, she was going to get a large dose of normal, Santora family normal, with Auntie Etta back on board. I closed my eyes for a moment, straining to hear the last sounds of them down the long hallway, melting away like distant music, most of all enjoying the distinctive soft sounds of Lorn trying to stuff down her delight. Something stirred deep in the pit of my stomach that felt like hope, if I could remember what the heck that was.

You Can Take the Actress
Out of the Nurse . . .

It was late and I was in the kitchen. If someone had been watching me, it would have appeared as if I were completely absorbed in the hunt for food, when actually I was most absorbed in congratulating myself on how I had successfully avoided Lorn over the past few days. As always, in the very heights of your best ego-driven moments, God finds a way to laugh in your face. It starts as an odd, prickling sensation and a warning that you are about to be taken down a peg or two when you realize the woman you were congratulating yourself for so deftly avoiding is standing behind you.

I spun around like a six-year-old Oreo thief.

"Can I help you find anything?" Lorn asked.

"I think I can find my way around my own kitchen."

"Of course you can," she said quietly. "I just meant that I shopped today." She stayed standing at the doorway. "I needed to make sure your mom and Aunt Etta have had enough fresh fruits and vegetables, less bread and pasta."

For a fleeting and logical moment, I knew I was being an ass, but I only nodded.

Lorn said, "You, on the other hand, should have all of those things. Bread, pasta, you should have whatever interests you."

I felt my stomach flip, and in an instant the ass was back when I shot at her, "You're not here for me, remember?"

It came out harsher than I intended, and I turned my head

so I could wince undetected into a cupboard. I continued to gather things I knew I would never eat.

"I remember," she said, and I hated how the richness of her voice still made me think she should be recorded whenever she spoke. I remembered how I would purposely ask her questions with long answers when we were lying in bed, the sound of her making me drift off to sleep in total contentment . . . or roll on top of her to achieve total contentment. I shivered a little. There must have been a chill in the kitchen.

It didn't escape me that with her robe-clad form in the doorway and my food-laden arms in the kitchen, we were looking like a scene from the movie *Desert Hearts* and we were playing the straight woman and the gay woman. Only I wouldn't be stupid enough to get onboard that train again. I knew from past experience it would be a train to nowhere, fast.

In an effort to soften my approach, I said, "You moved in quickly. Do you have everything you need, I mean, for your room?"

"I do," she said, and with those two words I wondered if she also was flashing back to a wedding in Jamaica so many years ago. Lorn's mother, Katharine, and my Uncle Tony had fallen in love at the same time we had met, and then gone back to be married there on the same day that Lorn had decided she wanted to risk us being a couple. The problem was, she had to commit to wanting to be a couple many more times after that. It had been a hellish pattern of leaving and crawling back, a time filled with pain as well as overwhelming passion.

I shook off that thought. Now, all I wanted was for her to commit to staying the hell out of my sight while she took care of my mother.

"Well, I'm glad to see you're eating," she said before disappearing back into the dark hallway.

Eating. Well, that hadn't occurred to me.

I was just doing what I had been doing for the past few weeks since my family all moved under one roof. Every night after Lisa had stocked the shelves each day, I would take a small amount of food and discreetly dispose of it. Now I was doing this with Lorn's shopping. Usually, I would bring it to a food donation place, but sometimes, if I was in a panic to get rid of it and didn't have the time to make the trip without risking my eagle-eye sister catching on, I would Frisbee some lunch meat and cheese into the woods, wondering what the wildlife made of the flying discs of salami and provolone. As a last resort, I had also flushed some slices of bread.

I remembered the day Eddie first saw me after Erica had gone. I was almost at my most gaunt version of myself as he looked me up and down with eyebrows pulled north by invisible puppet strings. "Honey, after all you've been through, can I just say, you look amazing." Leave it to a gay guy to appreciate the sight of a budding anorexic.

I answered, "Total Devastation Diet. It's easy; the weight just drops off." Eddie had laughed, which was my intention, but it spooked me how even a guy as shallow as him couldn't hide the unmistakable look of pity in his eyes. At that time, I asked myself if I was heading for a little trouble. And I was ten pounds heavier then.

Lorn had caught me in my fake kitchen raid and, as much as I wanted to, I couldn't kid myself I would get away with it. One by one I placed the food back, except for the Ben & Jerry's ice cream and the bag of Oreos, which made me think she intentionally put in front of me all the things I could never resist.

The following morning the producer arrived early at the house, unannounced. I answered the door and there was Sandra, briefcase in hand, looking quite ready to produce something. I wondered if this woman might actually give Lisa a run for her money.

"I don't think Lisa was expecting you," I lied. "She left about an hour ago."

Sandra pulled off her Ray-Bans and cursed. "What the fuck.

Your sister's dodging me. Does she have a habit of doing this?"

"Of doing what?"

"Avoiding amazing opportunities when they are thrown right at her feet."

"I'm pretty sure she thinks she's the amazing opportunity. Isn't that why you drove two hours from Boston at nine on a Saturday morning?"

Sandra didn't answer, but smirked and threw an eye roll in for good measure.

"Well, come on in; maybe she'll show up in a bit. Lisa probably has some leftovers lying around for lunch, and this way you can assure yourself the omelet wasn't just a fluke." Thankfully, I had not ditched any food the night before.

Sandra walked by me and I could feel her nerves also pass by in a vibrating wave. This was not a woman used to being stood up. Precisely why Lisa did it, I thought.

"Let me guess," I said. "Contract negotiations?"

She gave me a look that said, *why on earth would I discuss this with* you? But then she must have thought better of it, knowing I could give her the boot before she got any of my sister's leftovers. Sandra nodded. "Yes, the uncomfortable part where we talk about money." She sighed, and I offered her a seat at the kitchen bar. She perched what looked like a thousand-dollar briefcase perfectly disguised as a designer bag on the kitchen island.

"If you find anything with tons of meat in it, I'm a vegetarian . . . and a quitter."

I pulled out Lisa's bolognaise, knowing how great it was served cold and set her up as she refreshed her lipstick and checked her hair in her compact. Hmmm, I thought. Refreshing lipstick before eating? As I was getting her a glass of chilled white sangria, I heard the unmistakable sound of a compact hitting the floor, shattering.

I suspected the shocked look on Sandra's face was not from sending her Mac Mineralize Foundation NC15 shade to an early death on the kitchen tile.

"Everything okay?" I asked.

"Um . . . I don't want to alarm you, but I'm pretty sure I just saw a famous actress walking around in your house dressed like a nurse."

"She's not dressed like a nurse."

Sandra said in an excited whisper, "No, really . . . Lorn Elaine . . . down your corridor, right there, believe me; I know it was her!"

"That's no actress," I said. "That's my mother's nurse."

Sandra kept staring in the same spot as if the ghost might reappear. "What the . . ."

"Lorn is a nurse now. She's been helping to take care of our mother."

"You're *kidding* me."

"Nope. Nurse. No longer an actress."

"Who does that?" she said, her hand closing over her horrified open mouth as she stared down the hallway. Then, to herself she muttered, "Obviously she's not mentally ill, I mean if she's taking care of someone, but . . . why . . ."

Recognizing the symptoms, I said, "You're a fan."

"I'm not gonna lie, I am. One day she just disappeared from Hollywood. She used to be on one of my favorite shows . . . what the hell was it now . . ."

"*Razor Falls.*"

"Right! She played a real vixen on that show. Kind of rare for an older woman to score a part like that on television, and she played it hot. I admit, she was my one girl crush."

"Only one?" I teased, but she was still craning her neck down the hallway.

"Well, every straight girl has at least one, right?"

"I wouldn't know," and then couldn't resist. "Lorn had one too, a long time ago."

I could tell Sandra had forgotten I was in the room, but she hadn't forgotten how to eat bolognaise.

I teased her. "Looks like you will be done with lunch soon. If you want, I could introduce you?"

Sandra's eyes bugged out. "I just couldn't. I mean, she's busy.

116

I mean, I don't want to interrupt the whole . . . you know . . ." she said, crinkling her nose and waving the napkin in her hand as if she were holding a dirty hanky.

"Nursing thing?" I asked.

"But I dropped my compact—" she said, opting not to abandon her lunch to pick up the flesh-colored shards. "Well, if you think it would be okay? Yes." She dabbed at her lipstick with her napkin when it occurred to her to ask, "How is your mother?"

"Mom's great, thanks. Thankfully, she dodged a bullet."

I moved from the island to the corridor before I called out, "Lorn?" My raised voice appeared to scare the shit out of Sandra, who started panic-smoothing her hair, working her way down to smoothing her outfit. Diving, then not diving, to grab her shattered compact abandoned on the floor. I heard the scraping sound of her foot sliding it under her bar stool in case it would make a bad first impression.

"Lorn, can you spare a second to meet someone?"

Behind me, Sandra said, "Jesus, do I have bolognaise on my face? That lunch was outrageous, by the way."

There was a half bite left. "You didn't finish."

"I can't eat now . . ." she said, her thumb testing the waist of her tight skirt.

Lorn appeared in the kitchen doorway, setting off what was probably the first gasp Sandra had emitted in her entire life. I saw Lorn as Sandra was seeing her, and I had to admit, like it or not, she was pretty gasp-worthy standing there in her nursing whites, her hair loosely pulled back well past her shoulders, a few strands loose and framing her face, her nursing top tightly fitted, yet still professional, though open just low enough in the front to hint at a Hollywood past.

Sandra stood quickly with her mouth partly opened, frozen by the sight of the star of *Razor Falls*. Only Sandra's eyes moved, swiftly scanning Lorn's body, and I wondered if Sandra was also thinking a variation of Lisa's theory: you could take the actress out of the nurse, but you couldn't stop wanting to nurse the actress.

A distant and deeply intimate memory of Lorn tugged at me, forcing me to pull out a memory of Erica and set it front and center in my mind. *Take that. A clever block.* How I had enjoyed Erica . . . every inch of her . . . but with that memory came the backhand of the loss and what I would never have again. Bad block. When would I learn the memories of both Lorn and Erica were best buried?

Lorn looked at me expectantly, and I forgot for a moment why I had called to her.

"Oh, hello," Lorn said to the stranger in our kitchen.

"Lorn, this is Sandra. She's a producer and, unlike my mother, she is in the battle of her life."

Lorn smiled. "You're the producer considering working with Lisa?" she said.

Sandra smiled dumbly back.

I had seen this so many times before when Lorn and I were first together. Actually, when I first was with her, I had been that person, acting like an idiot around her because I had admired her work as an actress. Again, all roads led back to Erica and I thought about how much things had changed for me. Everything was so different now. There was nothing that seemed important about television, actresses, or fame that would make me act differently around anyone. Lorn had chosen the path where there was so much suffering . . . some people did not get as lucky as my mom . . . some people died while Lorn was on the job, unlike acting, where you might pretend to die on the job. She had chosen the opposite of fantasyland for the harsh reality of life and death.

And then the thought struck me: after experiencing her own loss, walking away from love in order to protect her career, I wondered for the first time, what had been Lorn's turning point? And for the first time I felt ashamed for not having asked her. Was I such an egomaniac that I thought her life change had been entirely driven by the chance of getting me back? She had answered that for me already, when I first opened the door to see her standing there. Why did I keep forgetting? She was not here for me.

The silence between the three of us was broken when the front door burst open, and Lisa barreled through.

"Oh hey, bitches," she said, as if she were fourteen and her old neighborhood guy friends had stopped by, waiting for Lisa to beat them to a pulp at street hockey. Or football. She strode past Sandra without a look and attended to the grocery bag filled with farmer's market veggies with the undue concentration of a botanist.

I said, "Lorn already shopped for Mom," but Lisa turned and quickly assessed the situation, her eyes flicking back and forth between Sandra and Lorn. "I see the producer's here . . . producing."

Sandra forced herself to look away from Lorn. "I came here looking for you, Lisa. We have business to discuss." Then she cleared her voice as a way to reset her nerves.

Lisa turned to me, pointed to Sandra, and said, "Another fan?"

"Yep," I said.

Lisa said, "How do you deal with this, Lorn? You spend years changing your career and still you get the annoying fans who would drag you back to Hollywood if they could. My sister always said that it was never about the fame to you, that it was just about the business."

Lorn stepped down off the landing to the hallway and when she walked towards Sandra, Lisa said, "Television is also Sandra's business."

Lorn extended a hand to her. Sandra shook her hand, the awestruck look returning to her face, blowing to hell Lisa's defense of her. "Nice to meet you. I'm the Visiting Nurse."

"Not really," I said, "she's the Staying Nurse."

Sandra swooned with Lorn at close range, and I knew from the look on my sister's face she was not amused. "Let's all have dinner tonight," Lisa said, and only I heard the twinge in her voice. When Lisa is threatened, she pulls the threat closer. When I am threatened, I toss it like a Frisbee into the woods.

I said, "I don't think that's a—"

"Sandy here and I have some business to conduct—," said Lisa.

"Sandra," the producer interrupted, staring at Lorn.

"—and Lorn hasn't had a day off in . . . well, since she got here, and Marie here obviously needs to eat." Lisa added, "Lorn, you're joining us."

Lorn said, "Oh, no, I can't, but thank you for asking."

"I didn't ask," Lisa said. That was true. Lisa tells people to eat.

Lorn smiled as Sandra piped up. "I really can't either. I have to get back to Boston after we finish our negotiations. I have another meeting later this afternoon . . . a dinner thing."

Lisa ignored Sandra, and turned to me. "You know how I am, sis. I can't negotiate anything on an empty stomach, but we can do it another day. Lorn, since the producer is busy, just you will join us. I'm cooking up something special."

She sure was, I thought.

Lorn looked over at me. For a sign of permission? "Why wouldn't you?" I said to her, managing a half smile.

"Thanks, Lisa, it actually sounds lovely. I've missed the days of your Camptown Ladies cooking."

Lorn looked at me again, so I gave another half smile, and I suppose that equaled a whole smile. I tried to remember a shared meal between us at Camptown Ladies but could not, as Lorn had already left in a closeted panic long before Camptown Ladies had opened. By the time word had got out that the best Italian dinner you could get your hands on was nestled deep in the woods and the campground started to take off, Lorn had missed it all. And by the time she tried one more time to come back, I had fallen head over heels with Erica.

In contrast, Erica and I had shared so many dinners at a private camp table for two under the tall pines of Camptown Ladies. Eating outside in private was near impossible with crowds of Lisa's dining fans around from spring through fall, so Erica had built a mini-picnic table for two, with no room for a spare Santora to join. It had been our private secret that it was built small exactly for that reason. I remembered the day Lorn had seen that table for the first time, the look of heartbreak when she saw the intimacy of the space Erica had built for us. The table was seated near a huge area of brush, which Erica carved into a crescent shape, just wide enough to tuck the two-person table inside, and we left the wild vegetation to curl around it like a natural cocoon.

I remembered when Lorn first saw it how her eyes darted from detail to detail. The tiki torches, the classic red-checkered picnic tablecloth, and our favorite red Coleman lantern. It sat between us for late night dining, along with the tiny matching tealight lantern we had named Dixie (after a hotel manager on Block Island, for a reason I could no longer remember.) In that moment I saw a glimpse on Lorn's face of how she wished it was all for her, and how for just a moment my stomach ached for what she had lost. What we had both lost. I could still feel her pain now as if a thread had not fully snapped between us, keeping us connected in some invisible way. Would it ever go away?

Sandra broke the silence. "Well, if Lorn is joining and Lisa is cooking, I guess I could make some calls, change a few plans."

Sandra stared at Lorn like a rabid fan; Lorn was looking everywhere except at me, and Lisa was staring at the producer as if she were an entrée. If there was something that thrilled Lisa more than cooking, or a woman who was a sure thing, it was cooking for a woman that wasn't.

And if our deck chairs had seat belts, I would have planned to fasten myself in for the evening.

Lakeside, Table for Two

Mom, Dad, and Aunt Etta had eaten hours ago. Lisa called it the Q-Tip hour because the early bird seating in restaurants made a room of gray-haired seniors look like a landscape of Q-Tips. The trio was already settled in to watch their favorite BBC series, *Last Tango in Halifax.* Dad claimed he liked watching it for the clever writing and multigenerational characters, but we all knew he was a fan of the hot lesbian kissing scenes, as were my sister and I.

Vince, who had been invited for dinner this evening, made a lame excuse by claiming he had to take his wife and son out, but his exact words upon departing were: "Confucius say: 'Man who gets in middle of hen fight, lose cock.'" To show my appreciation, I slapped him on the ass before he could escape out the door.

Since the kitchen was the forbidden zone when meals were being prepared, it was all on me to entertain the producer and the nurse while Lisa worked her magic. We took our drinks out to the big deck with the panoramic view of the lake shimmering beneath us for a last few moments of sun.

Sandra recovered from her starstruck silence by switching into business mode, asking Lorn to join her, resting her drink on the cocktail ledge of the deck railing so she could fire questions at her. I liked this idea and hovered in the closest chair, thinking I might get some of my own questions answered without having to ask.

Sandra asked, "What made you switch from acting to nursing when your career was going so great?" Strong opener, I thought, leaning back in my chair, trying not to look interested in an answer.

Lorn paused for a moment. "It sounds corny, but I suppose you could say I had a calling."

"Really?" Sandra said. "Like when a nun gets a calling to join the church?"

"Except my boss is more difficult," she said. Good one, I thought, but my laugh was drowned out by Sandra whose roar of a laugh echoed over the lake. I watched as she leaned closer to Lorn, resting her hand on Lorn's arm as if she was stopping her from lifting her drink.

"Really, though, what did you mean by a calling?"

Lorn looked over at me, then back out to the lake. Was she trying to remember, or pausing to censor what she was going to say?

Finally, she answered. "It started with this overwhelming feeling I was in the wrong place all the time. Everything I did, even if I was successful in my career, didn't feel right. It all felt as if I needed to change direction or I would suffocate. I asked for a sign ... which I didn't get until right after I had graduated nursing school, and that is when the first wave of Covid-19 hit ..."

"So, it's all your fault," I said, the joke falling flat.

Lorn smiled a familiar smile at me. She had spent several years getting used to the often-inappropriate Santora family sense of humor, doling out countless of those smiles, and I was thinking this as she said to Sandra, "The Santoras are mostly harmless and sometimes funny."

"Sorry. Maybe too soon," I said, and Lorn shook her head no at me, eyes sparkling.

Lorn led Sandra over to the table so we could all sit.

"I guess a calling is when you no longer have a choice, but it becomes clear that you need to change your path or risk losing your way. I had a lot more reasons, but that one makes me sound the most heroic, so that's the story I tell." Lorn laughed at herself,

123

and I found it hard to look away.

"Brave woman," Sandra said. "When everyone else was mostly running from cities and other people, you put yourself on the front line."

"Nah," Lorn said softly. "I was too afraid not to listen to the voices in my head."

I said, "Just warn us if they say 'Kill, kill, kill.'"

Lorn laughed again. "If this wine is good, I might give you a ten-second head start," she said, and I remembered how quickly she could dish back a comment. Lorn took a sip of her wine, and I waited to see her eyes close and hear her tiny "Mmmm" as she always did after swallowing her first sip. When she did it, I remembered the taste of wine on her lips.

When she opened her eyes, she looked away from us and stared out at the lake.

Aloof—admirable. An impressive woman . . . and still so attractive. Damn her.

"Is Hollywood like the mafia? Do they always try to pull you back in with another project?" Sandra's jarring question pulled me back to reality. "I mean, forgive me for being crass, but the money must have been hard to give up."

Lorn laughed at the question, and I thought about how for so many years I had worked to keep her laughing, just to hear that sound. "Nobody in Hollywood is saying, 'If only we had a few more forty-something women around for all these delicious roles.'"

"But you're a stunning woman," Sandra said cautiously, almost shy, and for a reason I didn't understand I wanted to smack the under-confident look off her face. Where the hell was the cocky producer we met in Boston? Lorn would not have liked that producer one bit. But this version . . . my palms were getting sweaty and I wondered why I wanted to wipe them on Sandra's face.

I chimed in. "I'm also finding it hard to believe they didn't try to pull her back into the fold. Lorn could always get all the men to drop at her feet."

Lorn looked away, and I could see the producer studying her. It was in that moment I could see something dawning on Sandra, as if she remembered when Lorn Elaine had been outed by the press. It was an easy one for me to remember. It had been at a family wedding in Jamaica when Lorn had recklessly kissed a woman without measuring what all the consequences could be, and that woman had been me.

When a straight woman kisses a lesbian and they both feel love, only two things can happen, and, unfortunately for us, both did. Like an explosion of the most remarkable kind we had connected, and she couldn't allow our connection to continue. As I sat there, watching her talk with the producer, it occurred to me for the first time that she had left all we had together in order to save a career she would eventually cast aside five years later. Of course, by then Erica had already confessed her love to me, and I had taken my chances on yet another straight woman.

And we all know the end of that story.

I noticed nobody was talking, and Sandra was looking to me for an answer to a question I had totally missed.

"I was just asking, what about you, Marie?" Sandra said.

My face must have said *Huh?* because Lorn jumped in, "Sandra was asking if you ever thought of making a change?"

"Me? I am not a fan of change, and yet it keeps happening to me. I attract change like a person petrified of dogs attracts Dobermans. You might guess that tragic endings of relationships are the worst endings, but I think the worst is women who dabble in the gay life, only to bail when things get difficult."

Lorn looked as if I had nailed her right in the chest.

Direct hit, I thought, but my stomach turned as if it was disgusted with me.

Sandra said quietly, "I meant if you ever considered a career change."

Oh.

"Well, I would have to have a career before I could change it. My house-flipping career died with Erica." I downed my drink, embarrassed by my ragged voice. "What about you, Sandra?

I'm thinking you probably thrive on the carnage of Boston city living . . . and producing." I tried to soften my voice, but it still left dangling an unmistakable edge. I sounded like a woman hating life, my life.

"Dinner's ready!" Lisa yelled as she stepped out on the deck, and I sprang from my chair as if the governor had just called at 11:59. I was hoping Lisa had not overheard my nasty tone. As she headed toward the table, I saw from her pleased admiration for her own dishes that she was far too distracted by her over-the-top presentation to pay attention to what we had been talking about. Lisa set the main tray down where the producer had the best view. When my sister flicked her eyes over to me, I realized I was wrong and she had observed the tense expressions on our faces.

"Looks like I picked the perfect dinner to serve: Quicksand!" she said.

Lisa was serving individual crock bowls of thick lobster bisque, each with two lobster claws sticking out of the sides of the bowl, grasping at the edge, giving the appearance of a lobster having been submerged in a quicksand of bisque. Alongside each bowl there was a large homemade Italian pepper biscuit shaped into a perfect ring just like a life preserver, tied with a tarragon rope, dangling over the edge of the bowls, and leaning barely out of reach of the hapless lobster.

"Wow," the producer said, "just . . . wow." At that moment, Lorn and I became Team Insignificant, and Sandra's attention landed back on her prize chef. My sister's smirk indicated she could hear the sound of the numbers on her contract ticking up several notches.

Lisa had also prepared four sample-sized seafood dishes for everyone to try, paired with her twice-baked potatoes, served in pairs, with a nipple-like dot of paprika on each. They were served with what she affectionately introduced as Stripper Corn, which was corn on the cob stripped bare, except for one long toga-like curl of unshucked leaf tied across the lower third like a toga. Lisa's idea of a vegetable side dish was a perfectly built

Jenga tower of alternating grilled zucchini and carrot sticks, constructed a lot like the bonfires we used to have at Camptown Ladies.

The puzzle towers of vegetables would have been plenty, but she also served up a long plate of spiced mini sushi rolls laid out on a bird nest-like bed of crispy thin noodles, for a dish Lisa named (right then, for Sandra's benefit): Rolls in the Hay.

I wasn't sure if the producer was panting for the food, my sister, a roll in the hay, or all three, but I did notice her focus shift abruptly away from Lorn. While we all were mesmerized by the hilarious artistry of the presentation and started in on the food, my sister shot me a cocky look that I pretended not to notice.

I attempted to start a new conversation since I was too full from my foot in my mouth to eat anything else just yet. I lobbed a question to the producer. "Sandra, tell us how you decided television was the business you wanted to be your career."

Lisa interrupted. "That slight condescension is my sister's attempt at humor. If she really wanted to be sarcastic, she could have asked you why you bothered to go into an industry designed to pitch hour-long infocommercials to a housewife market that simply doesn't exist anymore. Now that would have been some worthy sarcasm."

Sandra didn't bat an eyelash, and said, "I couldn't agree with you more. The days of generic TV programming are over. It's all about specializing, marketing to the fringe and taking risks to be the first . . . and the best, of course. That's why I'm considering a deal with you, Lisa."

My sister liked her approach. "Considering, huh?"

Sandy knew how to play the game with her. "Consumers have too many choices at their disposal so it's not enough for a channel to just be the best at what they do. You have to offer something so unique they can't get it anywhere else."

Lisa turned to me and said, "I'm unique."

"Heard it," I said as I poured Lorn and me another glass of wine. I felt Lorn look up at me, but I avoided her eyes. I am simply playing the good host, I thought.

Sandra answered, "One of a kind. That's how you grab any new market in any industry. Besides, I didn't pick TV. TV picked me."

"What do you mean?" I asked, disappointed that the producer was much more than a little interesting.

"I mean that the set of circumstances leading me to do what I do and be where I am were so . . ."

"Magical?" This was an especially strange word to say, and since Lorn and I asked this at exactly the same moment, all eyes landed on us.

Sandra said, "I was going to say bizarre, but I guess you could say magical . . . I suppose, yes. I had no choice but to follow the path put before me. And that led me to my success as a producer, which led me to Lisa and our tremendous opportunity for more success, and Lisa's somewhat difficult personality in holding out on the deal, which led me to this opportunity to be here tonight, with you."

Maybe she meant to say "with you all," but she had clearly said "with you" as her eyes were back on Lorn.

Lorn smiled back at her and said, "I believe that, too. Every moment, every meeting, every circumstance—I have to believe it's all part of a bigger plan."

Lisa said, "If so, then I believe that plan was drawn up by a crack addict architect."

We may have all been thinking collectively about Mom, but I also thought of Erica, and all the circumstances that seemed to have no logical plan. Or certainly not a plan I would have signed on to.

"Maybe," Lorn said. "But we can't pretend to understand the way of the originator of all things."

Lisa said, "Oh Jesus, I mean, Christ—I mean, really, is this turning into a conversation about God?"

Sandra turned to me to ask, "Is this the one topic too edgy for your sister?"

Honestly it was.

"Nothing's too edgy for me," my sister shot back. "We can

talk about the Easter Bunny next, if you like make-believe or . . . Santa?"

"Except he is real." We did it again. Lorn and I joined in with the same sentence.

My eyes darted to Lorn, and her eyes were already on me, trying to gauge my reaction. I smiled, telling her, "Lisa doesn't believe in magical things, even when they happen directly to her."

"Not true," Lisa said. "Once, I came three times in two minutes. Now that was some fucking magic."

Sandra bellowed a laugh before skimming a large spoonful of bisque into her mouth. Her eyes rolled back, and she tossed her head back and forth in ecstasy as if Lisa had inspired her as much with her words as her food. She was a beautiful woman, no denying that. A force to be reckoned with, and not just a little sexy. I glanced at Lorn, who was watching her too, and when her eyes stopped rolling back in her head in pleasure, Sandra said, "Lorn, please taste this! It's like sex . . ."

I felt another irritating stab of heat slice through my middle, and when the sound came from Sandra, my irritation flared back over to the producer . . . over Lorn's easy way of charming everyone she met. Either way, I had fantasies of dunking Sandra's head into a vat of Quicksand Bisque and holding her down with a lobster claw to the neck. Lisa, on the other hand, was thoroughly enjoying watching Sandra plummet deeper into ecstasy with every bite.

When Sandra stopped chewing, she glanced around at us as if she had been lost and was surprised we were all still at the table. "So, Lorn," she said, "I'd like to hear about how you made the switch."

"From gay back to straight?" I asked, enjoying the acid feel of the words on my tongue.

Sandra said, "Um, no, from award-winning actress to nurse. Though if she wants to tell us that other story, I am open to listening."

Lorn ignored my comment, but I had seen her flinch. And

I'd hoped it would feel better to witness than it did.

Lorn said, "I was led to nursing through no choice of my own."

"That's the part I want to hear about," Sandra said.

But Lorn politely shook her head and said, "I'm not ready to talk about that yet."

Lisa broke the silence. "So then, let's continue the 'women that dabble in lesbianism' conversation I heard when I first came outside."

Sandra liked this idea and said, "I'd like to know if there are two schools of thought about this. I've heard some of my gay friends say that if you go gay, you were always gay, but I'm not so sure about that."

Lisa said, "First off, of people we are talking about, how many drinks are there on the table? This is math that matters."

Sandra answered, "Just one. Each."

Lisa said, "All right, so the straight woman has a shot of keeping her clothes on."

I interrupted. "Can we talk about something else?"

The producer said, "Come on, Marie, what's more interesting than this?" Then she turned to Lorn and said, "What do you think?"

Lorn put her spoon down. "I know for a fact that anyone can fall in love with anyone. I'm also sure there are gay people who are born that way through and through." At this, I let out a whet-whoo whistle, and pointed to my sister as Lorn continued. "I also think you can fall for somebody you don't expect to, the same way you can fall for somebody you absolutely don't want to. If we were all in total control, life wouldn't be challenging."

Sandra smiled, in awe of her.

"Well, Lorn should know," I said. "She fell for someone she didn't expect to fall for and certainly someone she didn't want to fall for. Oh, and she definitely was not born gay. This woman is straight, through and through. Right, Lorn?"

Lorn wouldn't look at me, and I regretted saying it even before she stood up from the table and reached her hand out to shake the producer's hand. "I'm afraid I have to call it a night. Sandra, I enjoyed meeting you, and I wish you good luck on your negotiations. Nothing easy is worth it," she said, turning to my sister. "Lisa, as always, it was an amazing dinner. Thank you for everything."

I was finding God myself, praying she would not address me, but, keeping with the pattern of my life, no such luck.

"And, Marie, you're right. I'm not resentful that you and others were born knowing which road you wanted to take. I only wish I had been like you. Since we met so many years ago, I'd decided it was only fair that I stay off any of those roads altogether. So, you can relax in knowing that when it comes to me, you have the entire road all to yourself. And maybe that's how it should be. Leave it to the experts, right?" Lorn's voice was getting louder and more shaken. "No student drivers with their learning permits, especially older student drivers, bumping into things, making mistakes, leaving the scene of the crime. Who wants to be the person crashing into and hurting people, the one that caused another person to be bitter?"

Ouch. I felt my face turn red, but Lorn wasn't quite done.

She looked directly in my eyes as she finished. "I've almost forgiven myself, and all I wish for you is that someday you'll heal from everything you have been through, some of it what I put you though, and find a way to make a happy life with the road left in front of you."

I couldn't help noticing she was in front of me. She was standing still in front of me, challenging me to let all the heartbreak go and follow the road ahead to try to be happy again.

My face grew hotter still. Not with anger but with the burn of knowing she was right and I was wrong. Lisa was wrong, too, and I knew it because she was fussing with catching all the invisible crumbs on an outdoor table.

Lorn left us and when the door to the deck slid closed, the full impact of it hit me at last. Not just that I had been a total asshole—that was the easy part—but that she had been entirely alone all the years before, and since, we had been together.

While I had all the beautiful memories of my time with Erica, Lorn had likely not experienced any real happiness during all that time, and all she had to look back on was us, and that had been so long ago.

For the first time in almost a year I realized I was nowhere near the loneliest person I knew.

"Well, that was awkward," Sandra said, and I waited for her to take a shot at me for being a horrible person and for scaring off her eye candy. Instead, she turned to Lisa and said, "Now, about your contract . . ."

"What about it?" Lisa said, feigning boredom, but I knew Lisa was most impressed when women acted cold and impersonal, especially when they should be displaying compassion.

The producer said, "We're nailing this down tonight. The details are inconsequential because I don't play games. I want your show, and you want to do it. Which leaves only one question on the table, and it's not the money. The only question I ever ask in a negotiation: are you *in* or are you *out?*"

Lisa looked like she had gotten hit with a still-flapping piece of cod. Are you *in* or are you *out?* It was the family motto again, and a big magical sign. I knew my sister was most definitively *in* with Sandra.

The only question? Exactly how far *in*.

Open Legs & Closing Doors

I had been nearly killed this morning. And when your day starts out like that, you tend to evaluate things a bit more closely. It had been a bad night and now a bad day. I had left a store and had walked off to the side of the parking area, knowing I would have to pass in front of a UPS truck to get to my car. The engine was running, but the driver inside was looking down and writing in his clipboard, so I stepped down off the curb. Just then, something compelled me to jump backward. I wish I could say it had been my undying love of Erica that saved me, but I could claim no such thing. I had just hopped backward on nothing more than a hunch that I needed to do that. And, right at that moment, I realized the heat I had felt on the bottom of my legs had been the UPS truck, which I had assumed was parked, but which had lurched ahead while the driver's head was still down on his clipboard. The truck accelerated forward before he had even fully looked up to toss his clipboard into his passenger seat. He gunned the truck past me, probably without even noticing I had been about to be avocado toast on his windshield.

What had made this a rough day, a really rough day, was not the close call. I had had those before, and knew I would have them again. In fact, even in that moment I tried to take pleasure in the idea that maybe a guardian angel had orchestrated a miraculous save . . . but that is not where my mind would allow me to go.

133

Where my mind went, and stayed, was this niggling thought: *I had missed my chance.* Realizing that even for a second, I registered upset that the truck had not struck me, making me see a buried part of me that no longer wanted to live.

I had just admitted it for the first time, and in such an impactful way. I preferred to be a hood ornament rather than waste another moment on this planet without the woman I loved. Even now, as I rationally thought about it, I came to the same conclusion: Did I really prefer to be UPS windshield splatter than to feel this pain for one more day?

I had managed to stifle the worst of my crying until I reached home. It was a new skill. I could put off crying like nobody's business. If it wasn't the time or the place, I could politely postpone unleashing my tears to a time when there would be no chance of a witness. Nobody needed to witness this . . . least of all me. So I avoided mirrors like a vampire. Seeing my face twisted in all that pain made it that much more real, and this was about as real as I could take.

I was relieved that I had the house to myself. No sign of anyone. Had I been back at the cabin I would have gone to the kitchen sink to stand and stare out the window. It was where Erica loved to stand. She would stare out the kitchen window and seem so at peace. It was one of her favorite places in the house, so it had become one of mine. But I couldn't stand there anymore because I had moved out of that house.

Why did I do that? At that, the tears came, and I imagined the rippling lake I was staring at was my grief, and I had filled the lake myself and now it was up so high I felt I might drown.

I closed my eyes tightly, which made the tears splatter on my cheeks. "Please . . ." I whispered. "*Please.* I miss loving you. Erica, can you hear me? Can you please come back from wherever you are? Let me know you're still with me . . ."

I heard the sudden whirr of a motor behind me, which spun me around to look at the bottom of the kitchen island. Impossible, I thought. Completely impossible. It was the heater at the base of the island, which had turned itself on, only it could not have done so, as the switch to turn this on was right at the base of the island in plain view. Nobody else was in the house, and the switch was very difficult to flip. To prove this, I knelt down to the floor and flipped the heater off, then back on, and the switch required a heavy snap to turn it on. Maybe, somehow, had Erica heard me?

My smile turned into a laugh; my tears still flowed but now from a feeling of hope I hadn't felt in so long. I whispered out loud, "Is this a sign?"

Rising from my knees by pulling myself up from the side of the island, I noticed where my hand was resting—in the center of a heart-shaped cutting board, which was secured to the side of the island. It was one of the first things Erica and I had bought together for the cabin, and it was the first thing I had installed at Lakeside 2229.

I laughed out loud, remembering how we had once tried to find a replacement for it, but couldn't because the beating sun had created a bleached heart-shaped stencil on the side of the island where it hung. I thought about how the heart was in the kitchen, at the very heart of the house. Before I stood up completely, I stupidly kissed the center of the cutting board, my lipstick leaving a light imprint on the sliced wood. How sweet. How sad.

How unsanitary.

My normal mood came roaring back, and in frustration I grabbed the thing and hurled it into the sink where it landed like a wooden baseball bat against stainless steel. A loud, empty, hollow sound. I wiped my tears away, hoping I hadn't broken the cutting board when I realized that Lorn had been watching me from the hallway. For how long, I had no idea.

"I didn't know anyone was home," I said, stupidly. Then I thought about all the other things I had experienced, bizarre, heart-shaped clouds, following me home on my drives and crazy moments where I would think of Erica's love of something random, like ladybugs. Then, in the middle of winter, one would scurry across the top of my bedroom dresser.

I grabbed a rag, wiped my face first, then the kitchen island. "Lisa made a mess in here."

"Your sister keeps a perfectly clean kitchen," Lorn said. "I'm here if you want to talk?"

"About my hatred of cutting boards?"

She patiently kept her eyes on me until I slowly shook my head before retreating to my room.

Later, there was a knock at my bedroom door. The sound was so hesitant that I questioned whether I'd heard it at all. Until it came again. It was two o'clock in the morning, and I had assumed I was the last person still awake. Lisa had to go to Boston in the morning, Vince got up early with the kids, Mom and Dad had been sleeping later now that they were back in the same bed, and Auntie Etta was still catching up on her coma-deprived beauty sleep.

That left one person.

"Come in," I said, and Lorn peeped her head in.

"I saw your light," she said, but she didn't move past the doorway.

I signaled for her to come into the room and she did, just barely, take a step inside the door and close it behind her so the light would not drift down the hallway and wake anyone else.

"So?" I asked.

"So, I thought maybe you were having a rough night and might need to talk."

I paused for a second, hoping my gentler side would edit my words, but that side was nowhere to be found. "And you thought I'd want to talk with you?"

I noticed that Lorn's hand had never left the doorknob. Was I that predictable?

She quietly reopened the door. "I shouldn't have come."

"Wait. Please."

I hadn't planned to be such a bitch, and I hadn't planned to

136

stop her from going either. "I'm sorry, that was rude. I am rude all the time these days, not sure if you noticed?"

Lorn waited, but when I didn't say more, she said, "I'm thinking I was wrong and that I shouldn't have come."

"I said I was being rude, but if it's a real apology you're looking for, I can probably rustle one up—"

"I meant that I shouldn't have come here at all. I am thinking I should try to line up a replacement for your mother's care—"

I was such a stupid ass.

"No. Please. My mother needs you; please stay. Don't make me beg. I've been doing too much of that lately. You know, not out loud . . ."

She nodded. "Your mother is going to be fine. She's getting stronger every day."

I whispered without looking at her, "I'm not."

"You will. Everything takes time, and I don't think me being here is helping you. Quite the opposite in fact." As she turned to leave the room again, I felt my familiar, exaggerated panic welling up inside.

"Stay. Please."

"I'll think about it," she answered.

"No, I mean, stay . . . now," I said, a bit too loud, then softer. "Maybe I do need to talk." When she didn't move, I said, "Please."

I respected how easily she did what I never could have done. She gave this stupid ass another chance. As she closed the door and walked toward the bed where I was sitting, I took my first real look at her since she had come back. After all these years, I decided she looked exactly the same, as if no time at all had passed. Her gorgeous, thick hair was still as full, her face still defying her age, her body frozen in time, as if she had stepped out of a Rubens painting. Exactly the type that turned my head, back when my head could still be turned.

She clicked the door closed and surprised me by passing the chair and sitting right next to me on the bed. She was a nurse, I reminded myself, guessing a bed didn't have the same connotation to her as it might to the rest of the world. Especially me.

I could smell her perfume, and again I felt something familiar rising in me that I couldn't explain. More panic? Irritation that she would be brazen enough to sit on my bed . . . or maybe it was blunted anger that she wasn't Erica. Maybe because I was thinking, Erica who? An unfair pang of guilt stabbed through me.

I was grateful she looked nothing like Erica—in fact, quite opposite to her. She looked like nobody else and so she only reminded me of the Lorn I once knew, nothing of the past five years. The mere thought that she might enter a room used to make my heart pound. And I wondered now if that was why my heart had been keeping me awake lately. There always had been a heightened excitement to our relationship that made me wonder if it was because I never fully believed she would let herself stay. Unlike the Santora family motto, Lorn was never *in* or *out*, and the excitement of almost having her, having her, or losing her, was something that was so intoxicating at the time. I felt my stomach twist with the contrasting memory of never feeling that doubt with Erica. Once Erica and I began our life together, we were a sure thing, and that had a different, more pure excitement of its own. And yet, look where I was. I had lost that sure thing, and I had buried more than a few secrets along with that loss.

When I snapped out of my silence, I saw that Lorn had been staring at me. In what I recognized as her calming nurse voice, she said, "Tell me why you're not sleeping."

In that moment I realized I had been listening for that voice when she would talk to Mom. It soothed me as well as my mother to hear her ask questions like this. For the first time I admitted to myself the many times I had listened from the other room, sometimes sitting on the very piece of floor I had sunk to, fainting on the very first day Lorn had arrived when I found out why Mom needed her. That I may have needed her too.

"Pick your reason," I said a bit too casually.

"Is it your worry about your mother, or is it Erica, or maybe both?"

I stared at her then, channeling my sister. Her beauty is ridiculous, Lisa would say. What a waste that she wouldn't let herself stay in Hollywood to be admired by the whole world instead of the occasional freelance patient. What a waste that she wouldn't let herself be gay. I wished for a dollar for every time my sister had said our team had lost a rare beauty indeed.

I decided it had been irritation I was feeling, because here it was again, spiking up as I looked at her. "Random question, do you still date men?"

Lorn blinked as if I had spat the question into both of her eyes. I was embarrassed that the question had flown out of my mouth, but there was nothing to do now but go with it. "You said you're not going down any particular road, but do you consider yourself a person that would date men, or women? I want to know exactly how much I stupidly miscalculated our relationship."

"You are under a lot of stress," she said, Nurse Voice not wavering, "and I want you to know my honest opinion."

I waited for it.

"Marie, your mother is a strong woman of any age, and there is a great chance she is as cancer free as any of us, or that it was completely contained and she will be perfectly fine. Truthfully, I am more concerned about you . . . and your mental health."

I ignored this and prodded. "I mean, all things being equal, if you didn't have to worry about your acting career, and now you don't, what is your preference? It's men, right?"

"Your mother's preference would have been to keep the knowledge of her illness from you. The last thing she wanted was to add to your stress." Nurse Lorn Elaine now chose to rest her hand on my forearm. I hated the familiar warmth of her fingertips.

"Why won't you answer me? Did you date men after we broke up? I'm just curious."

"I'm not going to lie to you. Nothing is a sure bet when it comes to serious health issues, but my gut tells me your mom will be fine. You, I'm not sure about right now."

My tone got angrier. "Personally I don't think you should limit yourself. I mean, why not? Good for you if you can deal with guys and date both. Doubles your playing field. It's simple math. When I was in high school, I dated guys. I had some huge crushes on boys that—"

"I lied to you," Lorn said.

"Which time?" I snapped. "Was it the first time you came back to me, or the second, or was it the third?"

"I didn't come in here because I thought you needed to talk. I'm worried that your mother's health could be compromised if she continues to think that you've given up ... that you don't want to be here anymore."

I was afraid to blink, worried it would appear as a flinch. We stayed with eyes locked for a bit too long before I thought to derail her.

"I wouldn't leave this house or my family. I can handle Mom's illness if it were to come back. After losing Erica, I can handle anything."

"Can you handle just living?"

I opened my mouth to answer, but no words came out. I made a pathetic little sound from my tightened throat. It sounded like *ek*. And then, though I hadn't given permission, the tears came, and Lorn reached for me.

I deflected her hands by grabbing them both, finally finding my voice. "No," I said. "You don't get to comfort me. For any reason."

A rush of emotion came out with it, but I deftly stuffed it back down and my anger turned the tears off like a faucet. I met her gaze firmly, and I set my face close to hers and strongly gripped her hands. They were hands I knew too well. Hands I had held many times, in so many ways. Hands I had held carefully while she touched me timidly, learning how to love me. These were hands I had held so many times, held forcefully over her head while I took her before fear could take over ... hands that had held me deep inside.

It was this last thought that snapped something wild in me,

140

something I had kept back for so long. The wall that had been up for months and months with no passion, that stretched to over a year now after losing Erica, the wall (the dyke?) was now crumbling, and the pressure of it finally letting go snapped me forward toward her. I let go of Lorn's hands, but only so I could grab her face and pull her to me to kiss her hard on the mouth. It started as a kiss I used to give Erica long ago . . . then it was a longer ago kiss, still as familiar and warm, and I remembered how much I used to want Lorn, still wanted her. The feeling crashed over me, but I attempted to stop it by closing my eyes.

Could I instead imagine she was Erica? But then I wouldn't see Lorn, and I wanted to see her . . .

She tried to pull away at first, shocked that I had come at her like that, but then our kiss softened between us, and her hands went from trying to pry my face off hers, to gripping me, as if she were afraid I might let her go. I kissed her harder, and her refusal crumbled along with mine until her kiss met mine with a hunger that may have been equal . . . or maybe more?

I lied to myself that the familiar feel of her reminded me of Erica, and this feeling was not from what we shared so much longer ago. At the same time, we arrived at our familiar kiss, and then found the more frenzied version, the one that always resulted in equally frenzied sex. It was the sure thing from so many years ago, the exact kiss neither of us could turn back from.

Confident at this memory, I finally let go of her face, knowing I had her trapped in the kiss, our kiss, and I raked my hands down to her breasts, remembering how much she loved when I did that . . . and I remembered much more. Even before I heard her right then, I had remembered the sound that always escaped from her lips when my hands were on her. Now it was impossible to confuse the memory of Lorn with Erica. This was unmistakably Lorn, full-figured by contrast to Erica's more athletic build, and so my mind was reeling. I could not pretend anymore.

Never a quitter, I moved swiftly down, reaching between her legs, knowing I was going outrageously fast, but I was thinking

141

that this part might be more like my Erica; here it might be easier for her to be any woman I needed. My own body was now raging for sex and so I gripped her there, erasing any doubt about where I needed to go next. I felt through her clothes that she was insanely wet, and so I felt justified and amped up my aggression. Her breaths were matching mine, deep, fast. I would have her. I was totally confident nothing could stop us, right until Lorn grabbed my hand by the wrist and abruptly turned her head away from me, leaving my gaping kiss still searching for her mouth.

What the hell had happened?

She was breathless. "I don't know what this is, but I don't think it's real for you . . ."

I didn't let go of my hold of her, and I whispered back as I pushed more deeply between her legs, "This feels real."

"I don't think so, not for you," she said, breaking away from me, leaving me sitting on the edge of the bed, still panting, feeling like a lech. "This was my fault," she said, not turning toward me as she left the room, door closing between us. I stared at the emptiness of the room until I thought I heard the sound of her door shutting at the farthest end of house.

I lay back on my bed, waiting for my breathing to slow. Everywhere I went, doors were always closing. And then, a sound, close to my door. She had come back.

I slid off my bed before I could change my mind and flung open my door to find my sister, arms crossed across her chest, glaring at me.

"What?" I said, sounding accused and guilty.

"Our mom needs her nurse. Don't make me lock you in at night," she said.

I Think I'm Alone Now

Now, Lisa was gone. I was alone in my room. From the second I saw my sister's face I realized I had been crazy. My sister always knew when I was about to do something really stupid. Thankfully, Lorn had known too, and had pulled away before I did something excruciatingly dumb (like banging my mother's nurse). All prevented, no thanks to me, but the night had complicated things, and I took stock of it all like a child, counting on my fingers.

Number one, dead or not, I still loved Erica. Number two, Lorn was my mother's nurse. Three, as both Lorn and I repeatedly reminded myself, she was not here for me. Come to think of it, even back then, when she was there for me, she ended up not there for me. She had been the unavailable actress, unavailable girlfriend, and now would be the unavailable nurse to my mom if I didn't watch myself. Why was her unavailability so hard to understand? My sister would say it was because I, in contrast, was born available.

This was nothing I wanted. Granted, I had wanted it, and did just now want it, and I had wanted it more than I had wanted anything in a very long time, maybe ever if I were to be honest with myself. But why start now?

For this brief moment on a Ralph Lauren comforter I had, for the first time, skipped over the Erica Years as if they had never happened at all. As if my passion for Lorn had never stopped, as if it had been lying dormant in my body, ready to come crashing back, to the surface. But for what? Perhaps for my sister's amusement? I could see no other purpose.

I could not pretend that I didn't love Lorn back then. This was as hard to pretend as ignoring the feeling swirling in me now that this had been a small taste of something that had been building for a while now. The years had not weakened what was between us; it felt as strong as our first year together, which had been mind-blowing. I would have done anything to have her . . . to keep her. I couldn't let this be the case now.

Even as I slipped into bed, still scolding myself, I could feel that my body had still not returned to normal. Our kiss had been anything but tentative, and my hands had touched her, maybe even groped her. How had I let myself get so out of control? From the moment I lost Erica, I hadn't wanted sex, nor had I even thought about sex, except to marvel at the fact that I had felt no hunger for it. Like a desert down there. And now, as I checked, it was more like Desert Storm.

I was wide awake and my body was even more wide awake. I told myself that maybe this would calm me down. Maybe living like a nun was making me a bit crazy and I needed to simmer myself down the old-fashioned way. It wasn't so long ago that I could remember simmering myself down quite often. Those simmer-down times would happen most often when Erica would have to travel without me, usually to Italy, where her client base had grown, thanks to relatives and connections my family had there. I remembered many nights, sleepless and bored in my bed before the thought would occur to me: I knew how to help me sleep.

I grabbed the pillow and rolled onto it, hoping the coolness would chill me down, but it had the opposite effect—soft like *her*, but I wouldn't admit her name.

I would also not admit that some things had become remarkably clear, clearer than I would've liked. I was imagining Lorn beneath me, telling myself it was only human to remember such things, like the way her body enveloped me when I would roll on top of her. It was always her softness that got me. That, and her unmistakable passion. Since I had been the one to unleash her passion, it created a connection between us that was intoxicating, and I remembered this now as my body moved with the thought of her under me. I remembered, too, how she liked to hear me so I allowed myself a soft sound against Ralph.

I imagined looking down at her face, her eyes closed, her mouth slightly parted, her long auburn hair splayed out across the pillow like a mermaid or a goddess. She would say certain things to me, and I remembered all that now. She had softly whispered things only a straight girl would say to another woman in bed, not politically correct at all, but it made me crazy so I dared not correct her. She would beg me to fuck her, and of course I would, and she would ask me to come while inside her, and I believed I would.

Things were a lot more confusing after Desert Storm.

I tried the best I could to justify why this passion had suddenly surfaced, and attempted to chalk it up to being lonely. As I saw it, there was only one way for me to protect myself. I would have to find somebody perfect for Lorn. I had done it once before, hadn't I? Only problem was, it had been me . . . and now years later, with the second love of my life under my belt, I would have to do it all again so that I could be free of her.

Ideas rushed through my brain day and night, and this one had started that night even before my heartbeat and breathing had returned to normal. If Lisa wasn't into Sandra . . . maybe Lorn? Or, use the straight-girl bait, Dr. Dick? What to do, what to do.

All I knew was that I needed to do something soon.

Surgery Requires Balls

I had done pretty well till now, but there would be no avoiding Lorn on the day of Mom's surgery. I had seen her only in passing once this past week, but Mom had become more reliant on Lorn and insisted that she be by her side at the hospital along with Lisa, Vince and me. Mom had been smart enough to give Dad a task that would keep him back at the house watching my nephew, Buddy. It was really more to give Dad something to do, as he was beyond useless in a hospital.

Lorn left the house long before us, bed made by 6 a.m., not that I noticed. Our entourage descended upon the hospital like we had donated the entire cancer wing, and not just made a large donation from the Santora estate in order to secure VIP treatment of Mom. I wondered, as I saw the staff turning to see what the steadily rising audio disturbance was all about, if in retrospect the hospital thought our brand of Italian noise and chaos was really worth a cash bribe.

While we were waiting for Mom to be taken down to the surgical department, I started getting antsy that Lorn would show up, so I took a walk down the hall to avoid her and ran smack into her.

"Everything okay with your mom?" she asked.

"Yes, why?"

"You were almost running."

"I, Mom needs some water."

"Not right before surgery she doesn't," Lorn said.

You can't pull a fast one on a nurse. I had to come up with a health care-related lie?

"My sister is acting weird." This was true. "Weirder than usual. Anxious, worried, and strangely excited."

"Sounds normal. Could be all the young nurses."

I hated how lovely she was when she smirked.

"Why aren't you wearing your uniform?" I accused.

"Because I don't work here."

Made a lot of sense actually.

She looked me over. "You seem stressed."

"I'm not."

"She'll be okay."

That warm smile. I nodded at her, said, "I know," but I was selfishly not only worried about my mother. When I looked at Lorn, I wanted to run, and yet I was worried about facing yet another loss. So, I did the only thing I could think of to make me feel better. "Gotta run; be back in a bit."

I hurried away from her, down the corridor to God knows where, while feeling the pull of her behind me. Why did she have to come back?

I was different this morning. Something had shifted in me. For the first time I felt Erica was not the one so far away from me, but that it was me who was now so far away from her. Drinking a coffee at a corner table in the hospital cafeteria, I let myself admit that I had dreamt all night about a certain nurse with sad and kind green eyes, an open book to her heartbreaking life history of love.

My thoughts were interrupted by one of the cafeteria workers, a familiar and beefy older woman who somehow rocked her hairnet and plastic gloves.

"Is your last name Santora?" she asked.

I jumped up in a panic, and the woman read my thoughts as she said, "No, no, everything is fine. I just wanted to know if you were Chef Lisa's sister?"

I recognized her. She and her girlfriend had been regulars at

147

Camptown Ladies. "Oh, hi! Your hairnet threw me off!"

"Yeah, it's a look! I just wanted to say, it's really cool what you guys are doing today. Everyone at the hospital is excited about it."

Huh? Everyone was excited about my mother's surgery?

"Nice running into you; good luck with your mom." She lowered her voice. "I have to run. My boss in the kitchen can be such a bitch."

"I feel ya," I said. She hurried away as I asked, "Wait, what is everyone excited about?"

She turned halfway back as she rushed away across the cafeteria, and shouted back, "See you at noon!"

Why did I think this had to do with my sister? She had been acting very weird lately, and she had not been around much, and when she was, she seemed exhausted and strangely happy. I had assumed it might be the producer, but because I was avoiding Lorn, we hadn't had a moment alone so I could grill her about how the deal with Sandra was going.

When I finally came back, Lorn was not around, but my eyes darted around like an addict, looking for her everywhere. I noticed my sister studying me, looking like I was scanning all the corners of the drugs-within-reach rooms for a fix. With everything going on with Mom, one thought had eclipsed them all: would I see Lorn again today?

It doesn't happen again this quickly, does it?

"Where's Mom?" I asked, sporting some quick thinking right there.

"What's the matter with you?" Lisa said. "You're acting like a freak."

"I just went to get a drink. Maybe I am wired," I said.

"There's a bar in here?" Vince asked, and Lisa swatted him.

"It's seven o'clock in the morning, idiot. Marie has worse troubles than that . . . look at her; she's a friggin' mess."

"I'm standing right here," I said, not that this ever mattered. "What the heck is happening at noon?"

"I don't know what you are talking about," Lisa said.

"Is something happening?" Vince asked, but I caught a whiff of bad acting.

"Nothing for you two idiots to worry about," Lisa said. "Mom should be out of surgery by ten or eleven, and when we get the good news and that it all went fine, we can all celebrate."

I walked away from them and sat at the far corner of the waiting room so I could stare outside the window, my face unobserved.

Yes, I thought. It does happen this quickly; you can swap one pain for another this fast. Or faster, if I really wanted to admit it to myself . . . knowing I was doomed the moment I had opened my front door and seen her standing there.

My fingers dug into the greasy plush arms of the waiting room chair as if I was awaiting a stay of execution call from the governor. Why was I certain I would end up cooked? Maybe the grimy armchair would take me out with a nice virus. The sun from the window beat on my face and since I was turned away from my family, I let myself close my eyes for a moment. I breathed deeply and tried to imagine myself as a strong castle, with a deep protective moat dug out around me, wide and impassible, and filled with a thunderous flood of black water circling my fieldstone walls. I imagined I had a drawbridge too rusty to ever be lowered, its hinges ancient and fixed, knowing the best protection for my castle was not to let anyone *in* or *out*. I imagined our family motto sculpted in the ancient stone above the useless drawbridge door: *Either You Are IN or You Are OUT*, the posting caked with dried moss and mint green lichen.

When I opened my eyes, Lisa had disappeared, and I didn't bother to ask where she took off to. After a while Vince plopped down in the seat next to me and was thoughtful enough not to speak. It seemed we sat there for hours, both Vince and I watching the annoying cooking show on the TV above us, powerless to turn it off. I wondered if it was the most overbearing nurse that controlled the TV, the one who had doled out two ice cubes to my mother as if they were bricks of gold bullion.

"Wow. This show sucks," Vince finally said. "Lisa's show will

149

blow all of these idiots away."

"True story," I said. The earlier loudness of our family had disappeared along with Lisa, and Vince finally gave my knee a squeeze to signal he also was leaving the castle, for a pee and a walk. I continued to sit motionless in the chair as if I were strapped in, waiting for a horror movie to start. What if my mother didn't make it through the surgery? What if I didn't manage to avoid Lorn or, worse, the feelings taking hold of me? I realized I missed the protective numbness of the past year. Why did I have to be the only person in the world who missed days and nights of mind-numbing grief?

Quite some time later Vince and Lisa returned right before Dr. Dick paid a visit to the waiting area. He was smiling so we all collectively breathed a sigh of relief. I saw him visually taking a head count, looking about, and I knew he was fixated on Lorn missing from the group. As his smile faded, he delivered the good news that mom had sailed through the surgery.

"Although we still have to wait for the testing to confirm that what I removed was not cancer, things looked good when I was in there. If it is anything sneaky or nasty, it certainly was contained, and I got it all."

Great news. Still, I hated this guy.

If he could have patted himself on the back, he would have. "Now, don't quote me, but I believe I helped Momma Santora dodge a bullet," he said, between glances down the hallway. He seemed disappointed he had to deliver that particular line when Lorn was not around.

He saved my mother, I thought. Then I thought, what an ass.

"Your mother will be sleeping for the next several hours, so I recommend that you all go home and get some rest. She'll be sleeping till at least three."

"Nope, but thanks," Lisa answered casually, as if he had offered ketchup with her fries. "We're staying. My sister is going back to the house to get Dad and Buddy in about an hour." She turned to me with a quick toss of the head, her way of putting a period at the end of my objective, and then back to the doctor to notify him of his. "Just call me on my cell when we can see her. We will all stick around."

I said to her, "Why would we drag Dad down here before he can see Mom?"

"Just do it," Lisa answered. "It will be good for Dad and for Buddy, and when you get back, Vince and I can meet up with you in the parking lot." Vince nodded as if they already had agreed on it.

Dr. Dick finished with, "You all have plenty of time, and your mother needs to rest now."

He paused before leaving, but he couldn't drag out his speech any more. He looked visibly disappointed that Lorn had missed it. I had to admit that I also was shocked Lorn had not been here to hear the results. Those were my exact thoughts as I glanced down the hallway and spotted Lorn at the end of it, standing alone, before she turned and walked away.

"I'll be back," I said as I left my family to follow her down the corridor.

Lisa called after me, "I have to make some calls. See you later when you come back with Dad and Buddy!"

Even though she had quickened her pace, I easily caught up to Lorn and said to her back, "You should have been here with us." I hadn't intended to sound angry, but I did. She stopped without turning, and I took her by her arm to turn her to me. She had been crying, and my heart broke as I watched her attempt to brush away the evidence as a tear rolled over her hand.

My stomach sank further.

Aside from what I was seeing now, more memories flooded back to me of when she had been so scared as she tried to avoid the love that had grown between us. She had cried like this when she told me she had to leave, because she couldn't let this happen between us, and yet she had not been able to stop it from happening and cried again when her fame dragged both of us into the spotlight. Our relationship happened at the beginning of social media, barely born at that time, so the press hounded us

151

the old-fashioned way, showing up at every turn, camping out at our house. It was a different time then. Before Ellen . . . before gay marriage was legal in California, then made illegal, then legal again, and before other states had followed suit. The press had written endless stories, casting a light on us in ways you wouldn't wish on your worst enemy, and when they destroyed our chance at happiness and Lorn backed away to protect what was left of her career, they still had stalked us mercilessly, and peppered the rag mags with ridiculous articles the public ate up:

LOVERS' SPAT . . .
BREAKING UP IS HARD TO DO . . .
EXPLOSIVE PHOTOS: LORN ELAINE'S FEMALE LOVER
CAUGHT CHEATING!

Lies, all of it, yet they caused the breakup to be true. If social media had been then what it is today, I knew we wouldn't have lasted even the short time we did. It had made no difference how many times I told Lorn that I was in it for the long haul (not just the U-Haul) and that none of it mattered to me . . . I didn't realize how much it had mattered to her.

She looked then exactly as she did now, her face filled with sadness and regret. I held her by both arms now, to stop myself from holding her any other way.

I softened my voice. "You didn't want to be there to hear the news? Lorn . . . Mom is okay; the doctor said it looked totally contained, likely not cancer, but they will test it. Dr. D—Rick thinks Mom is going to be fine."

"I know. I could see," she said. "I'm so happy about that, I'm so happy for you," she said as her voice broke.

I softened my tone. "Why weren't you with us? We . . . Mom would have wanted you here."

"I was here. But I'm not a part of your family anymore, not sure I ever really was. I didn't feel I deserve to be—"

"Mom wants you here." I looked at her then, feeling a burn deep in my chest caused from swallowing the confession that

I, in fact, wanted her here. Instead, I added, "And that good-looking doctor was devastated you weren't around."

She tried to smile. "He'll be just fine. He always has a flock of—"

"Seagulls around him?" I finished.

The smile I had been waiting for finally came, with an adorable eye roll I had never witnessed before.

Her arms and soft skin abruptly felt familiar under my grip, and I flashed to the first time I had learned that gripping her wrists would send Lorn reeling in more intimate circumstances, and as if her skin had burned my palms, I let go of her arms.

I tried to sound casual. "Doctor Rick also told us what you did to get Mom into the study. You were the reason she got in. You pimped yourself!"

She could not help but laugh, and seeing her laughing eyes squeeze out one more tear made the pain in my chest ache further. While I was relieved to see her laugh, deep inside I heard a warning: not again. I knew this feeling all too well, and it was not going to end well for either of us—especially not for me. "Here is what I think," I said. "I think you should give the guy a fair shot. He's a big fan of yours and he pulled a lot of strings."

She smiled with only the corner of one side of her lips now, and I forced myself to look away, as she was pulling strings that made me want to lunge for her, or run. I swallowed hard, looked back, and said, "Will you please join us later when we go in to see Mom?"

She stood motionless, our eyes locked, my offer hanging between us.

Finally, she said, "I shouldn't . . . but I want to be there once she wakes."

I nodded, wishing this feeling would stop flooding through my veins; it scared me how it felt more like excitement than relief. All this flooding . . . perhaps this is what had filled the damned moat around my castle. I imagined the water rising above the green mold line . . . The emergency help I needed right now made me think I needed Doctor Dick on the case *stat*.

After we parted, I went back to find Lisa and Vince, but instead found an empty waiting room. One of the nurses left the station to find me there. "Do you need help?"

I sure did, I thought, but shook my head no, and thanked her. "What will you do with all this quiet?" I asked.

"Go take a walk outside and enjoy my lunch," the nurse said happily.

Special people, I thought.

Needing to walk off some anxiety, I stole the nurse's idea and decided to walk a few laps around the hospital building outside before heading out to get Dad and Buddy. As I walked, I wondered why my sister had pushed so hard for Dad to stay home to take care of Buddy, and then equally hard to get them to come back with me. I wondered if my sister had sensed Dad was too afraid to be here and had tossed him Buddy so he would have an excuse to stay home, but he had seemed in good spirits when we left, blowing kisses at Mom as we drove off. I realized only now this was probably just a big show for Buddy. As I walked around the meandering hospital buildings, hoping I could find my way back to where we had parked, I tried calling Dad at home. When I didn't reach him, I stalled my rising anxiety by reminding myself I was going home to deliver good news, and it would be better to deliver it in person with a big hug to both him and Buddy.

It was a longer walk than expected, and just as I feared I would not find my way back to the main parking lot, things started looking familiar. At last, I saw the Guest Parking sign indicating a turn at the next corner, but before I had even made the turn I could sense, and then hear, a commotion. I also heard familiar and faint music off in the distance. I whipped my head around as I turned the corner, and heard it more clearly, the song my family always played on repeat at every gathering:

C'è la luna mezz'o mare
Mamma mia me maritari,
Figghia mia, a cu te dari
Mamma mia pensaci tu.

154

The music was being played a respectable distance away from the hospital, and I traced the sound to the very back end of the parking lot, where the woods met asphalt, parted only by a dinky chain link fence where an opening was made by a fallen piece on the ground. This opening was right in front of three identical trucks, parked in a row and surrounded by a sea of green scrubs. I noticed then that this was the final destination of an ant trail of hospital staff heading out of the building and across the parking lot, along with others tagging along to see what the commotion was about. I was one of them.

As I got swept up in the ant trail leading to what looked like old vintage milk trucks, my first thought was how beautiful the scrubs looked against the retro cream color of the trucks with the scrub-matching mint green lettering, and set off by the vintage cherry red stripes of the awnings. Where had I just seen those exact colors?

One-third of the way across the parking lot, the smell of mouthwatering food collectively hit the crowd, and that is when I knew. Even before it occurred to me to actually read the sides of the three catering trucks, which read: *Momma Santora's BALLS.*

Of course, it was Lisa!

The heavenly smell was unmistakable now, my sister's famous Camptown Ladies marinara and arrabbiata spice wafting over the crowd, making all helpless to do other than follow, a steady stream of lunch-seeking zombies on the hunt for the blood-red sauce lunch. As I expected, herd mentality kicked in, even among health care professionals, and they instinctively sped up their walk. I knew I was thinking exactly what the crowd must be wondering: *would there be enough food?*

In the early days of Camptown Ladies this would happen, and I laughed at the silly thought. They didn't know Lisa if they feared there was not enough food. At this thought, I passed the cafeteria nurse floating behind, checking her phone, as if she had all the time in the world. And she did. She knew that no Camptown Ladies guest had ever gone without food, especially if they couldn't pay for it.

I realized now the three trucks were decked out in the exact colors of the flyers I had seen in the hospital corridor and lining the nurse's station. Earlier I had noticed they read: "All Employee Appreciation Lunch! Join us for the BEST food this side of Boston—" and I had stopped there when I thought, yeah right, hospital food, and felt sad for the hard-working staff.

As I walked nearer, I could see a news crew with a multi-camera team setting up in the thick of the growing crowd, next to a banner that hung on the fence: "First Responders Appreciation Lunch" and a second layer posted over it, in my sister's unmistakable chicken scratch: "ALL ARE WELCOME!" Given she was in full view of the main road, even I had a pang of worry whether the food would hold out. I spotted my sister hanging out of the first truck, handing out bowls and sandwiches to a pair of young nurses. The sandwiches were nestled in wax paper, striped in three wide colors to coordinate with the truck: green, white, red . . . the Italian flag, only depicted in my sister's retro tones and the word *BALLS* printed across the stripes. When she spotted me grinning as I approached, she gave a nonchalant toss of the head, as if I had pulled up while she was simply watering our lawn.

Even from this distance I could see the signature "hubba hubba" wiggle of her eyebrows as the young women gushed over her food. Lisa gave an Evita-like upturned hand wave to indicate the surroundings, in case I hadn't noticed the three *BALLS* trucks, the huge crowd, and the line of cars pulling over on the main road.

"Well, here's someone who lacks BALLS!! This is my sister, Mare!" The crowd clapped and Lisa bellowed, "What are you clapping for? She has done nothing on this project to get the balls rolling!" The crowd laughed as she returned effortlessly to work, taking orders, scooping balls, and chatting up the crowd with lightning speed since of course no money was changing hands. She would ask the orders of five people at a time, fill all of them and hand them out as if she had done this all her life. Of course, she had, in fact, done this all her life. From her home kitchen or at Camptown Ladies, Lisa was in her element feeding the masses, and the first of the masses had begun with her family, which was no small job indeed.

"Where can I help?" I yelled over the music.

Lisa held up the number three, pointing to the farthest truck before handing bowls and sandwiches out to her hungry public.

I knew before I even saw him that of course Vince would be working on one of the trucks, but to my surprise Buddy popped out the side door to give me a quick hug before proudly flashing his color-coordinated *BALLS* notebook and running back into the crowd. "Order ahead here, please!" he yelled, as he took some notes before running back to my brother and sister-in-law Katie, working happily in the truck.

How had Lisa pulled all this off?

As I approached the camera crew, I saw that (of course) this was not a news team, but Sandra and her studio production team, hijacked for the day to capture this guaranteed go-viral video. Sandra was too busy barking orders and staring up at food goddess Lisa and all her money-making future potential to notice me walk right past her.

Food and paper menus were everywhere, and I noticed not one menu was given back, thrown away, or carelessly dropped on the ground without being snapped up again. Most were tucked preciously in scrub pants pockets unless they were being held up and read aloud to laugh at the outrageous menu names. What Vince and I had laughed at in the car so long ago seemed like pretty genius marketing from where I stood now.

Vince waved me along, that they had it all handled, and I yelled to him he was in trouble for keeping secrets. "Chef Lisa said Snitches Get Stitches!" and I laughed and nodded as I walked along, drinking in the sights, sounds, and smells of the scene. I saw a flash of a warmer red color from under the awning of the last truck, and I heard my breath suck in as I stood still in my tracks as if I were stuck in mud. Lorn was leaning out to the cheering crowd, waving as they recognized her. She laughed as she signed the requested autographs on wax paper sandwich wraps, with the crowd handing her pens. Then she leaned her body way outside the food window of the truck for selfies. I could do nothing but be a witness, feeling my heart pounding so deeply I was relieved the place was filled with medics in case it finally gave out. I let myself remember loving her.

When Lorn leaned in my direction as she passed out meatball sandwiches, she saw me, and when I shrugged my hands in the air, she did the same, laughing like she had no idea how she got talked into going from actress to nurse to waitress. Before I could say a word to her, Dad poked his head out of the truck Lorn was in and shouted, "Sir! You can't leave without your BALLS!!" The crowd laughed as he twirled a pile of T-shirts he was giving out the back of the third truck. "Come 'round back to the speakeasy if you want to wear some BALLS!"

Somebody cranked up the music a bit louder (guess who), and I laughed as I heard my sister shouting over a loudspeaker the English lyrics over the Italian version:

> *There's a moon in the middle of the sea*
> *Mother, I must get married.*
> *My daughter, who do I get for you?*
> *Mother, I leave it up to you.*

Vince joined in, grabbing the loudspeaker and singing from the second truck the favorite verse of our family that he, Dad, and Lisa would always torture me with. Lisa joined in as both loudspeakers blared their voices, and they pointed over at me as the crowd went nuts:

> *Lazy Mary, you'd better get up.*
> *She answered back "I am not able."*
> *Lazy Mary, you'd better get up,*
> *we need the sheets for the table.*
>
> *Lazy Mary, you smoke in bed*
> *there's only one man you should marry . . .*

My advice to you would be
is to pay attention to me.

I turned back to see Lorn laughing, crying, and clapping along with the Italians in the crowd who knew the lyrics and were proudly joining in. Proof again that when you have a crazy Italian family and add piles of amazing food, everyone becomes part of the family. When Lorn looked over to laugh directly at me, I had never remembered seeing her look happier than at this very moment, and my heart warned me again with some dramatic thuds.

When the song ended and before it started again, Lisa bellowed out to me: "Hey, get your ass to truck three. Dad and the nurse are the weakest links!" I happily caught the sound of Lorn laughing as I scurried to the back of the truck with Dad to get him away from the balls before he started publicly double-dipping bread into the sauce, or worse. He needed to stay doing what he was best at, yukking it up with the crowd while throwing T-shirts.

Sandra threatened her camera crew to get the shot of him at the back of the truck or else, and her producer instincts paid off. When Dad couldn't reach everyone in the back of the growing crowd, he surprised the producer by whipping out a concert T-shirt gun and blasted a T-shirt into the face of anyone who had their hands up. I laughed at him trying to ignore the lawsuit possibilities, and joined Lorn inside the truck to work side by side.

Lisa had guerrilla-marketed the idea directly to the employees to get the flyers posted and had pulled the whole thing off without permission or a single permit. By the time the two-hour lunch event was winding down, it hadn't yet occurred to anyone to ask who at the hospital had agreed to this since all the office personnel were also stuffing meat and veggie balls in their mouths, or bringing them back to their coworkers manning patients or phones. I could hear Lisa all the way down at the first truck, bellowing that this would be the first of many pop-up

159

BALLS events. I could see by the way Sandra was admiring the scene that her only goal was to get it all captured on a video destined to go viral, and if the cops came to break it all up, even better.

I wasn't the best at my job, but it seemed Lorn had more hidden talents. Aside from thrilling people just by being her TV star self, damned if the woman wasn't quite handy with a ladle and torpedo rolls. She caught me admiring her ability to fill two rolls at once and shrugged.

"I played a waitress in a film once and learned a few tricks," she said, eyes sparkling when she turned toward the sun.

On several occasions we were so slammed I was able to forget for a few seconds the distracting thrill of being in such a small area with Lorn. But it came roaring back if she reached across me, or we accidentally grazed each other in the truck. It forced me to overconcentrate on stirring or serving from the vats of balls, and Lorn mistook that for a budding talent of my own.

"You're getting pretty good at this," she said, winking, which made my head spin. I told myself it was the steam from the six bubbling sauce pans, and my solution was to scrape every drop of sizzling sauce from the sides of the pans with the precision of a bomb disposal technician.

When the crowds finally began to thin and we had a moment to regroup, I looked up to see Lorn staring at me with heartbreaking green eyes. Before I could stop myself, I asked, "What's wrong?"

"I forgot what a good team we were," she said, her voice trailing off as she turned away to the service window.

My lips parted, but no words followed as I tried to ignore my stomach splitting into equal parts dread and hope.

After feeding every last employee and passerby alike, when the catering trucks had finally closed and Sandra's cleanup crew arrived, we finished up by handing out the last few *GOT*

BALLS? T-shirts. Within an hour the only task left was for the cleanup crew to reinstall the section of fence and drive away the catering trucks, taking Lisa up on her offer to enjoy any leftovers with their families.

This all happened before the local police could figure out the legality of the scene. When any cops came, Lisa had signaled for Buddy to run over to their cars to take their sandwich orders. She knew they would be much too busy eating to efficiently track down the hospital administrators, who were too far away from the food trucks. There was only one cop that got a bit too nosy for Lisa's comfort, and she squashed that quickly by calling over Lorn to distract him. Her actress fame worked like a charm, and by the time she finished chatting with him and taking selfies to show his kids, he was asking if we needed any help.

When the threat was over, Lisa said to Lorn, "Kind of handy to have an actress around," and she tossed Lorn a cleanup rag. "Just so you don't get too full of yourself—*wipe*."

Lorn just shook her head as she laughed and dutifully wiped tomato splatter at the service window. I wondered if she was thinking about all the times we had worked together in the kitchen, ending a fun night of entertaining, feeling tipsy and flirty, and feeling blessed and lucky.

Much later in the afternoon we were gathered, exhausted, in the lobby and finally we were allowed in to see Mom, two at a time. Lisa grabbed Vince and disappeared before I could stop her, leaving Lorn and I to look across at each other like the last two left without a gym class partner.

"I guess we're on deck," I said, and she nodded. I swallowed my pride and said, "Thanks so much for helping us today."

Before she could answer, Doctor Dick swooped in out of nowhere and Lorn stood up to greet him. I stayed seated, wondering if I was imagining that Lorn's face had brightened. Straight girl, I thought, or at least she wants to be.

Good, I reminded myself, even as my stomach twisted in that terrible and familiar way.

I stood up as Dr. Dick wrapped his magical surgeon hand

around Lorn's beautiful one in what he pretended was a polite shake. "Ms. Elaine, I was hoping I might see you here today."

I took a deep breath and felt better, if better was wanting to punch the man who had just saved my mother. "Lorn is going to let you take her to dinner," I said. "It's the least she could do for helping Mom in the way you did." From my peripheral, I saw Lorn's face turn to mine, but I kept my eyes locked on Dr. Dick.

"Well, I would love that," he said, and I was relieved for just a moment before scrutinizing his beaming schoolboy face.

I wanted to mess up that face. Calm down, I told myself, it's just a dinner . . . and isn't this what you wanted?

"But, Ms. Elaine, please don't feel obligated—"

"Please, call me Lorn, and no, that sounds nice, thank you," she said, as if speaking to a bank teller, but then she followed that with a warm smile, and I could see he was toast. "I'd like to continue our conversation from yesterday," she added.

Yesterday?

"All right then. Terrific. Are you free tonight?"

Tonight? This guy was pushing it.

I felt Lorn glance my way again, but I didn't look at her until she answered, "Yes. That would be perfect."

Perfect? Really?

Like a total nerd he handed her his card and said they could chat later to work out the particulars. Then he strode off like a twelve-year-old fisherman who had just caught his first fine-looking rainbow trout. Actually, no rainbow.

I was caught in that tiny space between relief and loss. "Good-looking guy," I said. "I hope you didn't mind me offering you up like that. I learned from my sister." When she said nothing, I said, "A nice choice, really. You know, if you want my opinion . . . but what do I know about men."

Now it was Lorn who wouldn't look at me, and I was thankful that Vince and Lisa came back right then to give me an excuse to end the awkward silence.

"How's Mom?" I asked.

"She's good, but they kicked us out," Lisa said. "They only

gave us five minutes to say hello; she's awake but drifting. She needs her rest." Lisa studied us, turning her eyes from me to Lorn and back again. "What the hell is up with you two?"

I said, "Nothing. Lorn has a date tonight with Mom's doctor, and I approve."

"Dr. Dick?" Lisa turned to Lorn. "Well, if my sister approves, that must be a relief." Lisa looked as if she didn't approve of me.

"Well, we're off to see Mom," I said, and when I walked away, Lorn stayed a step behind, leaving me to assume that she also must have heard Lisa mutter: "Weirdos."

Mom had fallen back to sleep when we walked in, and I was relieved she looked as if she had been napping, not as if they had cracked open her chest to remove a piece of her lung. Lorn and I flanked either side of her bed and when mom opened her eyes, she saw Lorn first.

"You're here," Mom mumbled to Lorn, "I was hoping you'd come back for her."

We both pretended we missed that one. "Mom, we're both here."

Mom looked over at me and then back to Lorn. "It's so good to see you together again."

"Momma Santora, you're on drugs," Lorn said as she chuckled. "We are just here to tell you to go back to sleep and that we both love you."

Mom looked at both of us and said, "I don't take drugs, just that one cigarette after my diagnosis. If I didn't look so cool, I would consider quitting."

Lorn and I both laughed, our eyes meeting across Mom's bed.

"Don't do anything rash, Mom," I said, but I was still looking at Lorn. Her eyes sparkled and filled, and I wondered why this woman had to be so damned attractive when she teared up. What point did that serve? Other than another way for God to mess with me.

"That's good you quit, Mom. Being a one-day smoker for a photo shoot could've done you in, but you made it. By the way,

Lisa said that post of your photo went viral."

"Viral is not good to hear when you're in a hospital," Mom said, in a voice less alert. Her eyes closed again.

I said, "Lisa put it on Insta."

"Gram," Mom finished.

I looked back at Lorn's sparkling eyes. "That's Mom's little joke."

Mom said, "I can hear you. People should not be dropping the word gram; it's ageist and sexist."

"She has a point," Lorn said, and I could tell by her squinting eyes that under her face mask she was smiling. Big. I hated how much I wished I could see it.

"Apparently sarcasm about the dangers of smoking works much better than lecturing. Young kids are passing your photo like crazy," I said.

Lorn said, "You're a celebrity. Careful, though, it's not all it is cracked up to be."

I looked back up at Lorn who was focused on Mom.

"The doctor says you'll be back home in no time," Lorn said.

"Yeah, that Doc must have a crush on you, too, Mom. He doesn't seem to leave this hallway."

Mom opened her eyes. "Don't be silly; he has his eye on Lorn." She turned to her, "Will you stay with us?" Mom asked. "You are a part of our family again . . . and I want you to stay. I know this is a good idea because when I was thinking about it earlier, I kept hearing *C'è la luna*." Mom drifted off to sleep.

My mother knew how to silence a room.

I had no idea what to say, so we both just stood there staring at Mom as she slept.

Finally, I said, "I guess you were wrong. You have to stay." An annoying feeling I could only vaguely identify as *hope* fluttered up to my chest.

Lorn nodded her head and said, "I'll stay . . . until she's well."

I hated hope. Hope never worked for me. "Thanks for being here for her," I said. When we reached the doorway to leave, I worked up my courage. "I mean, for all of us."

Lorn halted at the doorway for a second or two before heading out to the corridor where Dr. Dick was waiting nearby.

My sister intercepted me, and led me away from them down the corridor.

"You're a mess," she said.

"I got that. But at least I am not stalking the hallways like that—"

"I'll tell you what you need to do," Lisa said. "You need to break up with your girlfriend."

"Lorn isn't my girlfriend."

"No, idiot. Erica. The dead one. You need to break up with her."

"You're crazy."

Lisa said, "No, you're going crazy because you need to end it with Erica. You never really did. So, write a goddamned letter to your dead girlfriend that she won't ever read, and *you* tell *her* that its over. That you're done. Write it down, make it official, read it a few times, give it a kiss, and tuck it in that junk drawer of yours so you can stop acting fucking crazy and get on to living your next big mistake."

"Thanks, Dr. Lisa," I said, "if the cooking thing doesn't work out, you could write mental health brochures. There won't be another mistake." Even as I said it, I was thinking, there was a mistake right there.

Take a Letter, Marie, Address It to Your Wife

Dear Erica,

Even though you're dead, I'm in the pissed off at you phase, and my sister says I need to write this letter. You know her. As crazy as she is, she is not usually wrong. So, here I am. Writing.

This is stupid.

Although, I've been thinking it was time I started doing a few things I've put off . . . like letting go of you for a start. I don't know if I actually can, but I'm ready to admit that I at least want to. Even as I write this, knowing you will never read it, my stomach feels like I just ate a bag of jalapenos. I guess it's because I have never wanted to let go of you. But we don't always get what we want, do we?

When someone disappears off the face of this Earth, we are left with what we are left with, and nothing more, no matter how much we dwell on the loss. I was left with my crazy family and have grown to be more grateful for them every day. They have seen me at my worst, and that was losing you.

So. I guess this is the part where I tell you that Lorn is back.

I can imagine you laughing right now, but, trust me, it's really not that funny. And it's getting less funny every day. She snuck back into my life. (Someday I will rip my sneaky front door off its hinges and put a glass one in so I can always see what's coming.)

I wonder if I am writing this letter out of guilt?

If you could see me from wherever you are, it might look as if Lorn is tempting me again. I can't blame that on her, can I? I have always been responsible for my own temptations. I knew exactly what I was doing allowing her to get near me . . . allowing her in.

The truth is, once I saw her, I knew what was coming. I'm admitting that now. Both the beginning, and the end, and I still let her in.

Again.

It was the same with you. There is something about both of you I could never resist, even though I had every reason in the world to do so. Maybe there's something about me that insists on being with someone irresistible, and someone who can resist me? Each time I got taken in, I convinced myself this was the secret to life: to have an irresistible love.

But now I know.

I should never be with anyone that can resist me. That has been a repeating recipe for disaster, a death of its own kind, and a disaster that could be repeated if I am not careful. What was losing you, if not a disaster?

My choices have again and again brought me a shitstorm of pain, first with Lorn (several times in fact), then with you (several times in fact) as we each tried to resist the love we felt. With Lorn it was to spare the demise of her career and with you, Erica, to spare my brother's heart. He loved you first, but we all knew I loved you best.

Unlike you, Lorn is still here. This time, I am determined to resist, but I worry that this time, she seems so much stronger than me. These days, everyone seems stronger than me. Even Mom (thankful for that one).

I am writing not just because Lisa told me to, but because I finally accept that you are truly gone, dead . . . buried. I can't take credit for this new acceptance. I simply had no choice. I admit now that I have lied to myself for way too long, and my family has been my accomplice, sparing my feelings by not shaking me and screaming what I needed to hear: *It's done.*

What we had is dead, along with you. Sounds harsh . . . but I have to move on.

Or, at least try. As with you there's something about Lorn that I'll never stop being able to resist. Maybe writing this down may help? Isn't it good to put a name to what is happening so I can admit it and take control over it? Maybe I need to figure out how to help send her off once and for all. (You certainly didn't need my help there.) There must be something I can do.

I do realize just because I have decided something, this doesn't mean things will be easier. It might be harder at first, but at least it's a decision I have finally made. So why do I still feel that string tied to you connecting us, and maybe always? I finally have to admit I'm the only one holding on to that string . . . so I am the only one that can let it go. As I write these words, I envision the tattered and flimsy threadbare string flying from my hands like the end of a rogue kite—setting us both free.

If you can still hear my every thought like you used to, you must be pretty exhausted. I'm like that friend who still calls constantly on the phone even though the friendship has been over for years. "Shut up!" you must want to say. "Move on!"

This will be the last time I say it: I love you. (Just so you know, I said that part out loud.) And this too: From the day I first met you, standing on my kitchen counter in Hollywood, California, flinging that friggin' tape measure around like Xena Warrior Princess, I have had a love for you that never stopped.

Until now. I am letting go of that string.

I loved you. Loved. Look at me adding the *d* on the end of that word. *D* is for the end of love, for the end of end, and for Done and for Dead and for Dread. (When did I become Dr. Seuss?) I had such dread about letting you go. But there it is, in writing, right there on the paper, and maybe Lisa is right. Although it will be tucked in my junk drawer, it feels final, seeing it written in black and white.

(Here it is again)

I Loved You,

—Marie

———————

Lisa Santora
2229 Lakeside Drive
Coventry, RI 02816

Dear Doctor Rick,

I'm writing this letter to show my appreciation for all you have done for my mother and, in turn, for our whole family. If I seemed at all gruff when we last met, please forgive me. While I am not a doctor, I've actually been working on my bedside manner all my life.

I am writing to tell you the woman whose life you saved, my mother, is the heart of our family. Everyone assumes it is my dad because he is the loudest one (you might remember the sound of him attempting to juggle charts in my mother's room before they all crashed to the floor, sending your entire third-floor staff into a mad rush to the room), but Dad is not the pillar of strength that my mother is. I shudder to think of him having to do without her if you had not performed your Doc-magic.

Just so you know who we are dealing with, Dad asked if we could keep the scalpel you used on Mom to have as a memento. I think he wanted to add it to the tools in his man shed, and while you should consider this a high compliment, you should not feel obligated to hand over your scalpel although it would become Dad's most prized possession. It was a known fact he wouldn't have had the courage to actually be at the hospital during her surgery, but that didn't stop him from saying he would like to own the instrument that was able to keep Mom, the love of his life, quiet for a few hours. That is exactly our dad. So I'm writing this letter to thank you for him.

169

I also want to thank you on behalf of my two siblings, Marie and Vince. In case you were fooled by my elegant handwriting, I am Lisa, the butchy sister (now, don't pretend you didn't notice). Since my sister is still a mess from a long year of grieving and my brother is . . . well, Vince . . . incapable of communicating anything more detailed than an armpit fart, I am reaching out on behalf of them to thank you.

I share these family details, not because I think you have a lot of spare time in your surgical schedule to read about the quirks of my family members, but because Italians consider everyone of significance as a part of the family. I am speaking from all of us when I say we are all eternally grateful.

If there is anything we can do for you beyond the hospital donation enclosed, please don't hesitate to ask. As you probably heard, I sent the entire hospital staff a lunch that collectively blew their minds as I needed to test out my new food truck, *BALLS*. It's not a household name just yet, but my cooking show is about to launch, so this might be the last free meal I can serve for a while.

Respectfully,

—Lisa Santora
Celebrity Chef, *Girls Can Cook!*

PS. I shouldn't be sharing this, but Lorn Elaine has not stopped talking about you since you went out to dinner last week. Since she has already agreed to be auctioned off as a celebrity dinner date to help the new hospital wing, I could not help thinking how delighted she would be if you were the highest bidder. Good luck with that, and enjoy your GOT BALLS? T-shirt.

———

From the Desk of Sandra

Dear Lisa,

I was so very happy to hear your mother's surgery went beautifully. Please give her my best, and I'm so glad to hear she enjoyed the basket.

No one is more thrilled than I that you finally accepted our last contract offer. I have attached all the documents we spoke about below so your "crackerjack team of lawyers" can go over it once more with a fine-tooth comb. Lawyers always have one lying around.

At the risk of feeding an ego that has likely never missed a meal, I have been doing this a long time, and I can tell you I have never been more sure of producing a hit show than I am of yours. Your cooking prowess aside, you should know before I make my next request, that it is your personality, along with Eddie's of course, that sealed the deal with our network.

The aforementioned having been said, I find myself having to request that you curb some of your (more flattering) comments directed at me, at least in front of my lower-level staff. I hope you take this as it is intended, as I suspect you know the level of my tolerance for your teasing is quite high (and, truth be told, my enjoyment of your pet names) . . . however, "Sugar Tits" might send the wrong message to my interns and staff (as true of an accusation as it is).

I look forward to our project and the many years of success to follow.

—Sandra

PS. Perhaps addressing me by initials S.T. might be an adequate sugar substitute?

————

Dear Lorn,

At the risk of being a pest, please accept these flowers as my way of expressing once again how much I enjoyed our brief evening together a few (somewhat long) weeks ago. Should you possibly find a way to free up one evening away from taking care of Mrs. Santora, you will make me the happiest doctor at Dana-Farber. I will await your call.

Respectfully,

—Dr. Rick

———————

Dear S.T.

Why the S.T.?

I wasn't sure if this strict rule about not calling you Sugar Tits also applied to texts, but just to be safe. Looking forward to our taping, so psyched you were able to get the live audience my lawyers demanded, as well as the 200 pounds of my homemade chocolates for the audience warmup. Trust me, it will be worth it. I was looking to pass out something more potent, but my lawyers can be real sticklers, as you know firsthand.

Thank you for agreeing to my last stipulation of no rehearsals. I was born ready to be in front of a crowd; however, my sidekick, Eddie, has been primping nonstop. Last night he admitted he has slept in his "costume" a few nights, which he will not show in advance of our taping. (If Scooby Doo were here, he'd be giving us a Ruh-Roh.) Eddie has assured me only that he will perfectly match the theme of our first show. Just a heads-up to my (very) hotshot producer, since Eddie used the word *theme*, you may want to have a wardrobe and makeup team on high alert. I cannot predict, nor can I vouch for, whatever Eddie has come up with that might have to be dismantled before taping. Me, on the other hand—I will come as I am, which the ladies don't ever complain about. (Rosie O'Donnell's look, the early years.)

Thanks for all your help with the pop-up *BALLS* event; it

was what sealed the deal, if you didn't know. Along with the S.T.'s.

PS. I had a dream about you. I hope that doesn't make you blush? Beautiful hair & S.T.s flying everywhere. I'm such a romantic.

—Lisa,
Purveyor of Fine BALLS (. . . you will let me know if this title is too much)

———————

Posted: Man Shed Rules
(See Dad with any questions)

1. No Girls Allowed **
2. Do not wipe feet before entering. We are men.
3. Please ask before entering the pantry in the shed; some green leafy herbs can be confusing and are not for children.
4. Any tools must be signed out. (I plan to buy some tools.)
5. Restroom Rules: #1 only . . . and since we are men, B.Y.O.P. should you require it.

**Although girls are not allowed, I am pleased to announce there are now two versions of the orange traffic cones installed through the walls in case of an emergency. Girls are to use the traffic cone (behind the privacy screen), which has the wide end sticking out of the wall, while boys will continue to use the traffic cone with the narrow end sticking out the wall, unless further directed.*

—Dad

You were sleeping so well I didn't want to wake you. Marie said she would be in to check on you after she is back tonight from Boston, but if she is later than ten, please ring my cell. If I don't hear from you tonight, I hope you don't mind that I will quietly check on you anyway? We don't want to get behind on your pain meds.

Or, if you want me to just come in and sit, I am always happy to be in your company.

—Lorn

———

Dear Lorn,

This note is long overdue. Sorry I'm sliding it under your door so late, but I admit I am relieved to do so, rather than say this in person. I also admit I've had a few drinks, and I decided to stay up all night so I can punish myself in the morning with a well-deserved headache. I don't know how I can possibly thank you for taking such good care of our mother last night. I saw you with her after we got home; it was so late, and you had fallen asleep in the chair next to Mom and I saw your note to her and wondered if she had a rough night? I wondered if you did as well.

All I could think to do was put a blanket over you and let you rest. Should I have woken you instead? I checked on you both again much later but you had gone, and Mom was sleeping soundly and what looked like comfortably. You have been here for her without fail, and it occurred to me just tonight (yes, so embarrassing) that only my mother deserves what you have done for us, and least deserving of all, is me.

You and I have not crossed paths in a few days now. I'm sorry about that, and sorry also about the other night. Can we talk before we all leave for the hospital benefit tonight? The relieving nurse (Mom will not like her in loyalty to you . . . me neither; it's how we Italians roll) will be here around five, but we could get out of the house after Mom's bath in the morning. That usually tuckers her out, and Dad has been asking for something to do to help (amazing) so he can be assigned to stay close to her. I will set them up with a TV series . . . and a gummy.

Did I mention: if you agree, brunch is on me? (So lame, I know.)

—Marie

———————

Good morning,

Hope you got some sleep. I'm up and breakfast sounds good, but be warned. I may get the pricey eggs Benedict . . . and a cinnamon roll. (Not being an actress anymore, I can eat.) Looks like you have your Mom's schedule worked out, so any time works.

—L

I held the note for a long time in my hands and might have held it longer if my sister hadn't stomped down the hallway and come into my room without knocking. I tossed Lorn's note between my bed and the nightstand a second before she walked in.

"You look like an idiot with that smile," she said. "Did you read my note to Dr. Dick out on the table?" She laughed in her particularly proud of herself way.

"Sure did," I lied.

"Good stuff, right?" she said.

"Hysterical," I answered, shaking my head as she laughed.

"You're a riot," I said, hoping that whatever she said in her letter, she at least avoided his nickname.

"Something's going on," she said.

"With whom?"

"You, dumbass. Dressed up a bit for 10 a.m."

"I'm being careful," I said, because I knew I wasn't.

Lisa looked suspiciously at me before leaving the room. One second later she poked her head back in.

"Whore."

Switch Got Flipped

I interrupted Lorn coaching my dad as she prepared him for our brief escape.

"Remember, my cell phone number is here, and she likes this pillow the best, not this one; it's too thick behind her neck." She lowered her voice. "And even if she asks for it, don't give it to her or she will have trouble sleeping." She paused to give him a chance to absorb, then continued, "Always keep fresh water with a straw so she doesn't have to sit up each time to drink; this way she will drink more. Not as much as we will tonight, but it will be something." Dad chuckled. "I also record *Good Morning America* for her; you should watch it with her because she likes to chat about the stories, and sometimes I can convince her to let me give her a little foot rub to keep her circulation moving."

Dad was taking notes on a small pad. "GMA, got it. And a kinky foot rub."

"We won't be gone that long," I said. Lorn looked quickly at me and then tried to cover it by moving over to adjust Mom's side table by a quarter inch.

Mom said, "Oh Lorn, I'm fine, dear; go have fun for a change. You have been by my side constantly."

"We'll be back in just a few hours unless Lorn decides she needs to go shopping for an outfit." She looked at me with an amused and puzzled expression. "It's definitely a look you've got going there, but you can't go to a benefit gala wearing nurse scrubs."

"No?" she said, smiling and smoothing her uniform as if photographers were hounding her on a red carpet. My flipping stomach realized this was one of very few playful exchanges we had had since she arrived. And I realized what a shame it was that the world no longer got to see her walking one of those red carpets, and how I was feeling lucky that I got to witness her walk the halls of 2229 Lakeside Drive.

After Lorn changed and finally agreed that Mom had been carefully set up with a dummy-proofed caretaking mission for Dad, we finally made our way out the door. I insisted on driving together and instantly regretted it once the car doors closed and the familiar and heightened awareness of her closeness hit me. In a car you are trapped. There is no easing away to another room so you can breathe air that has not been filtered by the scent of her. As you drive you need to concentrate, but my concentration wanted to split to the passenger side.

"You'll like this place," I said, with no idea where I was taking her.

We were both silent on the drive, and I wondered if it was a sign of how breakfast would go. Finally, she said, "We could just go back to Bittersweet," and I thought, haven't I already? I had, in fact, spent a good chunk of adult life drowning in bittersweet.

"Sure."

"You always liked it there."

"I did."

I had not gone back to our favorite café since she had left, and I had never taken Erica there, only just now realizing I had been avoiding the ghost of Lorn. Yet it appeared, in my driving away from the nearest café to avoid the ghost of Erica, I had been heading there already. I spent a lot of time avoiding ghosts. I turned one corner and we were there, the sight of the place hitting me in the middle of my chest. The feeling was one of longing, as if she were not right by my side.

We found our usual seats, and as I watched her settle in I wondered why I already felt high on Bittersweet's strong coffee before even taking a sip. Of course, right then the sun had to streak in at just the right angle to light her hair ablaze and, oh yes, those damned green eyes. And now I felt I had already had one sip too many.

Add the damned coffee to my growing list of memories that haunted me, I thought, as I tried not to stare at her. "The usual?" I asked.

She may have nodded or even spoken, but I missed it since I had already popped out of my seat and fled to the counter to order, hoping at least there I would not have such a spectacular view of her.

I ordered us both eggs and coffee and knew I could risk peeking at her. She would be doing her usual surveying of the room and giving friendly nods to anyone that glanced her way. Straight actress, I thought. When most gay women enter a café (or any room) they attempt to take it by storm, as if proving they belong there. A gay woman plants a (rainbow) territorial flag, much the way almost all men do when entering a room. Straight women, on the other hand, plant a tiny white flag, surrendering an apology for the disruption their presence has caused by opening a door or moving a chair across the floor. They usually follow with a self-conscious nod of the head or a tight apologetic smile for interrupting the space with their femaleness.

Aside from her striking attractiveness, the people in the café were sizing her up, trying to figure out where they knew her from, or if she was "somebody." She was somebody all right. I had forgotten what a burden that seemed to her when we first met . . . and how it was heightened by the exposure she feared with our relationship. She was different now. Maybe it was the nurse overtaking the actress—of course a nurse belongs in any room she wants—or maybe she had just grown stronger while we were apart, while I had grown weaker.

I sat back down at the table with our coffees and said, "So."

"So," she answered back, just as she used to tease me.

I smiled and teased back. "Are you ready to be auctioned off tonight?"

"Can you ever be ready for that?"

"You tell me," I said.

She smiled and said, "I wish I could say this was my first experience being auctioned, but you would be surprised how often it happens in Hollywood."

I nodded and gratefully sipped the drink that now could legitimately be the blame for my thudding chest. I wondered if this felt as familiar to her as it did me, and she looked as if she was enjoying the (almost) comfortable silence.

"Thank you," I blurted out before I lost my nerve because for some reason I had wanted to say that again. "For what you have done for my mother through all this." She looked at me with such warmth that I nervously said, "I mean, selling yourself goes well beyond the call of duty, don't you think?"

"Former actress. It's what we do."

I nodded, mimicking her exaggerated seriousness as she chuckled, and the sound of her warmed me in that way that can make a person feel lucky, unlucky, or both.

We both looked around to assess how the place had changed and decided at the same moment to say "This place hasn't changed," and this time we laughed together. Finally, I thought, the ice was breaking between us . . . It was a day of firsts, and now I was wondering if maybe we could be friends.

Thinking this, I gave myself permission to ask a question you would ask a friend. "Certainly none of my business, but have you already gone out on a date with the Doctor D—Rick?"

"I did," she said. And it was fine," and I wondered if maybe there was more to this, but this was all I would get. She went out on a date with him, it was fine, and I was right when I said it was none of my business.

Our food was ready so I got up to get it, and I noticed she didn't move, just as she always didn't and just as I knew she wouldn't. In our past relationship I had been the "go get the food" one; she had been the "go cook the food" one. I got the same strange sensation I had always gotten around Lorn when we fell into our roles as a couple. As much of a lipstick lesbian as I may have appeared to the café-goers, when I got up to cross the room to get Lorn her breakfast, I felt the long forgotten masculine part of me rising up. I stole a glance back at her waiting at our table, and when I saw she was watching me, the feeling doubled. I wondered if this was similar to the pleasure men felt, but as an ache grew inside me, I suspected it was less an all-over flushed female thing, and more of a divining rod feeling I tried to deny. She had always been able to raise this feeling in me, and although I may not have showed it as outwardly and obviously as a man, what I felt seemed embarrassing like that.

I grabbed the plates, telling myself that it was not coming back, that overwhelming feeling of excitement, but as I headed back to the table to join her, my body didn't listen, just as it never does.

As passionate as my life had been with Erica, Lorn brought something out in me that only she could—and the tingling I was feeling was getting less all-over and more focused, and outrageously distracting. How had I completely forgotten this long-lost masculine feeling, as real as the tray I was holding, as I crossed the café with a heavier stride? What I felt growing inside me felt so real I feared it might also be visible to the public. Who was this Italian woman following a divining rod back to her table?

Seriously, who was I? I had completely forgotten this particular hold Lorn had on me. Or, had I merely buried it when Erica came along, then unburied it when Erica was buried? I had forgotten the mind-numbing details about how Lorn's over-the-top femaleness brought out the complete opposite side in me, stealthy as it was, or I thought it was, to the rest of the world.

When our eyes met across the room as I walked, I flashed back six years. I was no longer at the café. I was at the grocery store, watching her push a cart, and she was asking if I wanted anything special for her to cook me for dinner.

I was useless in a grocery store on a good day, but today I wondered if I had appeared more like a lumbering husband dying to get his girlfriend back home to bed. I recalled the pounding heat rising in me that was oh so distracting in the cereal aisle, and I had whispered to her, "you're so fucking gorgeous" and she had raised an eyebrow and one corner of a flirty smile and said, "No my dear, not me." And I could see I had flipped a switch also in her, as she said I always could, and I worried the heat between us might just boil the shelves of Cream of Wheat.

Remembering that day was not helping me now. We had a connection I had never had with anyone else, and knew I never would again. I chose to think of it more as yin-yang than the less politically correct male/female connection, but I wondered. From the moment we were first together we had this "thing" and I always wondered whether it was because she was outwardly such a feminine woman, an 80% straight girl to all who knew and saw her, catapulted me to be more masculine in response. I also wondered if the masculinity had always been there, but since my sister was dramatically more masculine than I was, I would never have recognized that in myself. I was the feminine one. That is, until Lorn. After meeting her, I realized I was both parts, fully feminine female combined with the (thankfully) harder to see sex-crazed core of a dude.

She was the one who had spotted this in me so long ago. She was the one who told me who I was. I joked at the time, heading home from the grocery, "Are you saying I'm Johnny Depp with tits?" And she joked, "You're Marie most of the time, but in the grocery store back there, I saw Mario." I laughed loudly in surprise, but then we both got quiet, silently measuring her playful accusation as we drove home that day, before following up with our hottest sex to date on the living room floor.

Now, I was in a café, faced with the knowledge of how much I had missed and wanted her. I also recognized how much I had missed my alter ego she had called Mario, and now there was no disconnecting the once again connected.

I held her eyes as I placed the tray down on the table, not even trying to hide how I was drowning in how ridiculously stunning she was, and marveled at how the simple act of delivering food to her in a café made me ache for everything we used to have. One time I had reached over in this very café and brazenly stolen a feel of her under the table, and watched as it set a firestorm in her Caribbean Ocean eyes. Something made me sure in this moment she was also remembering that exact day.

To try to diffuse the moment, I joked, "Can I bring you anything else, Miss?"

She looked at me, not fooled, and not smiling to let me know she knew exactly where I was. And who I was ... with her. She had always known when I was like this, and, unlike her, I was not a skilled actress and unable to hide it.

She said quietly, "Everything I need is here."

She knew. My switch had been flipped. In the past there was no use hiding it, and I wondered if she was with me now, remembering us on the floor and how it had been the first of many times I would do things to her I hadn't dared before.

I lowered myself back to my seat, pointlessly pretending nothing was going on, and we both tried to focus on our food, finally distracting myself with my enjoyment of watching her eat. I always loved watching her overly formal table manners, especially delightful if she was eating something casual, like a sandwich. Pinkies up, delicately, especially if she had to use her hands, but also when using smaller forks and spoons. Nibbling on tiny bites of her eggs Benedict, she looked like downright royalty.

With the food distracting us both, things got casual again, and in between bites we shared Do You Remembers, mostly about Bittersweet Café, and managed to steer clear of the other bittersweet variety. It felt more comfortable than I had been expecting, but I remembered it had always been that way with her. Easy breezy, then when I least expected it, fire like I had never known before or since.

Later, as we stood to leave, Lorn allowed me to stop her hand from taking her plate so I could take hers, and our eyes locked again with the ache roaring back before I could look away. It felt like everyone in the café watched me take her plate in silence and walk back to the table to leave together, and I wondered exactly what they saw. Did they see two girlfriends out to breakfast while their husbands were off playing golf? Did they see a familiar actress they could not place as Lorn Elaine, or maybe they were collectively surfing a wild attraction to a spectacular woman? That last one would be me.

I noticed one other thing.

If I could've called out one moment where my grief over losing Erica evaporated into thin air, I knew it was this very moment. As we left the café, I could not help myself and instinctively touched the small of her back as I opened the door for her. I was grateful not to feel my typical grief and instead feel the glorious sunshine of the day landing on me as I guided her out the door. But I was not so in my own head that I could ignore how my touch made Lorn flinch. But even this couldn't stop me from looking forward to more time with her at the benefit tonight.

As we left the café, even as I feared my switch had been flipped again for this mostly straight woman, at the moment I was simply grateful for the release she gave me from the pain of Erica. It had happened now, in an hour at Bittersweet Café, and stranger still was that the grief felt long ago and far away, as grief should feel when it is finally left behind.

My relief was short-lived since once we were back in the car, the closeness of her brought back the cautious warning from deep inside me: You may feel 100% grateful to be free of Erica, but clearly you are only 80% done with straight girls.

Going Once, Going Twice

Dad, Vince, Lisa, and I were like a pack of starving lions surrounding an ever-shrinking watering hole (disguised as a small plate of hard Italian cheese, pepperoni, tomato dipping sauce, and crusty bread that Lisa had whipped up). They were enjoying a pre-gala cocktail in the kitchen as I focused all my energy to be prepared for when Lorn joined us. When I finally heard Lorn's heels coming down the hallway, I tried to look casual by grabbing the last cracker as a prop and readied it for my mouth so I would not have to speak.

Lorn didn't need to go shopping for an outfit. She wore a black dress, similar to or actually *the* dress that was one of my favorites of hers back in the day. It was cut low in the front, tight at the waist, with cold shoulder sleeves allowing her softly freckled shoulders to peek out and taunt me. I remembered with stunning detail reaching with both hands under that similar/same dress, and in remembering I entirely missed my mouth with the cracker.

Vince and Lisa didn't miss a thing and snorted in unison.

"Wow, Lorn," Lisa said because, unlike me, she actually could speak.

"Well, we're all here; should we go?" I asked, hearing my rushed and awkward transition a few seconds too late.

"Hold your horses, Mare. Maybe Lorn wants to have a cocktail or a snack if you are done throwing crackers on the

185

floor," Lisa said.

"No, no, I'm perfect," she said to Lisa.

Damn right. I was screwed.

We had not even been at the hospital gala for five minutes, all of us looking around and listening to the music, when Dr. Dick descended upon Lorn like a seagull on a French fry. A quick look verified that Lorn seemed happy to see him, though she didn't move toward him. Strike one, pal.

Not that I should care.

My sister, who became the town mayor in any crowd, moved first to shake his hand, compliment his doctor skills, wink at him, and say, "Of course you remember our friend, Lorn. She's a big fan of yours as well."

I remembered when I was twelve and Lisa had tried to trap me under a beanbag chair, not knowing that the vinyl was smothering me. Strength came from nowhere as I had stood up, tossing her off me for the first time in my life. If I had a giant vinyl beanbag chair right about now, my sister would be wearing it like a hat.

He said, "Lorn, you look absolutely amazing. May I be so rude as to steal you away for a moment?" Yes, he would be so rude, I thought.

He put his hand out for her, and I saw my sister's attention flick toward me for my reaction. My beanbag fantasy shifted over to Dr. Dick, but I heard myself say, "Go on, Lorn. I'm sure you need a break from us. Don't worry, we won't leave without you."

Dr. Dick said to me directly, "It would be my pleasure to give Lorn a ride home."

He'd pulled a Rambo and drawn first blood. Since I saw this as ever-so-slightly fucking arrogant, I looked directly at him and said, "It's not the 1940s, Rick. You'll have to ask Lorn, not me." It felt good to drop his doctor title into an imaginary toilet, and

I saw him visibly prickle at the loss of it.

At first his eyes narrowed; then he seemed amused, and certainly not threatened, which made me instantly hate the same man who had saved my mother's life.

"Oh, I wasn't asking you," he said, "but I know you were only concerned for your friend." My strong dislike of him turned to white-hot hate.

Then Dr. Dick turned his back to me, and I wanted to backhand him across his emerging bald spot. His hand, still outstretched to her, said, "Lorn, will you honor me with a dance?"

"I think you're supposed to bid for that right," she answered.

Lisa laughed, and I wanted to hug Lorn. Until I realized she was being playful with him. Straight girl flirting. Was it this or my heightened hatred of him making the blood pound in my ears?

Lorn was hesitant, but as she took his hand, I felt a cord cut between us. Good-bye, I thought coldly. If I could have sneered without being seen, I would have. Things become so much simpler as people make their choices. It's the people who need to accept the choices that really have a job to do. Like me. I had a job now. I had to let whatever this was or wasn't between us go with Dr. Dick. I attempted to fool myself with a sigh of relief so my sister might hear it, but as he escorted Lorn away, I saw him touch the small of her back and my inner wild man sprang back to life, trying to gauge if a camouflaged fling of my drink was possible at this growing distance.

Instead, I attempted a playful yell after her. "Lorn, just text us a signal when you're bored!"

I didn't get to see if Lorn turned around because Lisa got right up in my face, her eyebrows up. My first indication that I'm being an idiot is always when the tables are turned and I shock my sister. My whole life this had been the key indicator of my being not in control of myself.

When Lisa nodded and said, "Easy, tiger," I was relieved she was smirking, as she typically would not come to the defense of an overconfident man. "What the hell is going on with you?"

"Nothing," I said. "You find him arrogant too."

"Of course. He's a surgeon. And he saved Mom's life. He has God's permission to be arrogant. Not sure about you, though. If I didn't know any better—"

"Oh, stop it."

"What happened this morning?" she barked over a painful Adele song. I was dying to flick my eyes past her to see them on the dance floor, but Lisa stayed close and I had to keep my eyes glued on hers. "Vince said you and Lorn went to breakfast." She moved even closer, almost nose to nose, totally blocking my view of the whole dance floor, and then used her pointed index finger to bridge the gap, resting the tip of it on the end of my nose. "This morning, did you eat a muffin?"

I shot Traitor Vince a look before slapping Lisa's finger off my nose. This act of aggression seemed to make her happy.

"You're being ridiculous. I'm still in love with Erica."

"She's dead," Lisa said. "Remember?"

"I remember."

"And you even broke up with her in a letter, right?"

I'm not sure how she knew I would actually do that, but I nodded yes. I could have tried to stare Lisa down, but it wouldn't have worked, and I knew the truth. "Oh fuck it," I said. "Let's all agree I'm an idiot and just get drunk." My sister and brother signed up for that idea by each raising their right hands, something we always did as kids in a *pick me* gesture. Dad copied, but I noticed he somehow already had a drink in his hand. "Nobody has to drive, so we can just leave the car and call a limo," I said. "We're fucking rich."

"And one of us already has a ride," she said, teasing to measure the look on my face, but I held steady with an I-don't-give-an-F shrug.

When that didn't work, Lisa poked me hard, her finger jabbing me, which hurt more with less dough around my middle. I was reminded that I needed to eat more Oreos and stop throwing them down the disposal in stacks of five each night while my family slept.

188

"Seriously, Mare, this could be good. If she likes him, it will remove any temptation for crushing on an *exceptionally straight nurse.*"

"There's no temptation," I said through gritted teeth.

Lisa backed up a bit, and I knew she would see me sneaking looks past her, but Lorn had evaporated with Dr. D. into the crowd. "You just feel like kicking Dr. Dick in the balls," Vince said.

I nodded. "I might need more than a few drinks."

Dad said, "Vince, for Christ sakes, get your sisters some drinks. What kind of man are you?"

As promised, we drank. Vince insisted on shots and I was enjoying the soft spin of the room until I heard the silent auction winners about to be announced. I pretended to chat with my family, but hearing Lorn's name over the loudspeaker broke my stride.

"And the winner of a dance and dinner date with Emmy award-winning actress Lorn Elaine is . . . Dr. Rick!"

Of course.

The announcer added, "I don't know if this should be allowed, folks. Is it me or have they already been dancing?"

I had to see this for myself, and when the music started, I slipped away to watch. They were easy to spot, this perfectly matched couple in the middle of the dance floor, which had cleared so the doctor could collect his winnings for all to see, not the least of all me. I didn't care that he had donated $5,000 for a hospital charity for this dance; he was an opportunist. An enemy. My enemy.

Easy, *tiger.*

I didn't want to admit they looked good together. As much as he had earned himself a kick in the balls, the doctor was a perfectly tall, dark complement to Lorn's fair beauty. I gritted my teeth again, seeing how well they danced together. There are some situations in this world where two women together are at a disadvantage. They can't, for example, go to a hospital fundraiser, no matter how much money one of the women may have to throw around, and can't bid on a dance and dinner date with another woman without creating a stir. Not quite here, not quite yet. Knowing this didn't help my dark mood.

I settled myself in a corner where I had a good view. Maybe too good. Lorn was smiling, and he took that as an invitation to pull her closer to him. Now that her head was resting on his shoulder, I saw her eyes scanning the crowd, and I pulled tighter against the shadow of the wall.

As I watched, I imagined what it would be like to dance with her in front of a crowd like this. Her left hand in mine, her body against me as she moved. I imagined discreetly sliding my hand from the middle of her back down to the small of her back, just as he was doing now. I would hold her firmly there until our eyes locked, much like their eyes seemed to be locking right now. Then she looked away. Was she nervous?

As they danced, she again pulled closer to him, but was it to scan the crowd? Could she be seeking her temporary Santora family, lost in a sea of doctors, nurses, and friends of the hospital? According to Mom, we were Lorn's family, no matter how temporary, at least until Mom was better. At this thought I felt as if Dr. Dick's gloved surgeon's hands were giving my heart a gripping squeeze. As the crowd joined them on the dance floor, he took the opportunity to give Lorn a light kiss on her cheek. As she looked over his shoulder, my eyes met hers.

I was surprised how the emotion rose in me as she kept looking ... was it sadness I saw in her eyes? What was she seeing in mine? I watched as they pulled closer, and I was no longer able to see her face.

As the song slowed to an end, and he bent to kiss her again, I tortured myself by standing my ground to watch. The song "Dancing on My Own" seemed to be playing just for me ...

My gut tightened as I made myself watch, torturing myself as he walked Lorn over to introduce her to a small group of men who looked identical to him. Handsome, confident, and each of them so much more appropriate for Lorn than I was.

Being only 80% done with straight girls meant I was still

paralyzed, and that damned 20% made me unable to drag myself from the scene. I reasoned that maybe if I let myself watch them, I could hit 100% done, and finally set myself free of both Lorn and Erica.

Or, maybe I just didn't want to walk away.

Even from this distance I could see the men eyeballing each other, and puffing up like they planned to arm wrestle Dr. Dick for a shot with Lorn. So much for the bro code. I imagined myself strolling over, hooking her arm in mine, and escorting her off without a word. Instead, I stood frozen in the corner. Why did I ever think for a second this could end any differently? Why did I think there was anything to end at all?

I needed to get away, and as I came out of my dark corner into the light, Lorn turned as if I had called her, which I had not. Truth was, I had whispered *good-bye*, only to myself and she was across the room, and my good-bye was drowned out by the music . . . and yet she was looking directly at me, as if she had somehow heard. Impossible.

The doctor was happily chatting up another doc, enjoying how he was impressing the guys with a celebrity actress on his arm. But she was looking at me, pal, and I wished he knew.

I finally came to my senses. This was childish. I gave Lorn the most genuine smile I could as if I was happy for her and followed that with a cheesy thumbs-up before I turned away as if it was the most perfect choice in the world for her to be with him. I headed back to find my family, tried not to look back, and failed. But the crowd had filled in, and we could no longer see each other. I had tortured myself enough for one night, I thought, as the song played out its last verse.

Had it been only one song since I had spotted her with him? If so, a lifetime of thoughts had whizzed through my head.

Enough. 100% DONE.

Lisa made me have one more drink so she could continue to cross-examine me about this morning. There was nothing to really confess. Nobody but me needed to know the crazy thoughts that had once again flooded my head. I told myself it didn't matter, even as I braced myself for the pain of leaving tonight without her.

The crowd dispersed a little, and we could all see Lorn from across the room where we stood. Even from a distance I could see she seemed a bit uncomfortable for a woman used to being the center of attention. People were coming up to her introducing themselves and shaking her hand, some asking for autographs. She was smiling and gracious, but something was off.

If she felt as lost as I did, hadn't it been her choice? She had walked off with him, just as it had been her choice to leave me so many times, and my choice to leave her now.

"Can we throw our donation in the bucket and get out of here?" I asked Lisa.

I didn't have to work too hard to convince them and we were barely to the door when Vince asked, "What about Lorn?"

"She's fine," I said. "She's where she wants to be."

Dad confessed he had only been drinking soda in case Mom needed him later, so he was our limo driver to take us home. Sitting in the back seat of the car I felt like I was in junior high school, disappointed once again by not fitting in at the school dance. Boy meets girl . . . boy dances with girl . . . and this girl goes home.

"Awfully quiet back there," Lisa said, eyeballing me in the rearview.

I just stared out the window. I could tell by the way Vince was fidgeting that he didn't want to leave Lorn there. "We should have checked with her first," he said again.

Lisa finally broke the silence that followed. "I told him to do it," she said.

"Told who?" Vince asked.

"The doctor. Dr. Rick-Dick. I told him that Lorn couldn't stop talking about him since their dinner date, and it worked like a charm."

I popped between the two front seats, hoping I had heard her wrong. "What? Why would you do that?" Vince instinctively grabbed my arm as if to stop me from jumping into the front seat between Lisa and Dad.

"I did it because you're stuck, and Lorn is not the answer, and you needed to let her go too. After the year you've had, you don't need to get mixed up in this and start the hurting all over again."

I swallowed hard, trying to keep my cool. "So, you're telling me we left Lorn back there with an extremely arrogant guy who's been told that she's really into him?"

"So? I thought they both needed a little convincing, and I think it worked—but he can go fuck off if he even thinks he can try something Lorn doesn't want—"

"Turn the fucking car around!" I yelled, and to my surprise Dad pulled a wild U-turn to avoid the light ahead and went speeding back across town.

When we arrived back at the gala, I told everyone to stay in the car even though Vince protested. "You don't want me as backup?" he asked, but Lisa didn't fight me on it. I ignored them all and charged back inside like one of the Brat Pack in the last ten minutes of an eighties movie.

Inside, I spotted the doctor immediately. He was alone and surveying the crowd with his nose up in the air. His face turned into a scowl when he saw me.

"You're back. Did you lose something?" he asked, though his confidence sounded forced.

"Looks like you might have. Where is she?"

"With your family, I thought. She said she couldn't stay. Listen, your sister said—"

"My sister says a lot of things; in fact, just a minute ago she said you should go fuck off." That'll teach him to listen to my sister, I thought, bolting from him.

There was no sign of Lorn. I was on my second lap of the dance floor without a glimpse of her, and then I thought the restroom was the one place I hadn't checked, and I would go stall by stall if I had to.

I didn't have to.

When I pushed open the ladies' room door, I found Lorn standing near the mirror, doing some repair to her makeup. She looked heartbreakingly beautiful . . . Had she been crying?

"Lorn—I'm sorry, we shouldn't have left. I didn't know my sister had told Dr.—"

She spun around, and her expression had turned to furious.

"Why did you bother coming back? Did you think I needed to be rescued?" She was working hard to be angry, but her eyes filled again.

I took a deep breath to slow my roll. "I could ask you the same question." I took a few steps toward her. "Why did you come back? Was it only for my mother? Or did you think I needed to be rescued? You said you weren't here for me, remember?"

Lorn said, "Please just leave. I can get myself home; I'm fine. I've been on my own for a long time. Always, in fact, if I were to be honest." The last part came as a whisper and it hit me straight in the heart.

Someone walked into the bathroom past us and stepped into a stall. I didn't care.

"What if I told you something . . . something I'm finding hard to admit . . . and then maybe you could be honest with me?"

She looked lost, not knowing how to answer, so I carefully took another step forward.

"I hated seeing him with you." I was losing the battle to control my voice from shaking. "I hated that he was dancing with you, touching you. I'm going to sound like an idiot now if I haven't from the moment I walked into this bathroom. I had to leave when I saw him kiss you."

The toilet flushed and a woman hurried out, not looking at us, high-tailing it after an unhealthy four-second hand wash.

I watched Lorn the whole time and could see her breathing had shifted from anger to something else. Before the woman could flee through the door, I said, "The doctor that saved my mother's life, well . . . I wanted to kick him in the balls. Even Lisa thought I was being outrageous."

She let out a tiny, stifled laugh and I saw her eyes fill up again.

Instead of thinking it, I whispered, "I don't know if there's anything more heartbreaking than a woman, certainly a woman who looks like you, trying not to cry."

I saw her catch her breath as she said, "Especially in a women's restroom."

I spoke slowly and gently, not knowing what I planned to say next. "I believed you when you said you weren't here for me . . . but if that isn't true, or if it's changed, I need you to tell me. I don't know if it will make any difference, but I'd like to know."

She whispered, "Do you need to hear it so you have a reason to run, like tonight?" When I didn't answer, she said, "Marie, I know this is unfair. How could I ask you to do this again?"

I said, "Are you asking?" She stayed quiet. "Because tonight I realized I've been worrying that you will disappear again."

She shook her head and said very quietly, "No. Just that first part, right there."

I moved toward her and reached for both her trembling hands, wet paper towels and all. "Please be honest with me."

She looked at me a long time before finally saying, "I'm not running anywhere. There are things you don't know. Like why I wanted out of Hollywood."

"That took some guts," I said.

"More than a few guts," she said with a small smile. "I would have given up everything to have another chance at a real life. To do it right this time and not have my career be my excuse to not have what I want."

"What do you want?" I asked, my heart pounding, not wanting to be the one to move first and close the small space between us.

As if she heard me, Lorn took the last step between us and lifted her head to mine.

I was petrified, so I stalled by whispering, "What if another toilet flushes . . ."

"I don't care," she braved, but one did flush right then, and we instinctively both covered each other's mouths with our hands. Neither of us had noticed the second door to the back of the bathroom. Our wide eyes and stifling laughs quickly shifted to more narrowed eyes and absolutely no laughing, and I knew the exact moment she was remembering from so long ago.

Long ago, before there was even a hint of the panic that would sweep her away from me, there was a night we had been making love—no, actually, we had been having some pretty crazy sex. Things had gotten a little crazy, and I was enjoying the sounds of her as we thrashed together in bed, yet we had still been sharing a house with Lisa and Vince so I covered her mouth with my hand as I took her. First came her wide-eyed surprise, followed by eyes that grew narrower, more knowing, then smoke-filled, before her eyes rolled back in her complete loss of control. I thought then, as I was thinking now, oh my, what have I discovered here?

Perhaps remembering too, she almost kissed me, sending my head spinning, but she pulled back when a lady emerged from a stall.

Except it was no lady.

"Are you two done making out in the friggin' bathroom?" Lisa said.

I was about to deny it, but there was something in the way Lorn was looking at me that stopped me from saying another word. Her mouth was parted as if she had been thinking how close we had come to doing exactly that. As we left the ladies' room, I pressed my hand to the small of her back, with a touch more contact than was required to lead her back home.

Do I Stay or Do I Go Now?

Lorn and I were both silent on the drive home. When we returned to the house, nobody took Lisa up on her idea for a nightcap, so we all retreated to our rooms. I sat on the edge of my bed, frozen, my heart pounding just as it had in that restroom. The two corridors and kitchen between us felt miles apart. How do you decide what to do at moments like this? Did I walk the distance between us? Or maybe the reason I was sitting here alone now was my answer? Had a few drinks made me imagine that she felt the same?

A great deal of time passed before a soft knock came at my door. Still, I didn't move, and Lorn surprised me by letting herself in. I remembered so long ago when we first met in Jamaica, Lorn was the one who had sat nervously on the bed. She was wondering about her fate after acknowledging the powerful attraction she had to me, to a woman, afraid to move after I had entered her room.

And now it was my turn.

She closed the door quietly behind her, and we looked at each other. Was she remembering, as I was, the many times we had been apart and come together, just like this? I had to admit, at this very second, I was more focused on how astonishing she looked in that dress. I crossed the room to meet her at the door.

"You again," I said, reaching until I had both of her hands

gently in my grasp. Then I held tight. Maybe in case she changed her mind?

She leaned slightly away from me until her back was planted firmly against the door and we both heard the click of the knob. We had done this scene a few times too, and the memories flooded back. She had been so afraid in the past, but her expression now, even as she leaned back, was different.

"And you again," she said.

In typical lesbian fashion of wanting to establish the entire relationship before it begins, I whispered, "Are we really starting again?"

"I'm not, no." she said, and at this I halted my plans to press her hard against the door with my body. She breathed deeply, and on her exhale she said, "I'm not starting again. I've only loved you. All this time, all these years. It's not starting again when all I've been doing is waiting for you."

If this was true, she had waited the five years for my time with Erica to end, then another year before she came to me. I searched her eyes as I said, "That was a long wait . . . So then, you did come back here for me?"

"I told myself I came for your mother because I promised myself that I would never come back after leaving the last time. And I still haven't come back to you because this is not to be my choice. It's entirely yours."

"Well, you came to my bedroom."

She softened with a faint smile as she said, "Who said I have to make it easy?"

I smiled at this, concentrating on keeping my eyes on hers and not allowing them to wander around her body. I had not forgotten that body, not one inch. I also couldn't forget that just a few hours ago she had been dancing with that doctor and that nobody in the room, including me, doubted they looked perfect for each other.

At the high risk of sounding pathetic, I said, "How do I know you're in this for the long game? That was a pretty good-looking guy you were dancing with tonight. I mean, maybe that feels right to you . . . more than this does."

Even saying it with such conviction, I could not forget what we had . . . yet. "You're still a wild card," I said. "The straight woman who only six years ago was terrified of the risk you were taking. The one who walked away, many times. I still have no idea what you want, so now I'm terrified of the risk I'm taking."

She looked me directly in the eyes. "Rick made me think about only one thing. How could I be dancing with him, so close—"

"I hadn't noticed," I said.

"His entire body was against me—"

"Too much information—"

"Yet I couldn't feel him. Not at all. But you can look at me from across a breakfast table, or a dance floor, or a bedroom, and you can physically touch me." She paused to take a deep breath at her confession.

I finally let myself move forward, pressed against her, watching for the flush of color I knew would rise from her beautiful neck, but missed it as I covered her mouth with a kiss. I felt Lorn's body reacting along the entire length of me as I pressed more firmly against her, making her change her stance as I got my leg against the middle of her. Warm, then hot.

Was this really happening?

We both remembered how we used to kiss, each time lingering longer, stronger, and I let go of her wrists to press her mouth harder to mine. We kissed until we were breathless, my head spinning as only she could make happen.

"I knew what was happening to you at the café," she whispered into my ear as if what she was thinking was so passionate that she had to protect its privacy, even in my bedroom. Her voice was ragged with a level of lust I had forgotten (or had I blocked it out?)

"And I know what is happening to you now," she said, and with that her hand skipped to the end goal, landing firmly between my legs—so unlike her, yet it was her I remembered now, and she held tight in just the way she knew would send me into a fury. The panic of wanting to take her quickly was intoxicating and familiar, and it was something I only ever had with her. I bent down and reached both my arms up the sides of her dress, my right hand able to go higher through the high slit on the side. She let out a groan that sounded both helpless and demanding. I dug my nails into her backside as she squirmed against me, not to get away, but to push harder. That's what I was looking for, that's what I needed, and this was yet another thing I had forgotten.

I gripped her harder, thinking of how I would not let her go, and then she breathed "Please take me" into my ear. Thankful I had taken my sister's advice and done some weight training to get my strength back, I was able to lift her up by her gorgeous ass as she wrapped her legs around me and carried her the few steps to my bed. I just barely got her there before we fell hard onto it. I was grateful I had not dropped her on the floor. It wouldn't have mattered, I thought, remembering more. We had done much worse on the floor before, but for our first time, *this* first time, the bed seemed a better choice.

Now on the bed, we both moved more frantically; my arms still cradling her middle, I slid myself down while sliding her dress up, surprised to find her already naked from the waist down as I buried my face into her, thankful my room was quite far away from the others as she let out a gasp. God, the taste of her.

While it was appreciated, she needn't have held my face down there. I wanted to finish her, but she groaned a soft "no, please" as she pulled me up. I took my time getting there, visiting like a frantic tourist before closing time all my favorite parts of her lightly freckled body. I had only thought I remembered her. My most favorite places on earth, I thought, as I drowned in the sounds of her repeating her earlier request.

As if it wasn't obvious, I told her I needed to be inside her as I kissed her breasts, her body shaking, so close to me and so close to the finish line. It's the details you remember at times like this and I knew if I touched her a few seconds more, she would be done.

My mouth found hers, and I smothered her with a long kiss as I took her, silencing her breathing. I thrust my knee against the back of my own hand as I went inside, jackhammer style until she finished. I remembered the first time I learned she wanted this, the first time I heard the same muffled screams and how they morphed to soft whimpers in my ear as I slowed, but did not stop. Who on earth wants to ever leave paradise? And, it turns out, paradise is not the sound of ocean waves; instead, it is exactly the sound of this woman, and this woman was mine.

I never felt so powerful as when I was taking her. Completely swept away, I could only come up with the obvious: "I love you."

It didn't matter that I hadn't planned it; it was my truth. I couldn't protect myself from the truth of it anymore—it had always been my truth—even in the beginning when I first started to feel something for Erica, I had still loved Lorn. It was during that time I realized that you could genuinely and completely love two people at the same time. They had overlapped each other, but the difference this time was that neither had eclipsed the other until this moment.

As if she heard my thoughts, Lorn whispered as tears rolled down her face, "I've only loved you."

"We've only just started," I said, wiping her tears.

She nodded, and I felt her tears against my neck, and I hoped she believed me. And I hoped I believed her.

Morning came and I woke up first to see the sun bathing her entire body, a sight that took my breath away, just as it always did. I couldn't help myself and traced the sun on her skin with my fingertips, and Lorn gave a slow smile before jumping up in a panic saying, "It's past time for your mother's shot—"

"Shhhhh," I said, "the temp nurse stayed overnight, remember?"

Lorn fell back into the bed with relief. My heart ached with love for how much she cared for my mother. As we stared at each other, I was thinking how nurses had to be the most amazing people on earth. I was also asking, how did I end up with the hottest one in my bed? I don't know what Lorn was thinking, but I melted at the feel of her breathing as it quickened, her chest falling and rising closer to me.

She whispered in her playful fake cocky way, "You want me again."

It was not a question. Just the damned truth.

"How do you know?" I whispered back, because I thought I was being so very cool. I wanted to laugh at that thought, and if my heart hadn't been pounding at the look in her eyes, I might have. I had never been cool for even one second around this woman.

"You have a tell," she whispered, "and it's very raw, and real ..."

I whispered back into her ear, "Tell me."

When she refused, with a small shake of her head, I knew it was because she couldn't find the words to speak. I was so thankful she could not read the many aggressive and filthy thoughts flying around in my head, then embarrassed when I realized that of course she could.

Lorn said, "I like being able to know things about you ... I'm keeping that secret to myself because I don't want it to change."

Her eyes gave her away again, and this was *her* tell, when her eyes appeared smoky and narrow, I knew she was trying to slow her breathing as I felt it quicken between us.

"Outrageous how much I want you," I said, with real concern in my voice.

"Then we're both doomed," she said, taking in the sharp breath she had been holding. I loved confession time.

I kissed her, fully waking us both. Her lips always gave me the sensation of diving head first into a stack of the softest pillows, drowning in the softness of her ... and it always made me think: what a way to go.

When she was able, she whispered, "You drive me crazy when you do that."

"This?" I said, trailing another kiss back to her lips.

"Well, yes, but the other thing . . . the one I won't tell you." Then she whispered into my ear what sounded like a warning, "I could go so crazy right now . . ."

What the hell was I doing?

And in considering this, my body went still. Aha, I thought. I hadn't even been aware how much I needed to move against her until I had stopped because clearly I couldn't manage two things at once.

"You mean this?" I whispered into her ear as I went back to the most natural movement in the world to me, a rocking movement with my hips against her, only realizing now that I likely did this whenever we were pressed close. I said, "Only you do this to me." And it was true.

She searched my eyes before saying, "I love *exactly* how you are."

Not that I had a choice, but this was perhaps the most erotic thing anyone had ever said to me, because only she really knew me. Lorn trembled with her confession, her hands now gripping my hips, making me push harder against the middle of her. I got up on my knees to straddle her, while keeping our bodies pressed together. She moved her hands down farther and pulled me closer, harder. I had forgotten how physically strong she was. It was another secret she hid completely from the world, but not from me.

Just barely into my shoulder she whispered, "Yes, please," before biting me there. Fuck. I had forgotten that too.

Locked on to each other, I could have rocked against her all day except the need for it all to end was so damned strong. She called it first, whispering to me, "Please . . . do it," and I remembered how she would always ask me to do exactly what I wanted to.

Going inside her was something that satisfied us both (possibly me a bit more) and a thing I wouldn't have understood needing so much before having *her*. "More," she whispered, and I gave her more. She was calling all the plays, switching up fast. "I need you, please," and I knew what that meant then too, a shorthand command that sent me diving down to her, keeping hold of her inside while I latched on to her with my mouth. Lorn's orgasm, fast as lightning and always explosive, had always shook us both, just as it did right now.

It was usually Lorn who got emotional right afterward, but not this time. I held on to her as if she was Kate Winslet sporting the only lifejacket and floating away from a sinking ship and asked her as I choked back tears, "Stay this time? Please."

She pulled me back up to her and nodded heavily against my forehead as she tightened her hold around my face. "I don't deserve this, but if you'll still have me—"

Well, let me think on that . . . And then, I found that maybe I could learn to do two things at once.

Another Door Opens

Lisa showed me an email she was about to fire off to her producer. Lisa, never one to be patient, was growing tired of waiting for her prize. The show was locked up, deal signed, yet still she had not landed Sandra. Lisa would not let me read over her shoulder as she preferred to read it to me out loud.

"Dear Sandra,

Thanks for all you have done to secure the show. Just as I know you do, I believe the show will be an instant hit. Speaking of hits, do you know I have been hitting on you? I can be subtle sometimes. Since you are the type to insist on everything in writing, there it is. My sister says I am as subtle as a sledgehammer, yet so far I haven't landed the girl. I'm not one to give up easily (I am like a dog with a boner), but I'm beginning to think this dog may be barking up the wrong tree. The last thing I want to do is compromise our working relationship, but I suppose I am willing to risk it."

"Wow," I said. "Dog with a boner. That line right there should work."

"Don't worry, it gets better," Lisa said as she kept reading.

"The thing is, life is short, and this train (which only becomes available about every five or six years) is planning to leave the station. The point is, you need to get on it."

"I'm guessing this is the subtle part?" I said, "You know, before you tell her what is what."

"Yeah, I'm not like you, Mare. I can't make goo-goo eyes for months or years before I dive in."

I didn't have the heart to tell her I had been diving in every night and morning for a week now, and frankly I was sore.

Lisa wasn't done.

"I know there is something between us, and I am never wrong about these things. Well, maybe once or twice, but telling you those stories would just muddy the waters. The point is, I'm into you, and I think you feel the same. However, I get that you have never gone this route before so I wanted to make sure we were up front with each other. I don't want to be like my sist—"

"Oh, I don't need to read that part," Lisa said as I slapped the back of her head and she skimmed down the letter to continue.

"You have used words like 'experiment' and 'explore,' but I'm not looking for someone with a Bunsen burner and a miner's helmet. I want someone who wants to be with me, and if that is not you, then okay. We can continue to work together, but I want to be blunt—"

"Uh-oh," I said. "Now comes the part where you get blunt?"

"Yep," Lisa said.

"Here's the thing . . ."

Uh, oh. Lisa's most shocking thoughts always come flying out of her mouth like shrapnel right after she says, "Here's the thing."

Lisa puffed up her chest and continued reading.

> "I'm a stallion at the gate, raring to go, and I have chosen you. If that makes you feel lucky in any way, then we should probably do something about this. However, if you are just playing or, worse, flirting to land a contract, I can cool my jets and gallop off to the next stall."

"Nice touch," I said. "Women love horse analogies."

"Next is the best part," Lisa said, grinning proudly. I held the edge of the table.

> "However, like my Dad always says, there are only two things in life, either you are in or you are out. If you are in, I will do things to you that no idiot man has ever dreamed of—"

"Oh, that should do it," I said.

> "I'm so sure I can give you what you need (and what you don't even know you need) and all you have to do to get it all is to say yes. I booked a dinner reservation for Saturday night at the Top of the Hub in Boston; the views are incredible and the food is great. Not as great as my cooking, of course, but you know that. After that, if you care to strap your miner's helmet on, you can explore for hours in the room I booked inside the Lenox Hotel . . . while I explore the inside of you."

I nodded, as if she would seriously consider my advice. "Maybe cut that last line?"

Lisa cackled, "What? I am like fucking Shakespeare, only without the spear. Of course, if she also wants that, this can easily be arranged." She broke her concentration to jot down a note on her grocery list. Good lord.

"Are you sure you don't want to edit out that last—"

"It's perfect. That's how you have to be with these straight girls. They don't know what the fuck they want until after you give it to them."

Well, she might have a point there.

"Poor thing," Lisa said. "She is risking losing me, so I had to point it out."

I could see she was truly worried for Sandra's loss. I tried once more. "You may want to consider waiting a day, you know, to reread it before sending it to her."

She looked at the printed email admiringly, and then surprised me by crumpling it up and bouncing it off my face.

"Good call," I said after it had clocked me in the nose. I was surprised she took my advice. Maybe my sister was—

"I emailed it at two in the morning," Lisa said. "I'll update you when she caves."

Later that day Lorn and I were sitting down by the lake in two Adirondack chairs while Mom took a nap. Mom was getting stronger each day and her naps were getting less frequent, so we took advantage of the time alone. At this time every day the lake reflected a vivid blue from the sky, instead of the usual lake-water brown, and the breeze was gentle enough to create a sparkling ripple on the surface. Lorn and I did not feel the need to speak; we were both taking it all in from our chairs. When I reached across for her hand, I heard her sigh.

"Perfect," she said, staring serenely before giving a quiet yelp when she spotted a hummingbird tasting each of the flowering plants hanging from the wood posts at the end of the dock.

"I haven't seen a hummingbird in so long," I said.

"Maybe you gave up looking. It's like magic. You have to be looking for it to see it." When I turned to her, she was looking at me with eyes so intense I would have leapt up if it wouldn't have scared the tiny bird. I could see from the expression on her face Lorn knew exactly what I was thinking, and what would happen next.

"Oh Jesus!" Lisa said from behind us, making us both jump. "I *knew* you were back at it. I just knew it!" Besides sounding like a know-it-all, I noticed Lisa also sounded happy, and I was filled with a sense of relief knowing my sister no longer had to worry about me.

"Will you two gluttons for punishment be able to stop gawking at each other long enough to watch my premiere tonight?"

"We can try," I said, but I still refused to look away from Lorn who was especially adorable when embarrassed.

"Any emails back from Sandra?" I asked casually, plotting our best escape to one of our bedrooms.

Lisa said, "Only that she would be coming tonight. Which was my plan anyway."

I ignored her but Lorn laughed, which of course encouraged Lisa to snort at her own joke. As Lisa walked away toward the house, she called back, "You two whores better get it on—only three hours before show time."

Our entire family, Lorn, plus a trembling-with-excitement Eddie and a trying-not-to-tremble producer Sandra all gathered in the living room as Lisa readied herself for her television debut. She was prancing around, confident as ever as she announced, "Maybe this could be my chance to do some good in the world; you know, with visibility like this, maybe I should run for office and represent the LGBTQWXYZwhatever-the-F community."

"There's your campaign slogan right there," Vince said, as Dad, seated on the couch next to Mom, cackled. Maybe it was the excitement of the debut, but Mom finally had all her color back. When I commented to Lorn that seeing her still so bright-eyed in the evening was something new, Lorn whispered back, "Such a great sign of progress . . . but I think you are seeing your mom happy for you."

A warm feeling spread inside me, and I gave Lorn's hand a squeeze. It occurred to me that with Mom doing so well, Lorn could have been thinking about leaving, instead of moving permanently into my bedroom. I held tighter.

Thinking back now, I was a total idiot. Of course, I had no choice but to fall completely in love with her again, even if she hadn't done so much to heal my mom. With the added magic of a nurse, I was toast. There had been a doctor too, but I couldn't recall his name right now. I zeroed in on Lorn, secretly squeezing my hand, her thumb sneaking to the center of my palm to give it a rub that simply placed my brain in a blender.

I watched as Dad handed Mom a little snack plate, stifling a laugh because Dad didn't notice he had used Lisa's favorite plate, which had a beautiful flower and bird on it, and the words: *Here Is Your Snack, Dumbass!* I watched the two of them as I nestled closer to Lorn in the big armchair we were sharing. I saw Vince's eyes flick over to mine, and he whispered something to his wife and they both winked at me like two idiots. I scrunched deeper into the chair, knowing the jig was up and we were the talk of Santora Town. I also went back and forth between thinking we needed more furniture for Lisa's TV screenings, and thinking the shortage of chairs was the perfect setup. The side of my body came completely alive as it was pressed next to Lorn's.

Lisa stopped pacing when she glanced at Lorn and me. Though I was sure she had already told the family about us, she looked like she was gearing up for a general announcement to Sandra and Eddie, so I deflected by tossing out a comment. "Dad, you must have missed sharing

210

a room with mom during all this."

Mom popped some fruit in her mouth as Dad laughed at me. "You kids don't know everything that goes on around here. We hardly spent one whole night apart!"

I looked over to smile at Vince and Lisa, who hadn't missed this bit of news.

"Your father is a sneaky devil," Mom said. "He would duck back into his room before any check-in from you girls." They laughed together on the couch as if they had pulled off a complex and rewarding heist, and maybe they had.

Auntie Etta perked up to add her two cents, "Those two were like a couple of panting teenage rabbits. How many times did I have to lie for you, Stan, when you were sneaking off into the woods—"

"Anything we should all know before the show starts?" Mom interrupted, as we all laughed. Meanwhile, Dad did his proud "heh, heh, heh" laugh under his breath, to assure us it was all true.

"Oh no, no, nothing you need to know about the show," Eddie sang out. "It's better we let it all unfold!" He gestured his last word by rolling up his arms, hands, and then unfurling each finger until he was in a full "Ta-Daaaaa" pose. I noticed something extra-giddy in his voice that made me laugh—and worry. History with Eddie had shown how often my sister and I could be the only ones thoroughly entertained by him. Would this be one of those times, only now in front of thousands of viewers?

I would have worried more if Lorn and I had not been buried under the same blanket and meshed into one chair. While my sister may have risked her TV career by adding Eddie, I couldn't help noticing that I was in heaven. I would have just as gladly watched a mind-numbing game show since, for the first time in over a year, I wanted to be nowhere else on earth than where I was right now. Here with a roomful of people, the warmth of Lorn's body pressed along my entire right side, I hovered somewhere between sleepy contentment and high alert. The last few days had been a blur, and as I waited with my family for the show to begin, I marveled at how quickly a person's entire world can change in a few weeks, or even a few minutes. Once again, Lorn had filled my life as if she had never left, only this time I believed in my heart it was different. Not because I wanted it to be, but because it simply was.

I believed Vince had found out about us this afternoon after Lisa let herself into my room without knocking. "*Oh, my eyes!!! I can't unsee that!!!,*" she yelled, backing out of the room as if she had been hit in the face with a can of mace or, more accurately, my naked ass. With eyes covered, and one free hand flailing, she dramatically backed out of the room, and theatrically smashed into a wall until, still blinding herself, she slammed the door closed. Behind the door the drama continued as she stomped with exaggerated childlike running footsteps as she yelled, "*Vince! Hey, guess what!*" Even though I could tell she faked the stomping run right by the door for our benefit, there was a chance my brother hadn't even stopped by the house, and I knew she would tell him as soon as she could.

At first, Lorn had been horrified and we dived back under the covers, muffling our laughs as we both imagined the view my sister must have taken in. Me, ass in the air, my face not visible (it was buried) and Lorn, wide-spread and white-knuckling the pillows, as if she were hanging on for dear life. I had given Lorn a few seconds to get over her embarrassment before diving, headfirst, back into paradise.

Now the vivid memory made me give her body a squeeze under the blanket, and when she gave me a side look at close range, my heart jumped back to the memory. A part of me was still grateful Lorn didn't fully understand her power over me, but I knew soon enough that jig would be up too.

Mom had a smile on her face every time she looked over at us. She looked a little smug too as if she was silently taking credit for her daughter's newfound happiness. As well she should, I thought. If she hadn't been so bold as to call Lorn to assist her, I wondered if I would have sat on this chair alone, getting skinnier by the day until I at last disappeared, just as Erica had. I whispered into Lorn's ear. "I love you . . . in case you were wondering."

"I sure was."

"*Quiet!*" Lisa yelled over her bowl of popcorn although she was the one who had been yapping loudly to Eddie. "I'm about to start!"

The credits came up, *"Italian Cooking . . . with Spirits! With Lisa Santora & Eddie."* As if we had witnessed a game-winning touchdown, we all wildly cheered.

"You changed the name of the show?" I asked Sandra.

"It was your sister's idea. I thought she was onto something." Lisa licked her lips at Sandra as if she had turned into a pork chop. She was onto something, all right.

"Holy shit, this is actually happening!" Vince said, as he thumped Lisa hard on the back.

Aunt Etta piped up, "When I was in the hospital, my sister told me over and over again that she wanted to teach you how to make her Italian egg biscuits the *right* way."

We all turned to her, then to each other. Since Aunt Etta came to live with us, she had continued to talk about her sister as if she was in the next room, and that she had spent every minute with her during her peaceful rest ("it was a cozy coma, best sleep I ever had"). She insisted her twin sister, Aunt Aggie, had never left her side. Turns out, the ghost of dead Aunt Aggie had an alive and well Italian egg biscuit agenda.

I noticed that Lisa looked pale, as if she was seeing a ghost right then, her face frozen and white as a sheet. Sandra noticed too and said, "I have never seen you look nervous, not even while we were taping live."

Sandra had a lot to learn if she thought my sister ever got nervous.

"Are you okay?" I asked Lisa.

Lisa said, "Auntie Etta, tell me——" but she was shushed by her sidekick, Eddie. "Look at my name!" he squealed, *"And Eddie!"* He was beaming, loose hand flopping against his heart,

"Hot damn! All the boys are going to have to treat me like the superstar I always told them I was!"

Lisa had told me about the early rehearsals, and I knew the show would start out with Lisa alone on the set, introducing her crew and the theme of her first show (all of which she kept a big secret) before bringing out Eddie. I was proud of her, not surprised, but so proud she had made this happen. Still, I agreed with Vince when he walked by and said quietly, "Why is Lisa so freaked out over Auntie Etta's dead sister's egg biscuits?"

Lisa had been sitting close to Sandra on the couch, and from the second the music started Sandra grabbed my sister's hand and held it tight.

I wondered if Sandra's newfound affection came from seeing my sister look so vulnerable that it finally warmed her heart ... or was Lisa spooked from Sandra's newfound affection? My sister's voice coming from the TV grabbed everyone's attention as she bounded onto the same home cooking stage we'd seen at the studio. Well, it wasn't exactly the same. It had been stripped bare of any feminine reminders of the blonde woman she replaced, with New England Patriots football-shaped cutting boards and our favorite bottles of Italian wine lined up along the faux kitchen window over the studio sink.

"Hi, everyone!" Lisa shouted over the applause, "Welcome to *Italian Cooking with Spirits!* I am Lisa Santora, and this is the show where we explore the answers to the following: how come at home almost all women do the cooking, yet all the richest chefs are male? Maybe we ought to stop cooking for free, huh girls?" The audience went bananas. "We will explore other things too, like taking on the mystery of how much booze you add to a dish before it is classified as a drink!" We all laughed along with the audience.

"Lastly, we will also explore how the spirits of my beloved Italian relatives still influence my cooking today. At the risk of being haunted, I plan to pass along *all* my Aunt Aggie's well-guarded secret recipes of the best authentic Italian cooking you have ever tasted!"

As the studio crowd applauded, I looked over at my sister, who shrugged at me, her face still frozen and freaked out. What the hell was going on?

Chef Lisa continued her intro to the live studio audience. "All great food for thought as we explore cooking without any men in the kitchen . . . (the crowd laughed) speaking of which, this is a perfect time to intro my friend and co-hostess: *Eddie!*"

And with that, the studio band played, accompanied by dual squealing, one squeal live from Eddie at 2229 Lakeside Drive and the other from the Boston TV studio as Eddie came flying out on stage . . . screaming for himself, dressed as a pink flamingo. To clarify, a six-foot flaming flamingo wearing a Santa hat, waving Fourth of July sparklers, and dancing toward Lisa with his long, gangly, perfectly shaved legs ending in giant pink flamingo feet.

The camera cut to Lisa's face, and I could tell by the way she was doubled over laughing on the cooking stage she had not seen his outfit prior to this moment. This turned out to be a good move since the audience was howling as much at Lisa's reaction as they were at the prancing flamingo. Here at home, we were also howling with the audience, and I saw Sandra was now rubbing Lisa's back. Lisa had a giant grin on her face, but still looked a bit as if she had seen a ghost. What the hell was up with her?

Chef Lisa the host finally stopped laughing so she could address her co-hostess. "Welcome, Eddie," she said, still doubled over toward the audience. "Did we discuss that you'd show up looking like Big Bird's gay brother who just flew in from Florida?!"

As the studio audience continued to go nuts, Mom said, "You're a hit!" and Dad said, "I need to get on that show!"

"Thanks so much for joining us on our first show, where, if my pal Eddie's getup didn't already give it away, our theme for today is Christmas in July!" The well-trained crowd clapped as if they had just been given a car. Lisa continued prepping her audience in her confident voice. "And if you come from an

Italian family, like I do, and love anything Italian, like Eddie does, (Eddie was hamming it up with a suggestive look that the audience ate up), "then you know no Christmas in July would be complete without Italian egg biscuits!" I turned to my sister as her TV voice said, "My Aunt Aggie used to make the best ones, and I feel my Aunt Aggie wants me to show you all her secrets!"

Auntie Etta leaned forward in her wheelchair with her fist up and yelled at the TV as if her long-lost sister was there in the room. "See? I told you! Aggie said it was one of her biggest regrets, not teaching you how to make those!" Then she followed it up with her signature cackling, spanking the tops of her own legs as she laughed. I had seen my sister do that move so many times. My brother too, in fact.

As I looked at my sister for an explanation, I felt a chill up my back, but it was oddly more like excitement. Lisa shrugged at me and pointed to the screen where she was explaining it to the audience. "I kept having vivid dreams of my Aunt Aggie teaching me how to make all her secret cookie recipes, which she never shared with me while she was alive. Just this morning, I woke up from a dream with her insisting I teach you all how to make her famous Italian egg biscuits."

Aunt Etta let out her cackling laugh and yelled at the Lisa on TV, "Welcome to my world, hotshot! The whole time I was sleeping in the hospital Aggie was yapping at me, telling me what to do, just like she always did." For the first time we all heard a little sadness in Aunt Etta's voice.

Lorn tapped me under the blanket and whispered, "What the . . .?"

I just shook my head.

I was not willing to share yet my similar experience years ago when I was convinced that Aunt Aggie came to me in a dream to tell me to go to Italy to find Erica after she had fled from what she felt for me. Back then, Erica left to protect me from hurting my brother who she was dating first. But here's the cool thing. I woke up from that dream knowing exactly where Erica was. It was the first time I had lost her, long before the final time.

Lisa said, "I assumed I had watched her when I was a kid and remembered it in a dream."

Aunt Etta corrected her. "Huh, that's rich! No way would she let any of the rug rats watch while she made her egg biscuits. Nobody was allowed in the kitchen when she made certain things, and cookies were at the top of the list."

When Aunt Etta said it, I remembered how us kids would get kicked out and how we would crawl under the kitchen table and hide out to see what all the secrets were about. We had always assumed it was to stop us from sticking our fingers in the batter bowls or stealing the tiny ball of rainbow sprinkles. I could see my sister was thinking the same thing.

The rest of the show was hilarious, with Lisa being Lisa and Eddie being, as Lisa called him on the show, "his flaming flamingo self" as her bungling assistant. The studio audience loved every minute of it, and Sandra proclaimed it a huge victory even before she got the call with viewer stats and the news of record-breaking social media posts. People were commenting all through the show that finally there was a cooking show as entertaining as late-night TV.

When Sandra finished her call with the studio execs congratulating her, she walked back over to Lisa, grabbed her by the face, and planted a kiss directly on her lips. That kiss flew well past the length of a friendly peck, and when Sandra pulled back, my sister looked stunned by her luck. Lisa had a hit on her hot little hands, and it appeared she might have a girlfriend as well.

Long after the show ended, Lorn and I still had not dislodged ourselves from the chair we were sharing. Eddie was long gone, off to find his adoring public, which had been texting him from a bar all through the show, and Mom and Dad had gone to bed. Vince also excused himself from our company to head home with Katie, but I don't remember when. I was too wrapped up in Lorn, still joined at my hip in the chair.

We could hear Sandra and Lisa having a deep conversation

in the kitchen while we were enjoying torturing each other alone in the room as we huddled closer. Just before the end of the show, I had thought Lorn was getting sleepy, so under the blanket I had grazed the back of my hand across her nipples, ignoring her attempts to stop me. I could not think of anything more enjoyable than torturing her this way until I had to finally stop, worried her squirming might get noticed. Lisa had already shot me a few "get a room" looks during the show.

Now we were alone in the room, and the privacy was delicious.

"Let's go to bed," she whispered, but I was enjoying teasing her right where we were.

"Let's stay . . . I can't move right now," I said, and she mirrored my evil grin.

"But why?" she said, cupping my crotch and giving me a firm squeeze that got my full attention. Now I was the one squirming. "Okay, lets go to your room," I whispered. Her eyes were filled with longing as she traced her fingers over the fabric around the folds of me, my head spinning from the light touch of her fingertips along with the hardness of her nails. I hated to admit how much the occasional graze of her nails was turning me into a liquid beast. "No, no, I think we should stay out here awhile," she said, and she got me to do that grinding into thin air thing I do when I'm losing my mind.

Lisa and Sandra were still whispering in the kitchen and doing God knows what out there, so my compromised logic made me take Lorn's hand down the front of my yoga pants, so I could grind against her more effectively. She groaned softly when she realized how much I needed her.

I grabbed her wrist to stop her. "Don't move," I said, looking at her, our eyes meeting as if we were in a deep kiss, but there was no kiss; there was simply too much going on. I held her hand still, though she fought me on this. When I had finally calmed a little, I let go of her hand, instantly knowing it was a mistake, but unable to stop myself as I moved against her in a quiet and agonizing slow speed until, without asking, she went deeper.

This turned a stationary chair into a rocking chair, and I was praying my sister was too wrapped up in Sandra to pay any attention to the creaking chair and deep breathing from our side of the living room.

Oh, we would need to go to her room for this next part.

"Let's go," I said, but she pushed deeper.

"Let me finish you . . ."

"No, please . . ."

As it would happen, my "please" didn't help, since it sounded like begging, which I was, so she tightened her grip on me until I finally stopped her. Lorn's eyes were on fire at first, then lit up with a spark of fury, as if I had stolen her lollipop.

"Please," she said into my ear, and I couldn't remember ever wanting anything more.

The need to touch her was unbearable. I would fight fire with fire, I thought, biting gently into her neck as I slid my hand down her backside, reaching under her to bury myself inside.

Lorn sucked in her breath as I pushed deeper, and I knew what she needed. What we both needed . . . and I took her that way. Things went in and out of control after that, just as they used to (maybe more?) until we were both left as a piled heap in the chair with me panting like the downward-facing dog I was.

Since this woman was officially driving me mad, I took her again, and Lorn surprised me by taking me at the same time. We both were in familiar territory, yet frantic, and we shook together until we collapsed again.

Contentment lasted for just a moment until I felt the need rising again, and I whispered, "Let's go to your room."

"We should stay out here awhile more; it's not even that late," she teased me, as she gripped my hips. She was studying my eyes, and I knew I would never be able to keep secrets from this woman, and knowing this was intoxicating. If she ever left me again, I would have to burn this chair in a campfire rather than be reminded of this magical night.

Mom, Dad, and Auntie Etta had long ago gone to bed, and Eddie had done his disappearing act, and I could still hear Lisa and Sandra having a deep conversation, or deep something, in the kitchen.

Lorn was teasing me under the blanket, mercilessly pulling me toward her, knowing I would have to grind against her in that *I have to have her* way that seemed to drive her crazy.

I heard a soft knock on the door. The timing of Eddie (or was it my brother?) made us both laugh. I whispered to Lorn as I pulled away from her, "I will wring his neck. You—stay."

She smiled that smile and I had to walk backward to the door at first, not wanting to take my eyes off Lorn curled up in the chair, the blanket still moving with her ragged breathing. The fiery connection between us was so powerful that it didn't seem real.

I floated across the room wondering, *Could it all be as perfect as it seems in this very moment?* Looking back at her once more, I wondered if this was the exact moment I could finally shake the fear of losing her. Or would there always be a part of me that believed however strong it felt, love could prove fragile again, just as before? I wanted to believe it was different this time, and my life yet again was taking a path I could not have imagined and could not have been happier to follow.

From across the room, everything in her eyes said, Yes, *this is real.* Actress Lorn had employed Nurse Lorn to heal my mother, heal me, and finally build a life together.

Reluctantly I reached the door and looked back once more to apologize for the interruption, but while I was keeping my eyes locked on hers as I opened the door, Lorn stood up, blanket tumbling to the floor, her jaw gaping and everything in her eyes saying, *No, this is not real.*

Had she figured out she'd made a mistake in the time it took me to walk across a room? The nursing and lesbo life were not for her?

It took several excruciating seconds for me to realize it

might be much worse than that.

I kept my hand on the door handle to steady myself: *Was she ill?* Now, when I felt all was perfect, was she going to drop dead? Were these the last few seconds of our happy life together?

I croaked a terrified whisper. "Lorn . . . *what?*"

Lorn was not looking at me; she was looking past me.

And, just like in every bad horror movie ever made, slowly I turned.

Erica stood in the doorway.

Guess Who's Back, Back Again

I was stunned silent. Behind me I heard Lorn whisper "She's . . . not . . ."

As usual, my sister stepped into the room to fill in the gaps when words failed me. Horrified, Lisa shouted, "No, no, no! She's dead to us!" Then she pointed her finger at Erica and barked, "Erica, you're dead to us. We all agreed. Even Mom."

Stunned, I remained silent, blinking as if my eyes were failing, as Lisa said, "Mare, she's dead to us, right? We all agreed."

Then Erica spoke. "Leaving like I did wasn't the right thing to do, but I had to—"

Lisa snapped at her. "You must be fucking crazy to come back like this." Erica took a step back behind the threshold again.

Erica, in a small voice I barely recognized, said, "I'm sorry, I do know this is a shock, but there was no way I could have known—"

"That you would shatter my sister's life?" Lisa spat, stepping in front of me. "Destroy her for the better part of a year?"

Erica slowly shook her head, looking past Lisa, her eyes locking onto mine. "If I ever thought I would live to see how much I hurt you—"

Lisa said, "You know what moment this is? It's the moment you won't live to see if you don't get the fuck out of here."

Somehow, Erica ignored my crazed sister and her balled-up fists, keeping her eyes steadily on me as she said, "I never would have left you if I didn't have to." She shook her head, starting to cry. "I love you and I *never* would have left us; somewhere inside you must know that."

"But you did," I managed to choke out, "and the only question is, why would you come back—"

"I didn't have a—"

Lisa whipped her head around to me, and said through clenched teeth, "Why the fuck is she still talking?"

Lisa was right, we had all agreed. Dead and buried. She was gone for so long she didn't get to come back . . . not ever. She was dead to us.

Without deciding to, I heard myself say, voice shaking, "After all this time, why—"

"—I had to," Erica said, tears tumbling. I noticed, even with her clothes hanging loosely from her, she was full-on quaking at her belly, and even with all the suffering she had caused me, I wanted to know why, I wanted to reach for her . . .

No.

This was the woman who had left me *forever*. She had been quite clear about that word on the last day I saw her. She was gone. *Left her phone, her clothes, her everything* gone.

Her words came back fresh as if no time had passed. *I just don't love you. I can't try to make this work, not even for another day. Please don't hate me.* Then the log cabin door closed between us.

But I did hate her.

I hated her still. The heat rose as hot in my face as it had in Lisa's. Yet when I saw her, almost not recognizing her for a split second . . . had cutting her hair so short been part of her need to start a new life? Cutting off something I had especially loved? I tried to blink away my thoughts, like she might disappear again and that maybe she was not really here at all.

And, just like that, the memory of the woman who had destroyed my life, a woman I had finally let go of, still had a hold on me. How could this be happening? I wanted to deny my heart was pounding as if something miraculous had just happened. As if a long-ago and long-given-up dream had come true . . . but there was something very bad about this . . . something I feared losing . . . if only I could think of what that was.

Lorn.

I spun around as if I had forgotten she was in the room (hadn't I?) in time to see Lorn backing slowly away from all of us as if the bus she had long been waiting for had finally arrived and rolled to a stop, and instead of opening its squeaky doors to welcome her aboard, she watched it explode right in front of her, its heat making her retreat.

I opened my mouth to say something to her, but no words came, and, worse, she saw me try. Lorn found something to say, but not to me. Her eyes were fixed on Erica, and it was her she spoke to. "I always felt you were still here. I thought of you every day, but you were supposed to be—"

"Dead to us!" Lisa yelled. "Lorn, she's dead to us. All of us. How many times do I have to say this?"

Lorn turned and walked away, heading toward her room as we all watched. Mom and Dad had come back, but I don't know when. Why were people leaving, coming back, and leaving again? My head spun, and I wished I could stop the world from moving another inch.

I wanted to call out after Lorn, but there were no words. How could I have known Erica would come back? How could I have known either of them would? I wanted to tell her I was as shocked as she was . . . but of course I wasn't.

Erica was not dead, and the lie our family had all agreed to tell ourselves had never included Lorn. Even I had only recently believed Erica was gone forever when I finally let her go.

I turned back to look at Erica to make sure she was really there, but Lisa blocked my view, stepping between us.

Lisa said, "Since you are dead to us, this night never happened. My sister can't go back to where she was when you left her, but you can. You know what we always say, either you are *in*, or you are *out*, and we all decided you are *out!*"

With that, Lisa slammed the door right in Erica's face, as if she were a Jehovah's Witness with a vacuum cleaner side hustle.

There was a finality to the sound of the door frame rattle that was comforting to my brain. It was done.

But it wasn't done. I was in deep trouble. I knew this because even as the door slam reverberated through the house, I was thinking: *Erica had come back for me.*

Lisa wiped her hands together with a few smacks as if it was handled and she was merely getting the last of the dust mites off. Then my sister got in my face and said, "The last thirty seconds never happened. Now don't be stupid, and go after Lorn."

With that, Lisa walked back into the kitchen, and I was left churning in the wake of her simple-as-that strut. I wished it were as simple as that. I froze, staring at the door while I imagined Erica walking away, down the long driveway. A fleeting sense of panic gripped me, *Could I catch her?* Even just to ask a few more questions?

I needed to go after Lorn.

But I couldn't move.

Lisa came back in from the kitchen and got right back in my face.

"Go," she said, pointing toward Lorn's room as if I were a child being punished. Our eyes locked. Lisa could still scare me when she wanted to, and right now she was pulling out all the stops. I went, but as I did, with each step I felt I was being pulled into two pieces: wanting to go comfort and reassure Lorn—and having the equally horrible feeling that Erica might disappear, never to be seen again (again).

When I reached Lorn's room, I found her standing inside her doorway as if she wasn't sure what she should be doing. Some drawers were open, her closet too, things tossed on the bed.

"Well, this complicates things, doesn't it?" she whispered at her pile of clothes.

Her voice was so different from Erica's, I thought as a sick feeling settled in my stomach. The comparisons had begun again. Well, yes, it did complicate things, but had she thought of leaving already?

Was she already packing?

Was Erica still outside somewhere?

Would Lorn disappear again?

Would Erica?

I was horrified she could hear my thoughts, and the silence between us felt like a drumroll.

"Why didn't you tell me?" Lorn whispered.

"I didn't know she would come back . . ."

"No. Why didn't you tell me she wasn't really dead to you, that you still loved her all this time?"

I slowly shook my head and worried I didn't sound convincing as I said, "Lorn, that door is closed."

"Only because your sister closed it. I don't think *you* would have."

I should have said something right then, anything, because my open mouth and silence were worse than if I had protested. Would I have been able to close the door? And why had there been even a few seconds when I had forgotten Lorn was in my life . . . and in the living room . . . and in that chair?

"I need to leave," Lorn said, turning back into her room.

"Don't," I said weakly from her doorway, but even as I spoke this word, I realized I would not have believed me either. All I could do was stand still until she closed a second door on me. And if she had expected me to open it, well, now I had failed her twice.

Mother, May I?

"Mom?"

"Come in, hun," Mom said. Her voice was tired and I knew she had not slept well again. Three nights in a row that I was aware of, but I wondered if she hadn't slept well for the last two weeks. I knew I might be just as much to blame for her insomnia as her struggle to adapt to her meds. For the hundredth time in the last few days, I fought the urge to call Lorn.

"You didn't sleep," I said.

"I slept enough," she said, smiling.

"You've been sleeping badly for weeks. Maybe I should call Lorn?" I said, sounding more hopeful than threatening. "I could tell her you may need something for sleep?"

"Hun, I can pick up a phone, and often I do." Mom gave a calculated pause. "Do you want to call Lorn?" When I didn't answer, she patted a spot near her and I sat on the edge of her bed. Mom waited. She is not like Lisa, my brother, or even Dad, who would have filled in any silence long before now, regardless whether any of them had anything to say.

When I realized she was holding her ground to get me to talk, I said softly, "I wouldn't know what to say to her."

"Do you know any better what you would say to Erica?"

I shook my head, feeling the sting of tears.

"You still miss her too. You miss them both," Mom said. I didn't want it to be that simple, but of course it was, and the simplicity was what made it so complicated. When I didn't respond, Mom said, "It took me a long while to learn that from great pain you can experience greater compassion, and from great sorrow, greater happiness."

I stayed quiet. Since when was my mother Confucius? I bit my tongue so I wouldn't tease her.

She smirked at me. "You know, from the darkest soil come the most beautiful flowers and all that shit . . . do you understand?"

"Yes," I said, laughing a little, "it means I'm knee-deep in fertilizer."

She snickered her masculine laugh as she patted my leg, in the less affectionate, more official way that was Mom's style. "I'm saying, people who have learned to love at the deepest levels have first traveled through the darkest times. These are the people you want to be surrounded by; these are the people you want to love and be loved by."

"What are you getting at, Mom? They both left me, many times in fact."

"Maybe they did years ago, but Lisa said you had let them both go."

That rat.

"Mom, Lisa slammed the door in Erica's face!"

"She was protecting you and Lorn. Your sister has always done that for you in her own unique way." Mom's smile was contagious, and I was certain Mom and I were both remembering the same Lisa moments: those times in Jamaica . . . that time in the rec hall at Campground Ladies . . . that time on the school track . . . and this time with our front door.

"I'm saying you're lucky if you can find even one person like that, and in your life you found two. You have to figure out what is the best decision for you . . . and for both girls."

Both girls. Mom had a way of cutting to the chase, and for the first time in my life I realized she had given that to my sister, only in a uniquely Lisa-like package. Regardless of the fact that Erica had left me, and I had let Lorn go, I missed them both. With Erica it was a distinctly more distant pain, but it was a longing that clearly never fully went away. There were too many perfect years spent together, too many questions about why we ended, and it was all amped up by the belief that I'd never see her again. With Lorn, the pain was crushing and raw as if I had finally been given a gift only to lose it again.

Mom said, "Remember weeks ago when you and Lorn took me for treatment and I slept the entire ride home?"

"You were stressed. You've been through so much."

Mom smirked at me. "Yeah, well, I wasn't sleeping."

"You sneak," I said.

Mom shrugged. "Lorn was talking about all her preparation to become a nurse, and how everyone tells you about the hard stuff, but she said nobody ever told her about the most beautiful, magical moments that you share with your patients."

I remembered looking over at Lorn when she said that, her voice trailing off, her eyes replaying scenes that Hollywood writers would have killed to have in their arsenal. I could feel my mother studying my face. Why couldn't she just tell me what to do?

As much as she might want to, I knew she wouldn't. Right there is where Mom and Lisa were the most different. Then she surprised me.

"Hun, go talk to Lorn," Mom said, giving my leg a decisive pat as if it were all settled.

I jumped up instinctively when she said it, as if I had been waiting for permission and now had my marching orders. When I hesitated, Mom said, "Remember, when Erica left, she didn't surface for almost a year. While it seems to me Lorn has been working her way back to you this whole time. She never really let you go, but she stayed out of your way so you could build a life with Erica."

"That's true." My heart sank. I should not have let Lorn go. "You need her, too," I said. "And you shouldn't suffer because of my stupidity."

Mom shook her head. "No, hun, don't go looking for her unless you can admit *you* need her, not me. All I need is for

229

you kids and for your father to be happy, and I need Lorn to be happy, too. Marie, you finally found each other again—"

"But you loved Erica too."

"Of course I did. I'll love whomever you love, whomever you choose . . . but you do have to choose."

"You've never told me what to do before, not about something like this."

"Well, you haven't done something this stupid before."

I nodded yes, and laughed at myself as a few tears tumbled down my face. My mind raced but doubt was seeping back in. It had been weeks, and for all I knew Lorn could be back in California, having ditched her real medical bag for a prop, playing a nurse on TV.

I remembered the time Lorn saw me sitting out by the lake on the Adirondack chair near our dock. I signaled for her to sit with me and we looked at each other, and I felt that when she was around magic happened. I marveled how her eyes were brighter than the sky, and I remember thinking this was the first moment I knew she belonged here with my family, that she belonged here with me. By this dock, by this lake. I knew that day that Lorn needed to be with my family who loved and needed her. I admitted to myself that I loved and needed her.

The memory left a such a pit in my stomach that I was attempting to avoid taking another risk on her. "She left you, too, Mom. She's your nurse and she's not even checking on you—-"

"Lorn calls me at least twice a day to be sure you're keeping up with my pill schedule," Mom said. "I told her you were, but neither daughter of mine poses a threat to her job security."

Right then Mom's phone vibrated beside her bed, and I glanced down to see the caller ID: *Lorn Elaine, Marie's Friend.*

It was exactly nine o'clock, time for Mom to take her medicine. Maybe it was time for me to take mine.

"Why don't you answer it?" Mom said.

I lunged for it on the third ring, and told myself it was because Lorn would be worried about why Mom wasn't answering.

"Hi, Lorn . . . it's me."

"Is your mom all right?" she asked, panic rising in her voice.

My eyes teared up at the sound of her and at her deep concern and love for my Mom. How could I have been so dumb? And was it too late?

"Mom is fine; she's right here." I smiled at Mom before walking out to the hallway. When I glanced back, Mom pretended to read the Martha Stewart magazine she kept by her bed. "Mom told me you've been checking up on my nursing skills."

Lorn was silent.

"Thank you," I said stupidly. "How are you?"

She stayed silent so I didn't wait for an answer. "Please come home," I blurted, walking farther down the hall so I could beg and still keep some dignity. I whispered into the phone, "I want you to please come home. Will you? Come back to Mom . . . come back to us?"

I closed my eyes to block out her screaming silence. When I opened them again, I caught Mom looking hopeful and walked slowly back to hand her the phone. I concentrated on stopping my tears as I shook my head. "She only wants to talk to you."

Mom made her *isn't life ridiculous* face as she took the phone.

"Hi, dear," she said. "Yes, yes, I'm fine . . . No, perfectly well . . . It could be better I suppose, but sleep is overrated, isn't it? . . . Okay, well, I stand corrected. You would know." I knew what was coming next, as Mom had been saying this as long as I could remember, to get our lazy asses out of bed. "Up and at 'em, plenty of time to sleep when we die."

I stayed standing near my mother's bed, knowing I should leave the room so they could speak privately, but selfishly wanting to hear Lorn's voice. I thought: I'm in love with her, and I'm an idiot. The return of Erica had rattled me, but it didn't change the fact that Erica had quit on us while Lorn's love had been unshakable.

"I will, I won't forget. Thank you, dear, for calling," and Mom ended the call before I could stop her.

I didn't plan to sound like a child who had lost their pet, but

231

my voice was shaky as I said, "You hung up. She said she couldn't come back, and she won't tell me where she is."

Mom calmly laid her phone down, saw me eyeball it, and knew I was considering a lunge.

"Hun, she's staying at the motel at the bottom of the hill. I told her not to stay in that dirty place, but you know Lorn; she didn't want to be too far in case we needed her. Which you do."

I kissed the top of Mom's head before flying out of the room. She called out after me, "Not sure, but I don't think I was supposed to tell you that!"

"Not sure my ass!" I called back, running like I was chasing a fugitive who could skip town at any moment.

Even My Mother Agrees

I pulled into the motel lot and parked alongside Lorn's rental car. I wanted to kiss that damned car. I wanted to kiss her. There were only eight cars in the unkept lot, so I took my best guess and knocked on the door closest to the car. I would knock on the entire row of doors if I had to.

When Lorn opened the door, I could see her sharply take in a breath. My throat tightened as if I might cry again. I was not prepared for how much I missed her face, how I had forgotten in just two weeks all the beautiful details.

"I love you," I said, thinking that at a time like this being direct was best after I had wasted two weeks of our lives.

She almost imperceptibly shook her head no, and it was all I could do to stop myself from reaching for her. How could I have risked losing her? I had not planned to still be standing in the motel doorway when I said it, but everything came tumbling out. "I shouldn't have let you go, and I never will again. Can you forgive me? Even my mother agrees I'm an idiot." When she said nothing, I added, "Do you think you could ever risk being with me again?"

I moved toward her, but her stepping back was clearly not an invitation. She had backed away much like Erica had before my sister slammed the door right in her face. Was a door in my face what was next for me? All I could think to do was plead.

"I'll find a way to earn your trust again. Whatever I have to do, I'll do it. However long it takes." I was well aware I sounded like the ending of a cheesy '80s movie, but what else could I do?

Lorn shook her head. "It's me I don't trust. You shouldn't be here."

I moved toward her again and she danced another step back. Just in case that wasn't clear enough, she put her hand up like a crossing guard and said, "No . . . I can't."

Well, that was pretty clear. But she wasn't done.

"I need to let you go to Erica. You should have gone to her long before now."

"I don't want to go anywhere," I said, trying not to shout. "I don't want to chase after someone who didn't want to be with me. I mean, I realize that's what I am doing right now, but that's beside the point." I could tell by the look on her face I was not getting through.

"Lorn, this is it for me. I know that now. You and I both have to learn to trust each other again. Believe me, I struggled with that one myself. But I know now you're the one I'm supposed to be with, to spend the rest of my life with. It's you that I want. You're perfect; I'm not, but please tell me you'll still have me?"

"You have no idea how not perfect I am."

"I chose to come to *you*."

"I'm guessing you don't know where Erica is."

She had me on that one, but to be fair to me, I hadn't even looked, and not only because my sister would have killed me. I started talking faster like it was 11:58 p.m., I was on death row, and the governor's phone was on the fritz.

"I know where I need to be, and it's with you. I don't care how long it takes, I'll convince you. It may not be right now, but I will . . . and I trust you won't leave because the nurse in you would not leave my mother until you see her completely well." I knew I was using my mother, but I saw her soften just a little. "I have at least that much time, right?" I tried to smile at her but I knew my ugly-cry face was mangling it.

Lorn whispered, "I'm sorry."

"Don't apologize to me. I should have told you about Erica—"

"No. I should have told you she was sick," Lorn said.

"I don't understand. You mean, my mother?"

"I should have given you the chance to go to her if that is what you would choose to do," Lorn said.

I stood frozen, unmoving, not understanding.

"I'm so sorry," Lorn said. "I didn't know where she was, but I knew she was sick. She heard I was a nurse, and she contacted me."

"My mother contacted you?" I asked quietly, but deep inside I already knew the truth before she said it.

Lorn said, "Listen to me. I knew Erica was sick. She and I both believed she had no chance of getting better."

"What . . .?" My voice cracked. I tried to figure out what she was talking about.

"Erica contacted me a long time ago, when you two were still together. She believed she was dying and there was nothing that could save her. I insisted she send me her records, to try to help with my medical contacts, but it was bad. Her doctors, Erica herself, and even I knew the terrible odds were that she would not survive the cancer. Over these past months you and your family talked as if she didn't survive, and I easily believed it—until, like a ghost, I saw her."

My head was spinning. I put my hand on the door to steady myself. It didn't work and I slid down against it until I sat sprawled on the floor, still in the doorway.

Lorn knelt in front of me and took both my hands to stop them from trembling. She waited until I looked her in the eyes, my own blinking in shock.

Then Lorn said, "You know how strong Erica is. She didn't want you to watch her die. She didn't want you to go through it, to grieve over her before she was gone. She wanted you to start a new life."

I could barely whisper, "What . . .?"

"That's why she left."

I was stunned. "She left me to go off and die alone?" I found it hard to breathe. None of this made sense. But actually it did. Erica's short hair (she hated short hair), the thinness of her . . . and I hadn't noticed then, but she had looked so pale. Only now could I finally see it, so late to the game, just as it had been with my mother. Can you ever notice something so gradual and terrible when it's happening to the people you love the most?

"Come inside," Lorn said, trying to help me up.

"No," I said, pulling her hand away. I hadn't meant to be so rough.

"I should have told you, but she swore me to patient confidentiality. She knew what she was doing. Still, it's no excuse. I wondered for so long if I should have told you, so you could say goodbye. She was very, very sick—"

"But she didn't die! Where is she now?" Nothing could mask the anger rising in my voice. "How about you finally do the right thing now, Lorn, and tell me where the fuck she is!"

Tears streamed down Lorn's face. "I promise you, this time I really don't know." I could see she was telling the truth. But it didn't matter. Because at that moment I let myself acknowledge that I knew exactly where Erica would be.

Forlorn

An hour later, after sitting, frozen, at the entrance to Camptown Ladies, staring at the gate and the sign swinging in the breeze, still making the same rusted cry as it squeaked on its hinges, I realized I didn't have a key with me. But I also knew I could easily smash the lock off the chain with one hit of a stone. Instead, I left my car at the entrance, and walked into the camp.

About a half mile down, where pavement was swallowed by dirt roads and branched out to all the rockier roads leading to the campsites, I walked straight through until I saw my cabin at the back of the campground. The thick canopy of pine trees where the cabin was nestled made it look like early evening rather than midmorning, but I had known it would. I remember feeling that the loss of sunlight was worth it in exchange for the feeling that the cabin was protected by a thick warm blanket of pine trees. As I approached, I saw the red solar camp lantern in the porch window flickering as it always did this time of day, with not enough sunlight to keep it on and charged to do any good in the evening. The front door was always unlocked, but now it was open. Erica appeared at the front door long before I reached it. How long had she been waiting?

How long had we both been waiting? It was the first time I realized our time apart was a loss for both of us. She looked small in the darkened doorway, her body always trim, but never skinny like this. The size of her revealed the horrors she had been through. I tried to read her face as I stepped up on the porch, but with the screen door between us it was too dark. I took a deep breath as I opened the door.

"Why didn't you let me take care of you?" I asked.

"Lorn told you." I nodded. "She could lose her nursing license for that," Erica said, "but I think she kept that secret long enough."

"She kept that secret way *too* long." I saw something flash in Erica's eyes: confused, sad, maybe hopeful?

"It's not her fault what I did," Erica whispered. "This was all me."

I wasn't sure in that moment who I was angrier at. "Why didn't you believe in me?" I asked, "Why wouldn't you let me take care of you?"

"There was nothing to take care of. I thought I was a goner," she said, trying to smile, but I saw her lips trembling. I strained to hear her when she said, "I couldn't have us end that way. Knowing I wouldn't survive—and worried I might take you down with me."

"You thought it was better to leave me thinking you just stopped loving me? That you had quit on us, and maybe there was someone else you loved more, and not this terrible thing—"

I stopped talking when I wondered whether she might have been right. After all, it had been the anger that helped replace the dark sadness when she left, followed by the distraction of my mother, and then the distraction of Lorn. If I had lost Erica to death, would I ever have healed?

I felt how deep a black hole would have been left. I might never have been strong enough to climb out. I knew as well as Erica did that I might not have. Just believing she fell out of love with me had nearly taken me down with her.

"I hoped in some way you would know in your heart that I never would have left unless I had to," Erica said.

I shook my head, "No, I never thought that even once. I thought there was someone else for the longest time; then I thought it was just me—"

"No," she said, "not you."

"Erica, I don't understand. You chose to shatter my life, our life together. Was it because you didn't trust I would have stayed by your side through . . . I don't even know what happened to you, because you didn't give me the chance. You still haven't."

"Marie, no. Just the opposite. I knew how much you loved me, and I knew you would be there for all of it, right down to the tragic end."

I barely whispered, "But it didn't end . . ."

"None of it ended. Not my life, not my love for you. When I didn't die when they said, and I miraculously started to turn the corner, I was consumed with living for you. Imagining the day I could come back is what kept me going. And when I started to believe I might actually make it, I fought being selfish every day. I wanted you to know I was still alive, still loving you, even if you had moved on . . . and you did move on. There is a part of me that is glad you did—"

"Only because I didn't know!"

Erica stared at me with eyes made more intense by the hollow of weight loss around them, still beautiful, just more heartbreaking. "In a million years, I would never have left you, not for any other reason."

"Other than to save me," I whispered, shaking my head, finally getting it.

"I don't want to complicate your life, Marie. I know what Lorn used to mean to you, and how she must have saved you. That's exactly why I sent her to you."

"I—don't understand . . ."

"Almost three months after I left you, over a year ago, I called your sister from the hospital. It was selfish, but I wanted to see if you were okay before I . . ."

"Died?"

"Yes," she said, "but she hung up on me, telling me to stop calling. I don't blame her."

That sounded like Lisa. Wait a minute.

I was horrified as I asked, "My sister knew you were sick?"

239

"No. Of course she would have told you, so I didn't tell her that. She wanted to protect you and asked me to stop calling, to stay away from you so you could heal, and before she hung up she let it slip she was now more worried about your mother."

My head was spinning as I was putting it together now—finally getting it.

"You contacted Lorn."

Erica nodded. "I asked Lorn to please go to your family. I knew you would need somebody if you were facing another loss, and maybe you would need Lorn even more than your mother did."

I said slowly, "So you shared your diagnosis, knowing Lorn would not be able to repeat it."

"I know it was a terrible thing to do, but I needed Lorn to go to you because I couldn't. She was the best person I could think of."

"But . . . you got better," I whispered.

She smiled sadly, nodding. "Yes. It made no sense; it wasn't supposed to happen, but it did. Knowing there was even a slight chance I might see you again started to make me stronger, but I was too weak to resist leaving you alone with your new life. I had to see it was over for us, so maybe I could move on someday too. But more than that I had to tell you why I left. And that I had never stopped loving you." I could see her body trembling; tears falling, we mirrored each other. I could barely hear her as she said, "Not for one second."

More than her body looking fragile, one of the strongest women I had ever known had had her spirit crushed along with her illness. She had thought I could move on, and I eventually thought I could as well.

She has no idea, I thought. So I told her. "I loved you more than life," I said, emotion flooding me as I attempted to cover my crying face, remembering how many times I had sworn it would be the last time I cried for her yet here I was again. Was it really true?

I had never really lost her.

240

For the second time that day, I was brought to my knees.

I felt Erica drop in front of me just as Lorn had as she pulled my hands from my face so I could see her. "I'm here," she whispered, "and I'm so sorry for what I did to you, and what I did to us. I'm sorry that I would do it all the same way again, knowing what I thought I knew then."

When our eyes met, I could see all the love was still there, just as it ever was, and what I felt in my heart I knew was the same in hers. I was feeling an anger for Lorn rising in me. "If Lorn had told me, I would have run to you, you know that. She never gave me the chance—"

"No, sweetheart, it was more than that. She had no reason to believe I would live. Nobody had any reason to believe that, least of all a nurse. She would have been breaking my last request to send you there, only to watch me die." Erica shook her head as if the painful memory had brought her right back and she needed to shake it from her. Her hold on my face weakened as she said, "There were several weeks, maybe months, where I was sure I was already dead. I don't remember a lot of it, and I'm glad. It's all so cloudy. The only thing that made it tolerable was knowing I was able to spare you from it all."

Erica rambled a bit, about the hospital she was in, the experimental treatments that seemed to be mercifully quickening her end, and she talked of a woman who came to visit her every day, who looked just like my Aunt Aggie. "Or, maybe it was a reoccurring dream," she said. "The woman looked just like her and kept telling me to come back here. That I had to live and to come back to you." Erica looked as confused as I was as she told the story. "Your Aunt Aggie died a long time ago. I feel like I went crazy during that time, like my brain will never be sharp again."

"You have many other skills," I said, and she melted me with her smile. But it soon faded.

"As surprised as you were to see me, I'm more shocked than anyone to still be here, except maybe my doctors, and except maybe Lorn."

My heart ached on hearing Lorn's name, and I wanted the anger to come back.

"Once I started to get better, so slowly, I was told by everyone how people don't survive the type of blood disease I had. You have to understand that Lorn knew too much about what I was facing. I was never supposed to be here."

I still couldn't wrap my mind around all this. All that time, I had been thinking I was the one suffering the most, and she had been to the brink of death while I had no idea.

Erica said, "I remember a little more each day, and I will tell you everything I can, but, Marie, I mean it when I tell you that you deserve to have a life with Lorn if that's what you want. I promise, I only want for you what makes you happy. I only came back because for some reason I needed you to know I was still here."

We were both crying hard now as her voice trailed off, and she let go of me, saying, "I think now it was so selfish of me to come back."

When she backed up a bit, I went into full panic mode. I reached for her face and pulled her to mine, fully remembering her kiss, even from a face now so hauntingly thin, but so beautiful, and a different body that seemed unfamiliar pressed against me. Her illness had not totally stripped the strength from her as she finally pulled me harder against her.

With perfect timing, as it had always been, we both came alive in our kiss.

I whispered against her lips, "Thank God," as memories flooded my heart and mind. How had I forgotten so much? "I'm so sorry . . . I didn't know . . . I should have known . . ."

How could I not still love her?

So many years ago I had been watching and resisting her for months, before we both had no choice in resisting anymore. Erica. The first woman my brother Vince had ever loved, the woman who had mended my broken heart after Lorn ran away in her midlife gay panic. Then she became Erica, the woman I realized I had fallen for. It had been a wonderful, glorious mess.

One that my brother Vince survived just fine, and one that led to what everyone thought would be my lifelong love. I remembered the years, months, minutes and moments we had, the electricity of that kiss and how it had ignited during a thunderstorm on a rooftop . . . It was all coming back to life on the same cabin floor she had built for me. For us.

I was finally allowing myself to experience the flood of memories I'd been fighting to keep from the surface during my life without her. I was trying not to remember the one day she had inexplicably started to pull away from me, being distant at first, followed by the nights where she picked fights with me so she could leave the table, and the dinners she would not eat, even when it was Lisa's cooking. I thought she had stopped loving me. I thought she hated me. She must have known the truth of her illness then.

Now that she was in my arms again, I could pinpoint the exact day with such clarity, the minute we had started to end and all the days that followed before the end. Why hadn't I seen it more clearly for what it was?

I broke away from Erica's kiss.

"It was that night, that dinner Lisa made that you refused to eat, or even look at me as we sat at the table not speaking. It was so easy to think maybe you loved someone else."

I pulled her to me into a tighter embrace as she whispered, "That was the day I found out."

"You stayed one more week before you left," I said.

"It was the worst week of my life, worse even than that moment at the doctor's office."

Of all the devastation I felt, it had been only the beginning of the horror facing her. And she had been alone.

"I had read about unproven treatments, doctors in Germany who were willing to give a few desperate treatments a try when all the doctors here gave me no hope. I had to try. But the doctors here told me I would be cutting the line, skipping treatment to go right to palliative care, the *keep you comfortable* care, and the next day I was flying like a bat out of hell to get as far away from you as I could, to try any experimental treatment for the 1% chance that someday I might see you again. Nobody, especially the doctors and nurses, including Lorn, ever thought I would get through it alive."

My heart sank again at the mention of Lorn's name, and Erica didn't miss this.

"You're not free to be with me, and I didn't expect you to be. I just couldn't live the rest of my life without telling you the truth. That I would never have quit on us, unless I thought . . ."

"That you were dying," I finished. "We were supposed to stay together for life. That was our plan, in sickness and in health, remember?"

"Except this wasn't sickness; this was death."

I gripped her by her shoulders and said, "Only it wasn't, and Lorn didn't give me the chance to be with you."

"Because I threatened her. She had to keep my confidentiality. I was supposed to be only weeks away from death, and I knew it would be easier if you thought I chose to leave you. I also knew if you could ever have the chance to feel love again after us, she was the only one. And, there's this: I know you love her."

"I love you," I said, trying to sound strong, knowing this was the truth but also that there was this other truth.

Erica said, "Lorn has come back into your life for a reason, and I'm not sure you can throw it all away."

"Like you did before?" I said. "Lorn and I only happened again because I didn't understand why you left, and that was her fault for not telling me. She just told me she always feared being with me because *she knew you might come back!*"

"She feared it because she loved you. Lorn never believed I would live, and we both knew she loved you all the time we were together—and she loves you still. And you love her."

I couldn't say a word to any of that. I looked down, not wanting her to see the truth of it all in my eyes.

"Marie, even if she had told you, and you were able to find me overseas to be by my side and watch me die, Lorn would've feared losing you forever to our memory. And you know that would have been true. You might not ever have recovered from the loss of us. It took a lot of convincing, but Lorn finally agreed she would keep my secret."

"Because she was a nurse and she couldn't tell me—"

"Do you understand it would have been much easier for her to tell you, but she knew how you would suffer? She didn't tell you *because she loves you.*"

I asked her in a desperate whisper, "Don't you think you lived so we could have this second chance?"

"No," she said. "It's a fact that I lived, but it doesn't guarantee a second chance for me at all. I always knew you loved her first. The second chance you're getting is with Lorn."

I couldn't say a word. She was right, and we both knew it.

"I knew if I came back, it might make things much more difficult for you, but that is where I was selfish. I told myself you had a right to know I was still out there, still loving you. And now you have two women who love you completely, with me placing you in this terrible position."

It was ridiculous, but now I mourned the simplicity of how I thought I had lost her, and how my anger had been healing.

I had missed so many signs. She had packed only one bag of clothes, and, besides us, she had left so many things behind. I'd stood in the doorway of our bedroom and accused her of the most awful things. Only a cheater would leave so suddenly, and Erica had not denied it when I accused her. People with a love like ours would take years to drift apart unless there was a third person involved. The explosion of us had been too complete, and the shrapnel had taken out everything in its wake. I was so sure there was nothing left. And my certainty made me never suspect anything else. Lisa had been the first to announce Erica was dead to us, and in solidarity the rest of my family had agreed.

And of course this wasn't Lorn's fault . . .

"If I only had known, none of this would have happened with—" I couldn't say Lorn's name. I knew it wasn't true. Even with Erica right in front of me, there was still a part of me that had felt Lorn was supposed to come back to me.

"If you had only told me," I whispered.

"I needed all the strength I had to leave. They told me there was no chance, but I had to try if ever I was—"

"To come back?" I asked. "Erica, how did you survive?"

She shook her head. "Who knows? Maybe the will to live? I like to think it was my love for you, but who knows? Maybe just dumb luck. I only came back to make sure you know I didn't stop loving you, not even for a second, and to gather some of my things if anything was still left."

It was all still here for her. I hadn't gotten rid of anything. I had simply abandoned the house and all our memories the way she had left it.

Erica's plan had worked. I was able to love Lorn again only because I thought Erica had let me go. I reached for Erica's hand and felt her trembling.

She took my face in her hands, and when she did, the hope sprung within me again, only to be crushed by memories flipping between Erica and then Lorn, the woman who I believed had saved me just a few weeks ago. And I believed I had saved Lorn, too.

This time when I looked at Erica, tears spilled from my eyes. I was so deeply thankful that she was alive, so deeply affected by the feelings that were flooding back. She had once rescued me from the pain of losing Lorn, my first love—and now, so many years later, it was Lorn's love that had stopped my spiraling down. I could not lie to myself that it was my love for Lorn that had lifted me back up and given me a second chance to be with my first love.

Erica nodded as if she heard my thoughts, felt my doubts, her eyes tearful along with mine. I said, "The truth is, Lorn rescued me, and my mother, and in some ways my whole family. She came back so closed off at first, until finally she trusted I could love her again, and she risked so much if I couldn't."

Erica gently let go of me. "But you did love her again. And you loved her first, and she is ready to be with you after all this time. I can't let you walk away from that."

A long silence passed between us before she spoke again. "If it's okay, I'll stay here for a little bit until I work out a plan. I might head back to California where some of my business contacts are," she said, and her attempt at a sad smile broke my heart as I imagined her thinner body attempting to do her house contracting work. I worried, stupidly: could she still climb a ladder with a five-gallon bucket of paint?

I finally rose to my feet, and reached down to pull her up with me, but she would not look up from the floor. "I'm sorry," she said. "I should not have come back. It was so selfish of me."

"So much has happened to you since you left, but there is so much I need to—"

"—Protect," she finished. I couldn't deny this was what I was thinking. "You should always protect the people you love," she said.

"Like you did for me," I said.

"And like Lorn did for you."

Let Me Tell You About My Sister

Lisa was stomping her way through the woods, and as she did, she imagined her forceful steps sending the wildlife scurrying for cover, just like the scene in the Lion King, and not just the squirrels and chipmunks, but the bigger beasts too. There is no bigger beast than me, she thought, and she imagined when she reached her destination in the woods that she might give a lecture that started this way.

"Let me tell you a few things about my sister Marie. Oh, I could tell you so many stories, because nobody knows Marie better than I do. *Nobody.* When she was little, we would fight so much, and Mom would say it was because we were only a year and four days apart. This kept the stakes high about everything from her borrowing my clothes to who gets the front seat (always no, and always me). Still today, if anyone observed us, they would never suspect we had not always been the best of friends. If she were sitting right here, she would laugh her head off if I said that out loud . . . but if she were sitting here, I wouldn't say it. But we both know it's true."

Lisa enjoyed imagining this scene. She loved taking charge, and storytelling was one of her favorite ways to direct a room. Her imagined lecture to nobody in particular continued.

"My sister Marie wrote a poem once when she was ten and I was eleven. I discovered it when by a stroke of luck, it fell from her notebook and I grabbed it before she dove for it. I have been faster than Marie all her life. Sure, the one year gave me a little head start, and I suppose if she had a different sister than me, she may have caught up, but she didn't. Most people didn't, in fact. I decided to read the poem out loud on our front porch steps so all the neighborhood kids could hear."

She smiled to herself as she imagined reading Marie's stolen poem:

> *I'm curious, not nosy, and not that bold,*
> *I plan to fix that, one day, when I'm old.*

Lisa imagined confessing to any hiding woodland animals:

"My baby sister interrupted with a few heroic attempts to shove me off the front steps, but I had a good hold of the railing with my other hand, and I've always been so much stronger. My sister never had the strength to move me unless I thought she might cry. Seeing Marie cry was always my kryptonite, but luckily she still has never figured this out. How could she, when 'Don't be a fucking wimp' was my go-to reply whenever things got dicey and I saw her bottom lip quiver?"

Lisa was thinking about how she had shouted out the rest of the poem that day, even as she knew she was being cruel because she was having way too much fun to stop:

> *A thought came to me,*
> *I'm exactly as I should be,*
> *I'm not the prettiest girl,*
> *but I'm smart in my heart.*
> *I'll have to take a different path,*
> *Truth is, I'm not so good at math.*

Lisa interrupted herself to laugh hysterically at that part, just as she had when she first read it. "Not so good at math— no shit!" Lisa yelled, wondering if a joke is told in the woods, and nobody is around to hear it, is it really a joke? Marie had clutched her arm that day when they were kids, flailing one unlanded punch after another in that helpless way a ten-year-old gay boy might do against his all-star athlete older brother. Lisa remembered how she had kept reading out loud as Marie's face turned a deeper shade of red.

> *I will follow my heart, no matter the cost,*
> *Following even when all is lost.*
> *I will love like it's the last thing to do on earth,*
> *I have been in love, even before birth.*

She did have regrets as she remembered how hard she had burst out laughing at the end, how she had wiped tears from her eyes, her laughter weakening her to the point where Marie finally was able to shove her off the steps and rip the poem away from her hand. It was okay, though, since Lisa had needed both her hands to pound the ground in her laughter, which was way beyond control.

Lisa thought, I should have known she would have love trouble from that day on. Lisa had a sister who loved love more than she loved food, and that was saying something. Lisa always worried this would be the thing that could devour Marie. Even at the age of ten, her sister was drowning in a passion for a love she hadn't even experienced yet. Lisa would wonder: what would happen when she finally connected with someone who also connected with her? Lisa wasn't afraid of much, but she was afraid of that.

When Marie first met Lorn Elaine, The Actress, Lorn's indecisiveness made Lisa want to beat her up. Anything to stop the push-pull that went on with her sister's heart. Marie was so in love that she lost all perspective, and Lisa had to be the one to snap her out of it. She was convinced Lorn was not good for her sister. But she had been wrong about that, and this was a fact she kept to herself.

It turned out that Lorn had been well worth the risk, and even after she hurt Marie yet again, Lisa had wondered if she was the one Marie should have waited for. Until Erica finally won Lisa over. As writer Amy Bloom would say, even a blind person could see how much Erica loved her sister.

Lisa chuckled, kicking a tree limb out of her way as she trudged along, thinking that everyone could see it except their dumb brother, who never saw it coming until he saw the two of them making out on a roof in the thunder and rain. And when all was finally out in the open with Vince, and Marie was healed by love again, Lisa realized she had been as much invested in finding love for Marie as her little sister had been in finding it for herself.

And now this freaking mess.

But, as usual, Lisa had it all figured out.

She always had to do the hard stuff when they were all growing up, and this would be no different. It was Lisa who had to go with Mom when they took their childhood dog for his last car ride, and it had been Lisa who didn't allow Marie to come along.

I'm not afraid of doing the tough things, she thought, and I'm not afraid of endings, especially when something needs to be put out of its misery. Enough of this. Both these women have yanked my sister around long enough, putting her through hell, and now she would have to put an end to it. Luckily, as usual, she knew she had the perfect plan.

Lisa thought that plans are a lot like cooking: you work up a menu and cook up the right ingredients, all to make the perfect result. She said out loud, "Some ingredients might hurt going down, and some ingredients can hurt you in the end if you get my drift." Lisa also knew sometimes things have to get much worse before they will get better.

Marie would say this was the case with most of Lisa's plans being a royal pain in the ass for everyone involved, but eventually Lisa knew everyone would see it her way. There is only one way out of this, she thought, knowing Marie wouldn't like her plan one little bit, and she was preparing herself during this stomp through the woods that, oh, it's going to be bad at first. Still, she knew they would be all in it before they really

251

knew what hit them.

And why was that? Lisa answered her question out loud: "I know what's right for my sister. Marie can't walk away from love, that part I'm sure of. She has never been able to. Erica knew that, and Lorn knows it too."

"Okay, pay attention," Lisa told herself now, "because I'm taking some deep breaths on this one since so much is out of my control. It could get ugly at first, but here we go." Slowly, Lisa walked deeper into the heart of Camptown Ladies . . .

"Well, I'll be damned," she whispered. "They both showed up." Lisa congratulated herself on how she had pulled her car into the front of the campground, parked far away, and walked herself in. The element of surprise was on her side as she approached the log cabin where both cars were parked out front.

Now, finally reaching the door, Lisa didn't want to give either of them a chance to say a word so she did her usual. She busted in talking.

"So happy to see you both! And on time. Are you ready to hear Lisa Santora's plan for what's going to happen with the rest of your lives?" Lisa liked to talk about herself in the third person occasionally when she needed to get right to the point.

When both of them said nothing, Lisa signaled with a finger point for Erica to scoot out of the best chair in the house so she would have to move to the only seat left, on the couch right next to Lorn. She was quiet for a bit, enjoying how the women looked like two lost girls, sitting cluelessly side by side, waiting for a bus on a federal holiday.

Lisa took it as a great sign how uncomfortable they were sitting so near each other, and she had to admit that until right then, she had been in *fake it till you make it* mode, and was not entirely sure her plan would work. But that never stopped her before, so she relaxed now, gave a big sigh, and could tell she was making them nervous as she smiled just a little too big.

Frequently Wrong, Never in Doubt

Lisa watched with fascination how both women bristled at the close proximity of sitting side by side each other on the couch. Could be promising, she thought, although she was secretly unsure if she even *had* a plan. Since "frequently wrong and never in doubt" was Lisa's normal mode, this predicament fascinated her because here she was, in doubt.

She smiled to herself. This must be how other people felt all the time.

Lisa would have loved to do this all day, but she finally stopped torturing the two women with her silence. "It's pretty simple: either you will or you won't work this out, but after all my sister has been through, she is not going to give up another fucking thing. Not if I have anything to do with it, which obviously I do. It will be up to both of you to work this out."

If that hadn't been clear enough to the two women, she finished with, "Nobody is leaving here until this is settled."

For dramatic effect, Lisa marched with heavy steps back to the front door of the log cabin and slowly turned to look at them both as she slid the dead bolt across the lock, enjoying the horror movie sound effect of metal on metal.

As Lisa turned to walk back to the women, Erica said, "You realize you locked the door from the inside."

The lovely nurse shot a look at Erica that said: *Bad move poking the bear. You're on your own.* Lisa smiled at Erica, amused.

253

"Yes, but I'm on the inside."

Erica's cockiness evaporated as Lisa walked back toward her, slower than she needed to, for full effect. When she was standing directly in front of her, she bent down until their noses were just inches apart. "Erica, you only thought you were close to kicking the bucket before."

Erica wasn't one to scare easily, but she made sure any last hint of her smirk vanished, just in case. Satisfied, Lisa went back to her seat, folded her hands in her lap just like Lorn, and directed her words to Erica.

"I know I caused all of this," Lisa said.

The nurse expected to be several steps behind Marie's sister, but she noticed Erica didn't look as confused as she was at Lisa's confession.

Lisa continued. "Erica, I didn't know you were sick; all I knew was that you appeared to be in love with my sister until the day you dumped her. I told Marie she needed to accept you were gone and to write a letter as if she was writing to you, to say good-bye. I thought writing it might bring closure, but she was in such a bad way that I decided to email a picture of it. You know, for real closure."

Lisa then turned to the nurse, "So you see, Lorn, this is all my fault. Maybe Erica would have stayed away for good if I hadn't sent that letter, but I did . . . before I knew Marie had started up with you again. Oops. My bad."

Lorn looked as if the missing puzzle piece had been found under a living room rug.

"Which brings us to now," Lisa said. "My sister loves you both, so the way I see it is you two will have to learn to be around each other, a lot, until she figures this all out."

The women stayed quiet, so Lisa said, "You know the saying that failure is not an option? If you didn't catch it yet, I'm saying that now. And Erica, I have a question for you," she said. "Who the hell finds out they're dying and slinks off without any explanation? Were you a friggin' cat in your past life?"

"No. I don't think I was a cat."

"Well, you're a goddamned pussy."

Erica opened her mouth, but never found an answer to that one.

Lisa watched as Lorn placed her hand protectively on Erica's arm, a signal of compassion for Erica, but Lorn realized this may have been the wrong move. It drew Lisa's attention to her earlier than planned, and now Lorn could only join Erica as a second deer in the headlights.

Sitting side by side like that, Lisa observed that in several ways the pair looked like a mirror image. Both fiercely independent, ridiculously attractive women, and both trying hard not to tip their hand. But Lisa could always smell fear, her favorite scent, and she was smelling it now in stereo. Intoxicating, she thought.

"Lorn, if you were to quit again on my sister, and you won't, that would land you in the double digits of how many times you've put my sister through hell." Lorn opened her mouth to protest, but Lisa drew in closer and said, "Shut it. I've been counting, and unlike Marie, I don't suck at math."

Lorn did shut it, and instinctively pulled back, but not before Erica put a protective arm across Lorn's front, as if they had been in a speeding car and the stoplight had just flashed red.

Lisa took only a second to register the implication of Erica's arm lying across Lorn's chest and smirked like a teenage boy.

"I'll cut to the chase. Actually, I'm cutting the chase. Neither of you have a decision to make because I'm putting an end to this right now. My sister will never walk away from love, so take some deep breaths, ladies, while I explain how it's all going to go down."

The ladies breathed as told.

"From this day on, you are both no longer allowed to think of my sister as your other half. That's over and done. Welcome to a new day. Do you both understand?"

"But Marie has to make the decision," Lorn said, instantly regretting it.

Lisa continued, "The two of you will be spending a lot of time together, so I'm confident you'll figure it out. Either you will agree, or I'll drive you both to the airport tonight, and off you both can go, back to the West Coast."

Erica gently asked, "How would we be spending time together?" Lisa could see that perhaps Lorn wanted to ask that, too.

"Mom still needs Lorn to help with Auntie Etta. And Erica, I have some jobs for you around the house, which is now becoming littered with old people. I need railings installed, walk-in showers with seating, that sort of thing. Now I know how fast you work as a contractor, so it's not a big job, but after that's done, and if my sister needs more time, I'll think of something."

"She could always work on Camptown Ladies renovations," Lorn said.

Erica and Lisa looked at the nurse as if she had lost her mind, but Lorn continued calmly, "With the huge popularity of your show, Camptown Ladies should be expanded, not merely renovated."

Lisa said, "Newsflash, Nurse Ratched. In case you hadn't heard, Camptown Ladies is long gone because Erica here dumped my sister, and I needed to get her away from those memories and this ridiculous cabin."

"I heard you were looking to sell it," Lorn said.

"And I did. So, tell me how, if I don't own it, am I supposed to hire pussy over here—"

"You're hired," Lorn said as she turned to Erica. "I own the campground. And if you want the job, we'll need a GC in charge of the expansion."

Lisa had never been stunned silent in her life, and her own silence was deafening to her as she put the pieces together.

Erica's mouth dropped open and Lisa finally spoke. "*You* bought Camptown Ladies?"

Lorn said, "I had an investment company buy it as soon as I heard it went up for sale."

"Why would you do that?" Lisa snapped, not liking the feeling of an unpredictable turn.

"Because I knew you and your sister would regret selling

it," Lorn answered simply, but she looked embarrassed. "Sorry. I guess I was keeping a close eye on things."

"While being a nurse?" Erica said, eyebrows up, stunned . . . and impressed.

Clever, clever woman, Lisa thought, her antennae gradually rising. Maybe the ex-actress turned nurse didn't mind the idea of Erica staying around. She watched as Erica turned to Lorn, "Do I have the contract?"

Lorn answered, "It's the very least I should give you back, but as far as I am concerned Camptown Ladies still belongs to Lisa, and I'm signing it back over to her."

Erica nodded slowly at Lorn, and Lisa noticed a hint of admiration. Erica had built Campground Ladies and now it would be expanded, and everyone in the room knew only one thing could have made Erica happier: Marie. But Lorn was not prepared to do that, and Erica didn't blame her.

Lisa clapped her hands together twice to get the attention of the room back. "Okay then," she shouted to an imaginary audience, "until my sister decides otherwise, I now pronounce my sister, Lorn, and Erica a threesome! Or, at least until she gives one of you the toss."

Lisa had gone off script, and this last comment had been a long shot even for her. As her joke hung between them, she wondered, would the two women dissolve into fits of laughter? Would they tell her to F-off, that their love lives were none of her business? After all, that's what she would have done. Or . . . Lisa thought, would they do exactly what they were doing right now: nothing? They were still sitting in wide-eyed silence, as if waiting to hear the particulars.

Well, now, Lisa thought, as she carefully observed them avoiding looking at each other, both looking petrified the other might think they were actually considering this crazy *one choice fits all* option.

Lisa realized she had totally underestimated her own brilliance. Everyone knows three is a crowd, and to Lorn and Erica it had to be a joke, an outrageous idea, but maybe it was a lot less crazy when it was *someone else's* idea. And less crazy still if the strongest person in the room was *giving you no choice.*

Erica and Lorn kept their poker faces on as they sat thinking and, more notably, not flinching at her wild announcement. Lisa slapped her thigh like a judge with a gavel, just as she always did when she felt a decision had been made and agreed to, and didn't she just nail it?

What Lisa didn't know was all the late nights Lorn had spent talking with Erica in the early days of her illness. And Erica never knew what her calls did to Lorn. It had been Erica's calls that encouraged Lorn to quit her first hospital position and switch her focus to hospice nursing. Erica's fate had helped Lorn want to help those going through end-of-life illness, especially if they were going through it alone.

Lorn had thought about Erica over the last year, especially when Erica's calls kept spacing out until they finally stopped altogether. Lorn, assuming Erica was gone, knew she was still ethically bound to respect her privacy. But then Erica called one last time, sounding so weak and frightened. "Please tell me where you are," Lorn said. "Let me come to you to help."

Erica had refused.

Lorn had agonized over telling Marie. Back then, when three months had passed after Erica's last call, and it was well past the red line Lorn had marked on her calendar, Lorn knew Erica could not possibly have lived past that date. She wondered if Erica had died completely alone, and this was when Lorn swore to herself that none of her patients would ever die alone. It didn't matter that Erica had not been her patient; regret had consumed her back then, and now, that she had not been strong enough to break the confidentiality law and let Marie know.

Lisa also had regrets.

She regretted that during what was probably in the thick

of Erica's illness, she had screamed at Erica to stop calling to check on Marie. Erica had dumped her baby sister, and Lisa was witnessing how it was destroying her. Lisa winced, remembering the last time she had spoken to Erica. She assumed this must have been Erica's last call to reach out to anyone, and Lisa had yelled into the phone that she was more worried about her mother's health than she was about Erica's gay breakup drama. And then she hung up on her.

Lisa was typically a stranger to guilt, but she did feel guilty about this. Even if she didn't know Erica was at death's door, she had hung up on a woman who was dying. She could have been Erica's last phone call.

Except, Erica's last call had not been to Lisa. Erica's last call many months ago had been to Lorn, telling her that her dying wish was that Lorn would go take care of Momma Santora and Marie. And that wish had sent Lorn off from California to Rhode Island, to offer her unwanted care to Marie and the family at 2229 Lakeside Drive.

Now, Lisa sat before these two women, snickering to herself how much this scene resembled a bad porn movie: the log cabin in the middle of the woods, perched on the only patch of land not sold with Camptown Ladies. There would be a threesome under duress. Lisa thought it would have made much better porn if Lorn were wearing her nurse's uniform.

Lisa smiled as her way of trying to comfort them because, as she saw it, at least this particular threesome in the room, herself, Erica and Lorn, were all aligned with the same goal. They all wanted Marie to get whatever she wanted, and there had only been one way Lisa could figure out to spare Marie any more loss. She only hoped these women would be up to the task.

And Marie didn't need to know about any of this.

Lisa planned that after several weeks of forcing these two idiots to spend some time together, she'd call a family meeting, figuring it would all be settled by then, one way or the other. It's the Italian way. Meaning that Lisa could hand back the control to her sister, and it would be up to her to tell the rest of the story.

There Are Only Two Things in Life

"Honestly, I'm feeling relieved," I said, and Lisa's response to me was a faint chuckle. "No, really, I'm glad it's going down this way," I said. "We are all getting along, and it doesn't make sense that I would be with either one of them when you really think about it."

"Right," Lisa said.

"There were way too many reasons why a life with either of them wouldn't have worked. Think about it: how many times has Lorn left?"

"But she's not leaving," Lisa said.

"She hasn't been around much the last two weeks . . . Erica, either. Maybe they're both done waiting around. It used to be Lorn with all the back and forth; now I can't make up my mind. And this whole thing with Erica—from the beginning, remember, you were the one that said it would never last."

Lisa said, "Yeah, well, she kind of proved me wrong on that one, don't you think? They kind of both did."

I couldn't have been more surprised if my sister had smacked me upside the head with a dead fish than hearing her admit she was wrong. "Wait a minute," I said. "You always said straight girls are trouble. It would never have worked out. You always said—"

Vince joined in as we all said it together: "There's just something about straight girls that you can't put your finger on."

Vince and I laughed, but I noticed my sister didn't laugh along this time.

"I did say that about Erica," Lisa said, "but she was with you for five perfect years and only left because she didn't want to put you through her own miserable death. God knows I'd like to be harder on the woman, but that should count for something."

I felt my face getting red and I looked at my sister's neck, wondering if I could get my hands comfortably around it to choke her. (No way.) Who the hell's side was she on? In the past, if I wanted in, Lisa was in. If I wanted out, Lisa was out. Whenever things went bad for me, I could always count on Lisa to slam doors in the all the right faces.

That is the version of my sister I needed right now, the same sister who declared the girlfriend who dumped me would be dead to our entire family. Sure, my sister kept me alive through all of that, but this new lack of loyalty was unacceptable. What was happening here?

I didn't say it as strongly as I had in my head, but I did barely squeak out, "Whose side are you on?"

"The side of reason," Lisa snapped. "You do what you need to do, Mare: walk away from Erica or Lorn, or walk away from both of them if that's what you want. I'll still be on your side."

"But you don't agree."

"I don't have to, but I'll go with whatever you decide," she said and started to walk toward the kitchen. I followed her because I knew she wasn't done, and there was a part of me that wanted her to be right.

As Lisa continued, she waved a wooden spoon a bit close and grazed the tip of my nose with a dash of hot red arrabbiata sauce. I could tell by the way my nostrils burned it would be a good one. "Just don't ask me to pretend that both women don't love the hell out of you, Mare. I can't be on board with that. Look what Lorn did for Mom. Look what Lorn did for you, for that matter. And how Erica suffered the brink of death alone to spare you so you might start your life again, which worked, because you had started to. If you ask me, these are both heroic women. The real question is, how does she smell to you?"

"Which one?" I asked in a daze.

"The sauce on your big Italian snout, you idiot."

I wiped my snout on a paper towel. "It's good," I said, because it was.

Lisa aggressively washed her hands at the kitchen sink as if my stupid thoughts had been on them. "Hey," she said, "you know what? Maybe they both deserve better."

I sized up her neck again, but admitted to myself that I lacked the skills. Besides, who would serve the meatballs? Dad was already hovering in the kitchen near the pots, sensing both Italian food and drama were well past the simmering point.

Lisa softened a little and turned me away from Dad to say more quietly, "I want you to consider the fact that maybe it's just shit luck that brought you back two amazing women, and now you have to choose. Or choose neither. Only don't be so sure that you'll get lucky a third time."

"Oh, I'm sure I wouldn't," I said. "Nothing about this makes any sense. We were always hurting each other; they each hurt me, and now I'm hurting them both. Isn't that a sign that it's all wrong?"

"It could be a sign you're a shithead," she said.

How could I argue?

When you get into a crazy situation again and again and then move on to the next person and get into that same situation, and then you go back to the first person . . . it becomes pretty clear who the shithead is. I looked at my sauce-freckled reflection in the glass pot lid, and thought: there she is.

As I was piecing this together, my sister said, "Last time I saw them both, they were fine. You're the one that can't figure it out. They know what they want. Face it, Mare, you're actually the ringmaster of this shitshow. There's only a couple of options. Either you figure out the shitshow, shut down the shitshow, or you go all Siegfried & Roy and keep ignoring the shitshow until a giant pussy devours your face."

I remained staring at my distorted face on the sauce-speckled lid. "Saw them both where?" I asked, but Lisa had darted away. Dad looked at me suspiciously, assuming I was guarding the meatballs, and wandered off in a huff as he muttered "Traitor" and made his way to the appetizer table to try his luck there.

When Lisa came back, she put her arm around me and said in a dramatically low voice, "I didn't want to tell you this . . . and she would *kill* me if she knew I was telling you this, but Mom still seems afraid you're going to let Lorn pack up and leave. I think she needs Lorn here indefinitely to help with Auntie Etta. You know she has been a handful since she busted out of her damned wheelchair. She is faster than Mom. But . . . if *you* think Mom will be okay without Lorn here to help, then cut her loose."

I knew Lisa was manipulating me, knowing I could not imagine letting either Lorn or Erica go, but I fell for it and my heart sank. Mom was changed after her recovery, and maybe her surgery had shaken her more deeply than any of us knew. But I feared her remaining stress was from worrying about me as much as about Auntie Etta. She acted as if giving obsessive care to Auntie Etta was to be her lot in life, her punishment for telling Auntie Etta's sister, Aggie, to drop dead and then getting her wish. Whenever Auntie Etta sarcastically called out "Nurse! Oh, Nurse!" Mom felt this debt was the least she could do, and she would come running.

Lisa seemed like she was still waiting for an answer from me. I could tell because she was tapping the wooden spoon against the pot in the *Jaws* theme.

Tap-tap . . . Tap-tap . . . Tap-tap, tap-tap tap tap tap . . .

"What am I supposed to do?" I said. "Am I supposed to ask Lorn to stay here with everything that's happened? She must already feel like I've betrayed her, and maybe I have. I've betrayed them both. Why on earth would either of them stay?"

"I forgot to mention that I already asked Lorn to stay and permanently take over Auntie Etta's care, at least till you make up your friggin' mind." I spun around in time to see my sister give a casual shrug. "Not everything is about you, hotshot, and caring for Auntie Etta was getting to be too much for Mom. Sorry. But right now, Mom comes first. I knew you would understand. Besides, Auntie Etta keeps asking for Lorn, talking crazy about how her dead sister Aggie wants Lorn to stay and be her nurse."

"She is getting more nuts by the day," I said, even as I swore I could feel her nutty DNA swirling inside me.

Lisa agreed. "Yeah, and remember, I did have those dreams that Aunt Aggie came back from the dead and wanted to keep sharing her recipes on my cooking show. I dreamed she was teaching me all the recipes that I never knew—but I do know them now. And how do you explain that Auntie Etta keeps saying it's her sister's cooking show?"

I couldn't explain it any more than I could the last time we watched Lisa's show together, and when the show started Auntie Etta kept yelling "Food fight! My sister Aggie says she wants a food fight!" and that was only seconds before one broke out on the show.

"What about the food fight? How do you explain that?"

Lisa went pale again. "That was weird," she agreed. "She couldn't have known Eddie and I were going to get into a little food fight that spread into the audience. Sandra had to leave it in the show because the audience went crazy for it, and the videos leaked online before we were even done filming."

"Do you think it is possible that Auntie Etta still hears her sister like she says she does?"

"From the grave?" Lisa asked as she stirred the pot. Then she said, stirring the pot further, "Yes, I do."

I believed it too.

Lisa said, "There have been too many things, like in the first show that detailed dream that Aunt Aggie taught me how to make her secret Italian egg biscuits. She said she would take two things to her grave, all her millions and her egg biscuit recipe."

"Turns out, she took neither," I said, and we both got quiet.

Lisa finally said, "Stranger things could happen, I guess."

"Not really," I said.

Lisa nodded in agreement. "The thing is, if I ever croak,

I know I would find a way to haunt you." We both burst out laughing, knowing if it had ever been true of two sisters, it would certainly be true of us.

"So if dead Aunt Aggie is insisting to her sister that Lorn is supposed to stay, does that mean she belongs here? And, if so, what about Erica? They are both already making themselves scarce."

Lisa put her hands up in surrender. "You're going to have to figure this out by yourself. I'm just saying, if you are hell-bent on avoiding them, that could be tricky." Something in my sister's eyes told me there was more to this story, and Lisa putting her hands up as if she had no control historically meant the exact opposite.

Lisa said, "And what the hell is Erica supposed to do while she is waiting around for you? She already outfitted this house with every handicap amenity there is for Auntie Etta and for our old-fart parents to grow into."

She had done a great job. I could not argue with that. And both Lorn and Erica had been much better at navigating all three of us under one roof than I was these days.

"Well, I have a much bigger project lined up, and it could take the better part of a year," Lisa said. "So if your plan is to avoid Erica, I'm just saying that also might be tricky. Sorry."

She wasn't.

The panic of losing control over my life again made me want to run from it. And yet the guarantee that Lorn and Erica could both be around for much longer came with a jittery feeling that was not completely unpleasant. It would have felt like relief if it didn't also feel like the moment right before a rollercoaster plunges, and you go from enjoying the scenery to thinking you are screwed, all in a matter of seconds.

I needed to distract myself so I walked over to the cupboard to grab a stack of dishes to set the table, only to find the entire stack was gone. Something was up. I could feel it, and I glanced at the table where the dishes were already set, taking a quick count before grabbing the weakest link to pump for information.

Dad was on his third trip to the cheese and pepperoni tray when I intercepted him by the arm. He looked panicked, and this was when I knew.

I spoke quietly so nobody would hear me grilling him. "Is this is a family meeting? And if so, what's with the extra plates?"

Dad's eyes were wide at first; then he smiled along with his usual apologetic shrug, the one that says *Sorry, but I thought we all agreed I lost control of this family years ago.* I stared at him, trying to figure out if he knew anything, and Dad was being patient because he was using me as a human shield to sneak more cheese. He was not going to talk while distracted by a platter of food. I glanced down to see one side of the antipasto was being picked clean of the Parmigiano-Reggiano chunks.

"It looks like a half-cheese pizza, Dad. You may want to spread out the evidence." He agreed and went to work, rearranging all the remaining cheese with his fingers. I gave up, knowing if there was a family meeting in the works, there was a good chance that both Dad and I were the last to know.

Mom surprised me by sneaking up behind me, catching Dad rearranging the cheese like pieces on a board game. "Stan! I would insist 'you touch it, you eat it,' but that would leave us nothing."

"Sorry," he mumbled, mid-picking, mouth filled.

Mom shook her head at him before taking me by the arm and walking me away. She gave my arm a squeeze and asked, "How are you, hun?" I silently thanked God that Mom's firm grip on my elbow felt back to full strength. Miserably, I thought I should also be thanking Lorn.

"Fine," I said.

"This must be so confusing for you."

But it wasn't, so I told her so. "Nope. There isn't one or the other that makes any more or less sense so . . . not confusion. I'm just stuck."

Mom put her hand on my shoulder, a rare occurrence indeed. "Then how about you stay where you are, and let Lorn and Erica decide what is best for each of them?"

With that, she gave my shoulder a pat-pat and walked away. My mother had changed so much through the years. Where was the mom with whom my siblings and I used to play passive-aggressive bingo whenever she gave her particular words of encouragement? Mom now delivered these gems swiftly and regularly. She had her hustle back. As she walked away from me, I imagined her pulling away the fog that had settled thickly in my head the moment Erica came back. Maybe Mom was right. I was enticed by Mom's suggestion to let it all go because likely this wasn't my choice.

Mom settled in at her rightful place by Dad's side, just in time to coach him how best to hold his overfilled plate of food. At least some things never changed.

I imagined what Mom would have said if she had counseled me a minute more, instead of running off to assist with Dad's balancing act, his stolen meatball hanging precariously on the edge of his plate. I imagined Mom would have said: "Why do you think the decision is all on you? You love them both, but it's not any more your decision than it is theirs. It is not like anyone is forcing them to stay. As I always tell your father, it's not all about you, honey." Then I imagined her kissing the top of Dad's head as they both said together "just, mostly."

I knew that someday, hopefully many, many years from now, when my mom was no longer with us, I would imagine all our conversations like this. I felt my eyes burn at the thought as I watched her fuss over Dad. The truth was I knew exactly what they both would say on nearly every subject. Mom would say, "Life has a way of leveling out the way it should," and Dad would chirp in, "Unless you fuck it up!" If we'd talked about this, have both chatted in the same matter-of-fact voice they would use talking about a neighbor's lawn as they would the probability that I might lose both the women I loved.

I shook my head to nobody in particular as I decided to stop torturing myself with the question because there was no solution I could think of that would not involve hurting someone—or hurting all three of us. Like with my past history with numbers, math never worked for me.

Weirdly, a vague feeling of relief flowed into my chest, thinking that someone other than me had to make this decision, and maybe my only role was to be all "Jesus Take the Wheel" about the whole damned thing. I knew my mother as well as I knew myself, and she didn't have to speak for me to know exactly what she would say, and someday after she was gone, I would always know exactly what her words would be in a crisis. The comfort in that finally soothed me, and I laughed as Mom rolled her eyes behind Dad's back as she hovered near his plate, wearing a large dinner napkin in hand like a catcher's mitt. Would I ever have someone waiting to catch my meatball?

Lisa handed me a glass of wine. I sipped the deep red pool of room-temperature Italian cabernet, and it tasted warm and rich, not unlike her sauce, which made me think maybe drinking was the best solution. I imagined that if Lorn and Erica had both been here, I would have handed them each a cocktail, telling them to get back to me with what they decided. Good plan, I thought, and sighed as the wine warmed my throat.

As if on cue, Erica stepped through the door without knocking and stood for a minute to hold the door open for Lorn. Both women were immersed in the golden hour of a late Sunday afternoon, and the sight of them brought the warmth in. Good thing because I was frozen solid, wine glass halfway to my face.

Erica moved swiftly over to Mom with her cocky stride. She had also got her hustle back, completely outrunning a disease that never had a chance against the strength of her.

I love her.

I also loved hiding behind my wineglass.

Erica's hustle contrasted with Lorn's more gentle approach, soundless as she entered any room, a perfect late-night nurse, except when she was decked out in a dress and heels. As always, I noticed how the blaze of her hair outshone the sun before she closed the door behind her. When the door closed, our eyes found each other across the room, and she gave a warm smile.

I love her.

I took another sip, hoping it would relax the double-pounding in my chest.

I looked towards the kitchen to my sister for answers as to why they were both here. Lisa was waving them in as if she were the burly usher at the show and they were late, the curtain already lifting on center stage. The room got quiet, and even Vince and my nephew Buddy stopped talking to stare at me. Maybe it was not Lisa's food, and I was the one on center stage?

Lorn hovered shyly near the door at first. I saw that her eyes stayed on mine in that same Lady Diana upward glance she sometimes gave when her emotions were running high and she couldn't look directly at me. By contrast, Erica challenged me with her stare, eyebrow arching as she smiled her trademark grin over Auntie Etta's shoulder, who had barreled in for one of her unsolicited hugs. When she finally got loose, Erica made her way back to the door to get Lorn, and I noticed she said something to her that made Lorn laugh, and when Lorn had leaned in, Erica's cheek had been close enough to catch the reflective warm glow from Lorn's hair, placing me on extreme high alert.

What was happening here?

Whenever I have this confused feeling, like the world plan was orchestrated on my day off, yet stars were lining up as if following a silent command, I instinctively turn to my sister to assess the look on her face. Lisa was purposely not looking at me, and I suspected that it was my sister who might actually be the legit ringleader of this particular shitshow.

Whatever direction this was going, I couldn't help but notice it was not extremely unpleasant to have both Erica and Lorn in the same room like this. It had happened a few times over the last few weeks, but the headiness of it had made me flee the room each time. This time I was not leaving. Having them both near would keep me stuck, but, if I were honest, my mind raced ahead to crazy thoughts I had buried, endless and tantalizingly unthinkable ideas that I had not acknowledged before now.

I downed the rest of my wine. Would it be drink number two making me decide I would be a willing captive to whatever plan was in my future, or perhaps drink number one had already done the trick? I caught my sister giving an arrogant nod to Vince, and my brother caught me watching them and attempted a casual sip of his own drink, though overly dramatic as if whiskey had burned his lips . . . except the dummy was sipping a light beer. If my sister was involved, then it was official; all that had to be done was for me to go along for the ride.

Mom warmly greeted Lorn with a hug, then the same to Erica, and was now pulling them farther into the room as if everyone had been waiting for them.

Mom said, "Lorn, hun, I missed you yesterday. Did you spend the day at the campground again?" I noticed Lorn didn't answer, but instead flicked her eyes over to me. Next, Mom folded both women into a tight hug that mingled their hair together. The beauty I witnessed could not have been captured by the finest artist's eye to get those colors just right. As I waited for them both, I didn't miss Lorn's hand rise to hold Erica's shoulder during the hug, and realized, as is often the case, it is not always the boldest who is the most brave.

There was something unmistakably at ease in the way Lorn's hand stayed on Erica's shoulder. Perhaps her nurse's training made touching automatic for her now, but also the ease in which Erica left Lorn's hand there caught my attention. Lorn was a nurse, and her compassionate touch was a way of life in her new vocation, and this should have shut down my dog-like impulse to put a different spin on the scene . . . yet . . . I was hearing a distinct call of my own, as if it was a dog whistle that, instead of sounding a high-pitched shriek, was playing "Unchained Melody." I watched and cocked my head like a dog, to try to catch the full meaning of this scene, as the soundtrack to *Ghost* played in my head.

I was such an idiot. I could feel my sister's name written all over this, and as if she heard my thoughts from across the room, she wasn't trying to hide her smug face. Her smile got wider, but it could have been from her spotting Sandra walking in the door as if it was her studio staff she was parting as she crossed the room. She tossed hellos behind her before joining her star chef at the stove. I knew from my sister's face that she was in love with this woman, as Lisa never had her face redden from the heat of her stove.

Momma bear led her catch of Lorn and Erica toward me as if they were two juicy salmons, offering them up to her thinnest cub with a gentle push, and as she did I swore I heard her chuckle.

Thanks Mom. I was now forced to greet Erica, then Lorn, at such close range I was compelled to give them each a kiss on the cheek, first-come, first-serve style, remembering how much I needed them both. I thought of how only a few months ago, I had been 80% done with straight girls. Now, as I looked at the two women, hopelessly in love with them both, that 80% seemed ridiculously high, and what I thought was panic was fluttering in my belly. I worried whether either one would wait long enough for me to make this impossible decision—if it was ever really mine to make.

I did what my sister would call Marie Math, adding misguided numbers into a failed formula, to equal a failed sum: 80% done with straight girls, x2, wanting both equally @ 50% each = 100% = me being in control: 0%.

Lorn and Erica's body language read equal parts petrified and electrified. Was it from being near me, or being near each other, or both? Would there be a duel? Would they accept the fact that I could not choose either one of them over the other? And, if so, where did that leave us? We three collectively each took a deep breath and laughed at the ridiculousness of our timing. Or maybe we were laughing at the ridiculousness of the whole damned scene.

Something in the way they both looked at me made me wonder . . . could this be a classic case of good luck, bad luck, good luck? What if our timing was not so horrible after all? This crazy thought made me fear they could now hear the pounding in my chest, my own personal *Jaws* theme rumbling inside. Would it eat me alive or send both women running? Or would my heart explode, the cardiac shrapnel taking the three of us out in one shot?

Impulsively I decided I would go down with a bang and not, as my sister would say, let my non-decision be the decision. It shocked both Lorn and Erica when I pulled them toward me into a three-way embrace, closing my eyes as I breathed them both in, just in case it might be my last sniff on earth. Then they both surprised me by holding on tight. Not only to me, but also to each other, leaving me shaking with possibilities I hadn't dared imagine . . .

When had I pinched a page directly from Dad's playbook? It was the realization that I also had lost control of my family years ago. And now, with these two women in my grip, it was the most stunning feeling I could never have imagined. I forgot my whole family was watching as I held on to both of them with equal desperation. Would my new path somehow include both of them? If so, how could one survive a life feeling so eternally grateful and ravenous? Helped by the wine, the room spun as a crazy thought formed . . .

What if I didn't have to choose?

I felt Lorn and Erica also trembling. What had Lisa done? It was my sister's profound joy in life to spot my most vulnerable frailties, identify all risks that could place me in harm's way, and then deftly, lovingly, craftily pluck off each problem, one by one, in order to save me from myself.

I looked over the shoulders of the two women in my grasp, breathing them in and watching my sister say something to Sandra; was it a proud confession? Had Lisa somehow orchestrated this? Just then she shot me a ridiculous wink and raised her eyebrows, not in surprise, but in victory. Whatever genius plan my sister might have pulled off now blurred into the background as I felt both women breathing rapidly so close to my neck as our hold on each other tightened.

Lisa yelled from the kitchen, *"There are only two things in life!"* and I heard the rest of my family join her. *"Either you are in . . . or you are out!"*

Dad, Auntie Etta, and my brother laughed identical Santora

cackles as much less innocent thoughts filled my head. Both Lorn and Erica's grip tightened on me. We stayed attached to each other, not one of the three of us willing to let go. Now, crying into their shoulders like an idiot, I thought, if this is the way it had to go down . . .

I was most definitely *in*.

From across the room, Lisa yelled out, *"Hey . . . maybe there are three things in life!"* and I drowned out the happy laughter in the room by pulling the three of us closer.

A Note from the Author

Proposed title for this book, December 3, 2011:

(1) *What's So Funny About Losing the Love of Your Life*
(2) *I Kissed an Urn, and I Liked It*

Before I came up with the title of *80% Done With Straight Girls*, those were a few working title ideas for this book. It may be the most accurate way for me to describe the state I was in at that time. If I am being honest, writing this book was what I hoped might save my own life after my partner, Kim, died on December 6, 2011. I felt my world had ended and I was in need of a major distraction, and I needed it fast. Spoiler alert: *It wasn't fast.*

At the time of this writing, ten years have now passed. Fun fact: the actual title came after reading a random review on *Goodread*s, where someone commented about a book she was reading, and that she was "80% done with *Dudes*" (or some other one-word hetero book title that I can't remember now, which had to do with single guys, or something equally dreadful). Something about that as a title made me laugh, and this was notable, since I had not laughed in a long time.

I was hoping to write a book that would sneak in all the ways I felt Kim was trying to communicate that she was still around, and maybe it would be a comfort to others. That was the

...dea anyway. The story you (hopefully) just finished came to me on my first commute back to work after Kim had passed away. Just like in this story, my odometer turned over to a significant number, and I felt it was a sign that I needed to write my next book in order to get back to living, or risk heading deeper into the dark place where I was spending most of my time. If you can imagine a giant-breasted Italian woman going down from 140 to 100 pounds—that was me, and things were not looking good for our fuzzy little hero. I felt quite a lot like it was do-or-die time, and writing seemed the easier choice. I may have been wrong, but I'm so happy I chose this path, and I wish that my readers will be as well.

What began as a desperate need to line up a project in order to preserve what was left of my sanity became much more than that. During that first long winter in 2011 it was only this book that made me believe I might actually get to the other side of the loss I had been through. The struggle was writing when I was busy wondering if I would ever find anything joyful or funny ever again. I also wondered if I could tolerate writing about my favorite subjects: love, sex, joy and family after feeling that I had lost them all. Thankfully, I felt the answers to those questions were: Well . . . fuck . . . *maybe?*

When I first started this book, I had intended on a different path for Erica, but it completely changed during my (highly unrecommended) method of letting the story just tell itself. I can't outline to save my life, so my process is to write with no plan and throw out hundreds of wasted pages and hours. Not a system likely to be part of a college curriculum, but I have come to learn that I needed all those throwaway parts just as much as what made it to these pages. (I can tell you with certainty that the morbidly sad stuff, which was written and eventually cut, nobody needed to read, except me.)

Typically, I write with the feeling that I am watching from a safe distance as the story unfolds, with me having very little to do with the plan, and have learned the hard way that I can only write when I have absolutely no clue what is going to happen in the story. (Speaking of losses, I mourn the loss of several decent story ideas that died at the hands of an outline. When I outline, it seems to pop a hole in my thought balloon, sending all the fun whooshing out, and I'm left only with the work that lies ahead.)

It became evident while I was writing that Erica's character needed to take a different turn. It also became evident that I was writing too close to home about death and maybe this was the reason it took almost a decade to finish this book. (Stopping here for a moment to be clear: This book is not anywhere good enough to have taken ten years to write. I am only stating that it did.) Shout-out and heartfelt thanks to the most patient publishers on earth, my friends at Bywater Books—Marianne, Salem, Kelly, and Fay. I am still amazed they even *answered* my email when I wrote to say I had finally completed the damned story and, by the way, did they still remember me? (Clearly, they *did*.)

So many things had happened after that winter of 2011, and my original thought was to capture at least some of them in a work of fiction, but my body just wouldn't let me do it. I would come crawling back to the story, attempt to write, and promptly fall asleep at the keyboard. No joke. I had never experienced anything like this before. For someone that does not sleep in general, sleeping sitting up while writing made me certain that my body wanted to shut the project down. It worked, and I gave up. Many times.

Because I have to always be doing something, during years of attempted writing, I switched back to drawing and painting, which was for me a much less intimate form of creating. I filled sketchbooks and canvases with beach paintings, wondering where it all would lead, and hoping it might heal my brain. It may have been an ego thing to prove that even if I could not write books, I was still out there making stuff. To keep me on track to work on art projects regularly, I started a YouTube channel (Artwork By Mari) with the thought I would teach others how I make art . . . until such time that my brain might finally wake up so I could write again. I didn't have much hope this plan would work.

I was haunted each time by the countless fails at my laptop, the stops and starts that went on for so many years, and I finally realized I was only able to write if I kept away from this particular story. I learned that my brain would function if I only worked on stories unrelated to these characters, all inspired by my family and by Kim. To avoid this book, I turned to screenplay writing, which filled the void for a long time. (This eventually led to a short film, now in postproduction, called *The Sibling Rule*. Two women fake a lesbian marriage in order to keep their children in the same school together, but complications arise when the marriage becomes real.)

In the end, I credit three things which led me to finally finish this novel: a broken ankle, my sister, and . . . Covid. First, my sister badgered me to please read an Amy Bloom book that she dropped off to me. She knew I would love Amy Bloom's voice, and I was losing my mind, unable to go to work at my corporate job with a shattered ankle (two years pre-Covid, this was a time when working from home was not an option). Here I was, trapped at home with my thoughts and the overwhelming feeling that I had bailed on some unfinished business, and the characters I loved. They were trapped in limbo along with me, so along with my grief I also felt guilt. You might ask, can you feel real guilt over characters stuck in an unfinished book? Why yes, I can.

As it turned out, my broken ankle kept me in my writing chair, my sister kept me inspired, and when Covid came along it reminded me once again how fragile and tragically short life could be. So what the hell was I waiting for? I started telling friends that I had to stop blaming a dead person for my comatose writing state—and just work through it, hoping if I spoke it out loud, I would hold myself accountable.

Yet I still fell asleep countless more times while attempting to write. The good news was that my boredom eventually outwitted my grief, and I was able to visit the characters again for at least a few minutes every day (before waking up with drool on my laptop). About halfway through the book my ankle healed, and I went back to work and stopped writing yet again. Until Covid hit. Along with everyone else, I had no work commute and no travel as the whole world hunkered down. Unlike our first responder heroes, all I had to do was follow the rules, stay home, get vaccinated, and ignore our then president.

I kept thinking, why not make the time count and complete something? Instead, I found a way to stall a bit longer in order to sew and donate Covid masks, since at the time they were not readily available (I stopped counting at 800 masks). Finally, when I could no longer use the excuse that homemade masks were still needed, I went back to writing with a goal of finishing the book before I would be called back into the office. *Who knew that would take so long?*

My partner, Marisa, and I had two friends in our Covid pod that we felt safe to have dinner with at home once a week, and Sue (Bootsie) and Sharon were encouraging me weekly to keep going with my writing, and finally they—along with friends Debbie, Natalie, and Rachel—celebrated along with me the news that Bywater would publish my third book and my fourth.

Which brings us here.

Thank you to my patient readers who have returned and a big hello to anyone new! Apologies in advance if you weren't expecting the swearing, sex, and Italian people to be so out there; there was a warning on my first book. You all will be the deciding factor as to whether I should ever go back to these characters again or leave them exactly where they are now. Either way, I'm happy to have been with the Santora family, who kept me distracted and mildly entertained during some dark days, and I hope you were happy to spend time with them again too.

Thanks in advance if you take the time to write me (artworkbymari@icloud.com) so I can personally thank you for waiting . . . and reading. If you were kind enough to have posted a review from long ago, or now, I thank you for that as well.

Sidebar: Don't believe any writer who tries to convince you that they don't see all reader reviews because we do. Every.

ngle. One. It was, in fact, rereading many of those reviews, some dating back to the publishing of my first book in 2007, which also made me want to try again, so I thank you for that. I know who you are! The (mostly) kind reviews made me want to connect with you all again through the Santora family. I sure hope I haven't overstayed my welcome, though that never stopped me before.

xoxo

Mari

About the Author

Novelist, filmmaker, screenplay writer & owner at Love Is Love Productions, Mari is best known for her romantic comedy novels, *Greetings From Jamaica, Wish You Were Queer* and *Camptown Ladies*. *Greetings From Jamaica* was released as an audiobook in 2021, and the audiobook for *Camptown Ladies* will be released in 2022.

She won a Golden Crown Literary Society Award for *Camptown Ladies* and her books were promoted by national magazines such as *The Advocate, On Our Backs,* and the online LBGTQ+ community AfterEllen.com, and on the *Howard Stern Show*. A graduate of Rhode Island School of Design, Mari is also a fine artist and has a YouTube channel: *Artwork By Mari,* teaching her viewers how to draw & paint. Mari's "day job" is with an international retail corporation as a Divisional Manager of Product Development (when she is not taking hilarious phone calls from her loud Italian family regarding her depiction of them.)

Mari wrote and directed her LGBTQ+ short film, *The Sibling Rule,* which was filmed in October 2021. The film is in post-production, and will be hitting the film festival circuit. (Two women fake a gay marriage to take advantage of The Sibling Rule, which will keep their kids in the same school, but complications arise when the marriage becomes a bit too real.) The screenplay has been recognized by the UK Film Festival,

, Apple, Flickers RI Film Festival, Female Voices Rock, and est Script Award Festival for the short & feature screenplay. *Greetings from Jamaica* is also a screenplay which was selected to be in the Toronto, Austin, Rome & Flickers RI film festivals. Mari's biggest dream is to make a feature film or series featuring her trilogy of Bywater Books.

Mari is also thrilled to write back to readers who enjoy her books, and asks (ok . . . begs) you to drop by to say hello at artworkbymari@icloud.com.

At Bywater, we love good books by and about women, just like you do. And we're committed to bringing the best of contemporary literature to an expanding community of readers. Our editorial team is dedicated to finding and developing outstanding writers who create books you won't want to put down.

For more information about Bywater Books, our authors, and our titles, please visit our website.

www.bywaterbooks.com

9 781612 942391